TALES OF MYSTERY &

GW00642363

General Editor: Da

THE BLACK VEIL

and other tales of
Supernatural Sleuths

The Black Veil

and other tales of
Supernatural Sleuths

Selected and introduced
by Mark Valentine

WORDSWORTH EDITIONS

In loving memory of
MICHAEL TRAYLER
the founder of Wordsworth Editions

ɪ

Readers who are interested in other titles from
Wordsworth Editions are invited to visit our website at
www.wordsworth-editions.com

For our latest list and a full mail-order service contact
Bibliophile Books, Unit 5 Datapoint,
South Crescent, London E16 4TL
Tel: +44 020 74 74 24 74
Fax: +44 020 74 74 85 89
orders@bibliophilebooks.com
www.bibliophilebooks.com

This edition published 2008 by
Wordsworth Editions Limited
8B East Street, Ware, Hertfordshire SG12 9HJ

ISBN 978 1 84022 088 9

Typeset in Great Britain by Roperford Editorial
Printed by Clays Ltd, St Ives plc

CONTENTS

INTRODUCTION

Detective stories involving crimes and conspiracies were well established in the story magazines and publishers' lists of the late Victorian and Edwardian period; the great success of Arthur Conan Doyle's Sherlock Holmes had assured that. And authors were alert to the possibilities of engaging the reader's interest with unusual variations on the form: so that Ernest Bramah wrote about a blind detective, in his Max Carrados stories; Victor L. Whitechurch about a railway detective, Thorpe Hazell; Baroness Orczy about a woman detective, Lady Molly of Scotland Yard; and so on. E.W. Hornung also hit upon the astute idea of telling a crime story from the villain's perspective, in his popular Raffles yarns.

At the same time, stories in which detectives encounter the eerie, macabre and seemingly supernatural, had been part of the techniques for building up mysterious atmosphere ever since the genre had begun – the cases of Poe's Auguste Dupin, and Wilkie Collins's *The Woman in White* and *The Moonstone*, being striking examples. Even Van Helsing, the vampire expert in *Dracula*, if not exactly a detective, is certainly a combative investigator who pursues the Count as any crimefighter would a master-criminal; while Dr Hesselius, in Sheridan Le Fanu's supernatural tales, is a medical man whose casebook also resembles that of a detective. And a surprising number of the Sherlock Holmes stories start with strong hints that some supernatural or uncanny agency is in play (*The Hound of the Baskervilles* most obviously, 'The Sussex Vampire' and 'The Devil's Foot', etc.), even if in the end these are always rationalised.

Moreover, the strong late-Victorian interest in spiritualism and apparent evidence of paranormal phenomena had led to the foundation of the Society for Psychical Research (SPR) in 1882 and the beginning of independent investigations into claimed 'real life' hauntings, manifestations, poltergeists, possessions and other phenomena. There was later an eager readership for 'haunted house' books, such as Elliott O'Donnell's accounts of supposedly authentic supernatural visitations, in *Some Haunted Houses of England and Wales* (1908), *Haunted Houses of London* (1909), and others. It was also a time when men and women of means were apt to become interested in the byways of history – in amateur archaeology, in folk-lore and legend, and in antiquarianism – and these could readily lead to speculations on the unseen world.

The great supernatural horror writer Arthur Machen worked for a time as a cataloguer of occult books and as a journalist for Walford's *Antiquarian Magazine*. His connoisseur of the curious, and sleuth of the singular, Mr Dyson, is drawn into networks of evil that include strange crimes, ancient talismans, and implications of the super-natural. He first made his appearance in 'The Inmost Light', a companion tale to Machen's notorious shocker *The Great God Pan* (1894), and was then the chief character in the author's *tour de force The Three Impostors* (1895), featuring the sinister Dr Lipsius. Mr Dyson's farewell came with the powerful tale of 'The Red Hand', which we include in this volume. It was first published in *Chapman's Magazine* of December 1895, and was collected in Machen's land-mark collection, *The House of Souls* (1906).

After these beginnings, authors began to explore different ways of combining detection and the occult, psychic or supernatural realms. Cases where these conceal more conventional crimes, where the uncanny is merely a disguise or a hoax, continued to occur. But increasingly, authors understood the dread allure and weird glamour of stories where such things are not explained away. Sometimes the occult detective character might have special gifts such as a sensitivity to the realms of the unseen such as Sax Rohmer's 'Dream Detective', Morris Klaw, who sleeps at the scene of a crime in order to discern visions of what has transpired. Or they might have a medical or psychology training, bringing them into contact with strange cases of obsession and possession, like Dion Fortune's Dr Taverner. These attributes might also be combined with arcane knowledge of occult history drawn from books of secret lore or from personal encounters with the darkness. Or all these could be combined to create a fully-fledged, active investigator of strange incidents.

So the stage was now set for the creation of a character that would draw together all of these strands – detection, ghosts and old legends – and seize the public imagination with fictional accounts of super-natural investigation. A few such attempts had been made in Victorian times. One of the first was *A Master of Mysteries* (1898), the collection of John Bell stories by Robert Eustace and L. T. Meade. Like the investigators of the SPR, though, Bell was mostly a 'ghost exposer', finding explanations for the apparently supernatural. We reprint here one of the strongest stories, 'The Warder of the Door'. Meade was an enormously prolific author, mostly of children's books, while Eustace, a doctor, is perhaps best known for his collaboration with Dorothy L. Sayers in *The Documents in the Case* (1930).

But perhaps the most successful Victorian examples of the supernatural sleuth were the Flaxman Low stories of E. and H. Heron (1899). The Heron pen-name disguised a mother and son literary partnership, Kate and Hesketh Prichard. The latter was a sportsman, soldier, hunter and prolific author, and the stories bear the impress of his vigorous character. We reprint 'The Story of Sevens Hall', a fine family curse story from the Flaxman Low collection.

A similar format to the Heron stories was offered by the Ghost Hunter stories of Allen Upward, which appeared in the *Royal Magazine* at the turn of the century. Upward was a colourful and curious character, who had been a Radical lawyer who stood unsuccessfully for Parliament, a gun-runner for the Macedonians in their struggle against the Turks, a colonial judge in Nigeria, and was later a scholar of Eastern philosophy and poetry.

It was Algernon Blackwood who was the first to earn fame in the occult detective field, with his *John Silence*. When the book was published in 1908, it was advertised on billboards and omnibuses, and soon became a great success. In his introduction to a reprint edition (1942), Blackwood reveals that these tales of his indomitable psychic investigator 'were originally separate studies of various "psychic" themes, and it was on the suggestion of Mr Nash, who had already published two books for me, that I grouped them under the common leadership of a single man, Dr John Silence.' It was a shrewd suggestion from his publisher, as the format gave a new shape and force to the author's otherwise somewhat diffuse studies in the supernatural.

But the best and strongest was yet to come. It may have been the recollection of Blackwood's success that prompted Willam Hope Hodgson, still determinedly finding his way as a working writer, to produce the series of Carnacki the Ghost-Finder stories for *The Idler* magazine, where five of them appeared from January 1910 onwards. Hodgson wrote for *The Idler* in what was to prove to be its last full year of existence: it folded in March 1911. Whether the stories had been devised with *The Idler* specifically in mind or not, they matched its tone well. It has been observed that the 'basic mood' of this periodical was 'the gentleman at leisure'. The framing of the Carnacki stories was therefore exactly apt for *The Idler*: a group of gentlemen gathered for dinner in comfortable and fashionable rooms on Cheyne Walk, The Embankment, Chelsea, to hear yarns from a host who is evidently himself a gentlemanly amateur.

The first published story, in the January 1910 issue, was 'The Gateway of the Monster', an excellent chiller fraught with suspense, which was a certain choice for this collection. The Carnacki stories are amongst the most powerful and intense depictions of personal terror in the face of supernatural evil by any author in the twentieth century. All of them offer plenty of narrative satisfaction, from the unusual ideas, strongly-realised central character, and energy in the telling, and this story is one of the most successful.

As shown in the exciting narrative thrust of 'The Gateway of the Monster', the Carnacki stories provided a format and framework well suited for channelling William Hope Hodgson's personal energy, robustness of character and striking imagination. It has been suggested that the stories drew on real incidents from Hodgson's life, but whether this is an important element or not, they certainly capture an attitude of courage, curiosity and determination that was true of the author himself, and which he sustained until his death in the First World War in 1917.

Hodgson adopted Conan Doyle's device of referring in passing to the other cases of his detective, yet to be told. It is a particular pleasure to include here the full details of a case mentioned in 'The Gateway of the Monster': the sinister affair of 'The Black Veil', which is faithfully evoked by contemporary author A. F. Kidd. This was first published in a collection of Carnacki tributes by A. F. Kidd and Rick Kennett, *No 472 Cheyne Walk*, published in 1992 by David Cowperthwaite on behalf of the Ghost Story Society.

One of the founders of *The Idler* (with Jerome K. Jerome) was Robert Barr, a versatile journalist and editor, who wrote for many of the short-story periodicals of the time. Though born in Glasgow, he was brought up in Canada, coming to England in 1881. He is mostly remembered today for creating Eugène Valmont, a French detective exiled in London who takes on cases privately. With his vanity, gallantry and precise reasoning, he has been seen as a model for Agatha Christie's more famous Belgian detective, Hercule Poirot. Here, from Barr's book *The Triumphs of Eugène Valmont* (1906), his dapper hero is brought up against a noble family's legendary ghost in 'The Ghost with the Club-Foot'.

Vernon Knowles was born in 1899 in Adelaide, South Australia of British parents but came to England as a young man, and wrote a handful of volumes of fantasies and fables, as well as poetry and eccentric novels. He had a light, wistful style and struggled to eke a living from his work, which deserves to be better known. It is pleasing to reprint here his poignant and wonderfully inventive tale, from *Two and Two Make Five* (1932), of Basil Thorpenden, who describes himself as an 'occult scientist' and invents strange ways of contacting the other world.

L. Adams Beck was another child of Empire: her father was the Admiral who gave his name to Port Moresby in Papua New Guinea. In the nineteen-twenties and -thirties she wrote popular historical romances under the name of 'E. Barrington', and a series of books exploring mystical adventures, inspired by the wisdom of the East, which are more thoughtful and with deeper characterisation than is common in this field. One of these was *The Openers of the Gate* (1930), sub-titled 'Stories of the Occult', which provides ten episodes in the career of Dr James Livingstone, a medical man but also an investigator of psychic incidents. 'Waste Manor', our selection, is a powerful tale of the endurance of a historical tragedy.

It is another great nation of the Empire, India, if not the entire Empire itself, that is at stake in Donald Campbell's breathless occult thriller 'The Necromancer' (1924), featuring his character Leslie Vane, a sort of James Bond of the jazz age. A secret service man, a sportsman, a fine shot and fencer, he can pilot a plane and race across the globe at the drop of a hat, and in this tale he is brought up against a reincarnation of Genghis Khan, and British cad and occultist Tristram Parr. Little is known of Campbell, who wrote for the Federation Press, renowned in the period for their brisk popular fiction.

Despite all these excellent examples, there have always been those who are unhappy about the hybrid that is the occult detective. When Ronald Knox put forward his 'Ten Commandments' of detective fiction in 1928, he stipulated that there should be no supernatural element. The Detection Club, with many of the great Golden Age writers of crime fiction as its members, put it more forcefully, ruling out what it called 'Mumbo-Jumbo, Jiggery-Pokery . . . or the Act of God'. On the other hand, neither have weird fiction savants been entirely happy that the sleuthing format works best for their field. The American supernatural horror genius H. P. Lovecraft was not ·

keen on the form, criticising the 'more or less conventional stock figure of the "infallible detective" type – the progeny of M. Dupin and Sherlock Holmes, and the close kin of Algernon Blackwood's John Silence – moving through scenes and events badly marred by an atmosphere of professional "occultism".'

Yet many disagree with these dismissals. The figure of the occult detective has remained persistently popular. Whether it is the trio of hapless paranormal investigators in the Hollywood comedy-action film *Ghostbusters* (1984), or the film-makers and folklore researchers in the enigmatic *The Blair Witch Project* (1999), cinema has always made use of the character, while TV has made its contribution in the Swinging Sixties series *Adam Adamant* (1966–7), about a revivified Edwardian investigator. Television has also provided numerous haunted house investigations, including some which led the viewer into thinking they were watching real supernatural incidents, such as Stephen Volk's *Ghostwatch* (1992). Sophisticated cosmic conspiracy series such as *The X Files* (1993 onwards) and *Millennium* (1996 onwards) also mixed the paranormal and intrepid investigators to great effect. Vintage occult detectives have also been revived through such concepts as the Wold Newton universe of fictional characters created by Philip José Farmer and his followers (1972 onwards), or the *League of Extraordinary Gentleman* comic book series written by Alan Moore (1999 onwards).

So supernatural sleuths continue to flourish in our own day, and we offer here a selection of more recent stories that serve the form well. One of the most admired in the field has been Mary Anne Allen's Jane Bradshawe, a church restorer who encounters ancient terrors during her visits to various parishes. Her stories were first brought together in *The Angry Dead* (1986) from Jeff Dempsey's Crimson Altar Press. In 'The Sheelagh-na-Gig', a calm economy in the telling of the tale belies the very strong implication of the ending. My own aesthetical occult detective, known only as The Connoisseur, recounts his experiences at the Isles of Fleet, off Galloway, South West Scotland, where he uncovers the secret of a lost domain. John Cooling evokes Norse mythology in his effective story featuring mythologist Dr Morrow, and inspired by the great sagas of the gods, while C. P. Langeveld introduces us to a splendid naval prognosticator of the psychic realm, Captain Thomas Gaunt, and his friend 'The Prefessor'. Psychics who claim to be able to help the police with clues to real crimes are still around today, and R. B. Russell recounts a bizarre and macabre case from the vintage files of one such. Our collection concludes by bringing the supernatural sleuth form right up to date in Rosalie Parker's chilling story of an internet investigation service and their cryptic messages to an embattled family.

Sherlock Holmes may have shunned all suggestion of supernatural agency, but thankfully his many rivals and literary descendants have not – so here is a casebook of the dark detectives for you to enjoy.

MARK VALENTINE

THE BLACK VEIL

and other tales of
Supernatural Sleuths

The Warder of the Door

ROBERT EUSTACE AND L. T. MEADE

'If you don't believe it, you can read it for yourself,' said Allen Clinton, climbing up the steps and searching among the volumes on the top shelf.

I lay back in my chair. The beams from the sinking sun shone through the stained glass of the windows of the old library, and dyed the rows of black leather volumes with bands of red and yellow.

'Here, Bell!'

I took a musty volume from Allen Clinton, which he had unearthed from its resting-place.

'It is about the middle of the book,' he continued eagerly. 'You will see it in big, black, old English letters.'

I turned over the pages containing the family tree and other archives of the Clintons till I came to the one I was seeking. It contained the curse which had rested on the family since 1400. Slowly and with difficulty I deciphered the words of this terrible denunciation.

And in this cell its coffin lieth, the coffin which hath not human shape, for which reason no holy ground receiveth it. Here shall it rest to curse the family of ye Clyntons from generation to generation. And for this reason, as soon as the soul shall pass from the body of each first-born, which is the heir, it shall become the warder of the door by day and by night. Day and night shall his spirit stand by the door, to keep the door closed till the son shall release the spirit of the father from the watch and take his place, till his son in turn shall die. And whoso entereth into the cell shall be the prisoner of the soul that guardeth the door till it shall let him go.

'What a ghastly idea!' I said, glancing up at the young man who was watching me as I read. 'But you say this cell has never been found. I should say its existence was a myth, and, of course, the curse on the soul of the first-born to keep the door shut as warder is absurd. Matter does not obey witchcraft.'

'The odd part of it is,' replied Allen, 'that every other detail of the Abbey referred to in this record has been identified; but this cell with its horrible contents has never been found.'

It certainly was a curious legend, and I allow it made some impression on me. I fancied, too, that somewhere I had heard something similar, but my memory failed to trace it.

I had come down to Clinton Abbey three days before for some pheasant shooting.

It was now Sunday afternoon. The family, with the exception of old Sir Henry, Allen, and myself, were at church. Sir Henry, now nearly eighty years of age and a chronic invalid, had retired to his room for his afternoon sleep. The younger Clinton and I had gone out for a stroll round the grounds, and since we returned our conversation had run upon the family history till it arrived at the legend of the family curse. Presently, the door of the library was slowly opened, and Sir Henry, in his black velvet coat, which formed such a striking contrast to his snowy white beard and hair, entered the room. I rose from my chair, and, giving him my arm, assisted him to his favourite couch. He sank down into its luxurious depths with a sigh, but as he did so his eyes caught the old volume which I had laid on the table beside it. He started forward, took the book in his hand, and looked across at his son.

'Did you take this book down?' he said sharply.

'Yes, father; I got it out to show it to Bell. He is interested in the history of the Abbey, and – '

'Then return it to its place at once,' interrupted the old man, his black eyes blazing with sudden passion. 'You know how I dislike having my books disarranged, and this one above all. Stay, give it to me.'

He struggled up from the couch, and, taking the volume, locked it up in one of the drawers of his writing-table, and then sat back again on the sofa. His hands were trembling, as if some sudden fear had taken possession of him.

'Did you say that Phyllis Curzon is coming tomorrow?' asked the old man presently of his son in an irritable voice.

'Yes, father, of course; don't you remember? Mrs Curzon and Phyllis are coming to stay for a fortnight; and, by the way,' he added, starting to his feet as he spoke, 'that reminds me I must go and tell Grace – '

The rest of the sentence was lost in the closing of the door. As soon as we were alone, Sir Henry looked across at me for a few moments without speaking. Then he said, 'I am sorry I was so short just now. I am not myself. I do not know what is the matter with me. I feel all to pieces. I cannot sleep. I do not think my time is very long now, and I am worried about Allen. The fact is, I would give anything to stop this engagement. I wish he would not marry.'

'I am sorry to hear you say that, sir,' I answered. 'I should have thought you would have been anxious to see your son happily married.'

'Most men would,' was the reply; 'but I have my reasons for wishing things otherwise.'

'What do you mean?' I could not help asking.

'I cannot explain myself; I wish I could. It would be best for Allen to let the old family die out. There, perhaps I am foolish about it, and of course I cannot really stop the marriage, but I am worried and troubled about many things.'

'I wish I could help you, sir,' I said impulsively. 'If there is anything I can possibly do, you know you have only to ask me.'

'Thank you, Bell, I know you would; but I cannot tell you. Some day I may. But there, I am afraid – horribly afraid.'

The trembling again seized him, and he put his hands over his eyes as if to shut out some terrible sight.

'Don't repeat a word of what I have told you to Allen or anyone else,' he said suddenly. 'It is possible that some day I may ask you to help me; and remember, Bell, I trust you.'

He held out his hand, which I took. In another moment the butler entered with the lamps, and I took advantage of the interruption to make my way to the drawing-room.

The next day the Curzons arrived, and a hasty glance showed me that Phyllis was a charming girl. She was tall, slightly built, with a figure both upright and graceful, and a handsome, somewhat proud face. When in perfect repose her expression was somewhat haughty; but the moment she spoke her face became vivacious, kindly, charming to an extraordinary degree; she had a gay laugh, a sweet smile, a sympathetic manner. I was certain she had the kindest of hearts, and was sure that Allen had made an admirable choice.

A few days went by, and at last the evening before the day when I was to return to London arrived. Phyllis's mother had gone to bed a short time before, as she had complained of headache, and Allen suddenly proposed, as the night was a perfect one, that we should go out and enjoy a moonlight stroll.

Phyllis laughed with glee at the suggestion, and ran at once into the hall to take a wrap from one of the pegs.

'Allen,' she said to her lover, who was following her, 'you and I will go first.'

'No, young lady, on this occasion you and I will have that privilege,' said Sir Henry. He had also come into the hall, and, to our astonishment, announced his intention of accompanying us in our walk.

Phyllis bestowed upon him a startled glance, then she laid her hand lightly on his arm, nodded back at Allen with a smile, and walked on in front somewhat rapidly. Allen and I followed in the rear.

'Now, what does my father mean by this?' said Allen to me. 'He never goes out at night; but he has not been well lately. I sometimes think he grows queerer every day.'

'He is very far from well, I am certain,' I answered.

We stayed out for about half an hour and returned home by a path which led into the house through a side entrance. Phyllis was waiting for us in the hall.

'Where is my father?' asked Allen, going up to her.

'He is tired and has gone to bed,' she answered. 'Good-night, Allen.'

'Won't you come into the drawing-room?' he asked in some astonishment.

'No, I am tired.'

She nodded to him without touching his hand; her eyes, I could not help noticing, had a queer expression. She ran upstairs.

I saw that Allen was startled by her manner; but as he did not say anything, neither did I.

The next day at breakfast I was told that the Curzons had already left the Abbey. Allen was full of astonishment and, I could see, a good deal annoyed. He and I breakfasted alone in the old library. His father was too ill to come downstairs.

An hour later I was on my way back to London. Many things there engaged my immediate attention, and Allen, his engagement, Sir Henry, and the old family curse, sank more or less into the background of my mind.

Three months afterwards, on the 7th of January, I saw to my sorrow in *The Times* the announcement of Sir Henry Clinton's death.

From time to time in the interim I had heard from the son, saying that his father was failing fast. He further mentioned that his own wedding was fixed for the twenty-first of the present month. Now, of course, it must be postponed. I felt truly sorry for Allen, and wrote immediately a long letter of condolence.

On the following day I received a wire from him, imploring me to go down to the Abbey as soon as possible, saying that he was in great difficulty.

I packed a few things hastily, and arrived at Clinton Abbey at six in the evening. The house was silent and subdued – the funeral was to take place the next day. Clinton came into the hall and gripped me warmly by the hand. I noticed at once how worn and worried he looked.

'This is good of you, Bell,' he said. 'I cannot tell you how grateful I am to you for coming. You are the one man who can help me, for I know you have had much experience in matters of this sort. Come into the library and I will tell you everything. We shall dine alone this evening, as my mother and the girls are keeping to their own apartments for tonight.'

As soon as we were seated, he plunged at once into his story.

'I must give you a sort of prelude to what has just occurred,' he began. 'You remember, when you were last here, how abruptly Phyllis and her mother left the Abbey?'

I nodded. I remembered well.

'On the morning after you had left us I had a long letter from Phyllis,' continued Allen. 'In it she told me of an extraordinary request my father had made to her during that moonlight walk – nothing more nor less than an earnest wish that she would herself terminate our engagement. She spoke quite frankly, as she always does, assuring me of her unalterable love and devotion, but saying that under the circumstances it was absolutely necessary to have an explanation. Frantic with almost ungovernable rage, I sought my father in his study. I laid Phyllis's letter before him and asked him what it meant. He looked at me with the most unutterable expression of weariness and pathos.

' "Yes, my boy, I did it," he said. "Phyllis is quite right. I did ask of her, as earnestly as a very old man could plead, that she would bring the engagement to an end."

' "But why?" I asked. "Why?"

' "That I am unable to tell you," he replied.

'I lost my temper and said some words to him which I now regret. He made no sort of reply. When I had done speaking he said slowly, "I make all allowance for your emotion, Allen; your feelings are no more than natural."

' "You have done me a very sore injury," I retorted. "What can Phyllis think of this? She will never be the same again. I am going to see her today."

'He did not utter another word, and I left him. I was absent from home for about a week. It took me nearly that time to induce Phyllis to overlook my father's extraordinary request, and to let matters go on exactly as they had done before.

'After fixing our engagement, if possible, more firmly than ever, and also arranging the date of our wedding, I returned home. When I did so I told my father what I had done.

' "As you will," he replied, and then he sank into great gloom. From that moment, although I watched him day and night, and did everything that love and tenderness could suggest, he never seemed to rally. He scarcely spoke, and remained, whenever we were together, bowed in deep and painful reverie. A week ago he took to his bed.'

Here Allen paused.

'I now come to events up to date,' he said. 'Of course, as you may suppose, I was with my father to the last. A few hours before he passed away he called me to his bedside, and to my astonishment began once more talking about my engagement. He implored me with the utmost earnestness even now at the eleventh hour to break it off. It was not too late, he said, and added further that nothing would give him ease in dying but the knowledge that I would promise him to remain single. Of course I tried to humour him. He took my hand, looked me in the eyes with an expression which I shall never forget, and said, "Allen, make me a solemn promise that you will never marry."

'This I naturally had to refuse, and then he told me that, expecting my obstinacy, he had written me a letter which I should find in his safe, but I was not to open it till after his death. I found it this morning. Bell, it is the most extraordinary communication, and either it is entirely a figment of his imagination, for his brain powers were failing very much at the last, or else it is the most awful thing I ever heard of. Here is the letter; read it for yourself.'

I took the paper from his hand and read the following matter in shaky, almost illegible writing: –

MY DEAR BOY, – When you read this I shall have passed away. For the last six months my life has been a living death. The horror began in the following way. You know what a deep interest I have always taken in the family history of our house. I have spent the latter years of my life in verifying each detail, and my intention was, had health been given me, to publish a great deal of it in a suitable volume.

On the special night to which I am about to allude, I sat up late in my study reading the book which I saw you show to Bell a short time ago. In particular, I was much attracted by the terrible curse which the old abbot in the fourteenth century had bestowed upon the family. I read the awful words again and again. I knew that all the other details in the volume had been verified, but that the vault with the coffin had never yet been found. Presently I grew drowsy, and I suppose I must have fallen asleep. In my sleep I had a dream; I thought that someone came into the room, touched me on the shoulder, and said 'Come'. I looked up; a tall figure beckoned to me. The voice and the figure belonged to my late father. In my dream I rose immediately, although I did not know why I went nor where I was going. The figure went on in front, it entered the hall. I took one of the candles from the table and the key of the chapel, unbolted the door and went out. Still the voice kept saying 'Come, come', and the figure of my father walked in front of me. I went across the quadrangle, unlocked the chapel door, and entered.

A death-like silence was around me. I crossed the nave to the north aisle; the figure still went in front of me; it entered the great pew which is said to be haunted, and walked straight up to the effigy of the old abbot who had pronounced the curse. This, as you know, is built into the opposite wall. Bending forward, the figure pressed the eyes of the old monk, and immediately a stone started out of its place, revealing a staircase behind. I was about to hurry forward, when I must have knocked against something. I felt a sensation of pain, and suddenly awoke. What was my amazement to find that I had acted on my dream, had crossed the quadrangle, and was in the chapel; in fact, was standing in the old pew! Of course there was no figure of any sort visible, but the moonlight shed a cold radiance over all the place. I felt very much startled and impressed, but was just about to return to the house in some wonder at the curious vision which I had experienced, when, raising my startled eyes, I saw that part of it at least was real. The old monk seemed to grin at me from his marble effigy, and beside him was a *blank open space*. I hurried to it and saw a narrow flight of stairs. I cannot explain what my emotions were, but my keenest feeling at that moment was a strong and horrible curiosity. Holding the candle in my hand, I went down the steps. They terminated at the beginning of a long passage. This I quickly traversed, and at last found myself beside an iron door. It was not locked, but hasped, and was very hard to open; in fact, it required nearly all my strength; at last I pulled it open towards me, and there in a small cell lay the coffin, as the words of the curse said. I gazed at it in horror. I did not dare to enter. It was a wedged-shaped coffin studded with great nails. But as I looked my blood froze within me, for slowly, very slowly, as if pushed by some unseen hand, the great heavy door began to close, quicker and quicker, until with a crash that echoed and re-echoed through the empty vault, it shut.

Terror-stricken, I rushed from the vault and reached my room once more.

Now I know that this great curse is true; that my father's spirit is there to guard the door and close it, for I saw it with my own eyes, and while you read this know that I am there. I charge you, therefore, not to marry – bring no child into the world to perpetuate this terrible curse. Let the family die out if you have the courage. It is much, I know, to ask; but whether you do or not, come to me there, and if by sign or word I can communicate with you I will do so, but hold the secret safe. Meet me there before my body is laid to rest, when body and soul are still not far from each other. Farewell.

Your loving father,
HENRY CLINTON

I read this strange letter over carefully twice, and laid it down. For a moment I hardly knew what to say. It was certainly the most uncanny thing I had ever come across.

'What do you think of it?' asked Allen at last.

'Well, of course there are only two possible solutions,' I answered. 'One is that your father not only dreamt the beginning of this story – which, remember, he allows himself – but the whole of it.'

'And the other?' asked Allen, seeing that I paused.

'The other,' I continued, 'I hardly know what to say yet. Of course we will investigate the whole thing, that is our only chance of arriving at a solution. It is absurd to let matters rest as they are. We had better try tonight.'

Clinton winced and hesitated.

'Something must be done, of course,' he answered; 'but the worst of it is Phyllis and her mother are coming here early tomorrow in time for the funeral, and I cannot meet her – no, I cannot, poor girl! – while I feel as I do.'

'We will go to the vault tonight,' I said.

Clinton rose from his chair and looked at me.

'I don't like this thing at all, Bell,' he continued. 'I am not by nature in any sense of the word a superstitious man, but I tell you frankly nothing would induce me to go alone into that chapel tonight; if you come with me, that, of course, alters matters. I know the pew my father refers to well; it is beneath the window of St Sebastian.'

Soon afterwards I went to my room and dressed; and Allen and I dined *tête-à-tête* in the great dining-room. The old butler waited on us with funereal solemnity, and I did all I could to lure Clinton's thoughts into a more cheerful and healthier channel.

I cannot say that I was very successful. I further noticed that he scarcely ate anything, and seemed altogether to be in a state of nervous tension painful to witness.

After dinner we went into the smoking-room, and at eleven o'clock I proposed that we should make a start.

Clinton braced himself together and we went out. He got the chapel keys, and then going to the stables we borrowed a lantern, and a moment afterwards found ourselves in the sacred edifice. The moon was at her full, and by the pale light which was diffused through the south windows the architecture of the interior could be faintly seen. The Gothic arches that flanked the centre aisle with their quaint pillars, each with a carved figure of one of the saints, were quite visible, and further in the darkness of the chancel the dim outlines of the choir and altar-table with its white marble reredos could be just discerned.

We closed the door softly and, Clinton leading the way with the lantern, we walked up the centre aisle paved with the brasses of his dead ancestors. We trod gently on tiptoe as one instinctively does at night. Turning beneath the little pulpit we reached the north transept, and here Clinton stopped and turned round. He was very white, but his voice was quiet.

'This is the pew,' he whispered. 'It has always been called the haunted pew of Sir Hugh Clinton.'

I took the lantern from him and we entered. I crossed the pew immediately and went up to the effigy of the old abbot.

'Let us examine him closely,' I said. I held up the lantern, getting it to shine on each part of the face, the vestments, and the figure. The eyes, although vacant, as in all statuary, seemed to me at that moment to be uncanny and peculiar. Giving Allen the lantern to hold, I placed a finger firmly on each. The next moment I could not refrain from an exclamation; a stone at the side immediately rolled back, revealing the steps which were spoken of by the old man in his narrative.

'It is true! It is true!' cried Clinton excitedly.

'It certainly looks like it,' I remarked: 'but never mind, we have the chance now of investigating this matter thoroughly.'

'Are you going down?' asked Clinton.

'Certainly I am,' I replied. 'Let us go together.'

Immediately afterwards we crept through the opening and began to descend. There was only just room to do so in single file, and I went first with the lantern. In another moment we were in the long passage, and soon we were confronted by a door in an arched stone framework. Up till now Clinton had shown little sign of alarm, but here, at the trysting-place to which his father's soul had summoned him, he seemed suddenly to lose his nerve. He leant against the wall and for a moment I thought he would have fallen. I held up the lantern and examined the door and walls carefully. Then approaching I lifted the iron latch of the heavy door. It was very hard to move, but at last by seizing the edge I dragged it open to its full against the wall of the passage. Having done so I peered inside, holding the lantern above my head. As I did so I heard Clinton cry out – 'Look, look,' he said, and turning I saw that the great door had swung back against me, almost shutting me within the cell.

Telling Clinton to hold it back by force, I stepped inside and saw at my feet the ghastly coffin. The legend then so far was true. I bent down and examined the queer, misshapen thing with great care. Its shape was that of an enormous wedge, and it was apparently made of some dark old wood, and was bound with iron at the corners. Having looked at it all round, I went out and, flinging back the door which Clinton had been holding open, stood aside to watch. Slowly, very slowly, as we both stood in the passage – slowly, as if pushed by some invisible hand, the door commenced to swing round, and, increasing in velocity, shut with a noisy clang.

Seizing it once again, I dragged it open and, while Clinton held it in that position, made a careful examination. Up to the present I saw nothing to be much alarmed about. There were fifty ways in which a door might shut of its own accord. There might be a hidden spring or tilted hinges; draught, of course, was out of the question. I looked at the hinges, they were of iron and set in the solid masonry. Nor could I discover any spring or hidden contrivance, as when the door was wide open there was an interval of several inches between it and the wall. We tried it again and again with the same result, and at last, as it was closing, I seized it to prevent it.

I now experienced a very odd sensation; I certainly felt as if I were resisting an unseen person who was pressing hard against the door at the other side. Directly it was released it continued its course. I allow I was quite unable to understand the mystery. Suddenly an idea struck me.

'What does the legend say?' I asked, turning to Clinton. '"That the soul is to guard the door, to close it upon the coffin?"'

'Those are the words,' answered Allen, speaking with some difficulty.

'Now if that is true,' I continued, 'and we take the coffin out, the spirit won't shut the door; if it does shut it, it disproves the whole thing at once, and shows it to be merely a clever mechanical contrivance. Come, Clinton, help me to get the coffin out.'

'I dare not, Bell,' he whispered hoarsely. 'I daren't go inside.'

'Nonsense, man,' I said, feeling now a little annoyed at the whole thing. 'Here, put the lantern down and hold the door back.' I stepped in and, getting behind the coffin, put out all my strength and shoved it into the passage.

'Now, then,' I cried, 'I'll bet you fifty pounds to five the door will shut just the same.' I dragged the coffin clear of the door and told him to let go. Clinton had scarcely done so before, stepping back, he clutched my arm.

'Look,' he whispered; 'do you see that it will not shut now? My father is waiting for the coffin to be put back. This is awful!'

I gazed at the door in horror; it was perfectly true, it remained wide open, and quite still. I sprang forward, seized it, and now endeavoured to close it. It was as if someone was trying to hold it open; it required considerable force to stir it, and it was only with difficulty I could move it at all. At last I managed to shut it, but the moment I let go it swung back open of its own accord and struck against the wall, where it remained just as before. In the dead silence that followed I could hear Clinton breathing quickly behind me, and I knew he was holding himself for all he was worth.

At that moment there suddenly came over me a sensation which I had once experienced before, and which I was twice destined to experience again. It is impossible to describe it, but it seized me, laying siege to my brain till I felt like a child in its power. It was as if

I were slowly drowning in the great ocean of silence that enveloped us. Time itself seemed to have disappeared. At my feet lay the mis-shapen thing, and the lantern behind it cast a fantastic shadow of its distorted outline on the cell wall before me.

'Speak; say something,' I cried to Clinton. The sharp sound of my voice broke the spell. I felt myself again, and smiled at the trick my nerves had played on me. I bent down and once more laid my hands on the coffin, but before I had time to push it back into its place Clinton had gone up the passage like a man who is flying to escape a hurled javelin.

Exerting all my force to prevent the door from swinging back by keeping my leg against it, I had just got the coffin into the cell and was going out, when I heard a shrill cry, and Clinton came tearing back down the passage.

'I can't get out! The stone has sunk into its place! We are locked in!' he screamed, and, wild with fear, he plunged headlong into the cell, upsetting me in his career before I could check him. I sprang back to the door as it was closing. I was too late. Before I could reach it, it had shut with a loud clang in obedience to the infernal witchcraft.

'You have done it now,' I cried angrily. 'Do you see? Why, man, we are buried alive in this ghastly hole!'

The lantern I had placed just inside the door, and by its dim light, as I looked at him, I saw the terror of a madman creep into Clinton's eyes.

'Buried alive!' he shouted, with a peal of hysterical laughter. 'Yes, and, Bell, it's your doing; you are a devil in human shape!' With a wild paroxysm of fury he flung himself upon me. There was the ferocity of a wild beast in his spring. He upset the lantern and left us in total darkness.

The struggle was short. We might be buried alive, but I was not going to die by his hand, and seizing him by the throat I pinned him against the wall.

'Keep quiet,' I shouted. 'It is your thundering stupidity that has caused all this. Stay where you are until I strike a match.'

I luckily had some vestas in the little silver box which I always carry on my watch-chain, and striking one I relit the lantern. Clinton's paroxysm was over, and sinking to the floor he lay there shivering and cowering.

It was a terrible situation, and I knew that our only hope was for me to keep my presence of mind. With a great effort I forced myself to think calmly over what could be done. To shout for help would have been but a useless waste of breath.

Suddenly an idea struck me. 'Have you got your father's letter?' I cried eagerly.

'I have,' he answered; 'it is in my pocket.'

My last ray of hope vanished. Our only chance was that if he had left it at the house someone might discover the letter and come to our rescue by its instructions. It had been a faint hope, and it disappeared almost as quickly as it had come to me. Without it no one would ever find the way to the vault that had remained a secret for ages. I was determined, however, not to die without a struggle for freedom. Taking the lantern, I examined every nook and cranny of the cell for some other exit. It was a fruitless search. No sign of any way out could I find, and we had absolutely no means to unfasten the door from the inner side. Taking a few short steps, I flung myself again and again at the heavy door. It never budged an inch, and, bruised and sweating at every pore, I sat down on the coffin and tried to collect all my faculties.

Clinton was silent, and seemed utterly stunned. He sat still, gazing with a vacant stare at the door.

The time dragged heavily, and there was nothing to do but to wait for a horrible death from starvation. It was more than likely, too, that Clinton would go mad; already his nerves were strained to the utmost. Altogether I had never found myself in a worse plight.

It seemed like an eternity that we sat there, neither of us speaking a word. Over and over again I repeated to myself the words of the terrible curse: 'And whoso entereth into the cell shall be the prisoner of the soul that guardeth the door till it shall let him go.' When would the shapeless form that was inside the coffin let us go? Doubtless when our bones were dry.

I looked at my watch. It was half-past eleven o'clock. Surely we had been more than ten minutes in this awful place! We had left the house at eleven, and I knew that must have been many hours ago. I glanced at the second hand. *The watch had stopped.*

'What is the time, Clinton?' I asked. 'My watch has stopped.'

'What does it matter?' he murmured. 'What is time to us now? The sooner we die the better.'

He pulled out his watch as he spoke, and held it to the lantern.

'Twenty-five minutes past eleven,' he murmured dreamily.

'Good heavens!' I cried, starting up. 'Has your watch stopped, too?'

Then, like the leap of a lightning flash, an idea struck me.

'I have got it; I have got it! My God! I believe I have got it!' I cried, seizing him by the arm.

'Got what?' he replied, staring wildly at me.

'Why, the secret – the curse – the door. Don't you see?'

I pulled out the large knife I always carry by a chain and swivel in my trouser pocket, and telling Clinton to hold the lantern, opened the little blade-saw and attacked the coffin with it.

'I believe the secret of our deliverance lies in this,' I panted, working away furiously.

In ten minutes I had sawn half through the wooden edge, then, handing my tool to Clinton, I told him to continue the work while I rested. After a few minutes I took the knife again, and at last, after nearly half an hour had gone by, succeeded in making a small hole in the lid. Inserting my two fingers, I felt some rough, uneven masses. I was now fearfully excited. Tearing at the opening like a madman, I enlarged it and extracted what looked like a large piece of coal. I knew in an instant what it was. It was magnetic iron-ore. Holding it down to my knife, the blade flew to it.

'Here is the mystery of the soul,' I cried; 'now we can use it to open the door.'

I had known a great conjurer once, who had deceived and puzzled his audience with a box trick on similar lines: the man opening the box from the inside by drawing down the lock with a magnet. Would this do the same? I felt that our lives hung on the next moment. Taking the mass, I pressed it against the door just opposite the hasp, and slid it up against the wood. My heart leapt as I heard the hasp fly up outside, and with a push the door opened.

'We are saved,' I shouted. 'We are saved by a miracle!'

'Bell, you are a genius,' gasped poor Clinton; 'but now, how about the stone at the end of the passage?'

'We will soon see about that,' I cried, taking the lantern. 'Half the danger is over, at any rate; and the worst half, too.'

We rushed along the passage and up the stair until we reached the top.

'Why, Clinton,' I cried, holding up the lantern, 'the place was not shut at all.'

Nor was it. In his terror he had imagined it.

'I could not see in the dark, and I was nearly dead with fright,' he said. 'Oh, Bell, let us get out of this as quickly as we can!'

We crushed through the aperture and once more stood in the chapel. I then pushed the stone back into its place.

Dawn was just breaking when we escaped from the chapel. We hastened across to the house. In the hall the clock pointed to five.

'Well, we have had an awful time,' I said, as we stood in the hall together; 'but at least, Clinton, the end was worth the ghastly terror. I have knocked the bottom out of your family legend for ever.'

'I don't even now quite understand,' he said.

'Don't you? – but it is so easy. That coffin never contained a body at all, but was filled, as you perceive, with fragments of magnetic iron ore. For what diabolical purposes the cell was intended, it is, of course, impossible to say; but that it must have been meant as a human trap there is little doubt. The inventor certainly exercised no small ingenuity when he devised his diabolical plot, for it was obvious that the door, which was made of iron, would swing towards the coffin wherever it happened to be placed. Thus the door would shut if the coffin were *inside the cell*, and would remain open if the coffin were *brought out*. A cleverer method for simulating a spiritual agency it would be hard to find. Of course, the monk must have known well that magnetic iron-ore never loses its quality and would ensure the deception remaining potent for ages.'

'But how did you discover by means of our watches?' asked Clinton.

'Anyone who understands magnetism can reply to that,' I said. 'It is a well-known fact that a strong magnet plays havoc with watches. The fact of both our watches going wrong first gave me a clue to the mystery.'

Later in the day the whole of this strange affair was explained to Miss Curzon, and not long afterwards the passage and entrance to the chapel were bricked up.

It is needless to add that six months later the pair were married, and, I believe, are as happy as they deserve.

The Story of Sevens Hall

E. AND H. HERON

'It may be quite true,' said Yarkindale gloomily; 'all that I can answer is that we always die the same way. Some of us choose, or are driven, to one form of suicide, and some to another, but the result is alike. For three generations every man of my family has died by his own hand. I have not come to you hoping for help, Mr Low, I merely want to tell the facts to a man who may possibly believe that we are not insane, that heredity and madness have nothing to do with our leaving the world; but that we are forced out of it by some external power acting upon us, I do not know how. If we inherit anything it is clear-headedness and strength of will, but this curse of ours is stronger. That is all.'

Flaxman Low kicked the fire into a blaze. It shone on the silver and china of the breakfast service, and on the sallow, despairing face of the man in the armchair opposite. He was still young, but already the cloud that rested upon his life had carved deep lines upon his forehead in addition to the long telltale groove from mouth to nostril.

'I conclude death does not occur without some premonition. Tell me something more. What precedes death?' inquired Flaxman Low.

'A regular and well-marked series of events – I insist upon calling them events,' replied Yarkindale. 'This is not a disease with a series of symptoms. Whatever it is it comes from the outside. First we fall into an indescribable depression, causeless except as being the beginning of the end, for we are all healthy men, fairly rich, and even lucky in the other affairs of life – and of love. Next comes the ghost or apparition or whatever you like to call it. Lastly we die by our own hands.' Yarkindale brought down a sinewy brown hand upon the arm of his chair. 'And because we have been powers in the land, and there must be as little scandal as possible, the doctors and the coroner's jury bring it in "Temporary insanity".'

'How long does this depression last before the end?' Flaxman Low's voice broke in upon the other's moody thinking.

'That varies, but the conclusion never. I am the last of the lot, and though I am full of life and health and resolve today. I don't give myself a week to live. It is ghastly! To kill oneself is bad enough, but to know that one is being driven to do it, to know that no power on earth can save us, is an outlook of which words can't give the colour.'

'But you have not yet seen the apparition – which is the second stage.'

'It will come today or tomorrow – as soon as I go back to Sevens Hall. I have watched two others of my family go through the same mill. This irresistible depression always comes first. I tell you, in two weeks I shall be dead. And the thought is maddening me!'

'I have a wife and child,' he went on after an interval; 'and to think of the poor little beggar growing up only to suffer this!'

'Where are they?' asked Low.

'I left them in Florence. I hope the truth can be kept from my wife; but that also is too much to hope. "Another suicide at Sevens Hall". I can see the headlines. Those rags of newspapers would sell their mothers for half-a-crown!'

'Then the other deaths took place at Sevens Hall?'

'All of them.' He stopped and looked hard at Mr Low.

'Tell me about your brothers,' said Low.

Yarkindale burst into laughter.

'Well done, Mr Low! Why didn't you advise me not to go back to Sevens Hall? That is the admirable counsel which the two brain specialists, whom I have seen since I came up to town, have given me. Go back to the Hall? Of course I shouldn't – if I could help it. That's the difficulty – I can't help it! I must go. They thought me mad!'

'I hardly wonder,' said Low calmly, 'if you exhibited the same excitement. Now, hear me. If, as you wish me to suppose, you are fighting against supernatural powers, the very first point is to keep a firm and calm control of your feelings and thoughts. It is possible that you and I together may be able to meet this trouble of yours in some new and possibly successful way. Tell me all you can remember with regard to the deaths of your brothers.'

'You are right,' said Yarkindale sadly enough. 'I am behaving like a maniac, and yet I'm sane, Heaven knows! – To begin with, there were three of us, and we made up our minds long ago when we were kids to see each other through to the last, and we determined not to yield to the influence without a good fight for it. Five years ago my eldest brother went to Somaliland on a shooting trip. He was a big, vigorous, self-willed man, and I was not anxious about him. My second brother, Jack, was an R. E., a clever, sensitive, quiet fellow, more likely to be affected by the tradition of the family. While he was out in Gib., Vane suddenly returned from Africa. I found him changed. He had become gloomy and abstracted, and kept saying that the curse was coming upon him. He insisted upon going down to Sevens Hall. I was savage with him. I thought he should have resisted the inclination; I know more about it now. One night he rushed into my bedroom, crying out: "He's come; he's come!" '

'Did he ever describe what he had seen?' asked Low.

'Never. None of us know definitely what shape the cursed thing takes. No one of us has ever seen it; or, at any rate, in time to describe it. But once it comes – and this is the horrible part – it never leaves us. Step by step it dogs us, till – ' Yarkindale stopped, and in a minute or two resumed. 'For two nights I sat up with him. He said very little, for Vane never talked much; but I saw the agony in his face, the fear, the loathing, the growing horror – he, who I believe, had never before feared anything in his life.

'The third night I fell asleep. I was worn out, though I don't offer that as an excuse. I am a light sleeper, yet while I slept Vane killed himself within six feet of me! At the inquest it was proved he had bought a silken waist-rope at Cairo, and it was contended that he must have concealed it from me, as I had never seen it. I found him with his head nearly twisted off, and a red rubbed weal across his face. He was lying in a heap upon the floor, for the rope was frayed and broken by his struggles. The theory was that he had hanged himself, and then repented of it, and in his efforts to get free had wrenched his head around, and scarred his face.'

Yarkindale stopped and shuddered violently.

'I tried to hush the matter up as well as I could, but of course the news of it reached Jack. Then a couple of years passed, and he went from Gib. to India, and wrote in splendid spirits, for he had met a girl he liked out there, and he had told me that there was never so happy a man on earth before. So you can fancy how I felt when I had a wire from the Hall imploring me to go down at once for Jack had arrived. It is very hard to tell you what he suffered.' Yarkindale broke off and wiped his forehead. 'For I have been through it all within the last two weeks myself. He cared for that girl beyond anything on earth; yet within a couple of days of their marriage, he had felt himself impelled to rush home to England without so much as bidding her goodbye, though he knew that at the end of his journey death was waiting for him. We talked it over rationally, Mr Low, and we determined to combine against the power, whatever it was, that was driving him out of the world. We are not monomaniacs. We want to live; we have all that makes life worth living; and yet I am going the same way, and not any effort or desire or resolution on my part can save me!'

'It is a pity you make up your mind to that,' said Flaxman Low. 'One will pitted against another will has at least a chance of success. And a second point I beg you will bear in mind. Good is always inherently stronger than evil. If, for instance, health were not, broadly speaking, stronger than disease, the poisonous germs floating about the world would kill off the human race inside twelve months.'

'Yes,' said Yarkindale; 'but where two of us failed before, it is not likely that I alone will succeed.'

'You need not be alone,' said Flaxman Low; 'for if you have no objection, I should be glad to accompany you to Sevens Hall, and to give you any aid that may be in my power.'

It is not necessary to record what Yarkindale had to say in answer to this offer. Presently he resumed his story.

'Jack was dispirited, and unlike Vane, desperately afraid of his fate. He hardly dared fall asleep. He recalled all he knew of our father's death, and tried to draw me on to describe Vane's, but I knew better than that. Still, with all my care, he went the same way! I did not trust my own watchfulness a second time; I had a man in the house who was a trained attendant. He sat outside Jack's door of nights. One morning early – it was summer-time, and he must have dropped into a doze – he was shoved over, chair and all, and before he could pick himself up, Jack had flung himself from the balcony outside one of the gallery windows.'

Sevens Hall is a large Elizabethan mansion hidden away among acres of rich pasture lands, where wild flowers bloom abundantly in their seasons and rooks build and caw in the great elms. But none of the natural beauties of the country were visible when Mr Low arrived late on a November evening with Yarkindale. The interior of the house, however, made up for the bleakness outside. Fires and lights blazed in the hall and in the principal rooms. During dinner, Yarkindale seemed to have relapsed into his most dejected mood. He scarcely opened his lips, and his face looked black, not only with depression, but anger. For he was by no means ready to give up life; he rebelled against his fate with the strenuous fury of a man whose pride and strength of will and nearest desires are baffled by an antagonist he cannot evade.

During the evening they played billiards, for Low was aware that the less his companion thought over his own position, the better.

Flaxman Low arranged to occupy a room opposite Yarkindale's. So far the latter was in the same state as on the day when he first saw Mr Low. He was conscious of the same deep and causeless depression, and the wish to return to Sevens Hall had grown beyond his power to resist. But the second of the fatal signs, the following footsteps, had not yet been heard.

During the next forenoon, to Yarkindale's surprise, Flaxman Low, instead of avoiding the subject, threshed out the details of the former deaths at Sevens Hall, especially those of which Yarkindale could give the fullest particulars. He examined the balcony from which Jack Yarkindale had thrown himself. The ironwork was wrenched and broken in one part.

'When did this happen?' asked Low, pointing to it.

'On the night that Jack died,' was the reply. 'I have been very little at home since, and I did not care at the time to bother about having it put right.'

'It looks,' said Flaxman Low, 'as if he had a struggle for his life, and clung to the upper bar here where it is bent outwards. He had wounds on his hands, had he not?' he continued looking at a dull long splash of rust upon the iron.

'Yes, his hands were bleeding.'

'Please try to recollect exactly. Were they cut or bruised upon the palm? Or was it on the back?'

'Now I come to think of it, his hands were a good deal injured, especially on the knuckles – one wrist was broken – by the fall no doubt.'

Flaxman Low made no remark.

Next they went into the spacious bedroom where Vane and more than one of those who went before him had died, and which Yarkindale now occupied. His companion asked to see the rope with which Vane had hanged himself. Most unwillingly Yarkindale brought it out. The two pieces, with their broken strands and brown stains, appeared to be of great interest to Low. He next saw the exact spot on the great bedstead from which it had been suspended, and searching along the back, he discovered the jagged edge of the wood against which Vane in his last agony had endeavoured to free himself by fraying the rope.

'We suppose the rope gave after he was dead, and that was because of his great weight,' said Yarkindale. 'This is the room in which most of the tragedies have taken place. You will probably witness the last one.'

'That will depend on yourself,' answered Flaxman Low. 'I am inclined to think there will be no tragedy if you will stiffen your back, and hold out. Did either of your brothers on waking complain of dreams?'

Yarkindale looked suspiciously at him under drawn brows. 'Yes,' he said harshly, 'they both spoke of tormenting dreams, which they could not recall after walking, but that was also taken as a symptom of brain disease by the experts. And now that you have learned about the matter, you, too, begin upon the old, worn theory.'

'On the contrary, my theory has nothing to do with insanity, though the phenomena connected with the deaths of your brothers seem to be closely associated with sleep. You tell me that your brother Jack was afraid to sleep. Your other brother awoke to find his death somehow. Therefore, we may be certain that at a certain stage of these series of events, as you call them, sleep becomes both a dread and a danger.'

Yarkindale shivered and glanced nervously over his shoulder.

'This room is growing very cold. Let us go down to the hall. As to sleep, I have been afraid of it for a long time.'

All the day Low noticed that his companion continued to look excessively pale and nervous. Every now and then he would turn his face round as if listening. In the evening they again played billiards late into the night. The house was full of silence before they went upstairs. A long strip of polished flooring led from the billiard-room door to the hall. Yarkindale motioned to Low to stand still while he walked slowly to the foot of the staircase. In the stillness Flaxman Low distinctly heard mingled steps, a softer tread following upon Yarkindale's purposely loud footfalls. The hall was in darkness with the exception of a gas jet at the staircase. Yarkindale stopped, leant heavily against the pillar of the balustrade, and with a ghastly face waited for Low to join him. Then he gripped Low by the arm and pointed downwards. Beside his shadow, a second dim, hooded, formless shadow showed faintly on the floor.

'Stage two,' said Yarkindale, 'You can see it is no fancy of our unhealthy brains.'

Mr Low has placed it upon record that the following week contained one of the most painful experiences through which it has been his lot to pass. Yarkindale fought doggedly for his life. He thrust aside his dejection. He followed the advice given him with marvellous courage. But still the ominous days dragged on, seeming at times too slow, at times too rapid in their passage. Yarkindale's physical strength began to fail – a mental battle is the most exhausting of all struggles.

'The next point in which you can help,' said Low on the eighth night, 'is to try to recollect what you have been dreaming of immediately before waking.'

Yarkindale shook his head despondently.

'I have tried over and over again, and though I wake in a cold sweat of terror, I cannot gather my senses quickly enough to seize the remembrance of the thing that has spoiled my sleep,' he answered with a pallid smile. 'You think the psychological moment with us is undoubtedly the first waking moment?'

Low admitted that he thought it was so.

'I understand now why you have emptied this room of everything except the two couches on which we lie. You are afraid I shall lay hands upon myself! I feel the danger and yet I have no suicidal desire. I want to live – Heaven, how I long to live! To be happy, and prosperous, and light-hearted as I was once was!'

Yarkindale lay back upon the couch.

'I wish I could give you the faintest notion of the desperate misery in my mind tonight! I could almost ask to die to escape from it!' he went on; 'the burden only appears to grow heavier and more unbearable every day – I sometimes feel I can no longer endure it.'

'Think, on the contrary, how much you have to live for. For your own self it matters less than for your boy. Your victory may mean his.'

'How? Tell me how?'

'It is rather a long explanation, and I think we had better defer it until I can form some definite ideas on the subject.'

'Very well.' Yarkindale turned his face from the light. 'I will try to sleep and forget all this wretchedness if I can. You will not leave me?'

Through the long winter night, Flaxman Low watched beside him. He felt he dared not leave him for one moment. The room was almost dark, for Yarkindale could not sleep otherwise. The flickering firelight died down, until nothing was left of the last layer of glowing wood ashes. The night lamp in a distant corner threw long shadows across the empty floor, that wavered now and then as if a wind touched the flame.

Outside the night was still and black; not a sound disturbed the silence except those strange unaccountable creakings and groanings which seem like inarticulate voices in an old house.

Yarkindale was sleeping heavily, and as the night deepened Low got up and walked about the room in circles, always keeping his face towards the sleeper. The air had grown very cold, and when he sat down again he drew a rug about him, and lit a cigar. The change in the atmosphere was sudden and peculiar, and he softly pulled his couch close to Yarkindale's and waited.

Creakings and groanings floated up and down the gaunt old corridors, the mystery and loneliness of night became oppressive. The shadow from the night lamp swayed and fluttered as if a door had been opened. Mr Low glanced at both doors. He had locked both, and both were closed, yet the flame bent and flickered until Low put his hand across his companion's chest, so that he might detect any waking movement, for the light had now become too dim to see by.

To his intense surprise he found his hand at once in the chill of a cold draught blowing on it from above. But Flaxman Low had no time to think about it, for a terrible feeling of cold and numbness was stealing upwards through his feet, and a sense of weighty and deadly chill seemed pressing in upon his shoulders and back. The back of his neck ached, his outstretched hand began to stiffen.

Yarkindale still slept heavily.

New sensations were borne in slowly upon Low. The chill around him was the repulsive clammy chill of a thing long dead. Desperate desires awoke in his mind; something that could almost be felt was beating down his will.

Then Yarkindale moved slightly in his sleep.

Low was conscious of a supreme struggle, whether of mind or body he does not know, but to him it appeared to extend to the ultimate effort a man can make. A hideous temptation rushed wildly across his thoughts to murder Yarkindale! A dreadful longing to feel the man's strong throat yielding and crushing under his own sinewy strangling fingers, was forced into his mind.

Suddenly, Low became aware that, although the couch and part of Yarkindale's figure were visible, his head and the upper part of his body were blotted out as if by some black intervening object. But there was no outline of the interposed form, nothing but a vague thick blackness.

He sprang to his feet as he heard an ominous choking gasp from Yarkindale, and with his swift hands he felt over the body through the darkness. Yarkindale lay tense and stiff.

'Yarkindale!' shouted Low, as his fingers felt the angle of an elbow, then hands upon Yarkindale's throat, hands that clutched savagely with fingers of iron.

'Wake man!' shouted Low again, trying to loosen the desperate clutch. Then he knew that the hands were Yarkindale's hands, and that the man was apparently strangling himself.

The ghastly struggle, that in the darkness seemed half a dream and half reality, ceased abruptly when Yarkindale moved and his hands fell limp and slack into Low's as the darkness between them cleared away.

'Are you awake?' Low called again.

'Yes. What is it? I feel as if I had been fighting for my life. Or have I been very ill?'

'Both, in a sense. You have passed the crisis, and you are still living. Hold on, the lamp's gone out.'

But, as he spoke, the light resumed its steady glimmer, and, when a couple of candles added their brightness, the room was shown bare and empty, and as securely closed as ever. The only change to be noted was that the temperature had risen.

A frosty sun was shining into the library windows next morning when Flaxman Low talked out the matter of the haunting presence which had exerted so sinister an influence upon generations of the Yarkindale family.

'Before you say anything, I wish to admit, Mr Low, that I, and no doubt those who have gone before me, have certainly suffered from a transient touch of suicidal mania,' began Yarkindale gloomily.

'And I am very sure you make a mistake,' replied Low. 'In suicidal mania the idea is not transient, but persistent, often extending over months, during which time the patient watches for an opportunity to make away with himself. In your case, when I woke you last night, you were aware of a desire to strangle yourself, but directly you became thoroughly awake, the idea left you?'

'That is so. Still – '

'You know that often when dreaming one imagines oneself to do many things which in the waking state would be entirely impossible, yet one continues subject to the idea for a moment or so during the intermittent stage between waking and sleeping. If one has a nightmare, one continues to feel a beating of the heart and a sensation of fright even for some interval after waking. Yours was an analogous condition.'

'But look here, Mr Low. How do you account for it that I, who at this moment have not the slightest desire to make away with myself, should, at the moment of awaking from sleep, be driven to doing that which I detest and wish to avoid?'

'In every particular,' said Flaxman Low, 'your brothers' cases were similar. Each of them attempted his life in that transient moment while the will and reason were still passive, and action was still subject to an abnormally vivid idea which had evidently been impressed upon the consciousness during sleep. We have clear proof of this, I say, in the struggles of each to save himself when actually *in extremis*. Contemporary psychology has arrived at the conclusion that every man possesses a subconscious as well as a conscious self,' added Low, after a pause. 'This second or submerged self appears to be infinitely more susceptible of spiritual influences than the conscious personality. Such influences work most strongly when the normal self is in abeyance during sleep, dreaming, or the hypnotic condition. In your own family you have an excellent example of the idea of self-destruction being suggested during sleep, and carried into action during the first confused, unmastered moments of waking.'

'But how do you account for the following footsteps? Whose wishes or suggestions do we obey?'

'I believe them to be different manifestations of the same evil intelligence. Ghosts sometimes, as possibly you are aware, pursue a purpose, and your family has been held in subjection by a malicious spirit that has goaded them on to destroy themselves. I could bring forward a number of other examples; there is the Black Friar of the Sinclairs and the Fox of the Oxenholms. To come back to your own case – do you remember of what you dreamed before I woke you?'

Yarkindale looked troubled.

'I have a dim recollection, but it eludes me. I cannot fix it.' He glanced round the room, as if searching for a reminder. Suddenly he sprang up and approached a picture on the wall – 'Here it is!' he shouted. 'I remember now. A dark figure stood over me; I saw the long face and the sinister eyes – Jules Cevaine!'

'You have not spoken of Cevaine before. Who was he?'

'He was the last of the old Cevaines. You know this house is called Sevens Hall – a popular corruption of the Norman name Cevaine. We Yarkindales were distant cousins, and inherited this place after the death of Jules Cevain, about a hundred years ago. He was said to have taken a prominent part – under another name – in the Reign of Terror. However that may be – he resented our inheriting the Hall.'

'He died here?' asked Flaxman Low.

'Yes.'

'His purpose in haunting you,' said Low, 'was doubtless the extermination of your family. His spirit lingers about this spot where the final intense passion of terror, pain, and hatred was felt. And you yourselves have unknowingly fostered his power by dwelling upon and dreading his influence, thus opening the way to spirit communication, until from time to time his disembodied will has superimposed itself upon your wills during the bewildered moment of waking, and the several successive tragedies of which you told me have been the result.'

'Then how can we ever escape?'

'You have already won one and your most important victory; for the rest, think of him as seldom as may be. Destroy this painting and any other articles that may have belonged to him; and if you take my advice you will travel for a while.'

In pursuance of Mr Flaxman Low's advice, Yarkindale went for the cold weather to India. He has had no recurrence of the old trouble, but he loathes Sevens Hall, and he is only waiting for his son to be old enough to break the entail, when the property will be placed on the market.

The Gateway of the Monster

WILLIAM HOPE HODGSON

In response to Carnacki's usual card of invitation to have dinner and listen to a story, I arrived promptly at 427 Cheyne Walk, to find the three others who were always invited to these happy little times, there before me. Five minutes later, Carnacki, Arkright, Jessop, Taylor, and I were all engaged in the 'pleasant occupation' of dining.

'You've not been long away, this time,' I remarked, as I finished my soup; forgetting momentarily Carnacki's dislike of being asked even to skirt the borders of his story until such time as he was ready. Then he would not stint words.

'That's all,' he replied, with brevity; and I changed the subject, remarking that I had been buying a new gun, to which piece of news he gave an intelligent nod, and a smile which I think showed a genuinely good-humoured appreciation of my intentional changing of the conversation. Later, when dinner was finished, Carnacki snugged himself comfortably down in his big chair, along with his pipe, and began his story, with very little circumlocution: 'As Dodgson was remarking just now, I've only been away a short time, and for a very good reason too – I've only been away a short distance. The exact locality I am afraid I must not tell you; but it is less than twenty miles from here; though, except for changing a name, that won't spoil the story. And it is a story too! One of the most extraordinary things ever I have run against.

'I received a letter a fortnight ago from a man I must call Anderson, asking for an appointment. I arranged a time, and when he came, I found that he wished me to investigate and see whether I could not clear up a long-standing and well – too well – authenticated case of what he termed "haunting". He gave me very full particulars, and, finally, as the case seemed to present something unique, I decided to take it up.

'Two days later, I drove to the house late in the afternoon. I found it a very old place, standing quite alone in its own grounds. Anderson had left a letter with the butler, I found, pleading excuses for his absence, and leaving the whole house at my disposal for my investigations. The butler evidently knew the object of my visit, and I questioned him pretty thoroughly during dinner, which I had in rather lonely state. He is an old and privileged servant, and had the history of the Grey Room exact in detail. From him I learned more particulars regarding two things that Anderson had mentioned in but a casual manner. The first was that the door of the Grey Room would be heard in the dead of night to open, and slam heavily, and this even though the butler knew it was locked, and the key on the bunch in his pantry. The second was that the bedclothes would always be found torn off the bed, and hurled in a heap into a corner.

'But it was the door slamming that chiefly bothered the old butler. Many and many a time, he told me, had he lain awake and just got shivering with fright, listening; for sometimes the door would be slammed time after time – thud! thud! thud! – so that sleep was impossible.

'From Anderson, I knew already that the room had a history extending back over a hundred and fifty years. Three people had been strangled in it – an ancestor of his and his wife and child. This is authentic, as I had taken very great pains to discover; so that you can imagine it was with a feeling I had a striking case to investigate that I went upstairs after dinner to have a look at the Grey Room.

'Peter, the old butler, was in rather a state about my going, and assured me with much solemnity that in all the twenty years of his service, no one had ever entered that room after nightfall. He begged me, in quite a fatherly way, to wait till the morning, when there would be no danger, and then he could accompany me himself.

'Of course, I smiled a little at him, and told him not to bother. I explained that I should do no more than look round a bit, and, perhaps, affix a few seals. He need not fear; I was used to that sort of thing.

'But he shook his head when I said that. "There isn't many ghosts like ours, sir," he assured me, with mournful pride. And, by Jove! he was right, as you will see.

'I took a couple of candles, and Peter followed with his bunch of keys. He unlocked the door; but would not come inside with me. He was evidently in a fright, and he renewed his request that I would put off my examination until daylight. Of course, I laughed at him again, and told him he could stand sentry at the door, and catch anything that came out.

' "It never comes outside, sir," he said, in his funny, old, solemn manner. Somehow, he managed to make me feel as if I were going to have the "creeps" right away. Anyway, it was one to him, you know.

'I left him there, and examined the room. It is a big apartment, and well furnished in the grand style, with a huge four-poster, which stands with its head to the end wall. There were two candles on the mantelpiece, and two on each of the three tables that were in the room. I lit the lot, and after that, the room felt a little less inhumanly dreary; though, mind you, it was quite fresh, and well kept in every way.

'After I had taken a good look round, I sealed lengths of baby ribbon across the windows, along the walls, over the pictures, and over the fireplace and the wall closets. All the time, as I worked, the butler stood just without the door, and I could not persuade him to enter; though I jested him a little, as I stretched the ribbons, and went here and there about my work. Every now and again, he would say: "You'll excuse me, I'm sure, sir; but I do wish you would come out, sir. I'm fair in a quake for you."

'I told him he need not wait; but he was loyal enough in his way to what he considered his duty. He said he could not go away and leave me all alone there. He apologised, but made it very clear that I did not realise the danger of the room; and I could see, generally, that he was in a pretty frightened state. All the same, I had to make the room so that I should know if anything material entered it; so I asked him not to bother me, unless he really heard or saw something. He was beginning to get on my nerves, and the "feel" of the room was bad enough, without making it any nastier.

'For a time further, I worked, stretching ribbons across the floor, and sealing them, so that the merest touch would have broken them, were anyone to venture into the room in the dark with the intention of playing the fool. All this had taken me far longer than I had anticipated; and, suddenly, I heard a clock strike eleven. I had taken off my coat soon after commencing work; now, however, as I had practically made an end of all that I intended to do, I walked across to the settee, and picked it up. I was in the act of getting into it, when the old butler's voice (he had not said a word for the last hour) came sharp and frightened: – "Come out, sir, quick! There's something going to happen!" Jove! but I jumped, and then, in the same moment, one of the candles on the table to the left went out. Now whether it was the wind, or what, I do not know; but, just for a moment, I was enough startled to make a run for the door, though I am glad to say that I pulled up before I reached it. I simply could not bunk out, with the butler standing there, after having, as it were, read him a sort of lesson on "bein' brave, y'know". So I just turned right round, picked up the two candles off the mantelpiece, and walked across to the table near the bed. Well, I saw nothing. I blew out the candle that was still alight; then I went to those on the two tables, and blew them out. Then, outside of the door, the old man called again: – "Oh! sir, do be told! Do be told!"

' "All right, Peter," I said, and by Jove, my voice was not as steady as I should have liked! I made for the door, and had a bit of work not to start running. I took some thundering long strides, as you can imagine. Near the door, I had a sudden feeling that there was a cold wind in the room. It was almost as if the window had been suddenly opened a little. I got to the door, and the old butler gave back a step, in a sort of instinctive way. "Collar the candles, Peter!" I said, pretty sharply, and shoved them into his hands. I turned, and caught the handle, and slammed the door shut, with a crash. Somehow, do you know, as I did so, I thought I felt something pull back on it; but it must have been only fancy. I turned the key in the lock, and then again, double-locking the door. I felt easier then, and set to and sealed the door. In addition, I put my card over the keyhole, and sealed it there; after which I pocketed the key, and went downstairs – with Peter, who was nervous and silent, leading the way. Poor old beggar! It had not struck me until that moment that he had been enduring a considerable strain during the last two or three hours.

'About midnight, I went to bed. My room lay at the end of the corridor upon which opens the door of the Grey Room. I counted the doors between it and mine, and found that five rooms lay between. And I am sure you can understand that I was not sorry. Then, just as I was beginning to undress, an idea came to me, and I took my candle and sealing wax, and sealed the doors of all five rooms. If any door slammed in the night, I should know just which one.

'I returned to my room, locked the door, and went to bed. I was waked suddenly from a deep sleep by a loud crash somewhere out in the passage.

I sat up in bed, and listened, but heard nothing. Then I lit my candle. I was in the very act of lighting it when there came the bang of a door being violently slammed, along the corridor. I jumped out of bed, and got my revolver. I unlocked the door, and went out into the passage, holding my candle high, and keeping the pistol ready. Then a queer thing happened. I could not go a step toward the Grey

Room. You all know I am not really a cowardly chap. I've gone into too many cases connected with ghostly things, to be accused of that; but I tell you I funked it; simply funked it, just like any blessed kid. There was something precious unholy in the air that night. I ran back into my bedroom, and shut and locked the door. Then I sat on the bed all night, and listened to the dismal thudding of a door up the corridor. The sound seemed to echo through all the house.

'Daylight came at last, and I washed and dressed. The door had not slammed for about an hour, and I was getting back my nerve again. I felt ashamed of myself, though in some ways that was silly; for when you're meddling with that sort of thing, your nerve is bound to go, sometimes.

And you just have to sit quiet and call yourself a coward until daylight.

Sometimes it is more than just cowardice, I fancy. I believe at times it is something warning you, and fighting *for* you. But, all the same, I always feel mean and miserable, after a time like that.

'When the day came properly, I opened my door, and, keeping my revolver handy, went quietly along the passage. I had to pass the head of the stairs, along the way, and who should I see coming up, but the old butler, carrying a cup of coffee. He had merely tucked his nightshirt into his trousers, and he had an old pair of carpet slippers on.

' "Hullo, Peter!" I said, feeling suddenly cheerful; for I was as glad as any lost child to have a live human being close to me. "Where are you off to with the refreshments?"

'The old man gave a start, and slopped some of the coffee. He stared up at me, and I could see that he looked white and done up. He came on up the stairs, and held out the little tray to me. "I'm very thankful indeed, sir, to see you safe and well," he said. "I feared, one time, you might risk going into the Grey Room, sir. I've lain awake all night, with the sound of the Door. And when it came light, I thought I'd make you a cup of coffee. I knew you would want to look at the seals, and somehow it seems safer if there's two, sir."

' "Peter," I said, "you're a brick. This is very thoughtful of you." And I drank the coffee. "Come along," I told him, and handed him back the tray. "I'm going to have a look at what the Brutes have been up to. I simply hadn't the pluck to in the night."

' "I'm very thankful, sir," he replied. "Flesh and blood can do nothing, sir, against devils; and that's what's in the Grey Room after dark."

'I examined the seals on all the doors, as I went along, and found them right; but when I got to the Grey Room, the seal was broken, though the card, over the keyhole, was untouched. I ripped it off, and unlocked the door, and went in, rather cautiously, as you can imagine; but the whole room was empty of anything to frighten one, and there was heaps of light.

I examined all my seals, and not a single one was disturbed. The old butler had followed me in, and, suddenly, he called out: – "The bedclothes, sir!"

'I ran up to the bed, and looked over; and, surely, they were lying in the corner to the left of the bed. Jove! you can imagine how queer I felt. Something *had* been in the room. I stared for a while, from the bed to the clothes on the floor. I had a feeling that I did not want to touch either. Old Peter, though, did not seem to be affected that way. He went over to the bed coverings, and was going to pick them up, as, doubtless, he had done every day these twenty years back; but I stopped him. I wanted nothing touched, until I had finished my examination. This, I must have spent a full hour over, and then I let Peter straighten up the bed; after which we went out, and I locked the door, for the room was getting on my nerves.

'I had a short walk, and then breakfast; after which I felt more my own man, and so returned to the Grey Room, and, with Peter's help, and one of the maids, I had everything taken out of the room, except the bed – even the very pictures. I examined the walls, floor and ceiling then, with probe, hammer and magnifying glass, but found nothing suspicious. And I can assure you, I began to realise, in very truth, that some incredible thing had been loose in the room during the past night. I sealed up everything again, and went out, locking and sealing the door, as before.

'After dinner, Peter and I unpacked some of my stuff, and I fixed up my camera and flashlight opposite to the door of the Grey Room, with a string from the trigger of the flashlight to the door. Then, you see, if the door were really opened, the flashlight would blare out, and there would be, possibly, a very queer picture to examine in the morning. The last thing I did, before leaving, was to uncap the lens; and after that I went off to my bedroom, and to bed; for I intended to be up at midnight; and to ensure this, I set my little alarm to call me; also I left my candle burning.

'The clock woke me at twelve, and I got up and into my dressing gown and slippers. I shoved my revolver into my right side-pocket, and opened my door. Then I lit my darkroom lamp, and withdrew the slide, so that it would give a clear light. I carried it up the corridor, about thirty feet, and put it down on the floor, with the open side away from me, so that it would show me anything that might approach along the dark passage. Then I went back, and sat in the doorway of my room, with my revolver handy, staring up the passage toward the place where I knew my camera stood outside the door of the Grey Room.

'I should think I had watched for about an hour and a half, when, suddenly, I heard a faint noise, away up the corridor. I was immediately conscious of a queer prickling sensation about the back of my head, and my hands began to sweat a little. The following instant, the whole end of the passage flicked into sight in the abrupt glare of the flashlight.

There came the succeeding darkness, and I peered nervously up the corridor, listening tensely, and trying to find what lay beyond the faint glow of my dark-lamp, which now seemed ridiculously dim by contrast with the tremendous blaze of the flash-power . . . And then, as I stooped forward, staring and listening, there came the crashing thud of the door of the Grey Room. The sound seemed to fill the whole of the large corridor, and go echoing hollowly through the house. I tell you, I felt horrible – as if my bones were water. Simply beastly. Jove! how I did stare, and how I listened. And then it came again – thud, thud, thud, and then a silence that was almost worse than the noise of the door; for I kept fancying that some awful thing was stealing upon me along the corridor. And then, suddenly, my lamp was put out, and I could not see a yard before me. I realised all at once that I was doing a very silly thing, sitting there, and I jumped up. Even as I did so, I *thought* I heard a sound in the passage, and quite *near* me. I made one backward spring into my room, and slammed and locked the door. I sat on my bed, and stared at the door. I had my revolver in my hand; but it seemed an abominably useless thing. I felt that there was something the other side of that door. For some unknown reason I *knew* it was pressed up against the door, and it was soft. That was just what I thought. Most extraordinary thing to think.

'Presently I got hold of myself a bit, and marked out a pentacle hurriedly with chalk on the polished floor; and there I sat in it almost until dawn. And all the time, away up the corridor, the door of the Grey Room thudded at solemn and horrid intervals. It was a miserable, brutal night.

'When the day began to break, the thudding of the door came gradually to an end, and, at last, I got hold of my courage, and went along the corridor in the half light to cap the lens of my camera. I can tell you, it took some doing; but if I had not done so my photograph would have been spoilt, and I was tremendously keen to save it. I got back to my room, and then set to and rubbed out the five-pointed star in which I had been sitting.

'Half an hour later there was a tap at my door. It was Peter with my coffee. When I had drunk it, we both went along to the Grey Room. As we went, I had a look at the seals on the other doors; but they were untouched. The seal on the door of the Grey Room was broken, as also was the string from the trigger of the flash-light; but the card over the keyhole was still there. I ripped it off, and opened the door. Nothing unusual was to be seen until we came to the bed; then I saw that, as on the previous day, the bedclothes had been torn off, and hurled into the left-hand corner, exactly where I had seen them before. I felt very queer, but I did not forget to look at all the seals, only to find that not one had been broken.

'Then I turned and looked at old Peter, and he looked at me, nodding his head.

' "Let's get out of here!" I said. "It's no place for any living human to enter, without proper protection."

'We went out then, and I locked and sealed the door, again.

'After breakfast, I developed the negative; but it showed only the door of the Grey Room, half opened. Then I left the house, as I wanted to get certain matters and implements that might be necessary to life, perhaps to the spirit; for I intended to spend the coming night in the Grey Room.

'I got back in a cab, about half-past five, with my apparatus, and this, Peter and I carried up to the Grey Room, where I piled it carefully in the centre of the floor. When everything was in the room, including a cat which I had brought, I locked and sealed the door, and went toward the bedroom, telling Peter I should not be down for dinner. He said, "Yes, sir," and went downstairs, thinking that I was going to turn in, which was what I wanted him to believe, as I knew he would have worried both me and himself, if he had known what I intended.

'But I merely got my camera and flashlight from my bedroom, and hurried back to the Grey Room. I locked and sealed myself in, and set to work, for I had a lot to do before it got dark.

'First, I cleared away all the ribbons across the floor; then I carried the cat – still fastened in its basket – over toward the far wall, and left it. I returned then to the centre of the room, and measured out a space twenty-one feet in diameter, which I swept with a "broom of hyssop".

About this, I drew a circle of chalk, taking care never to step over the circle. Beyond this I smudged, with a bunch of garlic, a broad belt right around the chalked circle, and when this was complete, I took from among my stores in the centre a small jar of a certain water. I broke away the parchment, and withdrew the stopper. Then, dipping my left forefinger in the little jar, I went round the circle again, making upon the floor, just within the line of chalk, the Second Sign of the Saaamaaa Ritual, and joining each Sign most carefully with the left-handed crescent. I can tell you, I felt easier when this was done, and the "water circle" complete. Then I unpacked some more of the stuff that I had brought, and placed a lighted candle in the "valley" of each Crescent. After that, I drew a Pentacle, so that each of the five points of the defensive star touched the chalk circle. In the five points of the star I placed five portions of the bread, each wrapped in linen, and in the five "vales" five opened jars of the water I had used to make the "water circle". And now I had my first protective barrier complete.

'Now, anyone, except you who know something of my methods of investigation, might consider all this a piece of useless and foolish superstition; but you all remember the Black Veil case, in which I believe my life was saved by a very similar form of protection, whilst Aster, who sneered at it, and would not come inside, died. I got the idea from the Sigsand MS., written, so far as I can make out, in the fourteenth century. At first, naturally, I imagined it was just an expression of the superstition of his time; and it was not until a year later that it occurred to me to test his "Defence", which I did, as I've just said, in that horrible Black Veil business. You know how *that* turned out. Later, I used it several times, and always I came through safe, until that Moving Fur case. It was only a partial "defence" therefore, and I nearly died in the pentacle. After that I came across Professor Garder's *Experiments with a Medium*. When they surrounded the medium with a current, in vacuum, he lost his power – almost as if it cut him off from the Immaterial. That made me think a lot; and that is how I came to make the Electric Pentacle, which is a most marvellous "Defence" against certain manifestations. I used the shape of the defensive star for this protection, because I have, personally, no doubt at all but that there is some extraordinary virtue in the old magic figure. Curious thing for a twentieth-century man to admit, is it not? But, then, as you all know, I never did, and never will, allow myself to be blinded by a little cheap laughter. I ask questions, and keep my eyes open.

'In this last case I had little doubt that I had run up against a supernatural monster, and I meant to take every possible care; for the danger is abominable.

'I turned to now to fit the Electric Pentacle, setting it so that each of its "points" and "vales" coincided exactly with the "points" and "vales" of the drawn pentagram upon the floor. Then I connected up the battery, and the next instant the pale blue glare from the inter-twining vacuum tubes shone out.

'I glanced about me then, with something of a sigh of relief, and realised suddenly that the dusk was upon me, for the window was grey and unfriendly. Then round at the big, empty room, over the double barrier of electric and candle light. I had an abrupt, extra-ordinary sense of weirdness thrust upon me – in the air, you know; as it were, a sense of something inhuman impending. The room was full of the stench of bruised garlic, a smell I hate.

'I turned now to the camera, and saw that it and the flashlight were in order. Then I tested my revolver, carefully, though I had little thought that it would be needed. Yet, to what extent materialisation of an ab-natural creature is possible, given favourable conditions, no one can say; and I had no idea what horrible thing I was going to see, or feel the presence of. I might, in the end, have to fight with a material-ised monster. I did not know, and could only be prepared. You see, I never forgot that three other people had been strangled in the bed close to me, and the fierce slamming of the door I had heard myself. I had no doubt that I was investigating a dangerous and ugly case.

'By this time, the night had come, though the room was very light with the burning candles; and I found myself glancing behind me, constantly, and then all round the room. It was nervy work waiting for that thing to come. Then, suddenly, I was aware of a little, cold wind sweeping over me, coming from behind. I gave one great nerve-thrill, and a prickly feeling went all over the back of my head. Then I hove myself round with a sort of stiff jerk, and stared straight against that queer wind. It seemed to come from the corner of the room to the left of the bed – the place where both times I had found the heap of tossed bedclothes. Yet, I could see nothing unusual; no opening – nothing! . . .

'Abruptly, I was aware that the candles were all a-flicker in that unnatural wind . . . I believe I just squatted there and stared in a horribly frightened, wooden way for some minutes. I shall never be able to let you know how disgustingly horrible it was sitting in that vile, cold wind! And then, flick! flick! flick! all the candles round the outer barrier went out; and there was I, locked and sealed in that room, and with no light beyond the weakish blue glare of the Electric Pentacle.

'A time of abominable tenseness passed, and still that wind blew upon me; and then, suddenly, I knew that something stirred in the corner to the left of the bed. I was made conscious of it, rather by some inward, unused sense than by either sight or sound; for the pale, short-radius glare of the Pentacle gave but a very poor light for seeing by. Yet, as I stared, something began slowly to grow upon my sight – a moving shadow, a little darker than the surrounding shadows. I lost the thing amid the vagueness, and for a moment or two I glanced swiftly from side to side, with a fresh, new sense of impending danger. Then my attention was directed to the bed. All the coverings were being drawn steadily off, with a hateful, stealthy sort of motion. I heard the slow, dragging slither of the clothes, but I could see nothing of the thing that pulled.

'I was aware in a funny, subconscious, introspective fashion that the "creep" had come upon me; yet that I was cooler mentally than I had been for some minutes, sufficiently so to feel that my hands were sweating coldly, and to shift my revolver, half-consciously, whilst I rubbed my right hand dry upon my knee; though never, for an instant, taking my gaze or my attention from those moving clothes.

'The faint noises from the bed ceased once, and there was a most intense silence, with only the sound of the blood beating in my head. Yet, immediately afterward, I heard again the slurring of the bedclothes being dragged off the bed. In the midst of my nervous tension I remembered the camera, and reached round for it, but without looking away from the bed.

And then, you know, all in a moment, the whole of the bed coverings were torn off with extraordinary violence, and I heard the flump they made as they were hurled into the corner.

'There was a time of absolute quietness then for perhaps a couple of minutes; and you can imagine how horrible I felt. The bedclothes had been thrown with such savageness! And then, again, the brutal unnaturalness of the thing that had just been done before me!

'Abruptly, over by the door, I heard a faint noise – a sort of crickling sound, and then a pitter or two upon the floor. A great nervous thrill swept over me, seeming to run up my spine and over the back of my head; for the seal that secured the door had just been broken. Something was there. I could not see the door; at least, I mean to say that it was impossible to say how much I actually saw, and how much my imagination supplied. I made it out, only as a continuation of the grey walls . . . And then it seemed to me that something dark and indistinct moved and wavered there among the shadows.

'Abruptly, I was aware that the door was opening, and with an effort I reached again for my camera; but before I could aim it the door was slammed with a terrific crash that filled the whole room with a sort of hollow thunder. I jumped, like a frightened child. There seemed such a power behind the noise; as though a vast, wanton Force were "out". Can you understand?

'The door was not touched again; but, directly afterward, I heard the basket, in which the cat lay, creak. I tell you, I fairly pringled all along my back. I knew that I was going to learn definitely whether whatever was abroad was dangerous to Life. From the cat there rose suddenly a hideous caterwaul, that ceased abruptly; and then – too late – I snapped on the flashlight. In the great glare, I saw that the basket had been overturned, and the lid was wrenched open, with the cat lying half in, and half out upon the floor. I saw nothing else, but I was full of the knowledge that I was in the presence of some Being or Thing that had power to destroy.

'During the next two or three minutes, there was an odd, noticeable quietness in the room, and you must remember I was half-blinded, for the time, because of the flashlight; so that the whole place seemed to be pitchy dark just beyond the shine of the Pentacle. I tell you it was most horrible. I just knelt there in the star, and whirled round, trying to see whether anything was coming at me.

'My power of sight came gradually, and I got a little hold of myself; and abruptly I saw the thing I was looking for, close to the "water circle". It was big and indistinct, and wavered curiously, as though the shadow of a vast spider hung suspended in the air, just beyond the barrier. It passed swiftly round the circle, and seemed to probe ever toward me; but only to draw back with extraordinary jerky movements, as might a living person if they touched the hot bar of a grate.

'Round and round it moved, and round and round I turned. Then, just opposite to one of the 'vales' in the pentacles, it seemed to pause, as though preliminary to a tremendous effort. It retired almost beyond the glow of the vacuum light, and then came straight toward me, appearing to gather form and solidity as it came. There seemed a vast, malign determination behind the movement, that must succeed. I was on my knees, and I jerked back, falling on to my left hand, and hip, in a wild endeavour to get back from the advancing thing. With my right hand I was grabbing madly for my revolver, which I had let slip. The brutal thing came with one great sweep straight over the garlic and the "water circle", almost to the vale of the pentacle. I believe I yelled. Then, just as suddenly as it had swept over, it seemed to be hurled back by some mighty, invisible force.

'It must have been some moments before I realised that I was safe; and then I got myself together in the middle of the pentacles, feeling horribly gone and shaken, and glancing round and round the barrier; but the thing had vanished. Yet I had learnt something, for I knew now that the Grey Room was haunted by a monstrous hand.

'Suddenly, as I crouched there, I saw what had so nearly given the monster an opening through the barrier. In my movements within the pentacle I must have touched one of the jars of water; for just where the thing had made its attack the jar that guarded the "deep" of the "vale" had been moved to one side, and this had left one of the "five doorways" unguarded. I put it back, quickly, and felt almost safe again, for I had found the cause, and the "defence" was still good. And I began to hope again that I should see the morning come in. When I saw that thing so nearly succeed, I had an awful, weak, overwhelming feeling that the "barriers" could never bring me safe through the night against such a Force. You can understand?

'For a long time I could not see the hand; but, presently, I thought I saw, once or twice, an odd wavering, over among the shadows near the door. A little later, as though in a sudden fit of malignant rage, the dead body of the cat was picked up, and beaten with dull, sickening blows against the solid floor. That made me feel rather queer.

'A minute afterward, the door was opened and slammed twice with tremendous force. The next instant the thing made one swift, vicious dart at me, from out of the shadows. Instinctively, I started sideways from it, and so plucked my hand from upon the Electric Pentacle, where – for a wickedly careless moment – I had placed it. The monster was hurled off from the neighbourhood of the pentacles; though – owing to my inconceivable foolishness – it had been enabled for a second time to pass the outer barriers. I can tell you, I shook for a time, with sheer funk. I moved right to the centre of the pentacles again, and knelt there, making myself as small and compact as possible.

'As I knelt, there came to me, presently, a vague wonder at the two "accidents" which had so nearly allowed the brute to get at me. Was I being *influenced* to unconscious voluntary actions that endangered me?

The thought took hold of me, and I watched my every movement. Abruptly, I stretched a tired leg, and knocked over one of the jars of water. Some was spilled; but, because of my suspicious watchfulness, I had it upright and back within the vale while yet some of the water remained. Even as I did so, the vast, black, half-materialised hand beat up at me out of the shadows, and seemed to leap almost into my face; so nearly did it approach; but for the third time it was thrown back by some altogether enormous, overmastering force. Yet, apart from the dazed fright in which it left me, I had for a moment that feeling of spiritual sickness, as if some delicate, beautiful, inward grace had suffered, which is felt only upon the too near approach of the ab-human, and is more dreadful, in a strange way, than any physical pain that can be suffered. I knew by this more of the extent and closeness of the danger; and for a long time I was simply cowed by the butt-headed brutality of that Force upon my spirit. I can put it no other way.

'I knelt again in the centre of the pentacles, watching myself with more fear, almost, than the monster; for I knew now that, unless I guarded myself from every sudden impulse that came to me, I might simply work my own destruction. Do you see how horrible it all was?

'I spent the rest of the night in a haze of sick fright, and so tense that I could not make a single movement naturally. I was in such fear that any desire for action that came to me might be prompted by the Influence that I knew was at work on me. And outside of the barrier that ghastly thing went round and round, grabbing and grabbing in the air at me. Twice more was the body of the dead cat molested. The second time, I heard every bone in its body scrunch and crack. And all the time the horrible wind was blowing upon me from the corner of the room to the left of the bed.

'Then, just as the first touch of dawn came into the sky, that unnatural wind ceased, in a single moment, and I could see no sign of the hand. The dawn came slowly, and presently the wan light filled all the room, and made the pale glare of the Electric Pentacle look more unearthly. Yet it was not until the day had fully come that I made any attempt to leave the barrier, for I did not know but that there was some method abroad, in the sudden stopping of that wind, to entice me from the pentacles.

'At last, when the dawn was strong and bright, I took one last look round, and ran for the door. I got it unlocked, in a nervous and clumsy fashion, then locked it hurriedly, and went to my bedroom, where I lay on the bed, and tried to steady my nerves. Peter came, presently, with the coffee, and when I had drunk it, I told him I meant to have a sleep, as I had been up all night. He took the tray, and went out quietly, and after I had locked my door I turned in properly, and at last got to sleep.

'I woke about midday, and after some lunch, went up to the Grey Room. I switched off the current from the Pentacle, which I had left on in my hurry; also, I removed the body of the cat. You can understand I did not want anyone to see the poor brute. After that, I made a very careful search of the corner where the bedclothes had been thrown. I made several holes, and probed, and found nothing. Then it occurred to me to try with my instrument under the skirting. I did so, and heard my wire ring on metal. I turned the hook end that way, and fished for the thing. At the second go, I got it. It was a small object, and I took it to the window. I found it to be a curious ring, made of some greying material. The curious thing about it was that it was made in the form of a pentagon; that is, the same shape as the inside of the magic pentacle, but without the "mounts", which form the points of the defensive star. It was free from all chasing or engraving.

'You will understand that I was excited, when I tell you that I felt sure I held in my hand the famous Luck Ring of the Anderson family; which, indeed, was of all things the one most intimately connected with the history of the haunting. This ring was handed on from father to son through generations, and always – in obedience to some ancient family tradition – each son had to promise never to wear the ring. The ring, I may say, was brought home by one of the Crusaders, under very peculiar circumstances; but the story is too long to go into here.

'It appears that young Sir Hulbert, an ancestor of Anderson's, made a bet, in drink, you know, that he would wear the ring that night. He did so, and in the morning his wife and child were found strangled in the bed, in the very room in which I stood. Many people, it would seem, thought young Sir Hulbert was guilty of having done the thing in drunken anger; and he, in an attempt to prove his innocence, slept a second night in the room. He also was strangled.

Since then, as you may imagine, no one has ever spent a night in the Grey Room, until I did so. The ring had been lost so long that it had become almost a myth; and it was most extraordinary to stand there, with the actual thing in my hand, as you can understand.

'It was whilst I stood there, looking at the ring, that I got an idea. Supposing that it were, in a way, a doorway – you see what I mean? A sort of gap in the world-hedge. It was a queer idea, I know, and probably was not my own, but came to me from the Outside. You see, the wind had come from that part of the room where the ring lay. I thought a lot about it. Then the shape – the inside of a pentacle. It had no "mounts", and without mounts, as the Sigsand MS. has it: "Thee mownts wych are thee Five Hills of safetie. To lack is to gyve pow'r to thee daemon; and surelie to fayvor the Evill Thynge." You see, the very shape of the ring was significant; and I determined to test it.

'I unmade the pentacle, for it must be made afresh *and around* the one to be protected. Then I went out and locked the door; after which I left the house, to get certain matters, for neither "yarbs nor fyre nor water" must be used a second time. I returned about seven thirty, and as soon as the things I had brought had been carried up to the Grey Room, I dismissed Peter for the night, just as I had done the evening before. When he had gone downstairs, I let myself into the room, and locked and sealed the door. I went to the place in the centre of the room where all the stuff had been packed, and set to work with all my speed to construct a barrier about me and the ring.

'I do not remember whether I explained it to you. But I had reasoned that, if the ring were in any way a "medium of admission", and it were enclosed with me in the Electric Pentacle, it would be, to express it loosely, insulated. Do you see? The Force, which had visible expression as a Hand, would have to stay beyond the Barrier which separates the Ab from the Normal; for the "gateway" would be removed from accessibility.

'As I was saying, I worked with all my speed to get the barrier completed about me and the ring, for it was already later than I cared to be in that room "unprotected". Also, I had a feeling that there would be a vast effort made that night to regain the use of the ring. For I had the strongest conviction that the ring was a necessity to materialisation. You will see whether I was right.

'I completed the barriers in about an hour, and you can imagine something of the relief I felt when I felt the pale glare of the Electric Pentacle once more all about me. From then, onward, for about two hours, I sat quietly, facing the corner from which the wind came. About eleven o'clock a queer knowledge came that something was near to me; yet nothing happened for a whole hour after that. Then, suddenly, I felt the cold, queer wind begin to blow upon me. To my astonishment, it seemed now to come from behind me, and I whipped round, with a hideous quake of fear. The wind met me in the face. It was blowing up from the floor close to me. I stared down, in a sickening maze of new frights. What on earth had I done now! The ring was there, close beside me, where I had put it. Suddenly, as I stared, bewildered, I was aware that there was something queer about the ring – funny shadowy movements and convolutions. I looked at them, stupidly. And then, abruptly, I knew that the wind was blowing up at me from the ring. A queer indistinct smoke became visible to me, seeming to pour upward through the ring, and mix with the moving shadows. Suddenly, I realised that I was in more than any mortal danger, for the convoluting shadows about the ring were taking shape, and the death-hand was forming *within* the Pentacle. My Goodness! do you realise it? I had brought the "gateway" into the pentacles, and the brute was coming through – pouring into the material world, as gas might pour out from the mouth of a pipe.

'I should think that I knelt for a moment in a sort of stunned fright. Then, with a mad, awkward movement, I snatched at the ring, intending to hurl it out of the Pentacle. Yet it eluded me, as though some invisible, living thing jerked it hither and thither. At last, I gripped it; yet, in the same instant, it was torn from my grasp with incredible and brutal force. A great, black shadow covered it, and rose into the air, and came at me. I saw that it was the Hand, vast and nearly perfect in form. I gave one crazy yell, and jumped over the Pentacle and the ring of burning candles, and ran despairingly for the door. I fumbled idiotically and ineffectually with the key, and all the time I stared, with a fear that was like insanity, toward the Barriers. The hand was plunging toward me; yet, even as it had been unable to pass into the Pentacle when the ring was without, so, now that the ring was within, it had no power to pass out. The monster was chained, as surely as any beast would be, were chains riveted upon it.

'Even then, I got a flash of this knowledge; but I was too utterly shaken with fright to reason; and the instant I managed to get the key turned, I sprang into the passage, and slammed the door with a crash. I locked it, and got to my room somehow; for I was trembling so that I could hardly stand, as you can imagine. I locked myself in, and managed to get the candle lit; then I lay down on my bed, and kept quiet for an hour or two, and so I got steadied.

'I got a little sleep, later; but woke when Peter brought my coffee. When I had drunk it I felt altogether better, and took the old man along with me whilst I had a look into the Grey Room. I opened the door, and peeped in. The candles were still burning, wan against the daylight; and behind them was the pale, glowing star of the Electric Pentacle. And there, in the middle, was the ring . . . the gateway of the monster, lying demure and ordinary.

'Nothing in the room was touched, and I knew that the brute had never managed to cross the Pentacles. Then I went out, and locked the door.

'After a sleep of some hours, I left the house. I returned in the afternoon in a cab. I had with me an oxy-hydrogen jet, and two cylinders, containing the gases. I carried the things into the Grey Room, and there, in the centre of the Electric Pentacle, I erected the little furnace. Five minutes later the Luck Ring, once the "luck" but now the "bane", of the Anderson family, was no more than a little solid splash of hot metal.'

Carnacki felt in his pocket, and pulled out something wrapped in tissue paper. He passed it to me. I opened it, and found a small circle of greyish metal, something like lead, only harder and rather brighter.

'Well?' I asked, at length, after examining it and handing it round to the others. 'Did that stop the haunting?'

Carnacki nodded. 'Yes,' he said. 'I slept three nights in the Grey Room, before I left. Old Peter nearly fainted when he knew that I meant to; but by the third night he seemed to realise that the house was just safe and ordinary. And, you know, I believe, in his heart, he hardly approved.'

Carnacki stood up and began to shake hands. 'Out you go!' he said, genially. And presently we went, pondering, to our various homes.

The Red Hand

ARTHUR MACHEN

The Problem of the Fish-hooks

'There can be no doubt whatever,' said Mr Phillipps, 'that my theory is the true one; these flints are prehistoric fish-hooks.'

'I dare say; but you know that in all probability the things were forged the other day with a door-key.'

'Stuff!' said Phillipps; 'I have some respect, Dyson, for your literary abilities, but your knowledge of ethnology is insignificant, or rather non-existent. These fish-hooks satisfy every test; they are perfectly genuine.'

'Possibly, but as I said just now, you go to work at the wrong end. You neglect the opportunities that confront you and await you, obvious, at every corner; you positively shrink from the chance of encountering primitive man in this whirling and mysterious city, and you pass the weary hours in your agreeable retirement of Red Lion Square fumbling with bits of flint, which are, as I said, in all probability, rank forgeries.'

Phillipps took one of the little objects, and held it up in exasperation.

'Look at that ridge,' he said. 'Did you ever see such a ridge as that on a forgery?'

Dyson merely grunted and lit his pipe, and the two sat smoking in rich silence, watching through the open window the children in the square as they flitted to and fro in the twilight of the lamps, as elusive as bats flying on the verge of a dark wood.

'Well,' said Phillipps at last, 'it is really a long time since you have been round. I suppose you have been working at your old task.'

'Yes,' said Dyson, 'always the chase of the phrase. I shall grow old in the hunt. But it is a great consolation to meditate on the fact that there are not a dozen people in England who know what style means.'

'I suppose not; for the matter of that, the study of ethnology is far from popular. And the difficulties! Primitive man stands dim and very far off across the great bridge of years.

'By the way,' he went on after a pause, 'what was that stuff you were talking just now about shrinking from the chance of encountering primitive man at the corner, or something of the kind? There are certainly people about here whose ideas are very primitive.'

'I wish, Phillipps, you would not rationalise my remarks. If I recollect the phrase correctly, I hinted that you shrank from the chance of encountering primitive man in this whirling and mysterious city, and I meant exactly what I said. Who can limit the age of survival? The troglodyte and the lake-dweller, perhaps representative of yet darker races, may very probably be lurking in our midst, rubbing shoulders with frock-coated and finely-draped humanity, ravening like wolves at heart and boiling with the foul passions of the swamp and the black cave. Now and then as I walk in Holborn or Fleet Street I see a face which I pronounce abhorred, and yet I could not give a reason for the thrill of loathing that stirs within me.'

'My dear Dyson, I refuse to enter myself in your literary "trying-on" department. I know that survivals do exist, but all things have a limit, and your speculations are absurd. You must catch me your troglodyte before I will believe in him.'

'I agree to that with all my heart,' said Dyson, chuckling at the ease with which he had succeeded in 'drawing' Phillipps. 'Nothing could be better. It's a fine night for a walk,' he added, taking up his hat.

'What nonsense you are talking, Dyson!' said Phillipps. 'However, I have no objection to taking a walk with you; as you say, it is a pleasant night.'

'Come along then,' said Dyson, grinning, 'but remember our bargain.'

The two men went out into the square, and threading one of the narrow passages that serve as exits, struck towards the north-east. As they passed along a flaring causeway they could hear at intervals between the clamour of the children and the triumphant *Gloria* played on a piano-organ the long deep hum and roll of the traffic in Holborn, a sound so persistent that it echoed like the turning of everlasting wheels. Dyson looked to right and left and conned the way, and presently they were passing through a more peaceful quarter, touching on deserted squares and silent streets black as midnight. Phillipps had lost all count of direction, and as by degrees the region of faded respectability gave place to the squalid, and dirty stucco offended the eye of the artistic observer, he merely ventured the remark that he had never seen a neighbourhood more unpleasant or more commonplace.

'More mysterious, you mean,' said Dyson. 'I warn you, Phillipps, we are now hot upon the scent.'

They dived yet deeper into the maze of brickwork; some time before they had crossed a noisy thoroughfare running east and west, and now the quarter seemed all amorphous, without character; here a decent house with sufficient garden, here a faded square, and here factories surrounded by high, blank walls, with blind passages and dark corners; but all ill-lighted and unfrequented and heavy with silence.

Presently, as they paced down a forlorn street of two-storey houses, Dyson caught sight of a dark and obscure turning.

'I like the look of that,' he said; 'it seems to me promising.' There was a street lamp at the entrance, and another, a mere glimmer, at the further end. Beneath the lamp, on the pavement, an artist had evidently established his academy in the daytime, for the stones were all a blur of crude colours rubbed into each other, and a few broken fragments of chalk lay in a little heap beneath the wall.

'You see people do occasionally pass this way,' said Dyson, pointing to the ruins of the screever's work. 'I confess I should not have thought it possible. Come, let us explore.'

On one side of this byway of communication was a great timber-yard, with vague piles of wood looming shapeless above the enclosing wall; and on the other side of the road a wall still higher seemed to enclose a garden, for there were shadows like trees, and a faint murmur of rustling leaves broke the silence. It was a moonless night, and clouds that had gathered after sunset had blackened, and midway between the feeble lamps the passage lay all dark and formless; and when one stopped and listened, and the sharp echo of reverberant footsteps ceased, there came from far away, as from beyond the hills, a faint roll of the noise of London. Phillipps was bolstering up his courage to declare that he had had enough of the excursion, when a loud cry from Dyson broke in upon his thoughts.

'Stop, stop, for Heaven's sake, or you will tread on it! There! almost under your feet!' Phillipps looked down, and saw a vague shape, dark, and framed in surrounding darkness, dropped strangely on the pavement, and then a white cuff glimmered for a moment as Dyson lit a match, which went out directly.

'It's a drunken man,' said Phillipps very coolly.

'It's a murdered man,' said Dyson, and he began to call for police with all his might, and soon from the distance running footsteps echoed and grew louder, and cries sounded.

A policeman was the first to come up.

'What's the matter?' he said, as he drew to a stand, panting. 'Anything amiss here?' for he had not seen what was on the pavement.

'Look!' said Dyson, speaking out of the gloom. 'Look there! My friend and I came down this place three minutes ago, and that is what we found.'

The man flashed his light on the dark shape and cried out.

'Why, it's murder,' he said; 'there's blood all about him, and a puddle of it in the gutter there. He's not dead long, either. Ah! there's the wound! It's in the neck.'

Dyson bent over what was lying there. He saw a prosperous gentleman, dressed in smooth, well-cut clothes. The neat whiskers were beginning to grizzle a little; he might have been forty-five an hour before; and a handsome gold watch had slipped out of his waistcoat pocket. And there in the flesh of the neck, between chin and ear, gaped a great wound, clean cut, but all clotted with drying blood, and the white of the cheeks shone like a lighted lamp above the red.

Dyson turned, and looked curiously about him; the dead man lay across the path with his head inclined towards the wall, and the blood from the wound streamed away across the pavement, and lay a dark puddle, as the policeman had said, in the gutter. Two more policemen had come up, the crowd gathered, humming from all quarters, and the officers had as much as they could do to keep the curious at a distance. The three lanterns were flashing here and there, searching for more evidence, and in the gleam of one of them Dyson caught sight of an object in the road, to which he called the attention of the policeman nearest to him.

'Look, Phillipps,' he said, when the man had secured it and held it up. 'Look, that should be something in your way!'

It was a dark flinty stone, gleaming like obsidian, and shaped to a broad edge something after the manner of an adze. One end was rough, and easily grasped in the hand, and the whole thing was hardly five inches long. The edge was thick with blood.

'What is that, Phillipps?' said Dyson; and Phillipps looked hard at it.

'It's a primitive flint knife,' he said. 'It was made about ten thousand years ago. One exactly like this was found near Avebury, in Wiltshire, and all the authorities gave it that age.'

The policeman stared astonished at such a development of the case; and Phillipps himself was all aghast at his own words. But Mr Dyson did not notice him. An inspector who had just come up and was listening to the outlines of the case, was holding a lantern to the dead man's head. Dyson, for his part, was staring with a white heat of curiosity at something he saw on the wall; just above where the man was lying, there were a few rude marks done in red chalk.

'This is a black business,' said the inspector at length; 'does anybody know who it is?'

A man stepped forward from the crowd. 'I do, governor,' he said, 'he's a big doctor, his name's Sir Thomas Vivian; I was in the 'orspital abart six months ago, and he used to come round; he was a very kind man.'

'Lord,' cried the inspector, 'this is a bad job indeed. Why, Sir Thomas Vivian goes to the Royal Family. And there's a watch worth a hundred guineas in his pocket, so it isn't robbery.'

Dyson and Phillipps gave their cards to the authority, and moved off, pushing with difficulty through the crowd that was still gathering, gathering fast; and the alley that had been lonely and desolate now swarmed with white staring faces and hummed with the buzz of rumour and horror, and rang with the commands of the officers of police. The two men once free from this swarming curiosity, stepped out briskly, but for twenty minutes neither spoke a word.

'Phillipps,' said Dyson, as they came into a small but cheerful street, clean and brightly lit, 'Phillipps, I owe you an apology. I was wrong to have spoken as I did tonight. Such infernal jesting,' he went on, with heat, 'as if there were no wholesome subjects for a joke. I feel as if I had raised an evil spirit.'

'For Heaven's sake say nothing more,' said Phillipps, choking down horror with visible effort. 'You told the truth to me in my room; the troglodyte, as you said, is still lurking about the earth, and in these very streets around us, slaying for mere lust of blood.'

'I will come up for a moment,' said Dyson when they reached Red Lion Square, 'I have something to ask you. I think there should be nothing hidden between us, at all events.'

Phillipps nodded gloomily, and they went up to the room, where everything hovered indistinct in the uncertain glimmer of the light from without. When the candle was lighted and the two men sat facing each other, Dyson spoke.

'Perhaps,' he began, 'you did not notice me peering at the wall just above the place where the head lay. The light from the inspector's lantern was shining full on it, and I saw something that looked queer to me, and I examined it closely. I found that someone had drawn in red chalk a rough outline of a hand – a human hand – upon the wall. But it was the curious position of the fingers that struck me; it was like this;' and he took a pencil and a piece of paper and drew rapidly, and then handed what he had done to Phillipps. It was a rough sketch of a hand seen from the back, with the fingers clenched, and the top of the thumb protruded between the first and second fingers, and pointed downwards, as if to something below.

'It was just like that,' said Dyson, as he saw Phillipps's face grow still whiter. 'The thumb pointed down as if to the body; it seemed almost a live hand in ghastly gesture. And just beneath there was a small mark with the powder of the chalk lying on it – as if someone had commenced a stroke and had broken the chalk in his hand. I saw the bit of chalk lying on the ground. But what do you make of it?'

'It's a horrible old sign,' said Phillipps – 'one of the most horrible signs connected with the theory of the evil eye. It is used still in Italy, but there can be no doubt that it has been known for ages. It is one of the survivals; you must look for the origin of it in the black swamp whence man first came.'

Dyson took up his hat to go.

'I think, jesting apart,' said he, 'that I kept my promise, and that we were and are hot on the scent, as I said. It seems as if I had really shown you primitive man, or his handiwork at all events.'

The Incident of the Letter

About a month after the extraordinary and mysterious murder of Sir Thomas Vivian, the well-known and universally respected specialist in heart disease, Mr Dyson called again on his friend Mr Phillipps, whom he found, not as usual, sunk deep in painful study, but re-clining in his easy-chair in an attitude of relaxation. He welcomed Dyson with cordiality.

'I am very glad you have come,' he began; 'I was thinking of looking you up. There is no longer the shadow of a doubt about the matter.'

'You mean the case of Sir Thomas Vivian?'

'Oh, no, not at all. I was referring to the problem of the fish-hooks. Between ourselves, I was a little too confident when you were here last, but since then other facts have turned up; and only yesterday I had a letter from a distinguished F.R.S. which quite settles the affair.'

I have been thinking what I should tackle next; and I am inclined to believe that there is a good deal to be done in the way of so-called undecipherable inscriptions.'

'Your line of study pleases me,' said Dyson. 'I think it may prove useful. But in the meantime, there was surely something extremely mysterious about the case of Sir Thomas Vivian.'

'Hardly, I think. I allowed myself to be frightened that night; but there can be no doubt that the facts are patient of a comparatively commonplace explanation.'

'Really! What is your theory then?'

'Well, I imagine that Vivian must have been mixed up at some period of his life in an adventure of a not very creditable description, and that he was murdered out of revenge by some Italian whom he had wronged.'

'Why Italian?'

'Because of the hand, the sign of the *mano in fica*. That gesture is now only used by Italians. So you see that what appeared the most obscure feature in the case turns out to be illuminant.'

'Yes, quite so. And the flint knife?'

'That is very simple. The man found the thing in Italy, or possibly stole it from some museum. Follow the line of least resistance, my dear fellow, and you will see there is no need to bring up primitive man from his secular grave beneath the hills.'

'There is some justice in what you say,' said Dyson. 'As I understand you, then, you think that your Italian, having murdered Vivian, kindly chalked up that hand as a guide to Scotland Yard?'

'Why not? Remember a murderer is always a madman. He may plot and contrive nine-tenths of his scheme with the acuteness and the grasp of a chess-player or a pure mathematician; but somewhere or other his wits leave him and he behaves like a fool. Then you must take into account the insane pride or vanity of the criminal; he likes to leave his mark, as it were, upon his handiwork.'

'Yes, it is all very ingenious; but have you read the reports of the inquest?'

'No, not a word. I simply gave my evidence, left the court, and dismissed the subject from my mind.'

'Quite so. Then if you don't object I should like to give you an account of the case. I have studied it rather deeply, and I confess it interests me extremely.'

'Very good. But I warn you I have done with mystery. We are to deal with facts now.'

'Yes, it is fact that I wish to put before you. And this is fact the first. When the police moved Sir Thomas Vivian's body they found an open knife beneath him. It was an ugly-looking thing such as sailors carry, with a blade that the mere opening rendered rigid, and there the blade was all ready, bare and gleaming, but without a trace of blood on it, and the knife was found to be quite new; it had never been used. Now, at the first glance it looks as if your imaginary Italian were just the man to have such a tool. But consider a moment. Would he be likely to buy a new knife expressly to commit murder? And, secondly, if he had such a knife, why didn't he use it, instead of that very odd flint instrument?

'And I want to put this to you. You think the murderer chalked up the hand after the murder as a sort of 'melodramatic Italian assassin his mark' touch. Passing over the question as to whether the real criminal ever does such a thing, I would point out that, on the medical evidence, Sir Thomas Vivian hadn't been dead for more than an hour. That would place the stroke at about a quarter to ten, and you know it was perfectly dark when we went out at 9.30. And that passage was singularly gloomy and ill-lighted, and the hand was drawn roughly, it is true, but correctly and without the bungling of strokes and the bad shots that are inevitable when one tries to draw in the dark or with shut eyes. Just try to draw such a simple figure as a square without looking at the paper, and then ask me to conceive that your Italian, with the rope waiting for his neck, could draw the hand on the wall so firmly and truly, in the black shadow of that alley. It is absurd. By consequence, then, the hand was drawn early in the evening, long before any murder was committed; or else – mark this, Phillipps – it was drawn by someone to whom darkness and gloom were familiar and habitual; by someone to whom the common dread of the rope was unknown!

'Again: a curious note was found in Sir Thomas Vivian's pocket. Envelope and paper were of a common make, and the stamp bore the West Central postmark. I will come to the nature of the contents later on, but it is the question of the handwriting that is so remarkable. The address on the outside was neatly written in a small clear hand, but the letter itself might have been written by a Persian who had learnt the English script. It was upright, and the letters were curiously contorted, with an affectation of dashes and backward curves which really reminded me of an Oriental manuscript, though it was all perfectly legible. But – and here comes the poser – on searching the dead man's waistcoat pockets a small memorandum book was found; it was almost filled with pencil jottings. These memoranda related chiefly to matters of a private as distinct from a professional nature; there were appointments to meet friends, notes of theatrical first-nights, the address of a good hotel in Tours, and the title of a new novel – nothing in any way intimate. And the whole of these jottings were written in a hand nearly identical with the writing of the note found in the dead man's coat pocket! There was just enough difference between them to enable the expert to swear that the two were not written by the same person. I will just read you so much of Lady Vivian's evidence as bears on this point of the writing; I have the printed slip with me. Here you see she says: 'I was married to my late husband seven years ago; I never saw any letter addressed to him in a hand at all resembling that on the envelope produced, nor have I ever seen writing like that in the letter before me. I never saw my late husband using the memorandum book, but I am sure he did write everything in it; I am certain of that because we stayed last May at the Hotel du Faisan, Rue Royale, Tours, the address of which is given in the book; I remember his getting the novel *A Sentinel* about six weeks ago. Sir Thomas Vivian never liked to miss the first-nights at the theatres. His usual hand was perfectly different from that used in the notebook.'

'And now, last of all, we come back to the note itself. Here it is in facsimile. My possession of it is due to the kindness of Inspector Cleeve, who is pleased to be amused at my amateur inquisitiveness. Read it, Phillipps; you tell me you are interested in obscure inscriptions; here is something for you to decipher.'

Mr Phillipps, absorbed in spite of himself in the strange circumstances Dyson had related, took the piece of paper, and scrutinised it closely. The handwriting was indeed bizarre in the extreme, and, as Dyson had noted, not unlike the Persian character in its general effect, but it was perfectly legible.

'Read it loud,' said Dyson, and Phillipps obeyed.

'Hand did not point in vain. The meaning of the stars is no longer obscure. Strangely enough, the black heaven vanished, or was stolen yesterday, but that does not matter in the least, as I have a celestial globe. Our old orbit remains unchanged; you have not forgotten the number of my sign, or will you appoint some other house? I have been on the other side of the moon, and can bring something to show you.'

'And what do you make of that?' said Dyson.

'It seems to me mere gibberish,' said Phillipps; 'you suppose it has a meaning?'

'Oh, surely; it was posted three days before the murder; it was found in the murdered man's pocket; it is written in a fantastic hand which the murdered man himself used for his private memoranda. There must be purpose under all this, and to my mind there is something ugly enough hidden under the circumstances of this case of Sir Thomas Vivian.'

'But what theory have you formed?'

'Oh, as to theories, I am still in a very early stage; it is too soon to state conclusions. But I think I have demolished your Italian. I tell you, Phillipps, again, the whole thing has an ugly look to my eyes. I cannot do as you do, and fortify myself with cast-iron propositions to the effect that this or that doesn't happen, and never has happened. You note that the first word in the letter is 'hand'. That seems to me, taken with what we know about the hand on the wall, significant enough, and what you yourself told me of the history and meaning of the symbol, its connection with a world-old belief and faiths of dim far-off years, all this speaks of mischief, for me at all events. No; I stand pretty well to what I said to you half in joke that night before we went out. There are sacraments of evil as well as of good about us, and we live and move to my belief in an unknown world, a place where there are caves and shadows and dwellers in twilight. It is possible that man may sometimes return on the track of evolution, and it is my belief that an awful lore is not yet dead.'

'I cannot follow you in all this,' said Phillipps; 'it seems to interest you strangely. What do you propose to do?'

'My dear Phillipps,' replied Dyson, speaking in a lighter tone, 'I am afraid I shall have to go down a little in the world. I have a prospect of visits to the pawnbrokers before me, and the publicans must not be neglected. I must cultivate a taste for four ale; shag tobacco I already love and esteem with all my heart.'

Search for the Vanished Heaven

For many days after the discussion with Phillipps, Mr Dyson was resolute in the line of research he had marked out for himself. A fervent curiosity and an innate liking for the obscure were great incentives, but especially in this case of Sir Thomas Vivian's death (for Dyson began to boggle a little at the word 'murder') there seemed to him an element that was more than curious. The sign of the red hand upon the wall, the tool of flint that had given death, the almost identity between the handwriting of the note and the fantastic script reserved religiously, as it appeared, by the doctor for trifling jottings, all these diverse and variegated threads joined to weave in his mind a strange and shadowy picture, with ghastly shapes dominant and deadly, and yet ill-defined, like the giant figures wavering in an ancient tapestry. He thought he had a clue to the meaning of the note, and in his resolute search for the 'black heaven', which had vanished, he beat furiously about the alleys and obscure streets of central London, making himself a familiar figure to the pawnbroker, and frequent guest at the more squalid pot-houses.

For a long time he was unsuccessful, and he trembled at the thought that the 'black heaven' might be hid in the coy retirements of Peckham, or lurk perchance in distant Willesden, but finally, improbability, in which he put his trust, came to the rescue. It was a dark and rainy night, with something in the unquiet and stirring gusts that savoured of approaching winter, and Dyson, beating up a narrow street not far from the Gray's Inn Road, took shelter in an extremely dirty 'public', and called for beer, forgetting for the moment his preoccupations, and only thinking of the sweep of the wind about the tiles and the hissing of the rain through the black and troubled air. At the bar there gathered the usual company: the frowsy women and the men in shiny black, those who appeared to mumble secretly together, others who wrangled in interminable argument, and a few shy drinkers who stood apart, each relishing his dose, and the rank and biting savour of cheap spirit. Dyson was wondering at the enjoyment of it all, when suddenly there came a sharper accent. The folding-doors swayed open, and a middle-aged woman staggered towards the bar, and clutched the pewter rim as if she stepped a deck in a roaring gale. Dyson glanced at her attentively as a pleasing specimen of her class; she was decently dressed in black, and carried a black bag of somewhat rusty leather, and her intoxication was apparent and far advanced. As she swayed at the bar, it was evidently all she could do to stand upright, and the barman, who had looked at her with disfavour, shook his head in reply to her thick-voiced demand for a drink. The woman glared at him, transformed in a moment to a fury, with bloodshot eyes, and poured forth a torrent of execration, a stream of blasphemies and early English phraseology.

'Get out of this,' said the man; 'shut up and be off, or I'll send for the police.'

'Police, you — ' bawled the woman, 'I'll — well give you something to fetch the police for!' and with a rapid dive into her bag she pulled out some object which she hurled furiously at the barman's head.

The man ducked down, and the missile flew over his head and smashed a bottle to fragments, while the woman with a peal of horrible laughter rushed to the door, and they could hear her steps pattering fast over the wet stones.

The barman looked ruefully about him.

'Not much good going after her,' he said, 'and I'm afraid what she's left won't pay for that bottle of whisky.' He fumbled amongst the fragments of broken glass, and drew out something dark, a kind of square stone it seemed, which he held up.

'Valuable cur'osity,' he said, 'any gent like to bid?'

The habitués had scarcely turned from their pots and glasses during these exciting incidents; they gazed a moment, fishily, when the bottle smashed, and that was all, and the mumble of the confidential was resumed and the jangle of the quarrelsome, and the shy and solitary sucked in their lips and relished again the rank flavour of the spirit.

Dyson looked quickly at what the barman held before him.

'Would you mind letting me see it?' he said; 'it's a queer-looking old thing, isn't it?'

It was a small black tablet, apparently of stone, about four inches long by two and a half broad, and as Dyson took it he felt rather than saw that he touched the secular with his flesh. There was some kind of carving on the surface, and, most conspicuous, a sign that made Dyson's heart leap.

'I don't mind taking it,' he said quietly. 'Would two shillings be enough?'

'Say half a dollar,' said the man, and the bargain was concluded. Dyson drained his pot of beer, finding it delicious, and lit his pipe, and went out deliberately soon after. When he reached his apartment he locked the door, and placed the tablet on his desk, and then fixed himself in his chair, as resolute as an army in its trenches before a beleaguered city. The tablet was full under the light of the shaded candle, and scrutinising it closely, Dyson saw first the sign of the hand with the thumb protruding between the fingers; it was cut finely and firmly on the dull black surface of the stone, and the thumb pointed downward to what was beneath.

'It is mere ornament,' said Dyson to himself; 'perhaps symbolical ornament, but surely not an inscription, or the signs of any words ever spoken.'

The hand pointed at a series of fantastic figures, spirals and whorls of the finest, most delicate lines, spaced at intervals over the remaining surface of the tablet. The marks were as intricate and seemed almost as much without design as the pattern of a thumb impressed upon a pane of glass.

'Is it some natural marking?' thought Dyson. 'There have been queer designs, likenesses of beasts and flowers, in stones with which man's hand had nothing to do'; and he bent over the stone with a magnifier, only to be convinced that no hazard of nature could have delineated these varied labyrinths of line. The whorls were of different sizes; some were less than the twelfth of an inch in diameter, and the largest was a little smaller than a sixpence, and under the glass the regularity and accuracy of the cutting were evident, and in the smaller spirals the lines were graduated at intervals of a hundredth of an inch. The whole thing had a marvellous and fantastic look, and gazing at the mystic whorls beneath the hand, Dyson became subdued with an impression of vast and far-off ages, and of a living being that had touched the stone with enigmas before the hills were formed, when the hard rocks still boiled with fervent heat.

'The "black heaven" is found again,' he said, 'but the meaning of the stars is likely to be obscure for everlasting so far as I am concerned.'

London stilled without, and a chill breath came into the room as Dyson sat gazing at the tablet shining duskily under the candle-light; and at last, as he closed the desk over the ancient stone, all his wonder at the case of Sir Thomas Vivian increased tenfold and he thought of the well-dressed prosperous gentleman lying dead mystically beneath the sign of the hand, and the insupportable conviction seized him that between the death of this fashionable West-end doctor and the weird spirals of the tablet there were most secret and unimaginable links.

For days he sat before his desk gazing at the tablet, unable to resist its lodestone fascination, and yet quite helpless, without even the hope of solving the symbols so secretly inscribed. At last, desperate, he called in Mr Phillipps in consultation, and told in brief the story of the finding of the stone.

'Dear me!' said Phillipps, 'this is extremely curious; you have had a find indeed. Why it looks to me even more ancient than the Hittite seal. I confess the character, if it is a character, is entirely strange to me. These whorls are really very quaint.'

'Yes, but I want to know what they mean. You must remember this tablet is the 'black heaven' of the letter found in Sir Thomas Vivian's pocket; it bears directly on his death.'

'Oh, no, that is nonsense! This is, no doubt, an extremely ancient tablet, which has been stolen from some collection. Yes, the hand makes an odd coincidence, but only a coincidence after all.'

'My dear Phillipps, you are a living example of the truth of the axiom that extreme scepticism is mere credulity. But can you decipher the inscription?'

'I undertake to decipher anything,' said Phillipps. 'I do not believe in the insoluble. These characters are curious, but I cannot fancy them to be inscrutable.'

'Then take the thing away with you and make what you can of it. It has begun to haunt me; I feel as if I had gazed too long into the eyes of the Sphinx.'

Phillipps departed with the tablet in an inner pocket. He had not much doubt of success, for he had evolved thirty-seven rules for the solution of inscriptions. Yet when a week had passed and he called to see Dyson there was no vestige of triumph on his features. He found his friend in a state of extreme irritation, pacing up and down in the room like a man in a passion. He turned with a start as the door opened.

'Well,' said Dyson, 'you have got it? What is it all about?'

'My dear fellow, I am sorry to say I have completely failed. I have tried every known device in vain. I have even been so officious as to submit it to a friend at the Museum, but he, though a man of prime authority on the subject, tells me he is quite at fault. It must be some wreckage of a vanished race, almost, I think – a fragment of another world than ours. I am not a superstitious man, Dyson, and you know that I have no truck with even the noble delusions, but I confess I yearn to be rid of this small square of blackish stone. Frankly, it has given me an ill week; it seems to me troglodytic and abhorred.'

Phillipps drew out the tablet and laid it on the desk before Dyson.

'By the way,' he went on, 'I was right at all events in one particular; it has formed part of some collection. There is a piece of grimy paper on the back that must have been a label.'

'Yes, I noticed that,' said Dyson, who had fallen into deepest disappointment; 'no doubt the paper is a label. But as I don't much care where the tablet originally came from, and only wish to know what the inscription means, I paid no attention to the paper. The thing is a hopeless riddle, I suppose, and yet it must surely be of the greatest importance.'

Phillipps left soon after, and Dyson, still despondent, took the tablet in his hand and carelessly turned it over. The label had so grimed that it seemed merely a dull stain, but as Dyson looked at it idly, and yet attentively, he could see pencil-marks, and he bent over it eagerly, with his glass to his eye. To his annoyance, he found that part of the paper had been torn away, and he could only with difficulty make out odd works and pieces of words. First he read something that looked like 'inroad', and then beneath, 'stony-hearted step' – and a tear cut off the rest. But in an instant a solution suggested itself, and he chuckled with huge delight.

'Certainly,' he said out loud, 'this is not only the most charming but the most convenient quarter in all London; here I am, allowing for the accidents of side streets, perched on a tower of observation.'

He glanced triumphant out of the window across the street to the gate of the British Museum. Sheltered by the boundary wall of that agreeable institution, a 'screever,' or artist in chalks, displayed his brilliant impressions on the pavement, soliciting the approval and the coppers of the gay and serious.

'This,' said Dyson, 'is more than delightful! An artist is provided to my hand.'

The Artist of the Pavement

Mr Phillipps, in spite of all disavowals – in spite of the wall of sense of whose enclosure and limit he was wont to make his boast – yet felt in his heart profoundly curious as to the case of Sir Thomas Vivian. Though he kept a brave face for his friend, his reason could not decently resist the conclusion that Dyson had enunciated, namely, that the whole affair had a look both ugly and mysterious. There was the weapon of a vanished race that had pierced the great arteries; the red hand, the symbol of a hideous faith, that pointed to the slain man; and then the tablet which Dyson declared he had expected to find, and had certainly found, bearing the ancient impress of the hand of malediction, and a legend written beneath in a character compared with which the most antique cuneiform was a thing of yesterday. Besides all this, there were other points that tortured and perplexed. How to account for the bare knife found unstained beneath the body? And the hint that the red hand upon the wall must have been drawn by someone whose life was passed in darkness thrilled him with a suggestion of dim and infinite horror. Hence he was in truth not a little curious as to what was to come, and some ten days after he had returned the tablet he again visited the 'mystery-man', as he privately named his friend.

Arrived in the grave and airy chambers in Great Russell Street, he found the moral atmosphere of the place had been transformed. All Dyson's irritation had disappeared, his brow was smoothed with complacency, and he sat at a table by the window gazing out into the street with an expression of grim enjoyment, a pile of books and papers lying unheeded before him.

'My dear Phillipps, I am delighted to see you! Pray excuse my moving. Draw your chair up here to the table, and try this admirable shag tobacco.'

'Thank you,' said Phillipps, 'judging by the flavour of the smoke, I should think it is a little strong. But what on earth is all this? What are you looking at?'

'I am on my watch-tower. I assure you that the time seems short while I contemplate this agreeable street and the classic grace of the Museum portico.'

'Your capacity for nonsense is amazing,' replied Phillipps, 'but have you succeeded in deciphering the tablet? It interests me.'

'I have not paid much attention to the tablet recently,' said Dyson. 'I believe the spiral character may wait.'

'Really! And how about the Vivian murder?'

'Ah, you do take an interest in that case? Well, after all, we cannot deny that it was a queer business. But is not "murder" rather a coarse word? It smacks a little, surely, of the police poster. Perhaps I am a trifle decadent, but I cannot help believing in the splendid word; "sacrifice," for example, is surely far finer than "murder".'

'I am all in the dark,' said Phillipps. 'I cannot even imagine by what track you are moving in this labyrinth.'

'I think that before very long the whole matter will be a good deal clearer for us both, but I doubt whether you will like hearing the story.'

Dyson lit his pipe afresh and leant back, not relaxing, however, in his scrutiny of the street. After a somewhat lengthy pause, he startled Phillipps by a loud breath of relief as he rose from the chair by the window and began to pace the floor.

'It's over for the day,' he said, 'and, after all, one gets a little tired.'

Phillipps looked with inquiry into the street. The evening was darkening, and the pile of the Museum was beginning to loom indistinct before the lighting of the lamps, but the pavements were thronged and busy. The artist in chalks across the way was gathering together his materials, and blurring all the brilliance of his designs, and a little lower down there was the clang of shutters being placed in position. Phillipps could see nothing to justify Mr Dyson's sudden abandonment of his attitude of surveillance, and grew a little irritated by all these thorny enigmas.

'Do you know, Phillipps,' said Dyson, as he strolled at ease up and down the room, 'I will tell you how I work. I go upon the theory of improbability. The theory is unknown to you? I will explain. Suppose I stand on the steps of St Paul's and look out for a blind man lame of the left leg to pass me, it is evidently highly improbable that I shall see such a person by waiting for an hour. If I wait two hours the improbability is diminished, but is still enormous, and a watch of a whole day would give little expectation of success. But suppose I take up the same position day after day, and week after week, don't you perceive that the improbability is lessening constantly – growing smaller day after day? Don't you see that two lines which are not parallel are gradually approaching one another, drawing nearer and nearer to a point of meeting, till at last they do meet, and improbability has vanished altogether? That is how I found the black tablet: I acted on the theory of improbability. It is the only scientific principle I know of which can enable one to pick out an unknown man from amongst five million.'

'And you expect to find the interpreter of the black tablet by this method?'

'Certainly.'

'And the murderer of Sir Thomas Vivian also?'

'Yes, I expect to lay my hands on the person concerned in the death of Sir Thomas Vivian in exactly the same way.'

The rest of the evening, after Phillipps had left, was devoted by Dyson to sauntering in the streets, and afterwards, when the night grew late, to his literary labours, or the chase of the phrase, as he called it. The next morning the station by the window was again resumed. His meals were brought to him at the table, and he ate with his eyes on the street. With briefest intervals, snatched reluctantly from time to time, he persisted in his survey throughout the day, and only at dusk, when the shutters were put up and the 'screever' ruthlessly deleted all his labour of the day, just before the gas lamps began to star the shadows, did he feel at liberty to quit his post. Day after day this ceaseless glance upon the street continued, till the landlady grew puzzled and aghast at such a profitless pertinacity.

But at last, one evening, when the play of lights and shadows was scarce beginning, and the clear cloudless air left all distinct and shining, there came the moment. A man of middle age, bearded and bowed, with a touch of grey about the ears, was strolling slowly along the northern pavement of Great Russell Street from the eastern end. He looked up at the Museum as he went by, and then glanced involuntarily at the art of the 'screever', and at the artist himself, who sat beside his pictures, hat in hand. The man with the beard stood still an instant, swaying slightly to and fro as if in thought, and Dyson saw his fists shut tight, and his back quivering, and the one side of his face in view twitched and grew contorted with the indescribable torment of approaching epilepsy. Dyson drew a soft hat from his pocket, and dashed the door open, taking the stair with a run.

When he reached the street the person he had seen so agitated had turned about, and, regardless of observation, was racing wildly towards Bloomsbury Square, with his back to his former course.

Mr Dyson went up to the artist of the pavement and gave him some money, observing quietly, 'You needn't trouble to draw that thing again.' Then he too turned about, and strolled idly down the street in the opposite direction to that taken by the fugitive. So the distance between Dyson and the man with the bowed head grew steadily greater.

Story of the Treasure House

'There are many reasons why I chose your rooms for the meeting in preference to my own. Chiefly, perhaps, because I thought the man would be more at his ease on neutral ground.'

'I confess, Dyson,' said Phillipps, 'that I feel both impatient and uneasy. You know my standpoint: hard matter of fact, materialism if you like, in its crudest form. But there is something about all this affair of Vivian that makes me a little restless. And how did you induce the man to come?'

'He has an exaggerated opinion of my powers. You remember what I said about the doctrine of improbability? When it does work out, it gives results which seem very amazing to a person who is not in the secret. That is eight striking, isn't it? And there goes the bell.'

They heard footsteps on the stair, and presently the door opened, and a middle-aged man, with a bowed head, bearded, and with a good deal of grizzling hair about his ears, came into the room. Phillipps glanced at his features, and recognised the lineaments of terror.

'Come in, Mr Selby,' said Dyson. 'This is Mr Phillipps, my intimate friend and our host for this evening. Will you take anything? Then perhaps we had better hear your story – a very singular one, I am sure.'

The man spoke in a voice hollow and a little quavering, and a fixed stare that never left his eyes seemed directed to something awful that was to remain before him by day and night for the rest of his life.

'You will, I am sure, excuse preliminaries,' he began; 'what I have to tell is best told quickly. I will say, then, that I was born in a remote part of the west of England, where the very outlines of the woods and hills, and the winding of the streams in the valleys, are apt to suggest the mystical to anyone strongly gifted with imagination. When I was quite a boy there were certain huge and rounded hills, certain depths of hanging wood, and secret valleys bastioned round on every side that filled me with fancies beyond the bourne of rational expression, and as I grew older and began to dip into my father's books, I went by instinct, like the bee, to all that would nourish fantasy. Thus, from a course of obsolete and occult reading, and from listening to certain wild legends in which the older people still secretly believed, I grew firmly convinced of the existence of treasure, the hoard of a race extinct for ages, still hidden beneath the hills, and my every thought was directed to the discovery of the golden heaps that lay, as I fancied, within a few feet of the green turf. To one spot, in especial, I was drawn as if by enchantment; it was a tumulus, the domed memorial of some forgotten people, crowning the crest of a vast mountain range; and I have often lingered there on summer evenings, sitting on the great block of limestone at the summit, and looking out far over the yellow sea towards the Devonshire coast. One day as I dug heedlessly with the ferrule of my stick at the mosses and lichens which grew rank over the stone, my eye was caught by what seemed a pattern beneath the growth of green; there was a curving line, and marks that did not look altogether the work of nature. At first I thought I had bared some rarer fossil, and I took out my knife and scraped away at the moss till a square foot was uncovered. Then I saw two signs which startled me; first, a closed hand, pointing downwards, the thumb protruding between the fingers, and beneath the hand a whorl or spiral, traced with exquisite accuracy in the hard surface of the rock. Here, I persuaded myself, was an index to the great secret, but I chilled at the recollection of the fact that some antiquarians had tunnelled the tumulus through and through, and had been a good deal surprised at not finding so much as an arrowhead within. Clearly, then, the signs on the limestone had no local significance; and I made up my mind that I must search abroad. By sheer accident I was in a measure successful in my quest. Strolling by a cottage, I saw some children playing by the roadside; one was holding up some object in his hand, and the rest were going through one of the many forms of elaborate pretence which make up a great part of the mystery of a child's life. Something in the object held by the little boy attracted me, and I asked him to let me see it. The plaything of these children consisted of an oblong tablet of black stone; and on it was inscribed the hand pointing downwards, just as I had seen it on the rock, while beneath, spaced over the tablet, were a number of whorls and spirals, cut, as it seemed to me, with the utmost care and nicety. I bought the toy for a couple of shillings; the woman of the house told me it had been lying about for years; she thought her husband had found it one day in the brook which ran in front of the cottage: it was a very hot summer, and the stream was almost dry, and he saw it amongst the stones. That day I tracked the brook to a well of water gushing up cold and clear at the head of a lonely glen in the mountain. That was twenty years ago, and I only succeeded in deciphering the mysterious inscription last August. I must not trouble you with irrelevant details of my life; it is enough for me to say that I was forced, like many another man, to leave my old home and come to London. Of money I had very little, and I was glad to find a cheap room in a squalid street off the Gray's Inn Road. The late Sir Thomas Vivian, then far poorer and more wretched than myself, had a garret in the same house, and before many months we became intimate friends, and I had confided to him the object of my life. I had at first great difficulty in persuading him that I was not giving my days and my nights to an inquiry altogether hopeless and chimerical; but when he was convinced he grew keener than myself, and glowed at the thought of the riches which were to be the prize of some ingenuity and patience. I liked the man intensely, and pitied his case; he had a strong desire to enter the medical profession, but he lacked the means to pay the smallest fees and indeed he was, not once or twice, but often reduced to the very verge of starvation. I freely and solemnly promised that, under whatever chances, he should share in my heaped fortune when it came, and this promise to one who had always been poor, and yet thirsted for wealth and pleasure in a manner unknown to me, was the strongest incentive. He threw himself into the task with eager interest, and applied a very acute intellect and unwearied patience to the solution of the characters on the tablet. I, like other ingenious young men, was curious in the matter of handwriting, and I had invented or adapted a fantastic script which I used occasionally, and which took Vivian so strongly that he was at the pains to imitate it. It was arranged between us that if we were ever parted, and had occasion to write on the affair that was so close to our hearts, this queer hand of my invention was to be used, and we also contrived a semi-cypher for the same purpose. Meanwhile we exhausted ourselves in efforts to get at the heart of the mystery, and after a couple of years had gone by I could see that Vivian began to sicken a little of the adventure, and one night he told me with some emotion that he feared both our lives were being passed away in idle and hopeless endeavour. Not many months afterwards he was so happy as to receive a considerable legacy from an aged and distant relative whose very existence had been almost forgotten by him; and with money at the bank, he became at once a stranger to me. He had passed his preliminary examination many years before, and he forthwith decided to enter at St Thomas's Hospital, and he told me that he must look out for a more convenient lodging. As we said goodbye, I reminded him of the promise I had given, and solemnly renewed it; but Vivian laughed with something between pity and contempt in his voice and expression as he thanked me. I need not dwell on the long struggle and misery of my existence, now doubly lonely; I never wearied or despaired of final success, and every day saw me at work, the tablet before me, and only at dusk would I go out and take my daily walk along Oxford Street, which attracted me I think by the noise and motion and glitter of lamps.

'This walk grew with me to a habit; every night, and in all weathers, I crossed the Gray's Inn Road and struck westward, sometimes choosing a northern track, by the Euston Road and Tottenham Court Road, sometimes I went by Holborn, and sometimes by way of Great Russell Street. Every night I walked for an hour to and fro on the northern pavement of Oxford Street, and the tale of De Quincey and his name for the street, "Stony-hearted stepmother", often recurred to my memory. Then I would return to my grimy den and spend hours more in endless analysis of the riddle before me.

'The answer came to me one night a few weeks ago; it flashed into my brain in a moment, and I read the inscription, and saw that after all I had not wasted my days. "The place of the treasure house of them that dwell below", were the first words I read, and then followed minute indications of the spot in my own country where the great works of gold were to be kept for ever. Such a track was to be followed, such a pitfall avoided; here the way narrowed almost to a fox's hole, and there it broadened, and so at last the chamber would be reached. I determined to lose no time in verifying my discovery – not that I doubted at that great moment, but I would not risk even the smallest chance of disappointing my old friend Vivian, now a rich and prosperous man. I took the train for the West, and one night, with chart in hand, traced out the passage of the hills, and went so far that I saw the gleam of gold before me. I would not go on; I resolved that Vivian must be with me; and I only brought away a strange knife of flint which lay on the path, as confirmation of what I had to tell. I returned to London, and was a good deal vexed to find the stone tablet had disappeared from my rooms. My landlady, an inveterate drunkard, denied all knowledge of the fact, but I have little doubt she had stolen the thing for the sake of the glass of whisky it might fetch. However, I knew what was written on the tablet by heart, and I had also made an exact facsimile of the characters, so the loss was not severe. Only one thing annoyed me: when I first came into possession of the stone, I had pasted a piece of paper on the back and had written down the date and place of finding, and later on I had scribbled a word or two, a trivial sentiment, the name of my street, and suchlike idle pencillings on the paper; and these memories of days that had seemed so hopeless were dear to me: I had thought they would help to remind me in the future of the hours when I had hoped against despair. However, I wrote at once to Sir Thomas Vivian, using the handwriting I have mentioned and also the quasi-cypher. I told him of my success, and after mentioning the loss of the tablet and the fact that I had a copy of the inscription, I reminded him once more of my promise, and asked him either to write or call. He replied that he would see me in a certain obscure passage in Clerkenwell well known to us both in the old days, and at seven o'clock one evening I went to meet him. At the corner of this by-way, as I was walking to and fro, I noticed the blurred pictures of some street artist, and I picked up a piece of chalk he had left behind him, not much thinking what I was doing. I paced up and down the passage, wondering a good deal as you may imagine, as to what manner of man I was to meet after so many years of parting, and the thoughts of the buried time coming thick upon me, I walked mechanically without raising my eyes from the ground. I was startled out of my reverie by an angry voice and a rough inquiry why I didn't keep to the right side of the pavement, and looking up I found I had confronted a prosperous and important gentleman, who eyed my poor appearance with a look of great dislike and contempt. I knew directly it was my old comrade, and when I recalled myself to him, he apologised with some show of regret, and began to thank me for my kindness, doubtfully, as if he hesitated to commit himself, and, as I could see, with the hint of a suspicion as to my sanity. I would have engaged him at first in reminiscences of our friendship, but I found Sir Thomas viewed those days with a good deal of distaste, and replying politely to my remarks, continually edged in "business matters", as he called them. I changed my topics, and told him in greater detail what I have told you. Then I saw his manner suddenly change; as I pulled out the flint knife to prove my journey "to the other side of the moon", as we called it in our jargon, there came over him a kind of choking eagerness, his features were some-what discomposed, and I thought I detected a shuddering horror, a clenched resolution, and the effort to keep quiet succeed one an-other in a manner that puzzled me. I had occasion to be a little precise in my particulars, and it being still light enough, I remem-bered the red chalk in my pocket, and drew the hand on the wall. "Here, you see, is the hand," I said, as I explained its true meaning, "note where the thumb issues from between the first and second fingers," and I would have gone on, and had applied the chalk to the wall to continue my diagram, when he struck my hand down, much to my surprise. "No, no," he said, "I do not want all that. And this place is not retired enough; let us walk on, and do you explain everything to me minutely." I complied readily enough, and he led me away, choosing the most unfrequented by-ways, while I drove in the plan of the hidden house word by word. Once or twice as I raised my eyes I caught Vivian looking strangely about him; he seemed to give a quick glint up and down, and glance at the houses; and there was a furtive and anxious air about him that displeased me. "Let us walk on to the north," he said at length, "we shall come to some pleasant lanes where we can discuss these matters, quietly; my night's rest is at your service." I declined, on the pretext that I could not dispense with my visit to Oxford Street, and went on till he understood every turning and winding and the minutest detail as well as myself. We had returned on our footsteps, and stood again in the dark passage, just where I had drawn the red hand on the wall, for I recognised the vague shape of the trees whose branches hung above us. "We have come back to our starting-point," I said; "I almost think I could put my finger on the wall where I drew the hand. And I am sure you could put your finger on the mystic hand in the hills as well as I. Remember between stream and stone."

'I was bending down, peering at what I thought must be my drawing, when I heard a sharp hiss of breath, and started up, and saw Vivian with his arm uplifted and a bare blade in his hand, and death threatening in his eyes. In sheer self-defence I caught at the flint weapon in my pocket, and dashed at him in blind fear of my life, and the next instant he lay dead upon the stones.

'I think that is all,' Mr Selby continued after a pause, 'and it only remains for me to say to you, Mr Dyson, that I cannot conceive what means enabled you to run me down.'

'I followed many indications,' said Dyson, 'and I am bound to disclaim all credit for astuteness, as I have made several gross blunders. Your celestial cypher did not, I confess, give me much trouble; I saw at once that terms of astronomy were substituted for common words and phrases. You had lost something black, or something black had been stolen from you; a celestial globe is a copy of the heavens, so I knew you meant you had a copy of what you had lost. Obviously, then, I came to the conclusion that you had lost a black object with characters or symbols written or inscribed on it, since the object in question certainly contained valuable information, and all information must be written or pictured. "Our old orbit remains unchanged"; evidently our old course or arrangement. "The number of my sign" must mean the number of my house, the allusion being to the signs of the zodiac. I need not say that "the other side of the moon" can stand for nothing but some place where no one else has been; and "some other house" is some other place of meeting, the "house" being the old term "house of the heavens." Then my next step was to find the "black heaven" that had been stolen, and by a process of exhaustion I did so.'

'You have got the tablet?'

'Certainly. And on the back of it, on the slip of paper you have mentioned, I read "inroad", which puzzled me a good deal, till I thought of Gray's Inn Road; you forgot the second n. "Stony-hearted step" immediately suggested the phrase of De Quincey you have alluded to; and I made the wild but correct shot, that you were a man that lived in or near the Gray's Inn Road, and had the habit of walking in Oxford Street, for you remember how the opium-eater dwells on his wearying promenades along that thoroughfare? On the theory of improbability, which I have explained to my friend here, I concluded that occasionally, at all events, you would choose the way by Guilford Street, Russell Square, and Great Russell Street, and I knew that if I watched long enough I should see you. But how was I to recognise my man? I noticed the screever opposite my rooms, and got him to draw every day a large hand, in the gesture so familiar to us all, upon the wall behind him. I thought that when the unknown person did pass he would certainly betray some emotion at the sudden vision of the sign, to him the most terrible of symbols. You know the rest. Ah, as to catching you an hour later, that was, I confess, a refinement. From the fact of your having occupied the same rooms for so many years, in a neighbourhood moreover where lodgers are migratory to excess, I drew the conclusion that you were a man of fixed habit, and I was sure that after you had got over your fright you would return for the walk down Oxford Street. You did, by way of New Oxford Street, and I was waiting at the corner.'

'Your conclusions are admirable,' said Mr Selby. 'I may tell you that I had my stroll down Oxford Street the night Sir Thomas Vivian died. And I think that is all I have to say.'

'Scarcely,' said Dyson. 'How about the treasure?'

'I had rather we did not speak of that,' said Mr Selby, with a whitening of the skin about the temples.

'Oh, nonsense, sir, we are not blackmailers. Besides, you know you are in our power.'

'Then, as you put it like that, Mr Dyson, I must tell you I returned to the place. I went on a little farther than before.'

The man stopped short; his mouth began to twitch, his lips moved apart, and he drew in quick breaths, sobbing.

'Well, well,' said Dyson, 'I dare say you have done comfortably.'

'Comfortably,' Selby went on, constraining himself with an effort, 'yes, so comfortably that hell burns hot within me for ever. I only brought one thing away from that awful house within the hills; it was lying just beyond the spot where I found the flint knife.'

'Why did you not bring more?'

The whole bodily frame of the wretched man visibly shrank and wasted; his face grew yellow as tallow, and the sweat dropped from his brows. The spectacle was both revolting and terrible, and when the voice came, it sounded like the hissing of a snake.

'Because the keepers are still there, and I saw them, and because of this,' and he pulled out a small piece of curious gold-work and held it up.

'There,' he said, 'that is the Pain of the Goat.'

Phillipps and Dyson cried out together in horror at the revolting obscenity of the thing.

'Put it away, man; hide it, for Heaven's sake, hide it!'

'I brought that with me; that is all,' he said. 'You do not wonder that I did not stay long in a place where those who live are a little higher than the beasts, and where what you have seen is surpassed a thousandfold?'

'Take this,' said Dyson, 'I brought it with me in case it might be useful;' and he drew out the black tablet, and handed it to the shaking, horrible man.

'And now,' said Dyson, 'will you go out?'

The two friends sat silent a little while, facing one another with restless eyes and lips that quivered.

'I wish to say that I believe him,' said Phillipps.

'My dear Phillipps,' said Dyson as he threw the windows wide open, 'I do not know that, after all, my blunders in this queer case were so very absurd.'

The Haunted Woman

ALLEN UPWARD

A month after the romantic adventure of Bewley Hall, I received the most extraordinary letter I have ever had in my life.

It was from a lady, and the envelope was marked *Private*. This is what I read.

The Abbey, Abbotsbury

DEAR SIR

I have seen in the *Journal of the Psychical Research Society* an account of some extraordinary discoveries made by you and a young lady named Sargent in connection with occult phenomena in old family mansions; and I am writing to ask you in confidence if you or she would be willing to come down here and see if you could do anything to put an end to a manifestation which has been going on for a considerable time.

I ought to explain that I am the only person in the house who has seen anything, and I have not mentioned it to anyone but my own maid, who can be trusted. I am *most anxious* that my son, Captain Throgmorton, should not hear anything about the matter, and therefore it is essential that no one should know why you are coming down. Some excuse will have to be thought of to account for your visit. My son is a widower, and has never recovered from the shock of losing his wife, and therefore you will understand that I must make it a point that *on no account* is he to be troubled.

I write to you in the greatest anxiety and distress of mind, and shall be prepared to pay liberally for your services and those of Miss Sargent, for which I shall be most grateful.

Trusting you will treat this matter as one *strictly* between ourselves,

I remain, yours truly,

(Lady) MARIA THROGMORTON

P.S. In replying, please do not use an envelope bearing the name of your firm, as the letter-bag is opened by Captain Throgmorton.

Had I listened to my first impulse, I should have written back firmly, declining to have anything to do with a matter which called for concealment, and especially when I was asked to visit a house under a false character.

Unfortunately, before replying, I showed the letter to Alwyne, whose curiosity was immediately aroused to the highest degree.

'I am certain there is more in this than meets the eye,' she declared. 'From the way this lady writes it is evident that she thinks there is some connection between what she has seen and her son – something which she is afraid to tell us. We must go down and find out at all events what the situation is, even if we go no further.'

The moment I heard her talk like that, I bitterly regretted having shown her Lady Throgmorton's letter. I knew Alwyne's courage too well by this time to have any hope of frightening her off from an adventure because it threatened to have some risk. The only argument I could think of was an appeal to the conventions.

'I could not think of letting you enter the house of people we know nothing about under a false name, or in some concealed character,' I said determinedly. 'I might consent to do such a thing, but my wife is different.'

'I am not your wife yet, you tyrant,' Alwyne retorted with a sly smile. 'If you show the cloven hoof like that I shall look out for some kind, good-natured husband who will not trample on me. But there is no need that I should take a false name, or do anything else that you don't like. Why shouldn't this lady advertise for a companion in the *Standard*, and I answer the advertisement, and go down on trial?'

I felt that I was no match for Alwyne's ready wit. She found a way out of every difficulty as soon as I stated it.

'Well, at all events, I shall insist on going down first, and finding out something more about these people,' I said. 'How do you suggest that *I* should manage?'

Alwyne considered for a minute.

'There is no reason why you should not go down in your own name, too,' she said at length, 'unless Captain Throgmorton has heard of you. You might find out that from Lady Throgmorton. I should think the simplest plan would be for her to send for you to advise her about some alteration in the house – those old places are always wanting repairs. Unless she can persuade her son to let it – he seems to be the master. You had better ask her for more information first.'

The upshot was that I answered Lady Throgmorton's letter as Alwyne wished. At the same time I looked up the family in the *Landed Gentry*.

The first result of these inquiries was the discovery that Lady Throgmorton was merely the captain's stepmother. She was the widow of one of our Ministers abroad, who had received the G.C.B., and Captain Throgmorton was his son by a former wife. Apparently, however, the stepmother and stepson had always been on the best of terms, and the widow of Sir Nicholas had remained on in the Abbey as its mistress until the captain's marriage, which had taken place about a year ago.

I could not learn anything about the wife's death, but it was clear that Lady Throgmorton had now resumed her old position.

At all events, she wrote back to me, saying that there was no need for me to drop my right name, and accepting the suggestion as to letting the house.

In due course I received a letter in her handwriting, but signed Arthur Throgmorton, in which I was formally invited to come down and see the property.

It was with very much more excitement than I usually feel on such occasions that I drove up to the main entrance of the Abbey, through an avenue whose yellowing leaves seemed ominous of some catastrophe.

I was first taken up to a comfortable bedroom on the second floor, and given some tea. Half-an-hour later, the footman who attended to me came back, and asked me to follow him down to her ladyship's room.

I could see from his manner that Lady Throgmorton had given orders that I was to be treated with all possible consideration.

The room into which he conducted me was one of a suite on the first floor, evidently appropriated to the mistress of the house. The furniture was almost new, and I hardly required to be told that the rooms had been prepared to receive the bride of Captain Throgmorton; they now seemed to have been relegated to his stepmother.

The appearance of my client startled me. She was a woman of fifty, still strikingly handsome, but disfigured by a too lavish use of cosmetics. She had assumed an artificial pose on a couch, beside which stood a table covered with smelling-bottles and such articles. As I entered, she raised a gold and tortoiseshell lorgnette to her eyes, and gave me almost a hostile scrutiny.

Behind her stood her maid, a tall, thin woman with pinched lips and half-shut eyes, who never moved nor spoke except to answer some question from her mistress or to hand her some scent or drug.

The sight of this rouged and laced-up figure, with its blackened eyelids and prominent nose, and the silent shadow in the background, made me feel as if I had stepped into the atmosphere of some place like Hamburg or Ostend, instead of an English country house.

'Sit down if you please, Mr Hargreaves. And speak softly, if you will be so good. My nerves are absolutely destroyed – Madeline, the essence!'

The silent maid chose one of the bottles, and began dabbing her mistress' forehead, taking care not to disturb the powder.

'The experience I have gone through has been most frightful,' Lady Throgmorton continued. 'Every night it has been the same. I cannot sleep without taking enough chloral to kill anyone unaccustomed to it. And when I do go off – *I dream*!'

She gave a shudder, and raised a bottle of salts to her nostrils. Even where I sat I could detect the odour; in fact, the air of the room was thick with scents.

I waited for her to explain the nature of her experiences.

'Every night since I have been back in these rooms it has come to me,' she went on. She seemed to have a difficulty in speaking out plainly. 'It is an apparition – or at least it seems to be one – the apparition of my son's wife.'

I thought it time to ask a question or two.

'Will you tell me a little more about the circumstances,' I said. 'When did Mrs Throgmorton die? And how?'

She darted a fierce glance at me as I put the concluding question.

'She died six weeks ago, of pneumonia, in the room I am now occupying. After her death my son could not bear to sleep in it, and I thought it best to return to these rooms, which had always been mine.'

'But if this apparition disturbs you there, why not try the effect of sleeping in some other part of the house?'

'Because it would be impossible to give any reason for changing again so soon. The servants would be inquisitive, and my son might suspect something.' She hesitated before adding: 'Someone else might take my place, and see what I have seen.'

'I suppose you are afraid that if Captain Throgmorton heard of this it might distress him?' I hazarded.

Again she fixed me with a threatening glance.

'Captain Throgmorton must *never* hear of it,' she responded. 'The shock would kill him.' She looked round at the maid for a moment. 'We are afraid that he has not been quite right in his mind since his wife's death.'

I could not conceal my consternation at this intelligence. I began to feel thankful that Alwyne had not come with me to such a house.

Lady Throgmorton saw that she must tell me something more.

'He would not believe that she was really dead, for a long time. Then he had a special coffin made for her, in the hope that she might come to life again. And he has told me that Eleanor would have appeared to him, if she really were dead, to assure him that she still remembered him in the other world.'

I considered these extraordinary statements in my mind before replying.

'And are you sure that it would not be the wisest course to let him know what has happened, and give him the chance of seeing whatever you have seen?'

Lady Throgmorton turned to the woman behind her, and made her administer a dose of some restorative, before she answered this question.

'I dare not run the risk. If he saw what I see every night it might unhinge his mind altogether. The apparition is – ' she paused, and seemed to pick her words – 'is not a natural one. It is – strange. And – and horrible.'

A convulsion passed across her face as she made this declaration. The rouge cracked on her cheeks, and the pearl powder went in flakes.

The maid interfered suddenly, addressing herself to me.

'I think you had better leave her ladyship now, sir. It will be bad for her to talk any more.'

I rose, murmuring some polite expression of regret, and got out of the room as best I could.

It seemed to me that I had got entangled in some very alarming mystery, and that the only prudent thing for me to do would be to quit the Abbey as soon as possible, and not return.

I passed the time before dinner in strolling through the grounds, as if in discharge of my commission to inspect the premises.

At the meal I met the master of the house for the first time. He was not a very young man – some age between thirty-five and forty – and his manner was subdued. But he appeared quite able to perform the duties of a host, and talked to me in a reasonable and businesslike spirit about the arrangements for letting the Abbey.

'Neither Lady Throgmorton nor myself find it a very cheerful place just at present,' he said. 'In fact, I am seriously uneasy about my mother's state of health. She has been accustomed to the bright society of foreign capitals, and the quiet, lonely life we lead here has got upon her nerves. I ought to take her to Paris, I expect, or the Riviera.'

I did not venture to make any direct reference to his dead wife, nor did he make any nearer allusion to the subject.

The only other thing of importance he had to tell me was that Lady Throgmorton would give me all necessary instructions.

'She has always managed everything here,' he explained, 'and I think it is a distraction for her just now to have the reins in her hands again. As for the shooting, it is not up to much, and the steward can tell you more about it than I can.'

Nothing that I saw of Captain Throgmorton was inconsistent with his being in full possession of his reason. But there are such people as monomaniacs, able to take their part in the world without giving any indication of eccentricity apart from their particular craze, and, of course, I could only suppose that my host was one of them.

But for the fact that the letting of the Abbey promised to be a piece of genuine business, I think I should have declined to have anything more to do with this family. As it was, I did not like to break with a client, and on my return to town I found Alwyne so keenly interested, and so determined to probe the matter to the very bottom, that I unwillingly gave way.

She went, as she had proposed, in the character of a prospective companion. I found it impossible to go with her, and could only urge her to wire me in case she felt the slightest uneasiness, and to come away instantly if things took an unpleasant turn

I waited with the greatest anxiety for her report, which reached me on the second morning after her departure.

I need only extract the important passages.

I arrived safely, and had what I suppose I must call a friendly reception from Lady Throgmorton. I did not see the Captain, as Lady Throgmorton's meals were served in her own boudoir, and I took mine with her.

I felt a great dislike for the maid, Madeline, who seemed to me to resent my coming. I fancied that she was playing on the fears of her mistress for some purpose of her own, and did not relish the idea of my doing anything to relieve them. In fact, I thought it quite possible, at first, that the apparition was the result of some trickery on her part.

I wish I could think so still. I wish I had never seen what I saw last night, and what I am afraid I shall never be able to forget.

When I say that I have seen it, I do not mean to be positive that it was an objective manifestation. My experience may have been purely subjective; that is to say, I may have been in sympathetic rapport with Lady Throgmorton, so that her vision was communicated to me.

That seems all the more probable because the maid, who has slept with Lady Throgmorton since these experiences began, declares that she has never seen anything.

Whichever it was, nothing would have induced me to face such a manifestation had I been warned of its character. But, as you know, I always consider it necessary that I should be told nothing in advance, in order to avoid the possibility of suggestion.

Lady Throgmorton struck me at the outset as a hysterical subject, just the sort of woman to be the victim of a nervous delusion, and therefore I did not much expect to find any reality in her experiences.

A bedroom had been prepared for me adjoining her own, but it was arranged that I should actually pass the night in a bed in her room, which was usually occupied by the maid. Madeline was to take the bed in my room in exchange.

I will not dwell upon the figure presented by Lady Throgmorton at night, without the paint and the powder which disguised her in the day. She had a table beside her bed for her sleeping-draughts and salts, and I noticed that she lay huddled on the very edge of the bed, as though to have her medicines within easier reach.

I wanted to have all the lights extinguished, but she insisted passionately on having a night-light, and as she assured me that she had had one burning every time the apparition visited her, I could not very well object.

Nothing happened till we had both been in bed for more than an hour. Lady Throgmorton seemed unable to sleep, and kept fidgeting with the bottles beside her, while I lay with my eyes half shut, watching the shadows on the ceiling, and listening to the restless movements of my unseen companion.

I was just dozing off when suddenly I heard an agonised gasp, almost a shriek, from the other bed.

In an instant I was wide-awake, and sitting up to look round. The first thing that met my eyes in the dim light was Lady

Throgmorton, stretched out stiffly in her place, with her head thrown back on the pillow, and her eyes fixed in a glassy stare, like a person undergoing a cataleptic seizure.

I followed the direction of her eyes without seeing anything more for the first few moments.

Then, as I withdrew my eyes from wandering about the room, to return to where she lay breathing convulsively, I saw the cause of her terror.

There was another person in the bed beside her.

I have said *in*, but I ought to have said *on*. The figure which met my sight was that of a woman prepared for burial. She lay stretched out in the rigid attitude of the dead, her face and form wrapped tightly round with white linen grave-clothes.

My heart nearly stopped beating at this silent invasion of the bed of the living by the dead.

But the worst was still to come.

While I watched, an awful change came over the spectral corpse. The linen wrappings appeared to decay by swift stages, and finally to fall away and hang in shreds from the appalling Thing – for all humanity had left it – which they had concealed.

What I then saw I can hardly bear to think of, much less to describe.

And imagine this horror seen lying side by side with a living woman who seemed to know it was there, and to feel the dreadful pollution of its touch!

I hardly know what I should have done if the sight had lasted a moment longer. But with the full revelation of its unutterable loathesomeness the Thing vanished – vanished from its place without any apparent movement, leaving me with the sickening dread of seeing it as suddenly return.

Common feeling compelled me to go to the assistance of Lady Throgmorton. I had hardly set foot on the floor when she began trembling all over, and calling out the name of her maid.

The woman, who had evidently been expecting a summons, opened the door immediately, and came in. She darted an inquisitive look at me, a look of distrust and even of alarm I fancied it, as she passed to the side of her mistress, to whom she began giving things out of the bottles.

I busied myself in lighting a pair of candles on the mantelshelf. As soon as Lady Throgmorton was able to speak I heard her demand anxiously: 'Has she seen it? Did you see anything?'

I turned towards the bed, and found mistress and maid waiting for my reply with apprehension.

'Yes, Lady Throgmorton. At least, I have seen something, which I expect is what you have seen. A dead body, lying beside you on the bed.'

She uttered a groan as she nodded her head in confirmation.

'And – and did anything happen to it?' she asked in a whisper.

I could not suppress a shudder as I answered: 'It assumed an appearance of decay.'

Mistress and maid exchanged glances of intelligence.

'I was right, you see, Madeline,' the lady said. And then she added, to my intense surprise: 'It has grown worse night after night. The first time I saw it, the shroud remained intact. Since then the change has gone on regularly.'

There was only one thing to say, and I said it.

'In my opinion you ought not to pass another night in that bed, nor in this room. Whatever be the real nature of this experience, it is clear that the only chance of its ceasing is for you to leave off sleeping here.'

In Lady Throgmorton's pitiable condition I hardly liked to question her on the subject of the spectre. But the idea had already presented itself to my own mind that the ghastly figure which was haunting her could only be that of her son's late wife, and the horrible changes it had undergone seemed to correspond with the decay of the actual corpse.

Having been assured that there was no chance of anything more occurring that night, I went back into my own room, leaving the maid to take my place.

This morning I have had a long talk with Lady Throgmorton, in the absence of her maid. She has told me quite frankly that she considers the apparition to be that of the late Mrs Throgmorton. She intends leaving for London today, on her way to Paris, and the Captain goes with her. She has pressed me very strongly to remain behind, and to pass at least one more night in the haunted room; and as I wish to ascertain whether my own experience of last night was objective or subjective, I think I shall consent.

But I dare not make the experiment alone, and as Lady Throgmorton is strongly opposed to any of the servants being made acquainted with the mystery, I have promised to ask you to join me here for the purpose.

Please wire.

So ended the report, with the exception of some personal messages of no interest to the public.

I need not remark on the courage of this brave girl in consenting to remain alone in a house where she had had such a frightful experience. I wired immediately to say I should arrive by the next train, and I was as good as my word.

I found Alwyne installed as Lady Throgmorton's deputy, in charge of the house and servants, who were all under notice to leave.

We decided to sit up till the hour at which the sepulchral figure would appear, if it appeared at all. In good time we moved into Lady Throgmorton's room, extinguished all the lights except the solitary night-light, and sat watching for what might happen.

A surprise awaited us.

We were ignorant of the exact minute at which the previous manifestation had occurred. But midnight came and passed without the slightest sign of anything uncanny.

I was just saying to Alwyne that I thought it useless to wait longer, when the silence of the night was broken by footsteps advancing suddenly along the corridor. In a moment the door was burst open, and we beheld on the threshold Captain Throgmorton, with a lighted lantern in one hand, and a revolver in the other.

'Explain the meaning of all this,' he demanded sternly, as we sprang to our feet.

I was at a loss what answer to make to him. But Alwyne was quick to assert herself.

'We are here in pursuance of instructions from Lady Throgmorton,' she said with dignity. 'Perhaps you will explain how it is that, after leaving the Abbey in my charge, you have returned in this manner and adopted such a tone towards me.'

The Captain was evidently not prepared for this retort, which at once subdued him.

'I will apologise, of course, if I am in the wrong,' he said, speaking more quietly. 'I came down here because my stepmother's action in leaving you here seemed to me eccentric. I felt more and more uneasy as I got further from home, and finally, after seeing her off to Paris, I decided to run down here again and make sure that all was right. I have only just walked over from the station, and seeing a light in this room, I suspected something wrong.'

He glanced round the room as he spoke with a mixture of curiosity and emotion.

I thought it was now time for me to speak.

'I trust my name, and the reputation of my firm, will be a sufficient guarantee that everything that has passed in your absence has been entirely in accordance with our instructions from Lady Throgmorton, to whom you may recollect you referred me. If you will now come with me into another room, I will tell you what those instructions were.'

Captain Throgmorton took us downstairs into his library, and there I told him the entire story, as I have told it here, only omitting for his own sake the hideous detail of the change which had followed the first appearance of the spectral corpse.

'Tonight we have seen nothing,' I said in conclusion. 'I think, therefore, you may rest assured that the whole thing is a diseased imagination on the part of Lady Throgmorton, due to the state of her nerves.'

The Captain listened with the closest attention, wincing more than once at the references I had made to his dead wife. At the close he said: 'I am infinitely obliged to you for telling me this. It is true that I had a special coffin constructed for my late wife, but it was in discharge of a solemn promise to her, as she entertained a morbid dread of being prematurely buried. I may add that I engaged a medical man to visit the vault every day for a week, when he reported to me that changes had taken place which rendered it utterly impossible to doubt the reality of the death.'

The reluctance with which he made this statement showed me that he knew what the doctor had seen. The changes were those which Alwyne had seen in the vision of Lady Throgmorton.

'Do you think there is any possibility that Lady Throgmorton may have heard of these visits?'

It was Alwyne who put the question. The Captain shook his head.

'I think not, Miss Sargent. Naturally I did not wish such a thing to be known, and I pledged the doctor to secrecy.'

He frowned as he added: 'It is a very serious thing if my step-mother has been representing that my intellect is disordered, as you say. I must consider what is my best course; but I think I shall have to follow her abroad, and perhaps to take the doctor with me.'

We separated for the night with mutual expressions of regret. In the morning Captain Throgmorton, opening the letter-bag as usual, found in it a telegram addressed to Alwyne.

It proved to be from Lady Throgmorton, who was staying at a hotel in the Avenue Friedland, and contained these words:

I HAVE SEEN IT HERE. COME IMMEDIATELY.

On reading this extraordinary dispatch, not one of us any longer doubted that the sender's mind was unhinged.

Captain Throgmorton at once sent a groom for the doctor, who arrived in the course of an hour.

When the doctor had been placed in possession of the whole of the facts – and this time I did not think it right to suppress anything – his manner became exceedingly grave.

'I will say nothing till I have seen Lady Throgmorton,' he declared. 'But I agree with you, Captain, that we ought both to go to Paris by tonight's boat.'

Before leaving, Captain Throgmorton and I exchanged promises, one of strict secrecy on my part, and on his own to communicate to me the final outcome of the affair.

That promise was never kept.

A brief note, so brief as to be almost discourteous, informed me that Lady Throgmorton had been confined, with her own consent, in a private asylum in the Department of Seine-et-Oise, and that is the last I have ever heard from the Throgmorton family.

The truth was revealed to me in a singular manner, some years after, by the last person from whom I ever expected to learn it – Lady Throgmorton's maid.

Having learnt that this woman had presumed to give my name as a reference, I found her out, and threatened her with proceedings. By way of excuse she pleaded that the death of her mistress had thrown her on the world without friends, Captain Throgmorton having refused to assist her because he suspected her of complicity in his wife's death.

That death, she now assured me, was the work of Lady Throgmorton, who was unable to endure the loss of her position as mistress of the Abbey, and of certain family jewels which went with the estate. It had been brought about, or at least hastened, by means of a drug which subsequently arrested the decomposition of the corpse.

The doctor, it appears, had already been struck by some unusual symptoms in the case, and again by certain unexpected signs in the decay of the body. On being informed of Lady Throgmorton's visions, or hallucinations, his suspicions were given definite shape, and a full confession was extracted from the wretched woman before her reason finally gave way.

Shortly after the somewhat abrupt conclusion of this adventure, a quiet wedding took place, and Alwyne Sargent became Alwyne Hargreaves. I do not think any explanation of my conduct in marrying my secretary is due from me, as a business man. Alwyne had materially assisted me to attain the prosperity I now enjoyed, and it was only right that she should share it.

Our Continental honeymoon helped to restore her health, which had been considerably impaired by the shocks to which she had been so frequently exposed.

I have now given up dealing in haunted property, and my wife will never in the future, I trust, be called upon to exercise her extra-ordinary gift of clairvoyance.

The Ghost with the Club-foot

ROBERT BARR

Celebrated critics have written with scorn of what they call 'the long arm of coincidence' in fiction. Coincidence is supposed to be the device of a novelist who does not possess ingenuity enough to construct a book without it. In France our incomparable writers pay no attention to this, because they are gifted with a keener insight into real life than is the case with the British. The superb Charles Dickens, possibly as well known in France as he is wherever the English language is read, and who loved French soil and the French people, probably probed deeper into the intricacies of human character than any other novelist of modern times, and if you read his works, you will see that he continually makes use of coincidence. The experience that has come to me throughout my own strange and varied career convinces me that coincidence happens in real life with exceeding frequency, and this fact is especially borne in upon me when I set out to relate my conflict with the Rantremly ghost, which wrought startling changes upon the lives of two people, one an objectionable, domineering man, and the other a humble and crushed woman. Of course, there was a third person, and the consequences that came to him were the most striking of all, as you will learn if you do me the honour to read this account of the episode.

So far as coincidence is concerned, there was first the arrival of the newspaper clipping, then the coming of Sophia Brooks, and when that much-injured woman left my flat I wrote down this sentence on a sheet of paper:

Before the week is out, I predict that Lord Rantremly himself will call to see me.

Next day my servant brought in the card of Lord Rantremly.

I must begin with the visit of Sophia Brooks, for though that comes second, yet I had paid no attention in particular to the newspaper clipping until the lady told her story. My man brought me a type-written sheet of paper on which were inscribed the words:

Sophia Brooks, *Typewriting and Translating Office*,
First Floor, No. 51 Beaumont Street, Strand, London, W.C.

I said to my servant, 'Tell the lady as kindly as possible that I have no typewriting work to give out, and that, in fact, I keep a steno-grapher and typewriting machine on the premises.'

A few moments later my man returned, and said the lady wished to see me, not about typewriting, but regarding a case in which she hoped to interest me. I was still in some hesitation about admitting her, for my transactions had now risen to a higher plane than when I was new to London. My expenses were naturally very heavy, and it was not possible for me, in justice to myself, to waste time in commissions from the poor, which even if they resulted success-fully meant little money added to my banking account, and often nothing at all, because the client was unable to pay. As I remarked before, I possess a heart the most tender, and therefore must greatly to my grief, steel myself against the enlisting of my sympathy, which, alas! has frequently led to my financial loss. Still, sometimes the apparently poor are involved in matters of extreme importance, and England is so eccentric a country that one may find himself at fault if he closes his door too harshly. Indeed, ever since my servant, in the utmost good faith, threw downstairs the persistent and tattered beggar-man, who he learned later to his sorrow was actually his Grace the Duke of Ventnor, I have always cautioned my subordinates not to judge too hastily from appearances.

'Show the lady in,' I said, and there came to me, hesitating, backward, abashed, a middle-aged woman, dressed with distressing plainness, when one thinks of the charming costumes to be seen on a Parisian boulevard. Her subdued manner was that of one to whom the world had been cruel. I rose, bowed profoundly, and placed a chair at her disposal, with the air I should have used if my caller had been a Royal Princess. I claim no credit for this; it is of my nature. There you behold Eugène Valmont. My visitor was a woman. *Voilà!*

'Madam,' I said politely, 'in what may I have the pleasure of serving you?'

The poor woman seemed for the moment confused, and was, I feared, on the verge of tears, but at last she spoke, and said, 'Perhaps you have read in the newspapers of the tragedy at Rantremly Castle?'

'The name, madam, remains in my memory, associated elusively with some hint of seriousness. Will you pardon me a moment?' and a vague thought that I had seen the castle mentioned either in a newspaper, or a clipping from one, caused me to pick up the latest bunch which had come from my agent. I am imbued with no vanity at all; still it is amusing to note what the newspapers say of one, and therefore I have subscribed to a clipping agency. In fact, I indulge in two subscriptions – one personal, the other calling for any pronouncement pertaining to the differences between England and France; for it is my determination yet to write a book on the comparative characteristics of the two people. I hold a theory that the English people are utterly incomprehensible to the rest of humanity, and this will be duly set out in my forthcoming volume.

I speedily found the clipping I was in search of. It proved to be a letter to *The Times*, and was headed: 'Proposed Destruction of Rantremly Castle'. The letter went on to say that this edifice was one of the most noted examples of Norman architecture in the north of England; that Charles II had hidden there for some days after his disastrous defeat at Worcester. Part of the castle had been battered down by Cromwell, and later it again proved the refuge of a Stuart when the Pretender made it a temporary place of concealment. The new Lord Rantremly, it seemed, had determined to demolish this ancient stronghold, so interesting architecturally and historically, and to build with its stones a modern residence. Against this act of vandalism the writer strongly protested, and suggested that England should acquire the power which France constantly exerts, in making an historical monument of an edifice so interwoven with the fortunes of the country.

'Well, madam,' I said, 'all this extract alludes to is the coming demolition of Rantremly Castle. Is that the tragedy of which you speak?'

'Oh no,' she exclaimed; 'I mean the death of the eleventh Lord Rantremly about six weeks ago. For ten years Lord Rantremly lived practically alone in the castle. Servants would not remain there because the place was haunted, and well it may be, for a terrible family the Rantremlys have been, and a cruel, as I shall be able to tell you. Up to a month and a half ago Lord Rantremly was waited on by a butler older than himself, and if possible, more wicked. One morning this old butler came up the stairs from the kitchen, with Lord Rantremly's breakfast on a silver tray, as was his custom. His lordship always partook of breakfast in his own room. It is not known how the accident happened, as the old servant was going up the stairs instead of coming down, but the steps are very smooth and slippery, and without a carpet; at any rate, he seems to have fallen from the top to the bottom, and lay there with a broken neck. Lord Rantremly, who was very deaf, seemingly did not hear the crash, and it is supposed that after ringing and ringing in vain, and doubtless working himself into a violent fit of temper – alas! too frequent an occurrence – the old nobleman got out of bed, and walked barefooted down the stair, coming at last upon the body of his ancient servant.

There the man who arrived every morning to light the fires found them, the servant dead, and Lord Rantremly helpless from an attack of paralysis. The physicians say that only his eyes seemed alive, and they were filled with a great fear, and indeed that is not to be wondered at, after his wicked, wicked life. His right hand was but partially disabled, and with that he tried to scribble something which proved indecipherable. And so he died, and those who attended him at his last moments say that if ever a soul had a taste of future punishment before it left this earth, it was the soul of Lord Rantremly as it shone through those terror-stricken eyes.'

Here the woman stopped, with a catch in her breath, as if the fear of that grim death-bed had communicated itself to her. I interjected calmness into an emotional situation by remarking in a common-place tone, 'And it is the present Lord Rantremly who proposes to destroy the Castle, I suppose?'

'Yes.'

'Is he the son of the late lord?'

'No; he is a distant relative. The branch of the family to which he belongs has been engaged in commerce, and, I believe, its members are very wealthy.'

'Well, madam, no doubt this is all extremely interesting, and rather gruesome. In what way are you concerned in these occurrences?'

'Ten years ago I replied to an advertisement, there being required one who knew shorthand, who possessed a typewriting machine and a knowledge of French, to act as secretary to a nobleman. I was at that time twenty-three years old, and for two years had been trying to earn my living in London through the typing of manuscript. But I was making a hard struggle of it, so I applied for this position and got it.

There are in the library of Rantremly Castle many documents relating to the Stuart exile in France. His lordship wished these documents sorted and catalogued, as well as copies taken of each. Many of the letters were in the French language, and these I was required to translate and type. It was a sombre place of residence, but the salary was good, and I saw before me work enough to keep me busy for years.

Besides this, the task was extremely congenial, and I became absorbed in it, being young and romantically inclined. Here I seemed to live in the midst of these wonderful intrigues of long ago. Documents passed through my hands whose very possession at one period meant capital danger, bringing up even now visions of block, axe, and masked headsman. It seemed strange to me that so sinister a man as Lord Rantremly, who, I had heard, cared for nothing but drink and gambling, should have desired to promote this historical research, and, indeed, I soon found he felt nothing but contempt for it. However, he had undertaken it at the instance of his only son, then a young man of my own age, at Oxford University.

'Lord Rantremly at that time was sixty-five years old. His countenance was dark, harsh, and imperious, and his language brutal. He indulged in frightful outbursts of temper, but he paid so well for service that there was no lack of it, as there has been since the ghost appeared some years ago. He was very tall, and of commanding appearance, but had a deformity in the shape of a club-foot, and walked with the halting step of those so afflicted. There were at that time servants in plenty at the castle, for although a tradition existed that the ghost of the founder of the house trod certain rooms, this ghost, it was said, never demonstrated its presence when the living representative of the family was a man with a club-foot. Tradition further affirmed that if this club-footed ghost allowed its halting footsteps to be heard while the reigning lord possessed a similar deformity, the conjunction foreshadowed the passing of title and estates to a stranger. The ghost haunted the castle only when it was occupied by a descendant whose two feet were normal. It seems that the founder of the house was a club-footed man, and this disagreeable peculiarity often missed one generation, and sometimes two, while at other times both father and son had club-feet, as was the case with the late Lord Rantremly and the young man at Oxford. I am not a believer in the supernatural, of course, but nevertheless it is strange that within the past few years everyone residing in the castle has heard the club-footed ghost, and now title and estates descend to a family that were utter strangers to the Rantremlys.'

'Well, madam, this also sounds most alluring, and were my time not taken up with affairs more material than those to which you allude, I should be content to listen all day, but as it is – ' I spread my hands and shrugged my shoulders.

The woman with a deep sigh said, 'I am sorry to have taken so long, but I wished you to understand the situation, and now I will come direct to the heart of the case. I worked alone in the library, as I told you, much interested in what I was doing. The chaplain, a great friend of Lord Rantremly's son, and, indeed, a former tutor of his, assisted me with the documents that were in Latin, and a friendship sprang up between us. He was an elderly man, and extremely unworldly. Lord Rantremly never concealed his scorn of this clergyman, but did not interfere with him because of the son.

'My work went on very pleasantly up to the time that Reginald, the heir of his lordship, came down from Oxford. Then began the happiest days of a life that has been otherwise full of hardships and distress.

Reginald was as different as possible from his father. In one respect only did he bear any resemblance to that terrible old man, and this resemblance was the deformity of a club-foot, a blemish which one soon forgot when one came to know the gentle and high-minded nature of the young man. As I have said, it was at his instance that Lord Rantremly had engaged me to set in order those historical papers. Reginald became enthusiastic at the progress I had made, and thus the young nobleman, the chaplain, and myself continued our work together with ever-increasing enthusiasm.

'To cut short a recital which must be trying to your patience, but which is necessary if you are to understand the situation, I may say that our companionship resulted in a proposal of marriage to me, which I, foolishly perhaps, and selfishly, it may be, accepted. Reginald knew that his father would never consent, but we enlisted the sympathy of the chaplain, and he, mild, unworldly man, married us one day in the consecrated chapel of the castle.

'As I have told you, the house at that time contained many servants, and I think, without being sure, that the butler, whom I feared even more than Lord Rantremly himself, got some inkling of what was going forward. But, be that as it may, he and his lordship entered the chapel just as the ceremony was finished, and there followed an agonising scene. His lordship flung the ancient chaplain from his place, and when Reginald attempted to interfere, the maddened nobleman struck his son full in the face with his clenched fist, and my husband lay as one dead on the stone floor of the chapel. By this time the butler had locked the doors, and had rudely torn the vestments from the aged, half-insensible clergyman, and with these tied him hand and foot. All this took place in a very few moments, and I stood there as one paralysed, unable either to speak or scream, not that screaming would have done me any good in that horrible place of thick walls. The butler produced a key, and unlocked a small, private door at the side of the chapel which led from the apartments of his lordship to the family pew. Then taking my husband by feet and shoulders, Lord Rantremly and the butler carried him out, locking the door, and leaving the clergyman and me prisoners in the chapel. The reverend old gentleman took no notice of me. He seemed to be dazed, and when at last I found my voice and addressed him, he merely murmured over and over texts of Scripture pertaining to the marriage service.

'In a short time I heard the key turn again in the lock of the private door, and the butler entered alone. He unloosened the bands around the clergyman's knees, escorted him out, and once more locked the door behind him. A third time that terrible servant came back, grasped me roughly by the wrist, and without a word dragged me with him, along a narrow passage, up a stair, and finally to the main hall, and so to my lord's private study, which adjoined his bedroom, and there on a table I found my typewriting machine brought up from the library.

'I have but the most confused recollection of what took place. I am not a courageous woman, and was in mortal terror both of Lord Rantremly and his attendant. His lordship was pacing up and down the room, and, when I came in, used the most unseemly language to me; then ordered me to write at his dictation, swearing that if I did not do exactly as he told me, he would finish his son, as he put it. I sat down at the machine, and he dictated a letter to himself, demanding two thousand pounds to be paid to me, otherwise I should claim that I was the wife of his son, secretly married. This, placing pen and ink before me, he compelled me to sign, and when I had done so, pleading to be allowed to see my husband, if only for a moment, I thought he was going to strike me, for he shook his fist in my face, and used words which were appalling to hear. That was the last I ever saw of Lord Rantremly, my husband, the clergyman, or the butler. I was at once sent off to London with my belongings, the butler himself buying my ticket, and flinging a handful of sovereigns into my lap as the train moved out.'

Here the woman stopped, buried her face in her hands, and began to weep.

'Have you done nothing about this for the past ten years?'

She shook her head.

'What could I do?' she gasped. 'I had little money, and no friends. Who would believe my story? Besides this, Lord Rantremly retained possession of a letter, signed by myself, that would convict me of attempted blackmail, while the butler would swear to anything against me.'

'You have no marriage certificate, of course?'

'No.'

'What has become of the clergyman?'

'I do not know.'

'And what of Lord Rantremly's son?'

'It was announced that he had gone on a voyage to Australia for his health in a sailing ship, which was wrecked on the African coast, and everyone on board lost.'

'What is your own theory?'

'Oh, my husband was killed by the blow given him in the chapel.'

'Madam, that does not seem credible. A blow from the fist seldom kills.'

'But he fell backwards, and his head struck the sharp stone steps at the foot of the altar. I know my husband was dead when the butler and his father carried him out.'

'You think the clergyman was also murdered?'

'I am sure of it. Both master and servant were capable of any crime or cruelty.'

'You received no letters from the young man?'

'No. You see, during our short friendship we were constantly together, and there was no need of correspondence.'

'Well, madam, what do you expect of me?'

'I hoped you would investigate, and find perhaps where Reginald and the clergyman are buried. I realise that I have no proof, but in that way my strange story will be corroborated.'

I leaned back in my chair and looked at her. Truth to tell, I only partially credited her story myself, and yet I was positive she believed every word of it. Ten years brooding on a fancied injustice by a woman living alone, and doubtless often in dire poverty, had mixed together the actual and the imaginary until now, what had possibly been an aimless flirtation on the part of the young man, unexpectedly discovered by the father, had formed itself into the tragedy which she had told me.

'Would it not be well,' I suggested, 'to lay the facts before the present Lord Rantremly?'

'I have done so,' she answered simply.

'With what result?'

'His lordship said my story was preposterous. In examining the late lord's private papers, he discovered the letter which I typed and signed. He said very coldly that the fact that I had waited until everyone who could corroborate or deny my story was dead, united with the improbability of the narrative itself, would very likely consign me to prison if I made public a statement so incredible.'

'Well, you know, madam, I think his lordship is right.'

'He offered me an annuity of fifty pounds, which I refused.'

'In that refusal, madam, I think you are wrong. If you take my advice, you will accept the annuity.'

The woman rose slowly to her feet.

'It is not money I am after,' she said, 'although, God knows, I have often been in sore need of it. But I am the Countess of Rantremly, and I wish my right to that name acknowledged. My character has been under an impalpable shadow for ten years. On several occasions mysterious hints have reached me that in some manner I left the castle under a cloud. If Lord Rantremly will destroy the letter which I was compelled to write under duress, and if he will give me written acknowledgment that there was nothing to be alleged against me during my stay in the castle, he may enjoy his money in peace for all of me. I want none of it.'

'Have you asked him to do this?'

'Yes. He refuses to give up or destroy the letter, although I told him in what circumstances it had been written. But, desiring to be fair, he said he would allow me a pound a week for life, entirely through his own generosity.'

'And this you refused?'

'Yes, I refused.'

'Madam, I regret to say that I cannot see my way to do anything with regard to what I admit is very unjust usage. We have absolutely nothing to go upon except your unsupported word. Lord Rantremly was perfectly right when he said no one would credit your story. I could not go down to Rantremly Castle and make investigations there. I should have no right upon the premises at all, and would get into instant trouble as an interfering trespasser. I beg you to heed my advice, and accept the annuity.'

Sophia Brooks, with that mild obstinacy of which I had received indications during her recital, slowly shook her head.

'You have been very kind to listen for so long,' she said, and then, with a curt 'Good-day!' turned and left the room. On the sheet of paper underneath her address, I wrote this prophecy: 'Before the week is out, I predict that Lord Rantremly himself will call to see me.'

*   *   *

Next morning, at almost the same hour that Miss Brooks had arrived the day before, the Earl of Rantremly's card was brought in to me.

His lordship proved to be an abrupt, ill-mannered, dapper business man; purse-proud, I should call him, as there was every reason he should be, for he had earned his own fortune. He was doubtless equally proud of his new title, which he was trying to live up to, assuming now and then a haughty, domineering attitude, and again relapsing into the keen, incisive manner of the man of affairs; shrewd financial sense waging a constant struggle with the glamour of an ancient name.

I am sure he would have shone to better advantage either as a financier or as a nobleman, but the combination was too much for him.

I formed an instinctive dislike to the man, which probably would not have happened had he been wearing the title for twenty years, or had I met him as a business man, with no thought of the aristocratic honour awaiting him. There seemed nothing in common between him and the former holder of the title. He had keen, ferrety eyes, a sharp financial nose, a thin-lipped line of mouth which indicated little of human kindness. He was short of stature, but he did not possess the club-foot, which was one advantage. He seated himself before I had time to offer him a chair, and kept on his hat in my presence, which he would not have done if he had either been a genuine nobleman or a courteous business man.

'I am Lord Rantremly,' he announced pompously, which announcement was quite unnecessary, because I held his card in my hand.

'Quite so, my lord. And you have come to learn whether or no I can lay the ghost in that old castle to the north which bears your name?'

'Well, I'm blessed!' cried his lordship, agape. 'How could you guess that?'

'Oh, it is not a guess, but rather a choice of two objects, either of which might bring you to my rooms. I chose the first motive because I thought you might prefer to arrange the second problem with your solicitor, and he doubtless told you that Miss Sophia Brooks's claim was absurd; that you were quite right in refusing to give up or destroy the typewritten letter she had signed ten years ago, and that it was weakness on your part, without consulting him, to offer her an annuity of fifty-two pounds a year.'

Long before this harangue was finished, which I uttered in an easy and nonchalant tone of voice, as if reciting something that everybody knew, his lordship stood on his feet again, staring at me like a man thunderstruck. This gave me the opportunity of exercising that politeness which his abrupt entrance and demeanour had forestalled. I rose, and bowing, said, 'I pray you to be seated, my lord.'

He dropped into the chair, rather than sat down in it.

'And now,' I continued, with the utmost suavity, stretching forth my hand, 'may I place your hat on this shelf out of the way, where it will not incommode you during our discourse?'

Like a man in a dream, he took his hat from his head, and passively handed it to me, and after placing it in safety I resumed my chair with the comfortable feeling that his lordship and I were much nearer a plane of equality than when he entered the room.

'How about the ghost with a club-foot, my lord?' said I genially. 'May I take it that in the City, that sensible, commercial portion of London, no spirits are believed in except those sold over the bars?'

'If you mean,' began his lordship, struggling to reach his dignity once more, 'if you mean to ask if there is any man fool enough to place credit in the story of a ghost, I answer no. I am a practical man, sir. I now possess in the north property representing, in farming lands, in shooting rights, and what not, a locked-up capital of many a thousand pounds. As you seem to know everything, sir, perhaps you are aware that I propose to build a modern mansion on the estate.'

'Yes; I saw the letter in *The Times*.'

'Very well, sir. It has come to a fine pass if, in this country of law and the rights of property, a man may not do what he pleases with his own.'

'I think, my lord, cases may be cited where the decisions of your courts have shown a man may not do what he likes with his own. Nevertheless, I am quite certain that if you level Rantremly Castle with the ground, and build a modern mansion in its place, the law will not hinder you.'

'I should hope not, sir, I should hope not,' said his lordship gruffly. 'Nevertheless, I am not one who wishes to ride roughshod over public opinion. 'I am chairman of several companies which depend more or less on popular favour for success. I deplore unnecessary antagonism. Technically, I might assert my right to destroy this ancient stronghold tomorrow if I wished to do so, and if that right were seriously disputed, I should, of course, stand firm. But it is not seriously disputed. The British nation, sir, is too sensible a people to object to the removal of an antiquated structure that has long out-lived its usefulness, and the erection of a mansion replete with all modern improvements would be a distinct addition to the country, sir. A few impertinent busybodies protest against the demolition of Rantremly Castle, but that is all.'

'Ah, then you *do* intend to destroy it?' I rejoined, and it is possible that a touch of regret was manifest in my tones.

'Not just at present; not until this vulgar clamour has had time to subside. Nevertheless, as a business man, I am forced to recognise that a large amount of unproductive capital is locked up in that property.'

'And why is it locked up?'

'Because of an absurd belief that the place is haunted. I could let it tomorrow at a good figure, if it were not for that rumour.'

'But surely sensible men do not pay any attention to such a rumour.'

'Sensible men may not, but sensible men are often married to silly women, and the women object. It is only the other day that I was in negotiation with Bates, of Bates, Sturgeon and Bates, a very wealthy man, quite able and willing to pay the price I demanded. He cared nothing about the alleged ghost, but his family absolutely refused to have anything to do with the place, and so the arrangement fell through.'

'What is your theory regarding this ghost, my lord?'

He answered me with some impatience.

'How can a sane man hold a theory about a ghost? I can, however, advance a theory regarding the noises heard in the castle. For years that place has been the resort of questionable characters.'

'I understand the Rantremly family is a very old one,' I commented innocently, but his lordship did not notice the innuendo.

'Yes, we are an old family,' he went on with great complacency. 'The castle, as perhaps you are aware, is a huge, ramshackle place, honeycombed underneath with cellars. I dare say in the old days some of these cellars and caves were the resort of smugglers, and the receptacle of their contraband wares, doubtless with the full knowledge of my ancestors, who, I regret to admit, as a business man, were not too particular in their respect for law. I make no doubt that the castle is now the refuge of a number of dangerous characters, who, knowing the legends of the place, frighten away fools by impersonating ghosts.'

'You wish me to uncover their retreat, then?'

'Precisely.'

'Could I get accommodation in the castle itself?'

'Lord bless you, no! Nor within two miles of it. You might secure bed and board at the porter's lodge, perhaps, or in the village, which is three miles distant.'

'I should prefer to live in the castle night and day, until the mystery is solved.'

'Ah, you are a practical man. That is a very sensible resolution. But you can persuade no one in that neighbourhood to bear you company. You would need to take some person down with you from London, and the chances are, that person will not stay long.'

'Perhaps, my lord, if you used your influence, the chief of police in the village might allow a constable to bear me company. I do not mind roughing it in the least, but I should like someone to prepare my meals, and to be on hand in case of a struggle, should your surmise concerning the ghost prove correct.'

'I regret to inform you,' said his lordship, 'that the police in that barbarous district are as superstitious as the peasantry. I myself told the chief constable my theory, and for six weeks he has been trying to run down the miscreants, who, I am sure, are making a rendezvous of the castle. Would you believe it, sir, that the constabulary, after a few nights' experience in the castle, threatened to resign in a body if they were placed on duty at Rantremly? They said they heard groans and shrieks, and the measured beat of a club-foot on the oaken floors. Perfectly absurd, of course, but there you are! Why, I cannot even get a charwoman or labourer to clear up the evidences of the tragedy which took place there six weeks ago. The beds are untouched, the broken china and the silver tray lie today at the foot of the stairway, and everything remains just as it was when the inquest took place.'

'Very well, my lord, the case presents many difficulties, and so, speaking as one business man to another, you will understand that my compensation must be correspondingly great.'

All the assumed dignity which straightened up this man whenever I addressed him as 'my lord', instantly fell from him when I enunciated the word 'compensation'. His eyes narrowed, and all the native shrewdness of an adept skinflint appeared in his face. I shall do him the justice to say that he drove the very best bargain he could with me, and I, on my part, very deftly concealed from him the fact that I was so much interested in the affair that I should have gone down to Rantremly for nothing rather than forego the privilege of ransacking Rantremly Castle.

When the new earl had taken his departure, walking to the door with the haughty air of a nobleman, then bowing to me with the affability of a business man, I left my flat, took a cab, and speedily found myself climbing the stair to the first floor of 51 Beaumont Street, Strand. As I paused at the door on which were painted the words, 'S. Brooks, Stenography, Typewriting, Translation', I heard the rapid click-click of a machine inside. Knocking at the door the writing ceased, and I was bidden to enter. The room was but meagrely furnished, and showed scant signs of prosperity. On a small side-table, clean but uncovered, the breakfast dishes, washed, but not yet put away, stood, and the kettle on the hob by the dying fire led me to infer that the typewriting woman was her own cook. I suspected that the awkward-looking sofa which partly occupied one side of the room, concealed a bed. By the lone front window stood the typewriting machine on a small stand, and in front of it sat the woman who had visited me the morning before. She was now gazing at me, probably hoping I was a customer, for there was no recognition in her eyes.

'Good morning, Lady Rantremly,' was my greeting, which caused her to spring immediately to her feet, with a little exclamation of surprise.

'Oh,' she said at last, 'you are Monsieur Valmont. Excuse me that I am so stupid. Will you take a chair?'

'Thank you, madam. It is I who should ask to be excused for so unceremonious a morning call. I have come to ask you a question. Can you cook?'

The lady looked at me with some surprise, mingled perhaps with so much of indignation as such a mild person could assume. She did not reply, but, glancing at the kettle, and then turning towards the breakfast dishes on the table by the wall, a slow flush of colour suffused her wan cheeks.

'My lady,' I said at last, as the silence became embarrassing, 'you must pardon the impulse of a foreigner who finds himself constantly brought into conflict with prejudices which he fails to understand. You are perhaps offended at my question. The last person of whom I made that inquiry was the young and beautiful Madame la Comtesse de Valérie-Moberanne, who enthusiastically clapped her hands with delight at the compliment, and replied impulsively, "Oh, Monsieur

Valmont, let me compose for you an omelette which will prove a dream," and she did. One should not forget that Louis XVIII himself cooked the *truffes à la purée d'ortolans* that caused the Duc d'Escars, who partook of the royal dish, to die of an indigestion. Cooking is a noble, yes, a regal art. I am a Frenchman, my lady, and, like all my countrymen, I regard the occupation of a *cuisinière* as infinitely superior to the manipulation of that machine, which is your profession, or the science of investigation, which is mine.'

'Sir,' she said, quite unmollified by my harangue, speaking with a lofty pride which somehow seemed much more natural than that so intermittently assumed by my recent visitor, 'Sir, have you come to offer me a situation as cook?'

'Yes, madam, at Rantremly Castle.'

'You are going there?' she demanded, almost breathlessly.

'Yes, madam, I leave on the ten o'clock train tomorrow morning. I am commissioned by Lord Rantremly to investigate the supposed presence of the ghost in that mouldering dwelling. I am allowed to bring with me whatever assistants I require, and am assured that no one in the neighbourhood can be retained who dare sleep in the castle. You know the place very well, having lived there, so I shall be glad of your assistance if you will come. If there is any person whom you can trust, and who is not afraid of ghosts, I shall be delighted to escort you both to Rantremly Castle tomorrow.'

'There is an old woman,' she said, 'who comes here to clear up my room, and do whatever I wish done. She is so deaf that she will hear no ghosts, and besides, monsieur, she can cook.'

I laughed in acknowledgment of this last sly hit at me, as the English say.

'That will do excellently,' I replied, rising, and placing a ten-pound note before her. 'I suggest, madam, that you purchase with this anything you may need. My man has instructions to send by passenger train a huge case of provisions, which should arrive there before us.

If you could make it convenient to meet me at Euston Station about a quarter of an hour before the train leaves, we may be able to discover all you wish to know regarding the mystery of Rantremly Castle.'

Sophia Brooks accepted the money without demur, and thanked me. I could see that her thin hands were trembling with excitement as she put the crackling banknote into her purse.

* * *

Darkness was coming on next evening before we were installed in the grim building, which at first sight seemed more like a fortress than a residence. I had telegraphed from London to order a wagonette for us, and in this vehicle we drove to the police station, where I presented the written order from Lord Rantremly for the keys of the castle. The chief constable himself, a stolid, taciturn person, exhibited, nevertheless, some interest in my mission, and he was good enough to take the fourth seat in the wagonette, and accompany us through the park to the castle, returning in that conveyance to the village as nightfall approached, and I could not but notice that this grave official betrayed some uneasiness to get off before dusk had completely set in. Silent as he was, I soon learned that he entirely disbelieved Lord Rantremly's theory that the castle harboured dangerous characters, yet so great was his inherent respect for the nobility that I could not induce him to dispute with any decisiveness his lordship's conjecture. It was plain to be seen, however, that the chief constable believed implicitly in the club-footed ghost. I asked him to return the next morning, as I should spend the night in investigation, and might possibly have some questions to ask him, questions which none but the chief constable could answer. The good man promised, and left us rather hurriedly, the driver of the wagonette galloping his horse down the long, sombre avenue towards the village outside the gates.

I found Sophia Brooks but a doleful companion, and of very little assistance that evening. She seemed overcome by her remembrances. She had visited the library where her former work was done, doubtless the scene of her brief love episode, and she returned with red eyes and trembling chin, telling me haltingly that the great tome from which she was working ten years ago, and which had been left open on the solid library table, was still there exactly as she had placed it before being forced to abandon her work. For a decade apparently no one had entered that library. I could not but sympathise with the poor lady, thus revisiting, almost herself like a ghost, the haunted arena of her short happiness. But though she proved so dismal a companion, the old woman who came with her was a treasure. Having lived all her life in some semi-slum near the Strand, and having rarely experienced more than a summer's-day glimpse of the country, the long journey had delighted her, and now this rambling old castle in the midst of the forest seemed to realise all the dreams which a perusal of halfpenny fiction had engendered in her imagination. She lit a fire, and cooked for us a very creditable supper, bustling about the place, singing to herself in a high key.

Shortly after supper Sophia Brooks, exhausted as much by her emotions and memories as by her long journey of that day, retired to rest.

After being left to myself I smoked some cigarettes, and finished a bottle of superb claret which stood at my elbow. A few hours before I had undoubtedly fallen in the estimation of the stolid constable when, instead of asking him questions regarding the tragedy, I had inquired the position of the wine cellar, and obtained possession of the key that opened its portal. The sight of bin after bin of dust-laden, cobwebbed bottles, did more than anything else to reconcile me to my lonely vigil. There were some notable vintages represented in that dismal cavern.

It was perhaps half-past ten or eleven o'clock when I began my investigations. I had taken the precaution to provide myself with half a dozen so-called electric torches before I left London. These give illumination for twenty or thirty hours steadily, and much longer if the flash is used only now and then. The torch is a thick tube, perhaps a foot and a half long, with a bull's-eye of glass at one end.

By pressing a spring the electric rays project like the illumination of an engine's headlight. A release of the spring causes instant darkness. I have found this invention useful in that it concentrates the light on any particular spot desired, leaving all the surroundings in gloom, so that the mind is not distracted, even unconsciously, by the eye beholding more than is necessary at the moment. One pours a white light over any particular substance as water is poured from the nozzle of a hose.

The great house was almost painfully silent. I took one of these torches, and went to the foot of the grand staircase where the wicked butler had met his death. There, as his lordship had said, lay the silver tray, and nearby a silver jug, a pair of spoons, a knife and fork, and scattered all around the fragments of broken plates, cups, and saucers. With an exclamation of surprise at the stupidity of the researchers who had preceded me, I ran up the stair two steps at a time, turned to the right, and along the corridor until I came to the room occupied by the late earl. The coverings of the bed lay turned down just as they were when his lordship sprang to the floor, doubt-less, in spite of his deafness, having heard faintly the fatal crash at the foot of the stairs. A great oaken chest stood at the head of the bed, perhaps six inches from the wall. Leaning against this chest at the edge of the bed inclined a small, round table, and the cover of the table had slipped from its sloping surface until it partly concealed the chest lid. I mounted on this carven box of old black oak and directed the rays of electric light into the chasm between it and the wall. Then I laughed aloud, and was somewhat startled to hear another laugh directly behind me. I jumped down on the floor again, and swung round my torch like a searchlight on a battleship at sea. There was no human presence in that chamber except myself. Of course, after my first moment of surprise, I realised that the laugh was but an echo of my own. The old walls of the old house were like sounding-boards. The place resembled an ancient fiddle, still tremulous with the music that had been played on it. It was easy to understand how a super-stitious population came to believe in its being haunted; in fact, I found by experiment that if one trod quickly along the uncovered floor of the corridor, and stopped suddenly, one seemed to hear the sound of steps still going on.

I now returned to the stair head, and examined the bare polished boards with most gratifying results. Amazed at having learnt so much in such a short time, I took from my pocket the paper on which the dying nobleman had attempted to write with his half-paralysed hand.

The chief constable had given the document to me, and I sat on the stair head, spread it out on the floor and scrutinised it. It was all but meaningless. Apparently two words and the initial letter of a third had been attempted. Now, however grotesque a piece of writing may be, you can sometimes decipher it by holding it at various angles, as those puzzles are solved which remain a mystery when gazed at direct. By partially closing the eyes you frequently catch the intent, as in those pictures where a human figure is concealed among the outlines of trees and leaves. I held the paper at arm's length, and with the electric light gleaming upon it, examined it at all angles, with eyes wide open, and eyes half closed. At last, inclining it away from me, I saw that the words were intended to mean, 'The Secret'. The secret, of course, was what he was trying to impart, but he had apparently got no further than the title of it. Deeply absorbed in my investigation, I was never more startled in my life than to hear in the stillness down the corridor the gasped words, '*Oh, God!*'

I swept round my light, and saw leaning against the wall, in an almost fainting condition, Sophia Brooks, her eyes staring like those of a demented person, and her face white as any ghost's could have been. Wrapped round her was a dressing-gown. I sprang to my feet.

'What are you doing there?' I cried.

'Oh, is that you, Monsieur Valmont? Thank God, thank God! I thought I was going insane. I saw a hand, a bodiless hand, holding a white sheet of paper.'

'The hand was far from bodiless, madam, for it belonged to me. But why are you here? It must be near midnight.'

'It *is* midnight,' answered the woman; 'I came here because I heard my husband call me three times distinctly, "Sophia, Sophia, Sophia!" just like that.'

'Nonsense, madam,' I said, with an asperity I seldom use where the fair sex is concerned; but I began to see that this hysterical creature was going to be in the way during a research that called for coolness and calmness. I was sorry I had invited her to come.

'Nonsense, madam, you have been dreaming.'

'Indeed, Monsieur Valmont, I have not. I have not even been asleep, and I heard the words quite plainly. You must not think I am either mad or superstitious.'

I thought she was both, and next moment she gave further evidence of it, running suddenly forward, and clutching me by the arm.

'Listen! listen!' she whispered. 'You hear nothing?'

'Nonsense!' I cried again, almost roughly, for my patience was at an end, and I wished to go on with my inquiry undisturbed.

'Hist, hist!' she whispered; 'listen!' holding up her finger. We both stood like statues, and suddenly I felt that curious creeping of the scalp which shows that even the most civilised among us have not yet eliminated superstitious fear. In the tense silence I heard someone slowly coming up the stair; I heard the halting step of a lame man. In the tension of the moment I had allowed the light to go out; now recovering myself, I pressed the spring, and waved its rays backward and forward down the stairway. The space was entirely empty, yet the hesitating footsteps approached us, up and up. I could almost have sworn on which step they last struck. At this interesting moment Sophia Brooks uttered a piercing shriek and collapsed into my arms, sending the electric torch rattling down the steps, and leaving us in impenetrable darkness. Really, I profess myself to be a gallant man, but there are situations which have a tendency to cause annoyance. I carried the limp creature cautiously down the stairs, fearing the fate of the butler, and at last got her into the dining-room, where I lit a candle, which gave a light less brilliant, perhaps, but more steady than my torch. I dashed some water in her face, and brought her to her senses, then uncorking another bottle of wine, I bade her drink a glassful, which she did.

'What was it?' she whispered.

'Madam, I do not know. Very possibly the club-footed ghost of Rantremly.'

'Do you believe in ghosts, Monsieur Valmont?'

'Last night I did not, but at this hour I believe in only one thing, which is that it is time everyone was asleep.'

She rose to her feet at this, and with a tremulous little laugh apologised for her terror, but I assured her that for the moment there were two panic-stricken persons at the stair head. Taking the candle, and recovering my electric torch, which luckily was un-injured by its roll down the incline the butler had taken, I escorted the lady to the door of her room, and bade her good-night, or rather, good-morning.

The rising sun dissipated a slight veil of mist which hung over the park, and also dissolved, so far as I was concerned, the phantoms which my imagination had conjured up at midnight. It was about half-past ten when the chief constable arrived. I flatter myself I put some life into that unimaginative man before I was done with him.

'What made you think that the butler was mounting the stair when he fell?'

'He was going up with my lord's breakfast,' replied the chief.

'Then did it not occur to you that if such were the case, the silver pitcher would not have been empty, and, besides the broken dishes, there would have been the rolls, butter, toast, or what not, strewn about the floor?'

The chief constable opened his eyes.

'There was no one else for him to bring breakfast to,' he objected.

'That is where you are very much mistaken. Bring me the boots the butler wore.'

'He did not wear boots, sir. He wore a pair of cloth slippers.'

'Do you know where they are?'

'Yes; they are in the boot closet.'

'Very well, bring them out, examine their soles, and sticking in one of them you will find a short sliver of pointed oak.'

The constable, looking slightly more stupefied than ever, brought the slippers, and I heard him ejaculate: 'Well, I'm blowed!' as he approached me. He handed me the slippers soles upward, and there, as I have stated, was the fragment of oak, which I pulled out.

'Now, if you take this piece of oak to the top of the stair, you will see that it fits exactly a slight interstice at the edge of one of the planks. It is as well to keep one's eyes open, constable, when investigating a case like this.'

'Well, I'm blowed!' he said again, as we walked up the stair together.

I showed him that the sliver taken from the slipper fitted exactly the interstice I had indicated.

'Now,' said I to him, 'the butler was not going up the stairs, but was coming down. When he fell headlong he must have made a fearful clatter. Shuffling along with his burden, his slipper was impaled by this sliver, and the butler's hands being full, he could not save himself, but went head foremost down the stair. The startling point, however, is the fact that he was *not* carrying my lord's breakfast to him, or taking it away from him, but that there is someone else in the castle for whom he was caterer. Who is that person?'

'I'm blessed if I know,' said the constable, 'but I think you are wrong there. He may not have been carrying up the breakfast, but he certainly was taking away the tray, as is shown by the empty dishes, which you have just a moment ago pointed out.'

'No, constable; when his lordship heard the crash, and sprang impulsively from his bed, he upset the little table on which had been placed his own tray; it shot over the oaken chest at the head of the bed, and if you look between it and the wall you will find tray, dishes, and the remnants of a breakfast.'

'Well, I'm blessed!' exclaimed the chief constable once again.

'The main point of all this,' I went on calmly, 'is not the disaster to the butler, nor even the shock to his lordship, but the fact that the tray the serving man carried brought food to a prisoner, who probably for six weeks has been without anything to eat.'

'Then,' said the constable, 'he is a dead man.'

'I find it easier,' said I, 'to believe in a living man than in a dead man's ghost. I think I heard his footsteps at midnight, and they seemed to me the footsteps of a person very nearly exhausted.

'Therefore, constable, I have awaited your arrival with some impatience. The words his late lordship endeavoured to write on the paper were "The Secret". I am sure that the hieroglyphics with which he ended his effort stood for the letter "R", and if he finished his sentence, it would have stood: "The Secret Room". Now, constable, it is a matter of legend that a secret room exists in this castle. Do you know where it is?'

'No one knows where the secret room is, or the way to enter it, except the Lords of Rantremly.'

'Well, I can assure you that the Lord of Rantremly who lives in London knows nothing about it. I have been up and about since daylight, taking some rough measurements by stepping off distances. I surmise that the secret room is to the left of this stairway. Probably a whole suite of rooms exists, for there is certainly a stair coinciding with this one, and up that stair at midnight I heard a club-footed man ascend. Either that, or the ghost that has frightened you all, and, as I have said, I believe in the man.'

Here the official made the first sensible remark I had yet heard him utter: 'If the walls are so thick that a prisoner's cry has not been heard, how could you hear his footsteps, which make much less noise?'

'That is very well put, constable, and when the same thing occurred to me earlier this morning, I began to study the architecture of this castle. In the first place, the entrance hall is double as wide at the big doors as it is near the stairway. If you stand with your back to the front door you will at once wonder why the builders made this curious and unnecessary right angle, narrowing the farther part of the hall to half its width. Then, as you gaze at the stair, and see that marvellous carved oak newel post standing like a monumental column, you guess, if you have any imagination, that the stairway, like the hall, was once double as wide as it is now. We are seeing only half of it, and doubtless we shall find a similar newel post within the hidden room. You must remember, constable, that these secret apartments are no small added chambers. Twice they have sheltered a king.'

The constable's head bent low at the mention of royalty. I saw that his insular prejudice against me and my methods was vanishing, and that he had come to look upon me with greater respect than was shown at first.

'The walls need not be thick to be impenetrable to sound. Two courses of brick, and a space between filled with deafening would do it. The secret apartment has been cut off from the rest of the house since the castle was built, and was not designed by the original architect. The partition was probably built in a hurry to fulfil a pressing need, and it was constructed straight up the middle of the stair, leaving the stout planks intact, each step passing thus, as it were, through the wall. Now, when a man walks up the secret stairway, his footsteps reverberate until one would swear that some unseen person was treading the visible boards on the outside.'

'By Jove!' said the constable, in an awed tone of voice.

'Now, officer, I have here a pickaxe and a crowbar. I propose that we settle the question at once.'

But to this proposal the constable demurred.

'You surely would not break the wall without permission from his lordship in London?'

'Constable, I suspect there is no Lord Rantremly in London, and that we will find a very emaciated but genuine Lord Rantremly within ten feet of us. I need not tell you that if you are instrumental in his immediate rescue without the exercise of too much red tape, your interests will not suffer because you the more speedily brought food and drink to the lord paramount of your district.'

'Right you are,' cried the constable, with an enthusiasm for which I was not prepared. 'Where shall we begin?'

'Oh, anywhere; this wall is all false from the entrance hall to some point up here. Still, as the butler was carrying the meal upstairs I think we shall save time if we begin on the landing.'

I found the constable's brawn much superior to his brain. He worked like a sansculotte on a barricade. When we had torn down part of the old oak panelling, which it seemed such a pity to mutilate with axe and crowbar, we came upon a brick wall, that quickly gave way before the strength of the constable. Then we pulled out some substance like matting, and found a second brick wall, beyond which was a further shell of panelling. The hole we made revealed nothing but darkness inside, and although we shouted, there was no answer. At last, when we had hewn it large enough for a man to enter, I took with me an electric torch, and stepped inside, the constable following, with crowbar still in hand. I learned, as I had surmised, that we were in the upper hall of a staircase nearly as wide as the one on the outside. A flash of the light showed a door corresponding with the fireplace of the upper landing, and this door not being locked, we entered a large room, rather dimly lighted by strongly barred windows that gave into a blind court-yard, of which there had been no indication heretofore, either outside or inside the castle. Broken glass crunched under our feet, and I saw that the floor was strewn with wine bottles whose necks had been snapped off to save the pulling of the cork. On a matt-ress at the farther end of the room lay a man with grey hair, and shaggy, unkempt iron-grey beard. He seemed either asleep or dead, but when I turned my electric light full on his face he proved to be still alive, for he rubbed his eyes languidly, and groaned, rather than spoke.

'Is that you at last, you beast of a butler? Bring me something to eat, in Heaven's name!'

I shook him wider awake. He seemed to be drowsed with drink, and was fearfully emaciated. When I got him on his feet, I noticed then the deformity that characterised one of them. We assisted him through the aperture, and down into the dining-room, where he cried out continually for something to eat, but when we placed food before him, he could scarcely touch it. He became more like a human being when he had drunk two glasses of wine, and I saw at once he was not as old as his grey hair seemed to indicate. There was a haunted look in his eyes, and he watched the door as if apprehensive.

'Where is that butler?' he asked at last.

'Dead,' I replied.

'Did I kill him?'

'No; he fell down the stairway and broke his neck.'

The man laughed harshly.

'Where is my father?'

'Who is your father?'

'Lord Rantremly.'

'He is dead also.'

'How came he to die?'

'He died from a stroke of paralysis on the morning the butler was killed.'

The rescued man made no comment on this, but turned and ate a little more of his food. Then he said to me: 'Do you know a girl named Sophia Brooks?'

'Yes. For ten years she thought you dead.'

'Ten years! Good God, do you mean to say I've been in there only ten years? Why, I'm an old man. I must be sixty at least.'

'No; you're not much over thirty.'

'Is Sophia – ' He stopped, and the haunted look came into his eyes again.

'No. She is all right, and she is here.'

'Here?'

'Somewhere in the grounds. I sent her and the servant out for a walk, and told them not to return till luncheon time, as the constable and I had something to do, and did not wish to be interrupted.'

The man ran his hand through his long tangled beard.

'I should like to be trimmed up a bit before I see Sophia,' he said.

'I can do that for you, my lord,' cried the constable.

'My lord?' echoed the man. 'Oh, yes, I understand. You are a policeman, are you not?'

'Yes, my lord, chief constable.'

'Then I shall give myself up to you. I killed the butler.'

'Oh, impossible, my lord!'

'No, it isn't. The beast, as I called him, was getting old, and one morning he forgot to close the door behind him. I followed him stealthily out, and at the head of the stair planted my foot in the small of his back, which sent him headlong. There was an infernal crash. I did not mean to kill the brute, but merely to escape, and just as I was about to run down the stairway, I was appalled to see my father looking like – looking like – well, I won't attempt to say what he looked like; but all my old fear of him returned. As he strode towards me, along the corridor, I was in such terror that I jumped through the secret door and slammed it shut.'

'Where is the secret door?' I asked.

'The secret door is that fireplace. The whole fireplace moves inward if you push aside the carved ornament at the left-hand corner.'

'Is it a dummy fireplace, then?'

'No, you may build a fire in it, and the smoke will escape up the chimney. But I killed the butler, constable, though not intending it, I swear.'

And now the constable shone forth like the real rough diamond he was. 'My lord, we'll say nothing about that. Legally you didn't do it. You see, there's been an inquest on the butler and the jury brought in the verdict, "Death by accident, through stumbling from the top of the stair." You can't go behind a coroner's inquest, my lord.'

'Indeed,' said his lordship, with the first laugh in which he had indulged for many a year. 'I don't want to go behind anything, constable, I've been behind that accursed chimney too long to wish any further imprisonment.'

The Curious Activities of Basil Thorpenden

VERNON KNOWLES

I

When I come to review my brief, but extraordinary, association with Basil Thorpenden, I appreciate at once how excellently the stage was set for his dramatic appearance and our meeting.

It was a wild October night. Ever since early afternoon the habitual gentle melancholy of autumn had been savaging to a frenzy, and now, close on midnight, the wind groaned and shrieked, as though bestridden with a flight of Furies; the rain beat on the window spasmodically, like a rattling of thin knuckles hopelessly imploring; and great drifts of leaves, snatched from the plane and chestnut, were flung, whirled and spun momently against the panes, then were lost again in the darkness.

I had drawn the curtains back, and for a time had regarded as much of the scene as the night would yield to the frail compulsion of my single green-shaded electric light.

But insidiously the sorrowful power of autumn entered my heart, and I thought on those things that may not be thought on without tears: of the swift passing of youth; of beauty that must die; of all that is lost when love is lost; of the innate loneliness, the groping, inarticulate unhappiness that hold us men – unendurable thoughts, all! And I gathered the curtains together again and turned to the fire. But – too late! autumn had overcome me; my peace was broken: a growing sense of strangeness seized on my mind: I felt withdrawn – far removed – from the world I knew: it lay remote, fantastic, dim-lighted and lapsing into shadow without me, and I, tremendous, a colossus, above it: pondering, sorrowing upon its inexplicable construction, its ways and its goal . . .

This was ill preparation for bed, and I knew it. If I continued in such fashion I should have little of sleep, and that little dream-ridden and unquiet. To shake off the mood I rose and sought a book from the shelves. In this operation I chanced to observe the hands of the clock: they pointed at one minute to midnight. Turning then toward the book-case, my gaze was abruptly arrested by an amazing sight: a pillar of faint mist was moving, very slowly and deliberately, from the direction of the closed door, along the wall; moving *en masse*, with an extreme of wholeness, no one portion of it swaying or stretching out, straying or eddying, as is the common way of mist . . . For a blank moment I stared, then bethought me. Had my eyes suddenly failed? were they focusing aright? But a quick glance at other objects about convinced me it was not a matter of focus. Was it misty outside? 'Season of mists' . . . I recollected. But – the absurdity of there being a mist in that raging wind! And beside, the rest of the room was quite free. Then – fire, somewhere in the house? This, a drifting of smoke? Absurd! There was no smell of fire; this was not smoke – this shapely, actually shapely, mist, growing denser, darker, but now become motionless . . .

And it grew denser and darker still.

I remained in my tense pose between fireplace and bookshelves, my head turned from the clock to this mysterious, incredible visitant.

Then the clock chimed; and as it did so, the mist drew itself even more compactly together and became a definite outline.

My brain strove abortively with the problem. An instant later, and no doubt I should have broken my pose, have struggled back to self-control, and stepped over to examine the phenomenon.

But the clock struck, and before my astounded gaze the outline became the outline of a man – in height and breadth. This suddenly was filled in, and without any commotion or disturbance whatsoever a middle-aged man stood before me.

'My dear sir!' he said, advancing.

Of course, for the moment I was, very properly, taken aback. Then I recovered.

'This is magic!' I cried.

'Well, in a kind of way, yes,' he agreed. 'And I must apologise. Really, I must beg your forgiveness. I do trust I have not startled you to the extent of inducing any harm?'

Drawing myself together I assured him that, startled indeed, curiosity was really the sole hurt I could confess I had sustained by his extraordinary appearance.

'I am most relieved,' he said. Then – 'Extraordinary? Well, unconventional, perhaps; yes, indeed.' He nodded several times, repeating 'Indeed, yes, indeed,' apparently in deep thought, then roused himself. 'I know exactly where I am. And I know what day it is.'

'You're at – ' I began.

'Eighty-four, Bishop's Road,' he interrupted; 'and it is now the tenth of October.'

A distinct note of triumph emerged in his voice.

'Correct,' I said. 'But how in the world – ?'

Outside, the wind groaned and shrieked, the rain beat against the window spasmodically. Ever since late afternoon all my thoughts had been strange and restless. On such a night, surely, might anything occur. The hours had mounted, tended, to some such extreme happening as had now come about – as inevitably (so it seemed to me) as a plant grows and attains to its blossom.

After such thorough preparation, how could it be expected of me to pay too high a price of wonder? But, in the interests of justice, I said, gesturing toward the window: 'Sir, allow me to congratulate you. Your appearance is most logical, apt and opportune.'

He smiled comprehendingly.

'Then, being logical, apt and opportune, it is forgiven?' he queried.

'Why, of course!' I said.

Thereupon we shook hands and sat down.

'Now, let me explain,' he said. 'My name is Basil Thorpenden – '

I interrupted with the information of my own; whereafter he continued: 'I am, by occupation – or perhaps I should say, by inclination – an occult scientist. And what I am going to tell you will, I fear, strain your credulity to breaking-point, yet' – he shrugged – 'you saw me, only a moment ago, appear out of the simple air – out of the future.'

'The future?' I exclaimed.

'Well, no. Of course I'm wrong. It *was* the future. Out of the present, I should have said.'

'How complicated,' I murmured.

He leaned forward with a smile.

'Let me continue, however . . . I must tell you that in my house at St John's Wood, I have a small room so fitted up – I am putting it crudely, for the sake of simplicity – fitted up with such apparatus as to enable me to enter, at will, into either the past or the future . . . You must understand that Time is not by any means one long road down which we progress, but rather a number of roads lying parallel to each other. All Time is, as it were, one great moment. Past, present and future co-exist. Today is not solely the today of the present, but is in reality composed as well of strata upon strata of todays – which, for the sake of convenience, we term the past and the future . . . Now, I regret to say that my apparatus is, as yet, only in the experimental stage. I am unable to pierce these strata very deeply, or, as we say, to go backward, or forward, in time farther than a mere five months or so. And, alas, it is not at all reliable even for such trifling excursions as these . . . But, to explain my presence here tonight – it was due to my apparatus unaccountably reversing the desired journey. I planned to go back three months and two days into the Past, to see my old friend Claston – since dead – who, before you, occupied this flat – '

'Yes, yes! he did,' I interrupted.

' – Instead, however, of entering the Past, I entered, to my intense chagrin, the Future. And, there being no means of returning to the Present, I necessarily had to wait until time caught me up, and released me. You see, quite simple . . . But – how intolerable it has been – the waiting! It is a marvel that I have managed to retain my sanity! For these last three months and two days, you must understand, I have had to endure living through *this* actual day, the tenth of October, over and over. I know precisely all that is to happen in it – what I shall say, what do; what you will say; your every movement . . . O, intolerable! . . . '

He fell silent; and I could only say: 'Extraordinary! how extraordinary!' my thoughts mounting excitedly. But, shortly gaining control over them, I questioned him closely about his apparatus, and about his other activities. He answered my curiosity with care and patience.

We sat with our chairs drawn up to the cheerful fire . . . And outside, October raged at her wildest: visiting the earth with her weapons of wind and rain; stripping the trees of their fine summer-won cloaks of yellow and russet and red . . .

I found myself considering Basil Thorpenden with more than a casual interest. I had liked him at once: liked his clear mind, his meticulous sense of values, his gentle sense of humour – as these were revealed to me. And then, his astonishing work: it interested me intensely. I found myself decidedly wishing to learn more about the man.

As he rose to go, he gratified me greatly by saying: 'Do dine with me one evening, will you? This week? Thursday, Friday? It is getting late now, and forgive me, I'm rather tired. These experiments are always wearying, you know; and especially when they go wrong.' He smiled, and I reproached myself for my lack of consideration. But he would not listen to apologies. 'Well, then, on Friday, at eight,' he said. 'We can talk, and I have one or two things to show that may interest you.'

So it was that I met him, and our brief, and strange, association began. Looking back now at that meeting. I appreciate at once how excellently that stage was set for his appearance, and how impeccably its drama consorted with his character, as I came to know him.

2

We had finished our coffee, and I had done examining a collection of spirit-photographs which Thorpenden had taken early that year – an interesting and quite convincing collection it was, too – when he rose and said: 'Come. I want you to see my Emotions Container.'

All through dinner I had had my first impression of him, as a remarkable and outstanding personality with unique mind and view-point, confirmed again and again. His conversation held me; and the references he made to his work – achievements and experiments – filled me with heightening curiosity and excitement. I had never before met a man like him. I felt it certainly would be impossible ever to meet his counterpart; such an experience, I told myself, comes but once in a lifetime. I was prepared to cultivate it to the full.

He took me by the arm and led me out: down a long passage and into a small room. It seemed a kind of laboratory. Against one wall were shelves holding much strange apparatus and machinery; the light glinted on polished metal and glass-tubing grotesquely twisted. Great earthenware jars stood about on the floor; on a central table liquids and solids in glass-stoppered bottles mingled with the usual chemist's varied assortment of test-tubes, retorts and Bunsen burners. Thorpenden went over to a corner and wheeled out with great care a wooden cabinet some four feet in height and two in width. Sliding back a panel in the top, he drew forth a short flexible tube to which was attached a mask – apparently. I was reminded at once of an anaesthetist's apparatus. Sliding back a panel in the front of the cabinet he revealed a complication of wheels, springs, glass-cylinders and what-not; my unscientific mind failed completely to ascertain, and differentiate between, all the details of the amazing mass.

'This,' said Thorpenden, 'is my Emotions Container: the work of a dozen years.'

I drew nearer.

'When you say your Emotions Container, do you mean that it is literally so?'

'Literally so,' he nodded. 'It came about thus. A dozen years ago, I became obsessed with the thought that many of my emotions, aroused suddenly – it may be, casually – in me, were often wasted because I had no object with which to engage them. This led me to consider what an appalling waste of fine emotion was undoubtedly going on throughout the world hourly. People experiencing this, or that – and the result a mere frittering-away and a loss. How good, I thought, if, instead of the emotion, unengaged, being irretrievably lost, it could be stored up, against a future time when it could be employed usefully! . . . So I came to tackle the problem, and eventually constructed this machine. It is, perhaps, one of the most delicate mechanisms in existence; for the subtlety of an emotion, do you know, is the subtlest of all subtle things . . . I must tell you that this Container takes only the Positive Emotions, such as Love, Delight, Enthusiasm, Happiness and so on. The Negative ones, of course – Fear, Hate, Sorrow, Greed and the like – are worthy only of destruction, not preservation . . . Imagine the use of the Container. You love, we'll say, and your love is not requited. With what an excess, then, is your heart charged! Applying the mouthpiece (see, it is within), you fit the mask over your face, then, just pulling this lever which opens the desired cylinder – the Love one, in this instance – a psychic suction ensues. Afterward, the lever is pulled again – this way, this time – thus hermetically sealing the cylinder. The mask is detached, and the cylinder remains stored with the unwanted emotion . . . Now, later – one day, some time – you chance to have need of some love: a little, perhaps; perhaps a considerable quantity. Going to the Container, you just depress this handle – thus reversing the procedure of the mechanism. Applying the mouthpiece, pulling the lever, the cylinder returns you the emotion to the extent you desire. Of course, it cannot exceed in quantity, all told, the amount you have previously given it.'

I stared from the invention to Thorpenden, and after a moment exclaimed: 'It's wonderful! Really – I say! But what a tremendous thing! A benefit, eh, to humanity? Making for happiness, everywhere!'

He smiled gently at my enthusiasm.

'I – wonder. It really *is* a big thing: that, I know. But it could be so dangerous. A trifling readjustment, and it could store up the Negative Emotions. Any amateur scientist could think of that readjustment, and carry it out. Then – what a force of hatred, greed, lust, murder, could inform men! Think of war – the next war! The mechanism has so many possibilities – too many possibilities – for evil, you see. And the way of the world, the way of human nature, is to degrade things slowly and surely; nothing is sacred! The good would be perverted to evil. I know it. I fear it . . . I shall keep the idea secret. I shall not let it pass out into the world.'

He replaced the mouthpiece-mask, slid back the two panels, and wheeled the machine into its corner.

'What a loss, then! What a loss!' I said.

He laid a hand on my shoulder, and regarded me.

'Perhaps the time will come – perhaps – when I shall perfect it to the extent of making it safe for the world. Although, maybe, before that . . . ' He broke off abruptly.

'Ah, then there's a chance – ?'

'Yes, a chance; just a chance.' He dropped his hand. 'But now, this way.' He opened the door and motioned me through. 'I've something else for you to see. Or, rather, to hear – my Hall of Footsteps.' He preceded me down the long passage, and at the end threw open a wide door.

3

It was a long hall into which we came, some fifteen yards in length and proportionately wide and high. There were no windows, the only other opening, beside the door by which we had entered, being another similar door at the far end. A series of pilasters upheld the ceiling, which was entirely unornamented and had, in its centre, a cluster of six electric lights. The floor was of parquet. The length, the height, the bareness – all conspired to give an impression of austerity and gravity. 'My Hall of Footsteps,' said Thorpenden. 'A sad, yet glad, place for me.' He paused a moment, then continued: 'I suppose all my life I have had every man's longing for immortality: to know, know for certain, that I would endure for ever. Like every man, too, I had my doubts. I turned at one time to religion, but could find no rest in it. Urged on, I came at length to think that the solution of the problem lay in – marriage. Having a child, was I not immortalising myself? Would I not endure, then, down the ages? . . . So I married; and I had a child: a boy. Yet I had not thought deeply enough on the problem, up to that point. I began to think again. And I saw that my solution was not a solution at all. One's child is but the half of oneself, for one thing; and for another, he might die prematurely, or die without issue – and then where is one's boast of immortality? . . . With something like desperation gradually rising in me I began to experiment, with the idea of finding some means of perpetuating myself, and those I loved. Yes, it was with a very

definite feeling of desperation that I began the work: I saw myself
warring with Time and Death. Not the first man thus to war, toward
just such an end! . . . The years went by. I could see no success ahead
of me. I began then to know the true power of my combatants. They
would win! I was impotent against them! . . . Then I made a slight
advance. I was able to immortalise certain sounds. And the first thing
I did was to immortalise the footsteps of my wife, and of my son . . .
That was nine years ago. I have done nothing since. You see, in the
very week that I had done this, the great catastrophe of my life
occurred.' He raised a hand to his eyes. 'My wife and boy were killed
in a railway accident. You remember? thc Orpington derailment:
one of the worst England has known . . . Nine years ago! . . . I gave
up my experiments at once. I suddenly lost heart . . . And, somehow,
the problem does not seem so urgent now; I am no longer racked
by it; the welling of desperation has quietly subsided. Perhaps I have
conquered my vanity, my self-love. I am content to trust now to my
old enemies, Time and Death. Who knows? Perhaps they will lead
one by the hand, gently as two children leading a child, and will bring
one into the land of heart's desire in the end, after all . . . But listen;
you shall hear what I did.'

He moved to the wall, and I saw for the first time two heavy scarlet
cords depending from the ceiling, beside the door. He pulled one
gently. 'My wife. Nine years ago.'

Immediately, from the far end of the hall, came a leisurely sound of
steps, calm and confident. They proceeded towards us . . . Nothing
else. Not the faintest shadowing of a figure, not the least disturbance
of the air.

I closed my eyes; and swift into my mind leapt a picture of the
woman, or so it seemed to me: the maternal-mouthed, gentle-eyed
wife . . . The steps rang louder, clearer; they were upon us. They
passed by . . . continued on, through the door, and were lost beyond.

There were tears in Thorpenden's eyes, and his mouth was grown
tight.

'Don't,' I said. 'Don't.' I gripped his arm. 'It hurts you too much.'

'No, no. It's all right. You must forgive me . . . Even yet, you see . . .
But listen to the boy.' He pulled the other cord.

There was a sudden swift pattering: click, click! went small heels:
the hurrying, eager walk of a child. Soon the walk quickened to a
run, then next instant – temptation of the glass-like surface of the
parquet-flooring – into a slide, long, swift, sweeping; it rushed past
us and on through the door, and finished without.

Instinctively I waited for the laugh that surely followed that exciting slide . . . But there was only silence.

I looked at Thorpenden. A wistful, half-wondering smile lightened his face.

'That is all,' he said. 'And yet – it is something.' I felt profoundly moved.

'Yet you've made up your mind? You won't go on with it?' I asked.

'No; I've no longer any desire. Maybe, above that sound of footsteps is the body of my wife, and my boy, and, maybe, patience and experiment could wrest them out of invisibility, yet – as I say, the problem no longer obsesses me, as it did.'

We went out.

'Was it not Whistler,' he queried, 'who ruled that when an artist ceases to be interested in the picture he is painting, the painting is finished?'

It was not until some time later that I took my departure. For my mind was full of questions on both the Emotions Container and the Hall of Footsteps, and on those other matters with which he had entertained me during dinner, and I was loath to leave without learning more from him. Eventually, when I came away, we had arranged another meeting in the following week.

4

When Thorpenden discovered that I appreciated port, he waxed very enthusiastic.

'My dear fellow,' he exclaimed, 'I'm delighted to hear it! I don't know what has come over England of late years – trouble at home and abroad: no end of it! – but I'm inclined to believe that had she only maintained her proper and decent taste for port, she would have avoided all this bickering and fuss, and be at peace now . . . But, really! Does it seem a very far-fetched notion to you? Believe me, I'm quite serious . . . However, here we are.' He went over to a small table whereon were set a decanter and glasses.

'And be careful,' he smiled. 'This is a test case. I warn you.' He handed me a glass.

And under his eye I drank it as port should be drunk: a savouring of the bouquet first; a slow sip; then a deeper and quicker one. Lowering the glass, I murmured: 'A rich, a magnificent, wine!'

'Ah,' said Thorpenden, nodding. 'You pass – with honours. It's Offley of '97.'

Thus, early in our so-brief friendship, was a further bond established between us. When two men agree upon the intricate question of port in all its details – shippers, years, decanting, temperature, even to the apparently small but really very important matter of the size and shape of the glass from which it should be, with gratitude and reverence, partaken – then, it is not too much to say they may completely, even bitterly, disagree upon such other, comparatively minor, questions as political partisanship and survival of personality after death. Their friendship is indeed an indestructible edifice reared upon an adamantine foundation . . .

We were lounging comfortably before the log-fire (pine-logs, they were, and the sweet searching scent of the resin took the room, underlying our tobacco-smoke perceptibly enough); and our conversation, from the topic of port, led slowly and inevitably to an exchange on Portugal, and thence on by easy stages to far cities and remote countries.

'There is one land,' said Thorpenden, 'that is not remote, yet is scarcely known personally to many. However, the mass of people have all heard tell of it. When I say it is not remote, perhaps I am giving only half the truth. In one sense, it is here;' (he waved a hand, indicating the room about us) 'in another, it is outside the world. I'm speaking of the Land of Ideas.'

I leant forward. 'I know something about it,' I said. 'Don't be surprised; not at first-hand: at second-hand. I've a friend, an author, who makes periodic excursions into the Land, and of one of those excursions* he has told me. I know about Tinsel and Sham; of the Field of Imperishable Irises over which hover the Dreams; and of the old Maker of the Gods . . . Oh, it must be marvellous, wandering there! But, of course, it is not for me . . . '

'No; I'm afraid not for you – a lawyer. For poets, authors, painters, musicians, sculptors, and, to end the list, scientists – yes. Near my bookshelves, upstairs, I have the secret door.'

'Will you not tell me,' I begged, 'of one of your visits?'

'Why, to be sure! Let me see . . . ' He fell into thought for a moment.

'I'll tell you of two,' he said at length. 'One of some considerable time back, and another, later, which turned out to be a sequel to it.'

I settled back in the deep chair and relinquishing the cigar-end took out my pipe. Thorpenden, selecting a cigar himself and lighting it carefully, began.

* This excursion may be found related in *Here and Otherwhere*.

'I remember that, feeling blunted by overmuch contact with the world, I had passed through into the Land of Ideas with my usual purpose in view: to seek out the Territory of Reality. Wandering along in a direction I had never taken before I came at length to the outskirts of a small town: a delightful haphazard clutter of buildings swarming up a hillside and crowning itself on the summit with a soaring tower of black and white stonework.

'As I proceeded, intent on exploration of the place, I became aware of a babble of voices from somewhere near at hand, and then, as I paused and listened, the ahs and m-ms of a gathered crowd.

'My curiosity was excited, and I turned aside, determined to learn the reason of the disturbance. Presently I came upon people, in twos and threes, hurrying in the same direction as myself. I was rapidly overtaking them when I myself was overtaken by a young man.

'I stretched out a hand, detaining him. "Tell me, what is the reason of all this hurry? And isn't that a crowd I hear yonder?"

' "It is indeed a crowd that you hear," he replied. "And I am in haste to join it, that I may not miss any of the song of Saedi."

'I asked: "Who is Saedi?"

'He looked at me. "You do not know of Saedi? You must be a stranger in this land?"

'I acknowledged: "I am, in truth, a stranger here."

' "Then, know: Saedi is a poet; he is the greatest poet we have." He broke off. "But let us continue, or we shall be late."

'We hastened on, and every minute the noise of the crowd grew in our ears.

'The young man, on my questioning him, said: "This is the hour of Saedi's singing. Every day at noon he appears with his lute; he stands at the porch of his house a while, the crowd acclaiming him; then he goes to a seat under a great magnolia-tree. And when there is silence, he sings. He sings until he can sing no more, when he retires. He is a man not come, as yet, to middle-age, and very tall, and of personal beauty. Not long ago he declared that the wonder and loveliness of the universe were become so increasingly urgent that nowhere could he look, nowhere, without the mood of song seizing him – his heart vexed, his mind aflame. There was never peace for him. And – how well he knew it! – wonder and loveliness sear the mind and scar it at length, and wear the heart away. There are things too powerful to be withstood by man – that break him as the mountain-fir is broken by the avalanche – and these are three: love and wonder and loveliness.

Wherefore, said Saedi, that he might not yet be broken, that he might escape this surely approaching fate – see! he would bind his eyes about with a cloth, and shield them. So much had they seen already – their pictures deeply stored in his heart – that he would never lack song, surely, till the day of his death. But in peace henceforth would he sing . . . And as he spoke, he bound a thick cloth securely over his eyes."

'At this moment we turned a corner and were almost immediately among the crowd. The young man plucked at my sleeve. "Follow me; there is a way that I know."

'And I followed him, and we drew away from the crowd, and took a path through a copse and presently emerged into a garden. Beside us flowed a small river; to the left a lawn stretched widely, broken by trees, and ending in a bank of canna-lilies and blue and white aga-panthus. Immediately ahead of us stood the great magnolia-tree with the seat beneath its boughs of which my companion had told me. A young wind brought to us, in gentle wafts, the sweet, cool perfume of its blossoms. From the porch of the house to the edge of a shrubbery adjoining the magnolia stretched the moving, murmuring ranks of the townspeople. We, close to the river, close to the magnolia's seat, were alone and hidden from view by a semicircle of oleanders and bougainvilleas.

' "I always come here," said the young man. "I never miss the hour of Saedi's singing. And yet" – his eyes clouded – "the length of Saedi's song shortens. I have noticed it. Every day, it shortens. Others have noticed it; and they are asking themselves – "

'He stopped abruptly; then he went on: "I had hoped, one day, to enter Saedi's house. For, you must know, he has always taken six youths who promised well in song, and trained them. Lately, he has taken but three."

' "Then,' I began, "does that mean – ?"

'But my question was lost in a sudden hubbub that swelled into shouts and cheers.

' "Saedi!" cried the young man, pointing.

'And there in the porch stood a fine, commanding figure dressed in white and scarlet. Thick yellow hair flowed to his shoulders, and among it was twined a wreath of roses. The eyes were bound with a purple cloth, beneath which, too, half the nose was concealed; the mouth showed firm and strong and tender.

' "Saedi, Saedi!" There was delight and adulation in the concourse of voices that greeted him.

'He stood a moment, then with bowed head was led by his three youths to his seat.

'The lute was placed in his hands, but he made no movement.

'The silence deepened.

'The crowd stared expectantly. And so intense became the silence that a bird's note trembled to my ears from far away, and the gentle clashing of the leaves, at the will of the breeze, sounded now harsh, now strident . . .

'And Saedi still made no move; his hands loosely held the lute; his head had fallen imperceptibly farther forward until his chin was sunken on his chest . . .

'And as I, within that semicircle of oleanders and bougainvilleas, waited too – all at once I knew. Yes, I knew. Saedi, with his bandaged eyes, had nothing left within him now to sing. He's not going to sing, I said to myself. Is this the first day upon which he has fallen silent? Then, it will not be the last . . . And I turned to my companion and whispered: "He's not going to sing. He has nothing left to sing."

'Then I saw tears were in his eyes. He said brokenly: "I felt it was coming to this. And what shall we do if it remains so? What shall we do if Saedi sings no more? Alas, I shall never now, never enter his house."

'And Saedi did not sing that day, and returned indoors, and the crowd dispersed perturbed and saddened.

'But the young man and I remained in our place. And I said to him: "It is that bandage of purple cloth about his eyes! If he were to tear it away, he would sing again. He must tear it away! Has he not guessed the truth? It's incredible, but if he has not guessed, he must be told."

' "He has been told," answered the young man. "When he first bound his eyes, a score of voices warned him. But he laughed. And he vowed to keep the cloth securely in place – so full were his heart and mind, he said, and so dear would be the growth of peace with the ever-fresh wonder and loveliness of the world waived."

' "Then," I shrugged, "Saedi will remain silent."

' "Still the people will continue to come," cried the young man. "For the people of this town own loyalty one of the chief virtues; and how could they ever forget Saedi? . . . And I shall continue to come. Each day, here in these bushes, I shall wait. And one day – I know, Saedi will sing again, and his voice will be even stronger and more beautiful. And then once more he will have six young men in his house – and I may be one of them."

'And then he rose up, and I rose up, and we parted."

Thorpenden paused, regarded the small stump of his cigar with whimsical regret and deposited it carefully in the ash-tray beside him.

'That is an account of the previous visit. And now to relate its sequel, contained in a later one.

'Once again I passed through into the Land of Ideas and wandered, seeking – as ever, keenly – that most elusive but most desirable of all places, the Territory of Reality. I bore to the left, and shortly, escaped from the path, crossed silent fields, and thus unexpectedly came upon the Two Valleys I had only once before entered. Descending into the first, I became aware of its nature – and remembered. A low, passionate-beating harmony filled the place, and reached to my heart gripping it ruthlessly: the music of Things Passing Away. My eyes filled with tears. Somewhere among those welling, throbbing strains sounded the ardent note of my own being. And the thought of this – once realised – leapt sadly in my mind with the insistence of a pulse . . .

'With what relief did I pass into the second Valley! The ineffable harmony that breathed there, tremulous and eager, caressed me like cool, sure hands. My tears were stemmed at their source, my heart. For this was the music of Things Coming To Life. And somewhere in its midst, I knew, small but sustained, purposeful and inevitable, rang the one note which was the springing centre of my being . . .

'In that strange, bare field that lies between the Two Valleys, these two conflicting harmonies meet. They meet, mingle and resist. They would fly from each other; they would overcome each other; they each long for supremacy, but may not achieve it: it is ordained that they meet and mingle and resist. And thus is existence maintained, nor may the perfect balance between the two harmonies be disturbed.

'As I turned away, I observed that at no great distance ahead rose a small town. And immediately on a close regard, though it was so long since I had last seen it, I recognised it – that delightful, haphazard clutter of buildings swarming up the hillside and crowning itself on the summit with a soaring tower of black and white stonework! This time, I averred to myself, I would explore the place . . . And then I thought: What of Saedi? And because the hour was close on noon, and the fount of my curiosity ever-springing, it seemed to me a more desirable thing first to see the silent Saedi once more. I could pass on to the town afterwards. I wondered if the people still thronged to the poet's garden daily. If so, I was certain they would not meet with song so long as Saedi suffered the purple cloth about his eyes . . .

'I pressed on, and soon reached the outskirts of the town. And once more I was one of the hurrying crowd, and I went with them. So, they were indeed loyal . . . Then, at that place of which I knew, I drew away, took the path through the copse and presently emerged into Saedi's garden. In that garden, it must be always summer. At the far end of the lawn, still the red and yellow canna-lilies mingled like a steady flaring of strong flames; with the blue and white globes of the agapanthus hanging as motionless before them, in a cool contrast. Still the great magnolia-tree was mooned with its blossoms, and all the air – hot, windless, in a tranced half-swoon – was heavy with their sweetness. I expected to find the young man of my previous visit already waiting in the little semicircle of oleanders and bougain-villeas, but was disappointed. Had he, as time passed, at length given up coming? The crowd, as before, stretched the whole way from the porch of the house to the edge of the shrubbery adjoining the mag-nolia, and was growing in size momently. I was surveying them idly, when a sudden movement took them, and I saw the door had opened. At the same moment, there was a rustle of the bushes and a sound of quick steps behind me, and the young man appeared. With what surprise he observed me, but with what warmth greeted me!

'Then you have not forgotten me?' I said.

'"No!" Then he motioned with his hand excitedly: "And look! Saedi!"

'The crowd was greeting him: "Saedi! Saedi!"

'I turned quickly. And there was Saedi, rose-crowned and white-and-scarlet dressed. Saedi: smiling gravely, standing with half-bowed head – and with the purple cloth gone from about his eyes.

' "Ah, the cloth," I said; "the purple cloth . . . Then he sings again? Was I not right, my friend?"

'The young man looked at me.

' "Yes, he sings again. And how he sings! . . . Yes, you were indeed right."

' "But how did it come about?" I asked. "For you told me he had vowed he would never tear the cloth away? I am curious to know," I said. Saedi had seated himself under the magnolia, and his six youths stood ranged behind him. He took his lute in hand, and the crowd, of a sudden, stood dumb.

' "Hush! Wait!" said my companion. "I will tell you afterwards how it came about."

'And then Saedi sang. And though I had not felt that my spirit was in need of any sustenance at all – yet Saedi's singing came to it as food and drink to a starving, thirsting man. And when he had done, I felt strengthened anew, and a divine comfort of happiness glowed in my heart. And I was trembling strangely, and unable for a time to speak. Saedi returned with his youths to the house: his path suddenly one of flowers, flung by the crowd. Soon the crowd, too, had gone; but the young man and I remained in our place; and at length I said to him: "And now, tell me how it came about?'

'He smiled. "In a very strange way. For a long time Saedi continued silent. But nevertheless each day the people came, always in hope; and each day Saedi appeared, and took his lute in hand. But weeks and months passed. The sorrow of the people was great, and always they were begging him to pluck off the purple cloth, but always he refused because of his vow. And then, when despair was at mortal grips with loyalty: one day – how well I remember! – Saedi broke his long silence with a little song. And very gradually thereafter the period of his singing lengthened; until now he sings as fully as before; and the golden voice is more wonderful than of old: it reaches straightly to the heart and raises those thoughts that, like heavy-bosomed clouds in their passing, rain tears; and it pierces through to the soul, knowing its way down those labyrinthine passages – stirring, with its poignant echoes, ghosts of the things long buried there . . . And all this came about because, with the passing of time, the purple cloth was wearing, thinning: allowing first a faint dawn of light to appear, which grew imperceptibly as the strength and thickness of the cloth yielded. Later, came a dim sight again of objects – and thus the song of Saedi began, and grew; and eventually the purple cloth broke its knot asunder, and Saedi was freed."

' "It is well," I said, after a moment. "It is well that it happened thus."

' "The gods are vigilant," responded the young man. "They answer the prayers of their people."

' "And as to yourself," I said, "you spoke of hoping, some day, to enter Saedi's house?"

' "The gods," replied the young man gently, "the gods are indeed vigilant. Next week I enter Saedi's house."

'Then he rose up, and I rose up, and we parted.'

Thorpenden, perceiving that my glass was empty, went over to the small table and fetched the decanter.

For a time we sipped and smoked and discussed the story of Saedi . . .

*   *   *

Eventually I said: 'Are you tired? Is it too much to ask you to recount another of your visits to that wonderful Land?'

'My dear fellow, I am not in the least tired! But what of yourself? I would not willingly lead you to even the beginnings of boredom?'

I assured him that his leadership to such beginnings was an impossibility.

'Then,' he smiled, 'in that case I shall continue . . . Let me think. I have entered the Land so often . . . '

He remained in thought for a few moments, then stirred.

'I must tell you something you will have gathered already from my talk. The one desire of my life has long been to attain to the Territory of Reality. The Territory lies in a remote corner of the Land of Ideas, and is most difficult to reach. When the day comes, if ever it does, that I pierce all the intervening difficulties (and of some of them I shall tell you) and come into Reality – I assure you that, from then on, I shall not return again to the world.

'The many times I have sought the way, unsuccessfully! But recently I have learned at last the direction – and that is a great achievement . . . However, I wish to tell you now of the Houses of Friendship: which I came upon during one of my unsuccessful attempts to locate the Territory. I was seeking the way, by asking all whom I encountered. Ah, then I didn't know that for every person the Territory existed in a different place, and though they indeed knew it well – being fortunate dwellers in the Land of Ideas, and different from myself, a mere visitor – they were totally unable to be of help to me. For a long time, attempting to follow their directions, I was thrown into confusion. Eventually the truth came to me, and I suddenly saw how profitless was all my questioning – since when I have surrendered myself to myself, and I alone guide myself, with such success up to the present that I have at length, as I said, learned the direction in which the Territory lies. And surely now one day I shall enter it . . .

'On the occasion of which I am telling, I had been directed by a lovely creature (who I afterward discovered was a Sculpture shortly to be created in the world) to take a path through a forest. When I at length emerged, it was to find before me a delightful prospect of garden-land stretching a great distance and apparently ending at the base of a line of purple-clad mountains. The trees and bushes were all a-blossom; between banks of lawn small streams ran their broken silver, or dropped over sudden little hills, like a fall of shining hair. A faint breeze blew: just enough aery motion above to keep the clouds changing their arabesques, and below to mingle a joyous pot-pourri of flowers' scent.

'I passed along slowly, and came shortly upon a little house that had, thrown about itself like a gay shawl, a wealth of wistaria, almost hiding it. Pausing a moment to admire, and wonder as to who its inhabitant was, I was a little surprised by the door being suddenly swung open and a young man appearing.

' "Yes; this path," he said, "and straight on."

'He pointed ahead to the line of purple-clad mountains.

' "But how did you know?" I asked curiously.

'The young man looked surprised.

' "Surely, everyone wishes to enter the Province of Beauty?" he said.

' "The Province of Beauty!" I exclaimed, and was disappointed. "No; you are wrong. I seek the Territory of Reality."

'It was his turn to look disappointed. Then he declared: "For me, Beauty is Reality."

'He was turning away, when I said: "Tell me, do you direct all passers-by to the Province of Beauty?"

'He nodded.

' "But I am only one of the guides. All this," he waved an arm, "is peopled by us – as far as those mountains. You see, we are the artists who died young. We can only point the way."

'With that, he returned to his house and shut the door, and I continued on.

'It was even as the young man said: on many a little house, thereafter, did I come, and from each emerged a young man with his direction. And I came at length to the line of purple-clad mountains, and I made that great journey over it, during which some strange experiences befell me, and I saw several wonderful things, but these I shall not tell now – Yet, stay! there is one that occurs to me specially I might mention.

'Somewhere in the midst of those mountains I came suddenly upon a vast level space that stretched away to right and left as far as the eye could see; and all the space was thronged with – what shall I call them? – Figures: I cannot describe them; they were like men, yet unlike. Indescribable in appearance! There were myriads of them: mingling, streaming to and fro; and their passage and talk – for they talked – made a long, low sighing, as it were a perpetual sad-thoughted wind had its proscribed abode there . . . I drew near in wonder and curiosity, and learned that they were all the Yesterdays the world had known. They asked my name, too; and when I told, swiftly it was passed among them, and shortly about me grew a commotion and a number of the Figures confronted me. And they murmured: "Look. Do you remember us?"

'And I looked – and recognised the Days of my past life. Each told its tale, under my scrutiny: and old joys and sorrows, triumphs, fears and disappointments took me again with their long-forgotten newness. I was turning away, unable longer to face the poignant record, when one Yesterday detached itself from the others and pressed against me. And I regarded it an instant, when all the undying bitterness and grief in my heart surged up anew, and I beat it off, crying out. For it was the saddest Day of my life: the Day on which my wife and child were killed . . . I turned aside blindly, intent on leaving the place at once. But soon I came to a terrible precipice opening widely and deeply in my path. Beyond it stretched a vast level space, similar to that in which I stood. And it, too, was crowded with myriads of Figures.

' "Who are they, yonder?" I asked. "Are they Yesterdays, as well?"
' "No, they are the Tomorrows," I was told.

'And I saw how impossible it was for the Tomorrows and the Yesterdays to meet – that precipice, whose depth held a roaring water, between them! That precipice – I shuddered; it was like a great jagged-toothed ogre-mouth; the rushing torrent like a black, darting tongue . . .

'After some search, I found a way out of that Place of Yesterdays; and came soon to a pass that brought me to foot-hills, from which I descended easily at length to gracious, silver-misted plains. I knew that now I was in the Province of Beauty, and that somewhere in the Province was the splendid circle of the Woods of Endless Song, within which lie the Meadows of the Undying Flowers, whose midmost Meadow holds the rose-coloured palace of Beauty herself: to which come all the prayers, desires and dreams of the world's artists. Beyond the Province of Beauty, somewhere far beyond, I was convinced lay the Territory of Reality. So, I was congratulating myself: at last I must be actually nearing my longed-for objective! . . .

'I passed by a little lake, and took a path that mounted a hill. On the summit I paused and surveyed the scene. Nearby, in the midst of a peaceful park stood a large, rambling house whose quiet loveliness seized on me with all the gentle, moving intensity of soft, stringed music. As I stared, there sounded a step on the path behind me, and I turned – to face an old man of very erect carriage, who approached me and nodded.

' "Yes, very lovely," he said. "But you should see the other house, beyond." And he pointed to the left. "It is second only to the palace of Beauty itself."

'Before I could make a reply he had nodded again and passed on, turning suddenly from the path and becoming hidden at once by the thick growth of bushes that clothed the hillside . . .

'It was only after considerable search that I came at last upon that other house. And surely the old man had spoken rightly: the palace of Beauty alone could exceed its perfection. It was built of stone that glowed with a dozen soft colours; and, surrounded by an expanse of lawn, it looked like a wonderful great opal set in jade.

'The veil of willow-branches beside me parted suddenly, and the old man of very erect carriage unexpectedly approached.

' "Was I not right?" he enquired.

' "Truly," I replied; and regarded it again. And the wonder of it took me with all the triumphing pain of a first love.

'Then I said; "Tell me of it." For I felt that of such a house much could be told. Nor was I wrong.

'The old man said: "The first house you saw is the House of Friendship. To it inevitably come all those destined to become friends. Within its walls they meet, acknowledge their mutual regard, then eventually pass out again and go their separate ways . . . And it is, indeed, a very lovely house: its quiet loveliness being the timeless gathering from the innumerable friends that have lodged there . . .

' "But this house that you now look upon, transcends the House of Friendship in loveliness by virtue of its superior qualities. For it is the House of Great Friendship. The splendour of its stone is caught from the splendour of the love within, and shines forth with ever-increasing strength. To this House – so difficult to reach: remote, and approached by the most desolate and hazardous paths – inevitably come all those destined to become great friends . . .

' "I shall tell you of two I knew; and their history is the history of all who enter there.

' "Koje was a young man who dwelt in the distant city of Lox: that quiet, crypess-crowned city of wisdom that is built on a mountain-top. And Koje early applied himself to books, as is the immemorial custom in Lox; and it was expected of him to become, in due time, an accepted and worthy citizen. But he grew very restless; and one day he declared that he could remain no longer in Lox. It was in vain that the old men remonstrated with him, and argued. At length they saw that he was not ordained to enter the service of

Wisdom; and they ceased forthwith to remonstrate and to argue. Then Koje departed from their midst; and he knew not whither he was going, nor why. All that he knew was the inner voice of his restlessness, and it sounded very sweet to him; and he allowed it dictate his path . . .

' "Now, there was another young man, named Nald, who lived in the city of Terg: the far-famed city of athletes. And Nald was a goodly son of Terg: combining beauty and strength perfectly – as do all in that city of the plains – but Nald was conspicuous, even so: he ran, drove, boxed, and did all other games excellently, while in the art of soldiery he was of the most courageous and enduring.

' "Imagine then with what sorrow Terg heard that the games and soldiering left Nald unsatisfied; and places beyond Terg called to him – and had long called – with voices of alluring persistence.

' "Before much could be said by the city in support of why he should disregard those calling voices, Nald had risen up and left . . . Much time passed with Koje travelling down from the North, and with Nald travelling up from the South. But at length, their feet found out those desolate and hazardous paths, which few men find – and sweeter to Koje came then the inner voice of his restlessness; and to Nald suddenly the voices of alluring persistence calling him became harmonised and simplified to a single gracious voice.

' "In thus wise they came to the House of Great Friendship, and entering, met. Then ensued that miracle which always ensues in that House: Koje and Nald on meeting mingled and melted into each other and became one person. Issuing forth again, the Two-In-One decided to return to the city of Lox. But when they reached it, all there would have nothing to do with them and drove them forth: 'You are not Koje!'

' "And then they went South, and came after long journeying to the city of Terg. But when they sought to enter, the gates of Terg were shut in their face: 'You are not Nald!'

' "Then the Two-In-One went far apart from all cities and all men, and built a house. 'This shall be our city,' they said; 'and it shall be called Loxterg.' And they abode in that house, and the divine two, Happiness and Content, gave it protection.

' "And it happened that, in the following years, others whose cities had disclaimed them similarly came by, and they also built houses, that today Loxterg is a magnificent city – and may it be your good fortune sometime to behold it."

'Abruptly as he had appeared, the old man turned from me with a nod of farewell, and parting the veil of willow-branches with sudden hand slipped through and disappeared . . .

'His tale rang strangely and wonderfully in my mind as I continued on: wandering this way and that, seeking, but vainly, the Territory of Reality. And after a period of such wandering I grew tired, and returned again to the world.'

Thorpenden lifted his glass, and looked across at me as he sipped. But for a while I was silent; then I sighed: 'Of course, you know I envy you?'

'Ah, my dear fellow! But you may very well envy me when I've found Reality.'

'That will surely be soon, now?' I queried.

'Perhaps, perhaps,' he said; and there was the sharpness of excitement in his tone. 'I know – yes, I'm sure! I'm very near it. Perhaps the next time – the very next visit – '

I had a curious sense of impending loss as I came away. O, he would find the Territory all right – nothing surer; and then – an end to our so brief, and for me so absorbing, friendship. I should never see him again . . .

I was about to ask him, as we stood at the door shaking hands: 'Tell me now – is this the last time we'll ever meet?'

But he forestalled me: 'Do come in next Monday?' Then, intuitively, he guessed what I was thinking. 'We'll see each other once more – at least,' he said gently.

Then I left him.

5

On the following Monday the maid admitted me with: 'The master said would you please wait for him in the study? He wouldn't be long.'

I went upstairs, and took a seat by the fire.

The late-March wind was loud outside and blew the rain in great pattering gusts against the window. Winter was doing its best to remain beyond its season: loath to yield to the first timid advances of Spring.

On just such a similar sort of night, I was thinking, had Thorpenden and I first met . . .

There sounded a sudden 'click!' behind me, and I turned quickly, to see Thorpenden emerge from beside his bookcase.

'Forgive me,' he said. 'I was afraid I would be late. I hurried.'

'Please! Don't apologise,' I protested.

He took my hand and said quietly: 'My friend, I've found it. I've found the Territory of Reality at last.'

'Ah! Then that means – that means – ?' I stammered.

'Goodbye to the world! – that's what it means.' He released my hand, and put an arm about my shoulder, 'Let us go downstairs to the sitting-room, and I shall tell you how it happened.'

When we were seated, he began: 'It is just by chance – the merest chance – that my search is ended. I had been in the Province of Beauty, pressing on and on, convinced – as I told you – that somewhere beyond it lay the Territory of Reality. At length, I saw ahead a great city built of silver, and walled around with a silver wall. My first thought was to pass it by: to go either to the right of it, or to the left. I felt that I must not waste time: I must go on. Immediately beyond the city rose a range of mountains, black and formidable, and it seemed to me that my way lay over them, and I should need all time and strength for the task. To tell the truth, I was not looking forward to the journey, despite the fact of my conviction that those forbidding mountains were the final obstacle to entry into the Territory . . .

'As I drew nearer the city, I saw numbers of people approaching it and entering in at its gates. And as I drew nearer yet, I observed that all the people were in very worn, ragged clothing. Perhaps partly because my curiosity was roused as to what was the name of the city, and as to why so many people were entering it, and none leaving, and partly too because I was dreading those threatening mountains – I decided to pause in my search. Thus, by a mere chance, did I take the right, the only, way to my goal! For that city, my friend, was the City of Love . . .

'At first, when I sought to enter, those that guarded the gate barred my way. But was I not a lover? Then they looked closer at me – and allowed me in. And I saw that, soon as the lovers entered, a transformation took place at once: gone were their worn, ragged clothes and they were dressed in velvet and silk, satin and brocade, all hung over with gems and gold. And everyone was at the peak of happiness. Music of the sweetest filled the air; and everywhere that one turned fine gardens met one with a greeting of odour and colour: a thousand varieties of flowers! I passed along with joy, and came eventually to another gate. From it led a road straight toward the nearby towering mountains. And I asked at the gate:

"Whither does the road lead?" And I was half-fearful of what they might answer.

'They said: "It leads direct to the Territory of Reality."

'Then I trembled, and could say nothing for a time. At length, regaining composure, I questioned: "Is this, then, the only road?" For suddenly I was thinking it must be.

'They answered: "Indeed, the only road."

'Then I told them: "I have been seeking this road for so long! To think that at last I have found it!"

'We conversed for a time; and I learned that had I passed by the City of Love, either to the right of it, or to the left – I had become lost for certain among those giant peaks, for there it is perpetual night, and one is preyed upon by the Dreads and Doubts, so that I had never won through to the Territory . . . '

Thorpenden paused. And in the pause – 'Once again,' I said, heavily, 'Once again, let me tell you I envy you.'

Then I remembered – and made congratulations . . .

And later I asked: 'And now – ?'

'And now,' said Thorpenden, 'I make my arrangements – at once. Goodbye to the world . . . O, you've no idea how eager I am to be in that Territory! . . . '

We talked on . . . But all the while I was thinking: 'I shall never see him again. We shall never meet again. This is the last time . . . ' And it was.

That evening closed my briefest and most fascinating friendship . . . We said 'Goodbye' at the door. I went away quickly, unwilling to linger; glad for Thorpenden, so sorry for myself . . .

A week later, passing along that street in a taxi, I glanced out as we breasted Thorpenden's house. It was forlornly empty, and had large 'For Sale' placards in all the front windows.

The Necromancer

DONALD CAMPBELL

Chapter 1

Leslie Vane, the famous young English explorer, had just returned from China, and was driving slowly along Knightsbridge, when his taxi was halted by a block in the traffic.

He was suddenly aware of a squat and evil-looking face gazing through the right-hand window of the vehicle. He jumped up, but the owner of the face had disappeared. 'A Tartar, a Red Tartar,' he said aloud. 'Whatever is the fellow doing in London?'

The explorer had been bidden to a certain quiet house in Sloane Street, where he was met by his old friend, Mr Winthorpe, a high government official.

Winthorpe's manner was never serious even at the most serious moments, but on this occasion he was not quite so jovial as usual.

'Vane, I am afraid we have another job for you,' he said. 'I want you to find out what is at the bottom of these rumours that an unknown Mongol chieftain is preaching the downfall of the British Empire in the East. He is said to be a lineal descendant of Genghis Khan, that great conqueror who, six hundred years ago, devastated great empires and slew millions of people. Two of our agents have been killed, and I have very little information to give you except that old Mustapha Ali takes the matter seriously, and, as you know, he is too well-informed to pay much heed to idle rumours. You will have an absolutely free hand. We are putting our regular Intelligence services to work on the case, but you will operate independently.'

So it was that Vane, who had not been twenty-four hours in England, departed that same evening for Paris to see Mustapha Ali. On the boat, he caught sight, for the fraction of a second, of the same evil Tartar face he had seen in Knightsbridge. Clearly he was under observation.

Vane was an extraordinarily young man to have reached the position he occupied. Although a scholar with a growing reputation for a very wide knowledge of Chinese and Tartar language and habits, he was also an all-round athlete. He had studied motoring and aviation as a necessary part of his work, but he was a hefty boxer, a useful swimmer, and an excellent cricketer.

He was a deadly shot, and an expert in the old-fashioned art of fencing. He was a tall, thin, sunburnt fellow of a usual English type that you will find among subalterns in the Indian Army and police. If he had one fault, it was a recklessness, a cool recklessness which landed him into predicaments that older and more cautious men would have avoided. The mailboat was in mid-Channel, and Leslie Vane, who was too fond of sea-air to take refuge in the cabins, was leaning over the side when he felt a remorseless grip, which he knew only too well, fasten on to him, and in the twinkling of an eye he was over the side. His well-trained brain told him to dive deep, and when he came to the surface again he saw the steamship fading away into the night. He shed his boots and other clothes, congratulating himself on his habit of always carrying his money in a belt next to the body, and swam slowly towards the French coast, about eight miles distant. He was not to suffer overmuch however, for he sighted a small French patrol boat moving at a snail-like pace on the smooth Channel waters. He hailed this, and soon was clambering up a rope ladder over the low side of the boat.

A young French naval sous-lieutenant greeted him with surprise. 'A Channel swimmer?' he asked, when he had regained his equilibrium.

'Unintentionally, m'sieu.'

'But how did you get here? People do not wander about the Channel for amusement.'

'Somebody kindly pushed me over the side of the packet-boat a few minutes ago.'

The naval officer whistled. 'Well, you had better come to my cabin and put on some clothes. I can land you in Dieppe in an hour or so. But what about clothes there?'

'I have a suitcase on the packet-boat, and there will be somebody to meet me.'

Leslie then introduced himself and the young Frenchman shook hands with enthusiasm.

'I was on the China station myself some six months ago, and met you at the Officers Circle at Saigon. I remember you quite well now, but you cannot blame me for not recognising you at first. It is not usual to have one's friends rising from the bosom of the vasty deep, as your poet says.'

The officer had heard much about Vane's adventures, and when they arrived in Dieppe harbour, sent a sailor to the passenger dock to

enquire for Vane's effects. These arrived, duly accompanied by a
moustachioed gendarme of the military police and a grinning negro.
This was Mustapha's confidential servant. Vane had to give a report
to the policeman, but he ascribed his involuntary plunge as due to an
accident so as not to have to wait while a tedious police enquiry was
made. Mustapha's servant had a highly-powered racing car waiting,
and Vane was on his way to Paris without any delay. Once at Mustapha's hotel, he washed and shaved, and then awaited the presence of
that most worthy Arab. Here let me interrupt the narrative to inform
you that Mustapha Ali, merchant of Algiers, with branch establish-
ments in Marseilles, Paris, Turin and Timbuctu, was a very old and
highly respected agent of the English government. Little passed in
that great port of the world inhabited by Mohammedans of which he
did not have news. Mustapha came to business without any of the
usual Eastern floridness.

'There is a Tartar chieftain, descendant of the great Genghis
Khan, and by name Kachgar, who has dreams of a great Yellow
Empire. He has money, arms, and thousands of adherents in Europe,
besides exercising a tremendous influence in that part of Asia which
stretches from European Russia to Siberia and Mongolia, to the
great wall of China and the mighty Himalayas. You will not only
have to face physical danger, but you will have to resist the uncanny
powers of the Magic which has been handed down among the Red
Tartars from time immemorial. Secondly, beware of one of your
fellow-countrymen named Tristram Parr, who has great knowledge
of evil. He is hand-in-glove with the Red Tartars and with Kachgar.
He, too, was an explorer, and in his travels picked up some of the
unholy secrets of the Hidden East.'

Vane then told of the mysterious Mongol whom he had seen
twice, and who, he was certain, had pitched him into the sea, using
an irresistible ju-jitsu hold. Mustapha rose to bid his young friend
godspeed, and handed him a little cross in brilliants.

'Wear this. It brings luck. It will also be recognised by any of my
people, who will help you if you are in difficulties.'

Chapter 2

As Leslie Vane walked out of the hotel on to the busy Boulevard, his keen eyes caught sight of the Tartar he had already seen
twice. The man had not seen him apparently, so the explorer followed him cautiously. Evidently the man thought his work was

accomplished, that he had put the interfering white man safely out of the way.

You may ask why did this Tartar spy on Vane before the latter had accepted the Government commission. The answer is simple. Kachgar's agents knew that the English Government had learnt of their leader's activities. They had killed two of these agents, and knew that the English would follow up the affair. In China they learnt that Leslie Vane, the explorer, was going back to England, and they knew that his own Government might employ his extraordinary knowledge of the East, so they resolved to track him.

Vane 'shadowed' the yellow man carefully and for a long distance right from the boulevards off into a dingy neighbourhood near the old fortifications, a neighbourhood where the sinister Apaches prowl at night, men who are more savage than the Red Indian tribe from which they derive their name. Vane saw the Tartar slink down a quiet street and then into the doorway of a dingy house, not the usual Paris apartment house, but a sort of dilapidated two-storeyed shack. The explorer hesitated. He was not a detective, it was not his business to do the donkey work of shadowing. He did not hesitate long, however, because a hefty blow on the back of the neck knocked him very nearly silly. Now, in dealing with the Parisian Apache, you cannot use Marquis of Queensberry rules. Vane did not try. He sprang forward, crouched as low as he could, bounded to one side, and turned around rapidly with his automatic held tight against his hip lest it should be kicked out of his hand. Then he fired, for he saw before him a typical 'killer', a slim, sallow-faced, cynical degenerate with the blood-lust and a drawn knife. The Apache went down like a stricken animal. Vane rarely missed.

Vane expected people to come out of the dingy houses, but only one man appeared, and he was evidently in no hurry, nor was he of the type you might expect to find in such a locality. He was a tallish man with enormous shoulders, rather bow legs, a face with high cheekbones and a peculiar brownish-red complexion not unlike that of certain Red Indians, a thin black moustache drooping at each end.

Vane waited for the stranger to approach, and then said: 'I have had to shoot a man in self-defence. Perhaps you will be good enough to witness that he still has a knife clutched in his hand. Possibly you saw the original assault.'

The stranger said never a word, but nodded, and smiled a cynical smile. Vane was trying to guess of what nationality he was, but he finally broke silence, and in very good English said: 'Well, Mr Vane, you did perfectly right to shoot this carrion. He was a clumsy bungler. So was the man who should have left you in the Channel to commune with the fishes. I see you are too good a man to be put away like any ordinary fool of a policeman. Allow me to introduce myself. You will probably know me under the name of Kachgar. This is not my full name, but as you probably do not know the language of my people, we will leave it at that.'

Vane found a peculiarly languorous feeling stealing over him. The grim, smiling and inscrutable face of the Tartar chief seemed to grow larger and larger. Then Vane remembered a remedy to this obvious Oriental hypnotic influence. He began to work out a mathematical problem, and so concentrated on figures to the exclusion of the face. When he had fully recovered himself, he turned and said to the Tartar: 'Very clever, Mr Kachgar. It is the old trick of using a man's imagination against himself.'

The Tartar smiled. 'You are a worthy foeman. It is a pity to have to kill a man of your brains. When I say "pity", I do not mean to use this word in the usual sense, for no strong man has pity.'

'And is that why your ancestor built the pyramid of a million heads?' asked Vane.

'Probably to impress his soldiers. Other and more modern people like the Bolsheviks in Russia have tried the same methods. When I rule, then I shall do the thing properly,' and Kachgar's eyes flashed.

'Well, good-day. I shall undoubtedly see you again soon,' said Vane, not quite knowing how to deal with one of the most extraordinary situations that had ever arisen in his young life.

'Not so quickly, Mr Vane . . . ' and the Tartar whistled. The first note had hardly disturbed the quiet air of the dingy street when half-a-dozen men dashed out of a nearby house and came full pelt at the two men. Vane dodged backwards and fired quickly. Two of the foremost assailants dropped in their tracks. He then turned on his heel and ran for dear life, oblivious of Kachgar. He sensed that he had been very nearly caught in a trap, and remaining in it would not have served him. This was a case of 'he who lives to run away will live to fight another day.'

He telephoned to Mustapha, who was surprised at the information the young explorer gave him. The old Arab then advised Vane: 'Go back to London immediately. I can see why Kachgar is over here. Keep your eyes on Tristram Parr. He is the weak link in a very dangerous chain. You will have to play these people at their own game. I shall not be able to help you much. They are sorcerers.'

You see, Mustapha, in spite of all his worldly wisdom, still remained a child of the desert, and believed most wholeheartedly in witchcraft and black magic. Vane smiled to himself. 'I think I can manage Mr Parr without very much loss of nervous energy; still, one never knows.' And so to the Gare St Lazare to catch the night train for London. There was no need for him to fly across the Channel. He argued that Kachgar's agents would be watching the aviation stations more than the railways.

Directly the explorer arrived in London he went to a dirty-looking house in Chinatown. Here was a man, Yun T'zu, who was a member of one of the famous Chinese Tongs or secret societies named the White Lily, and it happened that Vane was 'protected' by this Tong because of his kindness in China to certain Chinese who were in danger of death. Yun T'zu was a man of many parts. In a few words he grasped the situation, with the result that a tall Chinaman, who looked like one of the soldier-Manchus from the North, stole out of a house about two hundred yards away from that into which Vane had entered. He had with him a long strip of crimson flimsy paper on which were printed symbols in Indian ink. Vane was going to play a very dangerous game. Everything now rested on the chance of his being able to pass as a Chinaman from the North among a meeting of very clever men from the East. In short, he was going to visit the house of Tristram Parr, the meeting of the adherents of Kachgar, as a delegate from the White Lily Tong, which hitherto had been hostile to the blandishments of the Tartar chief.

He wondered how to get information through to Winthorpe without exciting suspicion, when to his delight he saw Old Bill 'Awkins, the veteran taxi-driver, prowling about the West India Dock Road, swearing in a loud tone at the ''eathern neighbourhood'. The Manchu lurched against his cab.

'Out of it, yer blinkin' chow-chow . . . ' began Bill, but his flow of language was stopped for a moment by a quiet voice saying to him: 'Keep on swearing, Bill, you old devil. This is Leslie Vane. Get back to Mr Winthorpe in Sloane Street as soon as you can, and tell him that I shall be at Parr's house near Oxford Street. Ask him to take precautions. He will understand. Go on swearing.'

'Lawluvaduk . . . Yus I understands . . . Go away, yer blinkin' rat-eater, else I'll kosh yer. 'Op it, Sing Loo, or whatever yer name is.

Fancy a blear-eyed Chink gettin' tight when an 'onest shofur who once erpon a time drove the Dook of Seven Dials carn't git a livin'.'

Bill's cab disappeared into the London night, and the drunken Manchu picked himself together, and vanished rapidly when he espied the advancing form of a policeman.

At the house near Oxford Street, a sleek servant of Oriental type, but in evening clothes, was opening the door to all sorts of visitors. There were bearded men in fur coats, obviously Russians, enigmatical Chinamen, grimacing Japanese, Arabs, Hindus, a negro or so, also a few white men. Mr Parr, the well-known Occultist, was giving a 'do', and the policeman on duty outside the house saluted several very distinguished people he recognised. He had previously been well 'tipped' by Parr's confidential servant.

In the large and luxurious hall on the ground floor of Parr's house was a species of altar erected in front of three thrones. The main body of the hall was occupied by chairs and divans. On the three thrones were seated Parr, Kachgar, and a very old, shrivelled-up man who looked as if he had lived a thousand years.

There was evidently to be some sort of religious ceremonial when the servant who had been admitting the guests came up to Parr, made obeisance, and said: 'Master, there is a strange Chinaman who demands admittance. He comes from this, so he says,' and the servant handed up to Parr a long strip of crimson flimsy paper inscribed with hieroglyphics. Parr knitted his brows for a moment, and then handed the strip over to Kachgar, who also looked puzzled. The Tartar chief in turn transferred the strip over to the aged man, a priest of the Ancient Wisdom of the Tartars. This veteran simply said in a cracked voice devoid of all tone and emotion: 'Admit the brother of the White Lily.'

The tall Manchu advanced towards the three Great Ones, and made obeisance in a perfunctory manner.

'Who are you, Manchu dog?' snarled the ancient priest.

'One who bears knowledge. I have come in search of knowledge, so that I may find the truth,' was the curious answer.

Parr, who understood the Mandarin dialect of Chinese in which this conversation had been held, was impressed. 'Kachgar, we have another wise man of the East. He has some of the Wisdom Which Is Not To Be Revealed. I can tell by his answer.'

The Tartar said little. 'I am not at all assured, my dear Parr. I do not understand this sudden sending of an emissary from the White Lily Tong.'

Parr smiled. 'Kachgar, you are of the East, eastern, but you are not a Chinaman. You are a fighting Tartar with little use for the wandering subtleties of the Chinaman, who is student more than a soldier. Even these Manchus, who came from the North, are now beneath contempt as soldiers. Let this fellow enter, and then impress him with your power. Thus you will make a convert to your cause, and add very valuable adherents to your forces.'

The Tartar smiled his grim smile. 'Cunning as ever, oh my friend the Sorcerer. Are you going to weave some of your magic spells?'

Parr laughed. 'To us has been given the ancient knowledge. Is there any reason why we should not use it. I dream of another Genghis Khan who will destroy this proud Empire, who will humiliate the men who have humiliated me . . . ' He jumped out of his seat, for the Manchu was intoning a chant, a chant which was old long before Julius Caesar landed in Britain, which was old before the Pharaohs of Egypt built the Pyramids, and many of the Orientals in the audience recognised it. He spoke to the Manchu in the sacred tongue, but that worthy took no notice of him whatsoever and went on chanting.

Kachgar's suspicions had been aroused, however, and he preferred his own judgment to that of Parr, the renegade Englishman.

'Look out! Behind you, Mr Vane,' he suddenly cried in English, but the stranger went on chanting without flicking an eyelid.

Several of the older men exchanged greetings with the chanter when he had finished, but Parr asked him to retire to an outer room while the council discussed private business.

Alone in a beautifully furnished room full of priceless Eastern antiquities, the stranger smiled ever so slightly.

He had recognised one of Mahomet's men among the secret council, and knew that he would now have information on which he could act. One of the Chinese or Tartar watchers at the entrance to the house came hurrying through the room, a look of fear on his face. It flashed across Vane's mind that this man had been informed or had seen some of Winthorpe's men, probably detectives from the special branch of Scotland Yard, so he waited until the man was passing him, and gripped him in a stranglehold. The man was helpless, and his body went limp, although he was not unconscious.

Vane speedily bound him with his own scarf, rammed a handkerchief into his mouth, and pushed him under a pile of silken stuffs on a couch in the corner of the room. He then hurried downstairs to see the other attendant gazing out of a spy hole in the door. With a flying leap, he landed on the Tartar, and his deadly ju-jitsu grip rendered the man unconscious. Vane then hurried out into the street and uttered a low moaning cry. A slim figure glided towards him. It was Smith of Scotland Yard, dressed like a street hawker. In the distance, Vane could see two burly workmen hustling a struggling form into a cab.

'We have collared one of the "look-outs", explained Smith.

'Quick, upstairs with you,' whispered the false Manchu. Two other men appeared like magic from nowhere, and following Vane installed themselves in the waiting room. 'It is no use trying the door which leads to the council chamber,' whispered the explorer. 'We must wait until I am summoned in again. Is there a cordon round the house?'

'Yes.'

The iron door which opened into the council room opened slowly, and Vane stalked up to it with dignity, though his heart was beating furiously. A voice bade him enter, and he was on the point of passing through when Kachgar in a voice ringing with fury, ordered 'Shut that door at once.' An alarm signal was ringing in a corner of the council chamber. Vane pushed against the door with all his might, and the three detectives came to his help. A desperate struggle ensued. At last when Vane felt that his strength was exhausted, the partially-opened door opened wide into the council chamber, where Parr was standing alone with a sardonic smile on his face.

'And what may this intrusion mean, gentlemen?' he asked with a sneer.

'Quick, sound the panels of the room. There is an emergency exit, probably into some adjoining house,' gasped Vane. He then spied a small piece of paper on the floor in the far corner of the room. He jumped to get it just as Parr moved towards it.

It was a message from Mahomet's man. 'Try third panel beyond this, and also raid next house,' read Vane. He turned to Smith and read the message to him. Instantly one of the detectives dashed out to notify the other police watchers, and Smith and the explorer began to search the carving on the third panel for a possible secret spring. The other detective interposed himself between Parr and the door. 'Detain Mr Parr,' ordered Vane. 'Yes, on my responsibility.' In speaking, he turned his head away from the panel on which was carved a wonderful Chinese figure of a dragon. His fingers touched and pressed its eyeball and the panel began to slide, leaving a blank. Smith switched on an electric torch, and Vane could see a flight of stairs. 'You stop here, Smith, and if you do not hear from me in half an hour, send reinforcements along. If it is a trap, it is not right for both of us to be caught.' Cautiously the explorer crept down the stairs. As he reached the last step, he placed his right foot very cautiously on the ground immediately below. Some half-forgotten memory of a secret passage in Italy had prompted him to do this, and very fortunate it was for him that he did. The square flag-stone gave to the pressure and sank, leaving a gap some seven feet by eight. At Vane's right hand was a blank wall, on his left a passage. In front of him, past the gap, another blank wall.

'Now, I wonder . . .' said the explorer to himself. 'To go up the passage would be obvious.' He pressed the wall on his right, reaching as far forward as he dared. The wall gave way suddenly, and a portion of it swung back, revealing a brilliantly lighted room furnished in a most comfortable English fashion. Vane leapt over the angle of the gap and advanced slowly.

To his alarm, he saw a huge mastiff of most savage aspect rise to its feet from behind some curtains which evidently concealed a door leading further on. Now, Vane had a curious gift which some people might term (and incorrectly) hypnotism. He could subdue most animals, probably because he liked animals and always treated them kindly. So he concentrated his will on the mastiff and stared at him for five long minutes. The animal came to him, sized him up, and licked his hand. As Vane advanced, so it came by his side, and seemed to wish to protect him rather than impede him. He thrust aside the curtains, and stepped into what was a sort of comfortable basement kitchen of the kind you can see in large London private houses. He then sought a staircase to the upper floors, the dog following him all the time. He found the staircase, and advanced cautiously, this time with an automatic gripped in his right hand. He emerged into a hallway, and tried the various doors on either side of this. He calculated that he was on the ground floor of the house, but could not see or find the front door. Hearing or seeing nothing to reveal the presence of the Tartar conspirators, he went on up the staircase to the next floor. He could hear a very faint sound of chanting, and smell incense. The dog thrust its muzzle into his left hand, and growled very faintly. 'All right, old chap,' whispered the explorer. 'We will go carefully.' He tried the handle of a door on his immediate right and opened it slowly and found himself in a little ante-room. It was then he remembered where he was.

Some years beforehand, a world-famous gambler had opened a gaming house which the police had never been able to raid success-fully. It was only on the death of the gambler that they had found that the house was divided into two absolutely separate halves. The entry to the back portion was down a passage leading from a mews. This was the passage Vane had already seen. He had been with the detectives on their tour of exploration and had come down that very passage. He remembered that the ante-room led into the principal gambling hall, once the ball-room of a great nobleman.

The door which separated the two had a spy-hole through which an attendant looked at every visitor, even those who were perfectly well known as patrons of the gambling establishment. Evidently the secret council of the Tartars was being held in the ballroom. Vane determined to return to Smith and get help. He had been away a bare quarter of an hour, but it seemed to him a lifetime. He crept cautiously back; as he began to descend the staircase, he was collared so that he could neither move or cry out. A most unexpected ally came to his rescue. With a savage growl, the mastiff sprang at Vane's silent assailant, who let go at once. The mastiff had him by the throat and was worrying him. Vane sped on his way, and met with no further opposition. Up the stone steps, he ran back into the original council chamber. Here he found a crowd of detectives and two or three men of the Government service, including Winthorpe in person.

'By George, laddie, we thought you were a goner, and were on the point of starting to avenge you . . . ' began that gentleman, when the explorer interrupted him:

'There is no time to be lost. Station men at once in Carbury mews and in the passage which leads to the back of the late Lord Carbury's house. Be careful of the death trap, which should still be open. Then enter the house from the front, which is in Wynter Street. Get axes, as you will have to chop through the partition between the two parts of the house. It is no good going to the house next to this. There is nothing there of interest to us.'

Several detectives departed at once, and then Vane said: 'Come along, Smith. We will go and investigate on our own.'

Half-a-dozen men crept after the explorer, and soon were in the Carbury mansion. There was no trace to be found of the mastiff, or of the man he had attacked. The investigators went through every room, including the big dance-room, where they found traces of a heathen ceremony, including an altar. They managed to open the door of this, which led to the front part of the house, and ran into the arms of another body of detectives. They were debating the next move, when one of the police watchers came running in.

'Some men have just gone out of the servants' entrance round corner and are getting into two large racing cars,' he gasped.

The detectives dashed off, and passers-by opened their eyes in astonishment as the Scotland Yard men clambered into their waiting cars, accompanied by a strange figure in Eastern dress.

'A film stunt,' declared a wise youth, but his words were belied by the yells of a tall, stout man who was endeavouring to get away from a mastiff who gripped him tightly by the left arm.

'That's Tristram Parr,' bawled Vane. But there was no need for the Scotland Yard car to stop. Two plainclothes policemen had already hold of Parr, and the dog reluctantly relinquished his grip. Smith did stop the car however, leaving the one ahead of them to carry on the chase. 'I must get back to give instructions so that the ports may be watched,' he told Vane. The explorer ran over to the little group of Parr and the two policemen. 'I want that dog,' he said, but he had no need to say much, for the mastiff bounded joyously over to him. Vane could understand the animal's mind. It had undoubtedly been brutally treated so as to make it savage, and it had turned against its masters and was ready to follow the human who would treat it kindly. The explorer chartered a taxi, and together with the mastiff returned to his rooms, which he always kept in London though he so rarely occupied them.

'Been to a fancy dress ball, sir?' asked the caretaker with a grin as he gave Vane the keys.

'Something like it,' replied Vane, with a smile.

Next evening the explorer, thoroughly recovered from the various incidents of the past few days, sauntered to his Club, dressed in the evening clothes of civilisation. The mastiff had escaped somehow, and insisted on following him, rather to Vane's annoyance, who reflected, however, that he could chain him up in an adjoining garage.

There had been no news of Kachgar and band. Parr was in hospital watched by the police, and had given no information. Vane took a short cut through Soho to the West End, and was going through a little-frequented passage near Berwick Street when he heard the mastiff growl, and turning, saw it spring at a man a few yards behind him. Another man then rushed at Vane, disabling his right arm with the vicious blow of a life-preserver of eel-skin and lead. Vane tried to break away from the savage blows which were raining down at him, but was in pretty bad shape when that most invaluable mastiff left the man he had attacked at first and sprang at Vane's assailant. It was all over bar the shouting.

Among the little crowd that had gathered was a detective, who sent a boy for a uniformed constable and an ambulance.

The two men were taken away, and the detective explained that he had received instructions to follow Vane in case the explorer should be attacked by the gang. Kachgar and company were probably endeavouring to escape by sea, but the minor agents of the conspiracy who were in London would still receive the orders of their masters. Picking up the life-preserver, the detective said: 'One hit of that across the skull or the neck and you would have been in very bad shape, Mr Vane.'

'Well, my arm feels pretty nearly broken as it is,' answered the explorer, who followed the sleuth to Charing Cross Hospital, where the doctor on duty after examination reported that there was nothing broken, but that the forearm had been very seriously bruised, and that Vane was not to use it for some time. Vane had taken the blow on his very well-developed muscle. Had he turned his forearm at all the bone would have been undoubtedly broken. 'They wanted to kill you without noise,' said the detective. 'I think you'd better go and stop at Mr Winthorpe's. He told me to ask you to go there in case of any trouble.'

Chapter 3

When Vane arrived at Mr Winthorpe's house in Sloane Street, he found the Government official looking very serious, a rare thing for him. He handed over to the explorer the *Evening News*, which had an account of the discovery of the body of a middle-aged Arab near Clacton. 'That was Mahomet's man,' said Winthorpe. 'It was very fortunate we broke up Kachgar's band. Let us be thankful for that. I have evidence here of a gigantic plot against England. As a matter of fact, Kachgar fixed this very day for a revolt to break out in India, where he has thousands of adherents. As far as we can judge, he has taken refuge on the East Coast, and is waiting to put out to sea. Now, the Air Ministry have offered to lend me a machine . . . '

Winthorpe hesitated. Vane understood that the Government official wished him to go out, yet did not like to ask him to do so because of his injured arm.

'Tell me something more definite,' he said.

'Well, there is a yacht cruising off the East Coast, and we have reason to believe that it belongs to Kachgar or one of his adherents. It is outside the three mile limit, so we can take no police action. I am asking you to break the law and take a big risk, but we want to deal with Kachgar. He is a very great danger.'

Vane jumped to his feet. 'I'm your man,' he cried. Two hours later he was standing by the side of a gigantic seaplane in which was seated a very well-known flying officer who originally had served in the Navy, where he was known by the nickname of 'Stinker'. There were thermos flasks full of hot coffee and a bundle of sandwiches on board. Vane clambered inside the machine, while a capable-looking young mechanic got into the observation seat. The seaplane was then pushed slowly down to the water, and soon rose. In a few minutes they were over the open sea, racing at full speed. The seaplane was a beauty, and was as docile as a well-trained lady's hack under 'Stinker's' expert and loving pilotage. They flew up the East Coast, keeping eyes open for a long, fast-looking, black yacht, which was suspected to be the vessel in which Kachgar was to escape from England so as to bring about his schemes for the destruction of the Empire. It was Vane who spotted a swift motor boat ploughing out to sea. The mechanic then espied the yacht, and the seaplane descended in a spiral flight. Aboard the motor boat was Kachgar threatening and cajoling the mechanic who was driving it. The Tartar chieftain heard the seaplane, and as it reached the water, he pulled out a Service revolver, and let drive at the 'plane and its occupants. Vane forgot all about his injured arm, and fired back. One of the crew of the boat threw up his arms and spun off into the water. Another dived overboard deliberately. Kachgar reloaded his revolver, and took a long aim at Vane. The 'plane was now floating on the water, and the motor boat was only a few yards from it. Vane unloosened the safety belt, threw off his heavy flying suit, and dived into the water. Before Kachgar had realised what was happening, Vane had grasped him, and dragged him over the side. The Tartar could not swim, and lost his nerve. Vane hit him a desperate punch so as to make him stop struggling, and swam with him back to the seaplane.

The observer was busy signalling, and the occupants of the motor boat did not stop to rescue Kachgar. They sped on their way to the yacht and safety.

The occupants of the seaplane did not have to wait long. A naval motor boat soon reached them, and took them aboard, towing the 'plane back to harbour.

The Tartar was still unconscious apparently, and watch over him was relaxed. Just before they got into harbour, he gave a convulsive spring and jumped into the sea. He rose twice, and the boat put about to rescue him. Two of the sailors jumped into the water, but they were too late to rescue the man who had wished to smash up England. He died bravely.

Tristram Parr, the renegade, was still in hospital, and as he had degenerated into a sort of imbecile, the Government decided not to prosecute. Vane treasures a diamond pin, the gift of a very great gentleman indeed, and Mr Winthorpe is as affable as ever. But Vane does not want any more 'special employment' for some time to come. He is having a really well-deserved holiday, and I dare say you could see him playing cricket any Saturday afternoon if you knew which ground to go to.

Waste Manor

L. ADAMS BECK

This story was told me by the man who had lived through its strange experiences. Part of it may be read, I think, by the light of modern western psychology, but the greater part stretches out into that vast ocean of wisdom of which India and her daughter-nations hold the chart – they and no others. For myself, I have long since formed my own opinion. I leave it to others to form theirs.

The man was a descendant of one of the old English families of Cumberland; by every instinct and tradition a gentleman. I met him on one of my many voyages from Marseilles to the East on a Japanese Nippon Yusen Kaisha liner which I shall call the *Hana Maru*.

To my secretary and me seats were allotted at a little table for three in the corner of the dining saloon. We looked at the third seat with the traveller's hope that something pleasant would come of its owner. That is always likely on board the Japanese boats, for the company is full of interest to those who love their Asia. Men of the great Japanese families, diplomats, soldiers, sailors, professors, students, artists, and many more are always coming and going on the long blue highway which begins in London and ends at Yokohama. I have made lasting friendships between port and port and have opened many a shut Asiatic door.

But it was an Englishman who walked quickly up to the table as the busy little waiters were serving the soup. He was of middle height, dark-haired with deep-set dark eyes under brows straight as bars across a noticeable forehead. The face was intellectual and over-sensitive. I felt certain of two things – that he had been ill recently and that he had hoped for Japanese company where ignorance of his language would leave him in untroubled quiet.

He bowed coldly, said his name was Wendover, and relapsed into silence.

But on such a voyage continued silence becomes impossible, and little interests sprang up along the Mediterranean as he realised gradually that we were harmless and had plenty of interests of our own to keep us going. The door of separation moved on its hinges. It appeared that he was in the Indian Civil Service, that he shared my love of Asiatic art, that he had of late taken up the study of Indian thought, and was a really deep student of history. These were bridges upon which real communion might pass to and fro, and I grew to like him, to understand that the realities which lie below the level of daily life were more to his taste than the surface which is enamelled so smoothly and coldly that not a living root may ever grow in it, nor flower blossom.

Sometimes he would sit with me on deck when stars were lucent in the black polished marble of the sea, silent more often than not in a world of his own, and I knew instinctively that he had thoughts worth hearing if ever they should float up to the surface, like bodies long drowned and lost to the world of the living. Indeed there was something poignant and melancholy about the man which marked him out from others.

We had long passed the narrow gut of the Suez Canal and were far down the Red Sea, ploughing past the wildly peaked and pinnacled islands which lie lonely as death with sundering seas washing on desolate shores. Weirdly coloured and beautiful they rise, flat against the sky as painted scenery from the harsh blue of the sea and pale sands.

It was sunset and they stood stark against the burning gold of the west. Oceans of gold billowed upon them from the sinking sun like a triumph of victorious gods. They took on splendour as though a flame in their hearts responded to the awful glory.

Wendover came along the deck and leaned his arms on the rail, absorbed, unconscious of any life about him.

Such a crisis of Nature's passion cannot last long, and very swiftly the wild pomp faded and night was gliding over the western sea to imprison the world in her net of stars. Then he turned and came slowly to me, his face still vibrant with a kind of pale triumph.

'That was orchestral. A mighty music!' he said.

The evening star emerged like a bird's clear song after thunder. He listened to its unstruck music for a moment, then spoke again abruptly: 'I've had a strange experience in England. That appealed to it.'

'And you are coming back to India for the clue?' I asked. 'She holds all the clues of the soul.'

'That's true. True.'

It is indeed. How many have I known coming consciously or unconsciously that India may unravel their destiny and free them from the complexities of the West! There they may sit, holding the hand of the Mighty Mother, looking from beneath her brooding brows into the all-revealing mirror where each man may, to his peace or terror, see himself as he is in naked truth.

That night he began the story which I am permitted to tell here. I give it in my own words because it came by fits and starts as if some inward spring welled and subsided. There were hints, implications, and these he looked to me to understand. Sometimes a word helped him to understand himself and he would look at me gratefully and say: 'Yes – that's it. That explains.'

So, though I add nothing whatever, I give here and there a little comprehension. But I am a voice, no more. The story is not mine. I shall give his name as Stephen Wendover. Obviously it cannot be the real one. His age was thirty-eight. The family house and lands had been sold in his boyhood. He had but one relation – a sister living in Australia whom he had not seen for twenty years. These are the preliminaries.

Rather more than a year before our meeting he was in England on a year's leave after a sharp attack of malaria, and needing rest of all things he went down to Tanswyke, a small village under the Sussex Downs for a couple of month's fishing. That was the excuse. Drowsing and dreaming in the great woods which clothe the valleys beneath the downs were the real aim.

It was that rare delight in England, a perfect summer, calm and laden with country scents, the flowers in cottage gardens floating like birds upon still air. In that of the old inn, old as the Plantagenets, where he lived they were almost unbearably sweet.

He had a little guide-book of the district for his strolls and noted in it the names of the stately parks and manors carved out of what appeared to have once been the mighty inheritance of one family – the Thorolds of Bydon.

'The Thorolds of Bydon,' said the little book, 'seem for the last three hundred years to have chosen the losing side in war and politics. They had already incurred the wrath of Henry VIII and Elizabeth, and in her reign the great Tudor mansion was dismantled and from the remains were built great walls enclosing a much reduced park and a comparatively small but beautiful house suited to their fallen fortunes. In their later misfortunes this house also fell into ruin, the estate dwindled into four acres of garden, and this patch of ground has lately been bought by Lord Wickington, first baron and owner of Wickington Park, once a part of the great Thorold estates. But a very curious fact is that the family has always attributed its ill luck to the marriage of a Thorold in the reign of Henry III with an heiress of the Tracy family whose father had led three knights to the murder of the saint and archbishop Thomas à Becket in Canterbury Cathedral in the year 1170. It is well known that a curse was pronounced on the de Tracy family that neither they nor any of their descendants should ever know prosperity thereafter, and it is certain that the Thorolds never throve after the de Tracy blood ran in their veins. Waste Manor is now a fern-clad heap of ruins. *Sic transit gloria mundi*.' With this Latin tag the guide-book story ended as guide-books will.

But it left a kind of dim pity on Wendover's mind as he thought of the stately houses in their waving woods and acred gardens flaming with blossom, flaring with hothouses, where the new-made knights and peers whose glories were founded on bacon and oil and alcohol, shone resplendent, and the last four acres of the Thorolds were swallowed up by Lord Wickington, formerly Jimmy Jicks, proprietor of Jicks's Vitamin Cattle-Food.

'Lord save us!' said Wendover to himself. 'I wonder if the Thorold ghosts come and gibber at night in at Jimmy's windows. I would if it were me.'

He sat in the little coffee-room of the Crosslets under the pewter plates in glimmering rows on the rough oak dresser, as Mrs Eves, the landlady, came in with a question about his day's fishing.

'Too much sunshine, and water as clear as a looking-glass. Nothing doing,' he said. But he hadn't wanted to do anything except lie under the hazels and blink at the shining little river. He had hidden his basket and rod and forgotten them and drowsed away the day except when he ate his luncheon and flung his crumbs to the Jicks pheasants, tame as the fowls at the Jicks model farm. Something in him thrilled responsive to something in the green solitude, and he camped there and drowsed until dusk hung in the trees like smoke.

'It looks as if the whole countryside had been forest,' he said to Mrs Eves. 'Did it all belong to the Thorolds?'

The taproom was full of babbling rustics, but she had a spare minute. 'Lord, yes, sir! They owned from here to Corrington in the old ancient days, but they never had no luck after one of them married a Tracy. It's said the Tracys killed some bishop down to Canterbury and they got a curse on them heavy enough to sink a man-of-war. Anyhow it sank the Thorolds all right. They was great court cards once. Lord Wickington bought the last four acres from Mr Thorold before he died.'

'And whereabouts was Waste Manor?' Wendover was glad to hear Thorold was dead. That would be less bitter than life for a man who honoured the past.

'That's hard to make out unless you know the lie of the land. It's to the west through the park, all overgrown with trees, and you come on it all of a sudden. But there's nothing to see, without it's great heaps of old bricks all overgrown with bushes and stuff.'

Wendover sat alone, smoking and thinking until the moon came lamping over the woods, drowning the stars in pale glory.

'Queen and Huntress, chaste and fair' – he could picture her glimmering through the long glades and wished he could follow her flying feet. At last he turned in, with a window wide to the moonlight and fruit-smelling honeysuckle and roses, and slept in a maze of dreams changing as softly as the shadows of breathing boughs on the walls.

Next day it seemed necessary to retrieve the basket and rod, and a notion possessed him that he would like to see that pathetic little four acres, now swept into the rich man's pocket with all the rest. He thought of the curse as he went up the narrow winding lane between deep clematis-wreathed hedges and so into the woods. Remember he had lived in India where the curse of a holy man may be a thing more real than the food you eat. In the girdling of the Himalayas it would not seem strange that it should blot out the light from the eyes of the murderer's descendants. Why not? In the reckoning of the gods is neither past nor future. For them the spilt blood still lay in pools on the pavement, the consequences of the deed still rippled outward like the rings in rudely disturbed water. Crime is the root, and misery the blossoming, of that deadly nightshade. It is impossible to live in India with open eyes and miss these implications. Even if you do not believe them, they colour all the air.

So thinking, he went to the nook of meadowsweet where he had left his basket. It was gone. Some mischievous boy must have made his own of it. No matter. Wendover got out his book – the *Chronicle of Walter of Lincoln*, an old monkish history – and half read, half dreamed the hours away in a spot where the ancient chronicler himself might have fished for the abbot's Friday dinner. Rest sank into his blood as he followed the story of the red Plantagenet, Henry II. 'A king very passionate, round-headed, showing a lionous visage, strong, light, hardy, and amorous with women,' the lover of Fair Rosamond and many more. He turned to the scene where the fierce anger of Henry blazed out against the unyielding archbishop, Thomas à Becket, and grinding his teeth until the foam-flakes fell from his lips he summoned de Tracy and his three knights, de Morville, le Breton, and Fitzurse, crying, 'Who will rid me of this proud priest?'

Without let or halt they mounted and galloped to Canterbury, and there in his own cathedral, before the very face of the Crucified God upon the altar, they closed round him as he stood haughty on the steps above them, and they broke his skull and pierced his heart and left him lying in his blood before the unchanging gaze of God.

A great story, greatly told in the sonorous monkish Latin. It possessed Wendover.

He laid the book on the grass and dreamed awake of the noble arcades of the vast cathedral echoing to the onset, for Thomas had defended himself with his crosier like a man of the Lord of Hosts Who is the God of Battles. He could see the four, maddened by their own blood-lust, devil-driven, hacking with Norman swords at the dying man, wild with hurry lest the awful Figure on the Cross should strike them into worse than death and drive them shrieking from the holy precincts.

Now it was done, and the unchanging Face followed them as with slowly invading terror rising about them like chill water, the tumult of their yells died in the dead quiet of the church, and they rode back for their reward. They received instead wrath and curses from the king turned craven at the thought of the wide world's horror. Outcast they would live, outcast die. Did any Nemesis haunt them in careless England later or did all the hate and fear drift into nothingness?

He sat and thought of these things and ate his food and drowsed again in the heavenly cool of leaves, and the shadows lengthened, and at last some shadow of pain or fear startled him awake to see day dead, the dusk in the trees, and a woman in white coming down the long glade. She carried his basket. Still weak from illness he got on his feet and went to meet her.

It seemed that they met in the deeps of a green ocean. The topmost leaves swaying in twilight were the ripple of the surface. The shadows below were its profundities. He thought she seemed to float in dim green light as she came on. Perhaps he was still a little confused with sleep.

(I remember Wendover paused here as the moonlight swept the flying waves with silver and a lost island drifted by us like a ghost. I asked if she were beautiful – a woman's question. He could not say. It was certain he had never seen anyone who conveyed the same impression, and that impression he was quite unable to define. She was pale and her eyes extinguished all the rest but the black background of her hair. They conveyed absolute and watchful stillness like those of a wild creature on guard – unwavering and fixed but intensely alert. That was all he could tell me, except that his feeling was one of extreme constraint amounting almost to a slight repulsion.)

'We found your basket in the copse last night and kept it for you. One of us saw you hide it and knew it was yours.' She tendered it gravely. Her words gave him a strange sensation. He had thought himself absolutely alone all day and had taken his ease as a man does in solitude. No one likes to think that curious eyes have been upon him in those conditions.

'I'm extremely grateful,' he said with reserve, 'especially since you've been good enough to bring it to me. I hope it wasn't much trouble. Do you live near?'

'Near,' she answered. Then, looking at him with a steadiness that caught his eyes and held them: 'You should not sleep here. It is dangerous.'

He noticed then that she spoke with a curious deliberation which seemed foreign, avoiding all the little contractions of daily speech. It was as though she repeated a lesson and with some effort. But the matter of her words took his attention from the manner.

'Dangerous? But how could that be?' he asked in astonishment.

'Perhaps you would not understand. One of us watched you all the time.'

One of 'us'? Of what strange family? She added: 'There are heavy dews here. Your clothes are wet, and as you have been ill – '

He stared at her in ever-growing amazement. Certainly there was a drenching dew, but why should she care and –

'How do you know I've been ill?' he asked suspiciously. The interview grew stranger every moment.

'You are ill now. You should not sleep here. It is dangerous. You should come and sleep in our house.'

She spoke with a kind of authority, her face and figure growing dimmer in the dusk. His astonishment was so great that it took the form of deep anxiety, as if he must safeguard himself from some danger. And yet there was nothing alarming in her words. They were unusual. That was all.

'I'm really very much obliged, but as it's getting dark I must be moving on. It's four miles to the village and – '

'It is much more than four miles. You would be unlikely to reach the village before tomorrow morning. Perhaps not then. You do not know the place.'

'I beg your pardon. I come here often. I know the way as well as I know – ' His voice failed suddenly. Was he so sure he knew? Something was closing in upon him. Perhaps the coming dark gave the trees the effect of marching, of drawing nearer and nearer. That something in him was himself yet not himself and it began to be afraid.

She replied: 'We know you come here. We have seen you. But you would not know the way back. You had better come with me.'

'But I beg your pardon. I go down here and turn to the left and – ' She drew back as if to let him pass.

'Try.'

Wendover made a few steps forward. Did he recognise that huge clump of pyramidal hollies, stiff as if shears had trimmed them? Did he know that alley of yews clipped into fantastic shapes? A thin light stole through the trees from a rising moon. Could that be a lawn – and a sun-dial? No, surely. Impossible. Only vague shadows. But he halted and turned, confused.

'You're right. Sorry. Somehow I don't know. But unless I walked in my sleep – ' He hesitated.

'We know you did not do that. The forest changes at night. It is better for strangers not to stay out in it . . . '

She was standing some paces from him. Her voice sounded cold and strange as the sound of a distant bell. The sense of a far greater distance than appeared crept from the inmost of the outer self and gripped him – something alien such as a man might feel on landing in an utterly unknown country among people inhumanly different. But her attitude had nothing menacing. It seemed to be watchfully passive. She waited.

'But the thing's ridiculous!' he said loudly, to hearten himself. 'Of course I know the way. You go down that glade, and turn to the left – no, to the right. No – not that glade. That one. At least – ' He turned about helplessly. His brain swam, and it was growing dark. What was he fighting against? Resisting, and uselessly?

'Couldn't one of you show me the way?' It became of immense importance to him that he should get back, yet he could not tell why.

'We never go to the village. The roads are not safe. You are in danger at this moment.'

They stood looking at one another. Were they testing each other's strength? He could not even be sure she looked at him at all. It was too dark. He spoke at last with difficulty, conquered.

'It's really very good of you and I suppose I must accept your hospitality. I mean I'm most grateful, but a stranger doesn't like to give so much trouble, and if you had a gardener or anybody who could come as far as the – '

'The gardeners all went a long time ago. You are not a stranger. We saw the name on your basket. Wendover. One of our people married a Wendover – a great many years ago. Do you remember?'

(He stopped here to tell me he had never been a man who cared for pedigrees and such things. There was a pedigree at his lawyer's office in London, but he had never looked at it.)

He shook his head helplessly at her question. 'Sorry. I don't know a thing about it. Who was it? Perhaps I've heard.'

She moved slowly towards the clipped yews, if yews they were, and he could do nothing but follow. She spoke over her shoulder. Was he walking in sleep? The air was heavy with dream.

'It was in 1624. Your ancestress Sophia Wendover. She married one of us – Sir Aylmer Tracy. Her daughter Cicely Tracy married her cousin, a Wendover. No, you are not a stranger.'

He could neither contradict nor assent, but it seemed to matter to him more than anything in his life – more even than the terrible strangeness of his loneliness with this unknown guide in the night and the phantasmal unreality of the tall hollies and clipped bushes shining in vague moonlight through which they passed. A lawn with the rabbits loping over it – could it be? Never – that was the glade down which he passed daily to the village. But the village seemed as distant now as the cold moon lost in arid space.

'Is this the garden?' he asked at last.

'It is what you see.' She went steadily onward.

'And the house? We seem to be going deep into the wood.'

'It is beyond those black hollies. You would never find it. People never come here. I am often in the wood at night but no one comes.'

'But you said the wood was dangerous.'

'Not for us,' she said and added strangely, and with what he took for glee, 'But the people at the big house find it dangerous. Lord Wickington is rotting with cancer. The heir is demented and the daughter is worse. I tell you the place is dangerous.'

She turned and looked at him, and so strange a light gleamed from her eyes that he shrank. She grew bolder now that they were in unknown ways. But he was too bewildered to think of flight.

Was it a garden or a long grassy glade? To use Wendover's strange phrase, it appeared to pulsate between the one and the other and he could not tell from one moment to the next. There were great walls of ancient brick mossed and plumed with fern. Were they broken here or there or lost in gulfs of darkness? He thought, but was not sure, that there were gaps filled with hazels and tangled rose-bushes, wild and tall. Half circling the walls ran a little river – the one in which he had fished so often, but it looked strange in the moonlight.

There were dim relics of splendour, a noble iron gate where gilding glittered still on the bars. It was two-winged and pillared, and on either pillar a stealthy griffin drenched his recumbent stone coils in shadow. Trees, trees, everywhere drowning out the light. The place had gathered ill about it, an opiate breath unlike the pure air breathing in the woods outside.

She led the way over a bridge that crossed the river and they stood in the inner garden. Inexpressible repugnance loaded Wendover's feet, but he went on. If he had stepped over the confines of the world into blank space he could not have been more utterly lost and be-wildered. Under the moon, now bright, the house appeared a huddle of shapes, rooms, roofs, blocked out with ruin. Impossible to say how much was lived in, how much given over to desolation. There was a broken balustrade from one corner, and from the gutters of the roof leaned gargoyle heads grinning down. What had they seen? What could their stony out-thrust tongues tell if in the darkness they came awake and yelled horror through the trembling woods? Below them was a sluggish lake choked with great lily leaves.

Wendover made one last struggle to be normal, to convince himself that all was well. 'It's a large garden,' he said as loudly as he dared.

'Four acres,' she answered, leading on to the gate.

She was right. Instantly he knew he was no stranger. They entered, and as it swung creaking behind him, he remembered. He had seen those windows lit, raying out light into the black woods. People had come riding, in coaches, haughty cold people who lived their lives in disdain of those who only existed to serve them. He saw the house no longer ruined but with a stately air befitting that of a great family, and the moon was glittering like a silver fish in the lily pool before the great front. She spoke again: 'This is the house. It is here you must sleep. Those woods are full of – '

'Of what?' He stopped and looked into her glittering eyes with chilling fear.

'You know. At night they wake and lie in wait.'

'And you?'

'I wake all night.' She turned and went on.

(It may seem a strange thing, but when Wendover repeated those words to me, though couples were pacing the deck and the gramophone on the other side brazened out the last Charleston, I forgot them all. My nerves tingled. The sinister secret words lent voice to the awful loneliness of ocean and hid beneath its vast veils of darkness.)

She walked up a wide flight of steps to where the hall door stood blackly opened, and as she set foot on them suddenly the dead house sprang into lights as for a festival. Lights broke forth at every window and poured like revelation into the black garden, showing crowded dreadful faces, slinking things, half-shaped forms that fled the light. A woman towered above them on the uppermost step as if for welcome. Her look was hideous and inhuman.

Wendover halted on the lowest. Strength returned to him. He cried aloud: 'I'll go no farther. Not a step. I know now I often felt you in the woods. And there are more of you. Your name is legion – Devils! In God's name, who are you?'

There was a muttering of distant thunder. It grew and grew, swelling into such a roar as when lions answer each other in reverberating deserts. It shattered in his brain.

The woman descended the steps to him, menacing, burning with evil passions. Her eyes shot out the flames of hell. Her hand stretched out to claim her own blood in him. It passed human endurance. The world rushed from him on thundering wings that sounded in and outside his tortured brain and through the universe. His senses broke and he knew nothing more.

(Here it will be said: could such a wild dream be taken seriously without assuming lunacy in the man who said he saw? Yes. I have heard darker stories than this where ancestral memory broke through the bars and invaded the present. Psychologists know them well and are helpless before them. But this experience has a stranger ending than any for which the West has any explanation.)

Morning – Wendover waked as if from tortured sleep in a strange place, a whitewashed room with jars and bottles ranged on shelves. A little country surgery. He lay on a long couch, his head propped on pillows, and beside him was a girl holding a bottle of some restorative. The air was still pungent with it. A man stood behind her, obviously a doctor, bending forward to see. He straightened up as Wendover opened his eyes.

'That's all right. He'll do now, Miss Thorold. Lucky you found him, though! It thundered and rained last night, and it doesn't do to lie out in the woods if a man's not too strong to start with.'

'It was good that you had the ambulance ready when I telephoned from the lodge,' she answered in a clear low voice. One knows those clear-cut voices and trusts them.

Silence. They both stood looking at him. He could feel it through closed eyelids. He tried to pull himself together, weakened by a great shock, unaware of its cause, quivering in every nerve. At last he dragged himself up on his elbow.

'I'm most awfully ashamed, and I don't know what happened. I've been ill and I suppose I fainted. After that I knew nothing. Where was I?'

'This young lady found you on her morning walk in Wickington Park. You were lying under the trees near the East Gate close by here and we brought you to my house in the ambulance. She is Miss Thorold. I am Dr Bowstead.'

I pass over the thanks and protestations. The girl had slipped away before they were ended, and Wendover was alone with the doctor.

'I'll take you back to the Crosslets presently, Mr Wendover. You're all right but I may as well say you're not a well man yet and must be careful.'

'But I never fainted in my life before. I can't imagine how it happened.'

'You never must again if it's going to involve lying out all night in Wickington Park. Why didn't you knock at the lodge door if you were feeling seedy?'

'I never thought of that. Indeed, I didn't see it,' Wendover said in a low voice.

He remembered no details of the shock, but knew that consciousness left him in the wood at least six miles from the East Gate. How had he come there? What had transported him. Was it his own feet fleeing from unbearable terror? Or something mysterious and terrible which had possessed his soul? But he was silent, and the good doctor motored him to the Crosslets and left, recommending at least two days' rest.

He felt the want of it himself, and besides it would give him time to think and remember. To that task he set himself.

Two days later he asked Mrs Eves, the landlady, for some particulars of his rescuer. Did she live in the village? Now that he had recovered he must surely go to offer his gratitude. Mrs Eves, comfortably flashing her knitting-needles over a cup of tea in the bar parlour, was perfectly ready to dispense information.

'Why, as to that, sir, Miss Cicely Thorold and her ma live very retired in the Cottage beyond the church, and a very nice-brought-up young lady as you'd wish to see. They belong to the old ancient Thorolds that owned Waste Manor when there was a house there long ago, but the money's gone and her brother in India – '

For a moment Wendover heard no word she said though there were many. Waste Manor. The desolate name, lightly spoken though it was, unlocked the floodgates of memory, and the torrent rolled again through the dry channels of his brain, bringing strange jetsam with it. Again he saw the white figure moving down the glade to meet him, he heard the ambiguous, sinister replies, he saw the trap laid into which his bewildered brain had driven him. How nearly its jaws had snapped he knew with terror. What had saved him from the madness of herding for a loathsome night with the powers of evil he could not tell, but believed it was some strong gesture of the invincible human will, which is in its foundation divine and free. That did not as yet matter – he was saved. But had the experience left any mark? What had *they* done with him while he lay unconscious and at their mercy? Who were they – what?

With these and many other questions rushing through his brain he never asked himself if the whole thing had been a hallucination rising like miasma from his attack of malaria, for he was as sure as of life and death that his eyes had seen, his ears heard, though in some deeper sense than the ordinary vision and hearing. Still, being human, he would seek for corroboration. He would find it also, he was certain. Slowly his mind returned to cognition of Mrs Eves's discourse.

'And her father had an appointment in India, sir, and come home and died, and her mother's an invalid, and if ever a girl's home was as dull as ditchwater it's hers. So she has a kind of solitary way with her and keeps herself to herself as the saying is. You won't see her if you go sudden. She'll like a note first.'

Before they parted he asked Mrs Eves a question which had its importance to him.

'I hear Lord Wickington is in bad health. Is that true? And his only son out of his mind?'

'Lord Wickington? Why, sir, a healthier stronger man doesn't walk on ten toes! I won't say he's got a nice temper. He don't seem a happy man for all his money. But as well as well! You could light a fire at his face it's that rosy. The son – ah that's a bad business. His horse bolted four years ago at something that frightened it in the woods, and he was dragged and his head smashed something awful and he's never had his senses since. He lives with a doctor up in a

village on Shackleton Down. There's no heir. And the daughter – '
She shook her head.

This was corroboration with a vengeance in its circumstance and
otherwise. He noted it and in spite of Mrs Eves's opinion would have
refused an insurance on Lord Wickington's life.

Alone again, he sat down and wrote a letter to his solicitor in
London:

DEAR THICKNESSE

I remember that before his death my father deposited in your
care our family pedigree and some miniatures and other little
relics for safe-keeping. I do not wish to remove them from your
care, for I am returning to India before long, but I wish to ask
two questions.

Can you have the pedigree looked through and inform me if
you can find my ancestress in the reign of Charles the First, born
Sophia Wendover, and tell me who her husband was? I also wish
to know who her daughter Cicely married. If there were more
than one it would probably be the elder daughter. My second
question is – are there among the miniatures any likenesses of
this ancestress and her husband? Because if so I wish to examine
them and if you send them down I will return them immediately.

(This letter and the reply were shown me on board the *Hana Maru*
by Mr Wendover.)

Having written to Miss Thorold and received permission he went
next day to the Church and through the little rose-garlanded church-
yard, lost in its dream of heaven, to the cottage which lay a quarter of
a mile beyond down a green byway.

It stood in a great copse of beech and elm trees which half hid it,
and not only was the seclusion cloistral but the church appeared to
rear its medieval barrier between it and all the life of the tiny village.
The garden was walled with old brick mossed and plumed with fern.
Tiny toad-flax grew along the upper ledge and fruit trees showed
above it. Wendover noted also that a brook, crystal-clear, ran over
bright pebbles before the garden and a little rustic bridge led to the
gate. This strengthened the impression of a dwelling set apart by
choice and circumstance.

He crossed the bridge with some diffidence and as he did so saw
Miss Thorold coming down the little path between the rose-standards
to meet him. She wore a white dress and was bare-headed, and a kind
of shuddering memory ran through him of another woman also in

white and bare-headed who had come down a long glade to meet him. It was strange that this dwelling reproduced in a little the features of the den of darkness once known as Waste Manor. Trees stood about this also, clouding it with shadow. Water cut it off from the commonplace world. The cottage was hundreds of years old, beamed and tiled and modernised with difficulty. A woman in white had drawn him to either.

Yet the width of the spiritual world lay between the two. The eyes raised to Wendover's were so frank and lucent in their serenity that had he known nothing else of her they would have won his eternal confidence. Here, too, he was not a stranger – but with how great a difference! Difference and coincidence repeated themselves all through that strange but happy interview. After he had left he asked himself if she had beauty in addition to her mystic charm and could not answer the question. When there is instant assimilation and union how can a man stand off to criticise and appraise? And that was his case. Neither then nor after could he inventory her face and presence. He tried to – that I might understand – but I could only gain the impression of selfless quiet, of something refined almost to tenuity, of utterly elusive beauty, if beauty there were. Brown-eyed, brown-haired, a little wistful, but with a kindling smile. I must leave it where Wendover left it – an impression. No more.

But in his mind, he said, the name 'Cicely Thorold' was like music, and it recalled strange evanescent pictures, painted by Rossetti and his school, of maidens lily-pure and solitary, mysteriously secluded amid holy emblems in lost churches and castles, like still white flames burning in the dark.

After greetings and inquiries and thanks she led him up the little garden to the low cottage.

'I wish I could introduce you to my mother, but I can't. She's a great invalid and as she never sleeps at night it must be in the day – when she can. She is asleep now.'

They passed two yews bowed blackly into an arbour, and within Wendover saw dimly a couch and the outline of a woman's figure lying upon it like one at rest or dead. Their footsteps made no sound on the grass as they went by. It emphasised the great quiet of the place.

The drawing room was larger than could have been expected. Two rooms had evidently been thrown into one; the ceiling was strengthened by rough but magnificently carpentered beams, and two stout pillars of cedar supported the plain arch which united the rooms.

The furniture was scanty but extremely beautiful and ancient, the whole room possessing an atmosphere of distinction which impressed Wendover very powerfully.

It was not until near the end of his visit that anything interesting transpired, but when it did it was startling.

Cicely Thorold said gently: 'There is a curious thing, Mr Wendover, about which I will ask you a question if I may. Your name isn't a common one and in our pedigree there is a marriage which connects us with it. May I tell you? We have the pedigree here.'

It may be imagined how the rush of blood quickened Wendover's heartbeat. He laid his cup down with a shaking hand and looked at her.

'An ancestress of mine was Cicely Tracy, daughter of a marriage between Sophia Wendover and Sir Aylmer Tracy. Cicely married her cousin Stephen Wendover of Casson Hall, Cumberland. Does that mean anything to you?'

He answered with an attempt at composure: 'It means a lot. I am Stephen Wendover of Casson, though the house is gone. I believe Cicely Wendover was an ancestress.'

They sat looking at each other with great eyes as those who wake from a dream.

'Wonderful!' she said in a low voice, and he echoed the word. Presently she added: 'Then we are far, far off cousins and you are a Tracy too. Her daughter married a Thorold. I never thought you were a stranger – '

'Something spoke,' he said slowly. 'It spoke in me too.'

There fell a silence between them. The old clock which had measured out the lives of the Thorolds and Wendovers ticked loudly beside them in its recess, allotting and resuming their minutes of life.

'May I come again?' he asked in a low voice as if it were a secret between them. 'I'm a very lonely man. Not a soul belonging to me but a sister in Australia. Don't shut me out.'

If his pleading was a shade too urgent she forgave it. She granted his wish. He might come in four days. Perhaps her mother would see him, knowing the kinship. As he stood on the little bridge watching her go up the garden another thought struck him. He had spent that afternoon in the fairy land of the ancient *Morte d'Arthur*. He had emerged 'from the Forest Perilous guided by the Strange Damsel and had entered the House of Adventure set in a right fair woodland and surrounded by running waters and girdled of high walls.'

(At this part of the story came reserves. I think Wendover did not wish me to know how closely his heart had clung to this sweet woman of his own blood – a plant of the same root, whose white blossom lit his loneliness like a star. Yet I read the story rightly, I am sure, when in my mind I divorced it from all sexual hope and experience. It was love untainted by any covetousness of earthly expression.)

He paid two visits before Mrs Thorold saw him – surely the frailest thing that could breathe and live, a body holding the spirit as insecurely as a cobweb holds a dew-drop.

Her black hair was oxydised with silver, her sad gray eyes as blackly lashed as her daughter's, but the look of wan suffering was her own. She met Wendover kindly but with a touch of pity.

'So you share the unhappy Tracy blood with us, Mr Wendover? Tell me, if you can, has it used you better than it has us?'

Difficult question to answer! He hurriedly reviewed his own life. Loneliness, the loss of house and lands, exile, health none too strong, a solitary future. And yet –

'Is life ever entirely happy for anyone?' he asked. 'Have the Tracys more to complain of than others? Would you say so? I think the root of our trouble lies deeper still.'

He saw Cicely's eyes quicken and shine. Mrs Thorold shook her head sadly. 'No, our forefather committed a wicked and most sacrilegious murder. We all pay for his devil's temperament.'

'It seems a little unjust!' he said thoughtfully. 'And I know many worse off than the Tracys.'

A little more passed and then she was wearied and closed exhausted eyes. Cicely took him to the quiet drawing-room with its air of breathless ancientry and pale distinction.

'My mother might be well if she could escape from that belief,' she said sadly. 'But she never will. It has doomed her. Is that part of the Tracy curse? I think not.'

What could Wendover say? His experiences in the Perilous Wood coloured all his thoughts with fatalism. He had told her of his letter to the lawyer; now he held out the answer. It confirmed his own vision and Cicely's facts completely. There the marriages of Sophia Wendover with Sir Aylmer Tracy and of Cicely Tracy with Stephen Wendover stared him in the face with legal precision.

'As to the miniature,' wrote Mr Thicknesse, 'we hold a miniature of Lady Tracy and one of Mrs Wendover. The latter is extremely attractive; the former I own is not to my taste. I shall send both down by a confidential clerk for your inspection on receiving your authority.'

Silently Cicely rose and opened a cabinet of ancient English oak barred with iron hinges. She took two miniatures from it and laid them on the table.

'Copies,' she said. 'We didn't even know the originals existed.'

Copies, but fine ones.

The face of Cicely Wendover reminded her descendant of Cicely Thorold's. The same delicate and pensive grace, brown-eyed, faintly smiling. But the other! The corpulence, the retracted nostrils and flat sensuous mouth were the woman of his horrible vision branded in upon his brain by revelation. She was magnificent in brocade and pearls with a high fan-shaped lace ornament upon her heart – the Lust of the Flesh, the Pride of Life, the Desire of the Eyes, made visible in a gross body. And she had married a Tracy – two meeting streams of evil.

Cicely looked at it shuddering. 'The vile woman. I've asked mother to let me burn it and she won't. It's like an evil influence in the house.'

'Yours will hold it at bay,' Wendover said. He pushed it from him with loathing, and it slid on the polished table and crashed on the floor. It was painted on thick glass after an old Dutch fashion and it flew into flinders. The thing was gone.

The joy in Cicely's face balanced his consternation.

'Thank heaven! If I had had the courage – No, I don't want yours, thank you! The original that that woman sat for and saw with her own eyes would be worse than the copy. Mother need never know.'

That day too he left with a bewildered sense of the ways of fate that nothing could explain. What are the blendings of heredity? What the doom they impose? The riddle was beyond him.

The time was drawing near when he must leave Tanswyke and prepare for his return to India, and each day Cicely grew dearer to him. He loved her not as men commonly love, but dearly. We are ill served by words where this passion is concerned. The same term must widen to wings that overarch the heavens and shrink to the fan-flutter of a base little flirtation.

He met her sometimes moving quietly along the sun-flecked forest paths on the near side of the park. Though he had said nothing, some delicate instinct in her divined that the other must not be spoken of. It held some instinctive horror for both – some racial nerve that quivered with the same wound.

Then she would stop and smile and they would fall into step for a while and then sit under the listening trees. It must have been a relief to her. Her life was so lonely; her mother's stark conclusions so unlike the fine intuitions that built her own strength. Once or twice he ventured to hint at the desolation of her life. Must it always be like this – always?

'One gets used to it,' was all she answered.

'But here? In this prison of a place? Surely the wide world – '

'Wherever we went it would be the same. After all, we are Tracys. We can't evade our doom. It has taken us all in turn. My father – my brother – my mother. Have you ever heard a verse of the song about us?'

He shook his head. She laid her small hands quietly in her lap and repeated without any inflection:

> Woe to the unborn sons of the Tracys
> (Say what redemption is left through all time?)
> O, could they win to the land where God's grace is,
> Baffled and faint with the storm-wind's embraces,
> (The wind that wails for their forefather's crime)
> With ever the wind and the rain in their faces –
> Never again, till the end of time.

Silence. They were sitting under a great beech by a pool starred with white cups and buds of lilies. Not a leaf stirred, and the quiet was cloistral. He looked at her and again the thought of the story of the Grail floated from the deeps of his mind.

'So Sir Percival looked on the maiden and had great pity of her, for so well shapen was she of limb and body as that nature might not better have fashioned her, and all the beauty that may be in woman's body was in her and all the sweetness and simpleness.'

It protested against her hard fate with a voice sadder than tears. He tried to remonstrate against his own conviction.

'But surely you can't believe that a long-ago crime of one of your ancestors could crush you like this? Life has hardships and contradictions, but such a cruel injustice would be impossible in any world not ruled by devils.'

'There are many strange things we don't understand. The consequences – the way things are bound together – ' she said.

'The very belief in it, the very life here, are enough to bring about the certainty of doom and insure its fulfilment. You ought not to be here: you and your mother – it's horribly bad for you. Couldn't you get away? Forgive me for venturing to say this, but we are friends.'

'I know. I'm grateful. But there's nothing to be done. We have no money. You could never think how little it costs to live here. And if we can save anything it must go to my brother. He has married unhappily. He – '

It dawned dimly on him then that he had heard of a Thorold – Tracy Thorold – who had been in one of the native regiments, who had mysteriously left it and vanished. Men said he had gone Indian. They say that sometimes when they can account for strange things in no other way. Wendover resolved he would hear more when he got back. Now he slid past the subject.

'But you?'

She saw he cared and looked up at him with the hidden soul in her eyes. He had never seen any so strangely beautiful. Clear as deep gray water set in the midnight of blackest lashes they had a magnetic power that sent a faint tingling along his veins.

'Don't be sorry for me. I have compensations,' she said and paused, then added: 'You have been so kind to us. Shall I tell you? One may be a Tracy and yet find wings.'

He caught at that. It is impossible to say how much the place and the two women interested him. No – that is too cold a word. They pulled on something in his heart. He understood. They were in the same plane though he could not define what and where it might be. Wings? And a Tracy?

'You will believe it,' she said, and seemed to search for words to express an experience too great for her. 'I was born in India, and mother and I came back when I was eighteen months old. She was too ill to stay there. You will see I could remember nothing of the country. A strange thing happened six months before we left. The wife of a Brahmin near us, who had no children of her own, was very fond of me. When my ayah took me to the grove near the temple of Vishnu the Preserver she was nearly always there. My mother says she was a beautiful young woman, very silent and gentle. She interested her husband in me. He was always at the temple and he would come out and stand looking down upon me, lost in thought. One day my mother asked him to say what was in his mind, for many people knew he could see hidden things. You will think it strange, but he said a wonderful thing.'

'Why should I think it strange?' Wendover said. 'Don't I know India? Sometimes I think the only clear sight in all the world is there.'

'Then you'll understand. He said: "Looking at this child I see strange joys and griefs. I see a vast building of the gods, as it were a mountain of stone carved in noble shapes. Dark inside – dark, set with small lights and I see a great Rishi [a holy sage] proud and terrible of aspect mounting some steps to the altar. And four men armed wait for him in the dimness." '

She paused and looked at Wendover with a question. He answered: 'But yet – might not the story of your family connection with the Great Murder have got about? I know from my own knowledge that there is some secret wireless in India we've never fathomed.'

She made no comment, but went on: 'And he said: "I hear them cry aloud to him and he fearing nothing – as how should he? – answers: 'Here am I. No evil-doer but a Priest of Him that Is.' And the wicked Four try to drag him from that holiest place, but he will not and resists like a warrior, and since the gods wait their time the evil-doers have their will and slaughter him. And so, to meet their doom." '

Again she paused and said: 'Have you thought it strange he should see Canterbury Cathedral in darkness?'

'Does it invalidate the time?'

'No, it confirms it most strangely. Thomas à Becket was murdered at five o'clock in the afternoon of December 29th. It would be black dark in the great cathedral then, but in India it would be light. That is the true sight. Then he said: "For this child because she has been swept into the karma of the great murderer there can be none of the transitory joys that men follow to their destruction. Alone she shall live, alone she shall die. Yet that Eternal within her shall take wings and escape, and the night repay the sorrows of the day." '

'They should never have told you!' Wendover interrupted with indignation. 'It was to doom you. They must have been mad.'

She looked at him strangely.

'They never did. You shall hear. Then he did a thing almost impossible for a Brahmin. He took a little stem of the sacred *tulsi* plant and dipping it in water traced the symbol of Vishnu the Preserver on my forehead saying: "Come home, poor child, one day from the cruel West. Your peace lies here." My mother was furious. She rubbed the mark dry, glaring at him, but he turned away smiling like a man who makes allowances. "What is done, is done" – that was all. But I was never taken there again.'

(It is hard to describe the interest with which I heard this part of Wendover's story. No more incredible thing could ever have been told of a Brahmin and a priest. But it elucidated much that followed, for I saw plainly that he had followed the girl's rebirths and recognised her as a daughter of India swept by a faulty karma or some need of her soul into the vortex of the Tracy curse. This should be borne in mind.)

'But what happened? What did it mean?' asked Wendover, bewildered. He had felt in her an almost visible dedication, but to what? To whom? He begged her to tell him more.

'I began an inner life when I was very young, I can never remember a time when the nights were blank. Directly I fell asleep the doors opened. I was much in India – I saw, I knew. I walked along the roads and few saw me. Here and there one who had the sight smiled and blessed me. That was my real life. I saw no reason in it; no child does, but it was life. The day was a dull dream. I awoke in the night. When I was six I saw the Brahmin and knew what he had said and told my mother. She was terrified, but would say nothing. Much later she owned it. She hated my dreams as she called them. But *I* know I only dream in the day. I wake all night.'

She smiled as one who has a secret to keep. Her face had taken a strange expression – her eyes like the luminous depths in some sea-cave obscurely dark. They seemed to ally her to strange secrets of nature, to wake a nameless fear in the man who heard her. Was it a dawning likeness to his strange guide in the Wood Perilous? Did the tangling fibres of kindred blood go as deeply and terribly as that? Were there dark possibilities as well as noble? There was power in her as well as delicacy, and power is a two-edged knife.

'Gradually I saw connection in my pictures. Certain currents played upon me – not others. I saw what the opening of the door meant. I know now that all the thoughts, ideas, of the world are real and eternal. They never pass away, but are a great store of knowledge which anyone may use who can, according to his own self-knowledge. Well, I have the key of a room in that palace of power and I know enough to be certain there are rooms upstairs to which I can't climb yet – but they are there. Every day it grows clearer as my inner and outer life blend.'

He repeated the famous prayer of Socrates aloud to see if she would recognise the thought.

' "Beloved Pan and all ye other gods who haunt this place, give me beauty in the inward soul, and may the outward and inward man be at one." '

'I know – I know! The woods are full of lovely Presences, but they never come inside this garden except when I open the gate to them at night. We are too sad. Then the inward and outward are at one without contradiction. That's just what I wanted to say.' She stopped and added: 'Did you know there is a saying of a great prophet, "When the outside becomes the inside then the Kingdom of Heaven is come"?'

He had never heard it, but it reached his heart. The wisdom of the subconscious uniting with reason and the intellectual forces. Yes, that would be the Kingdom of Heaven indeed.

There was a long silence. What right had he to intrude into the secret places of her soul? And yet there were things he burned to ask. He had been a student of these things in India. He knew some of the teachings of the ancient and modern schools of thought. It can be imagined with what interest he heard her young lips uttering the mysteries which bewilder the wise. He ventured a step farther.

'I can quite believe it is possible that pictures of the past are mysteriously preserved, amazing as it is. But the future? The past *may* – I don't say it is – be traceable to latent or hereditary knowledge of your own. But the future? That's the test!'

'Not as you think. In the world where I live time is not marked off as we have it here. The present and future are pictures in exactly the same way.'

'Can you give me any proof of that? What have you seen?'

'Proof?' she said. 'There's no proof about it. That belongs to earth. Things there *are*.'

Something in her manner impressed Wendover more than her words. She was careless whether an outsider believed or no. She knew.

'I have seen pictures of you.' she added. 'I saw you in a tent on the mountains somewhere with a dark man behind you in a green turban, and another man, light-haired and very tall, came up to you, and the dark man brought a table and chairs out of the tent and you both spread out a map and marked it. There were acres of forget-me-nots all round you as if the sky had fallen and made blue pools of peace. The mountain had two peaks like the Breasts of Sheba in *King Solomon's Mines*, and a huge overhanging ice-cave pushing forward into the valley, and a river running from it. Do you remember?'

Remember? Wendover was pale with memory. Kolahoi, the great snout of the glacier, the cold river. And Edmond Hall had run over from Aru, and they had planned to trek from there to the Sind by Khem Sar and Zaiwan, and he remembered in a flash that this Hall had said to him idly: 'I never see Kolahoi that I don't think of the Breasts of Sheba in Haggard's book.'

Wendover pulled himself together. 'Can you tell whether you saw this in the past or future?'

'Not in the least. I tell you time has no meaning to me there. But it will certainly happen if it hasn't come already, for it *is*.'

'Have you seen more of me?'

'Yes, much more. That's why I know we are tied together by something more than blood. All the people I see have touched or will touch me. I saw you here – walking in the garden. The house weighed on you like lead. It would on me if I had to live in it. But I escape.'

'You must know your own future from your past and present,' he said earnestly. 'Tell me – shall you escape for good? Will your life be cast in brighter surroundings?'

'They are bright as stars!' she answered with her inscrutable smile. 'But I shall never have what people call a good time. It will be better than that. Much better. Remember this life is a very short act of the play. Sometimes I can't tell whether what I see belongs to this act or the one before or to come. How can I? You outside people all look on this as something to be made use of, to be planned into this life as if one had a telephone fitted or any other convenience. I can't make you see how little account it takes of the kind of life we live in the day. That's only like the little bit of an island peak that shows above the sea with the rest of the continent drowned in deep water. *We* know which matters.'

The thought struck Wendover then that he had lit by chance on the most wonderful medium – invaluable in the desperate quest of the Dark Continent which lies beyond our ocean of thought. He told her a little of what the wise men of the day are seeking, hoping to interest her. She shook it off her as a wind-wafted rose shakes rain.

'I have nothing to do with all that,' she said. 'It sounds horrible to me. My world is quite different. I don't care whether they succeed or no. These things come to the people who need them. They make us make beautiful thought-forms – but I can't explain, and it doesn't matter. What does matter is that one sees all life is law and you build your nest straw by straw like a bird and if the wind blows it away it's because you built badly. Build again! I've built this wonderful House of life for myself and I am content with it. The next will be higher up on the mountain above the clouds.'

He entreated her to tell him more, though he saw very well he was not to hear the things which most concerned her. Indeed she said one thing which he held for true in all relations of life.

'You can never truly hear anything unless you know it already yourself. What's the good of telling? Perhaps I should not have said as much as this.'

They walked back slowly through a grave sunset in wind-washed trees, and he little thought this would be the last chapter in a very wonderful experience. He counted upon some parting confidence before he left in two days, which might clear the outlook for both. But it was not to be. At the bridge she stopped and held out her hand.

'You have been so kind – and the only one of my own blood – that I will tell you that when my mother dies I believe I shall go to Burma and wait and see what happens. I have money enough for that. Do you laugh? Ah, I want only work and thought. The vision draws me that way.'

He would have interrupted with some eager protest about money but she smiled and went quickly up the garden.

Next day came a note to say her mother was so ill that there could not be a minute for meeting.

But I wish you all good. May I call you Stephen, for I think of you in that way, and we shall never meet again. Our lives have touched very strangely. We are bound by the fetter of a great wrong, but it can be slipped. I have seen your fate – peace like mine and perfect release from things which do not matter and vex the quiet of our souls. I send my love and hope to you. The wind and rain may blow in the faces of our people, but they will not vex you and me. We have known the secret and have found our way to the back of the North Wind.

Here Wendover's story ended, for a few weeks after he embarked upon the liner where I met him. Gliding over the surface of the Indian ocean we often sat at night watching the moon and stars drift by in solemn procession; and I did my best to learn from him what conclusion he had come to about the vision, if so it can be counted, of what he called the Wood Perilous. He believed it was a true sight, that it had in truth happened, that for an hour he had been swept into the world of spirits and had there been a spectator of the strange drama eternally surrounding us and rarely visible. This he thought received confirmation from the fact that we met one day at the board for wireless news and there read together the information that Lord Wickington had died under an operation for cancer of the throat.

'And who will they strike at next?' he asked as he turned away.

'They?' I could get no definite opinion from him on that point, though it was obvious that he leaned to the spirit hypothesis. To me it appeared rather a mystery play of evil passions still sending their vibrations through a place which had been their playground for many centuries. The kindred blood in Wendover and something sensitively responsive in him to these aerial messages had dramatised a dead and living evil into human-seeming forms. In this connection I noted keenly that the out-of-the-world seclusion of Cicely Thorold's home and many other incidents, including her strange saying, 'I wake all night', repeated, as it were, on a noble plane his meeting with the embodied evil of the Perilous Wood. I believe this foretold the trans-mutation of the curse centred in Waste Manor, that one day larks will sing about it and doves dream on the tiles of the ancient roof and happy children will play in the pleached alleys of yew and the dead evil blossom as the rose in fragrance and innocent beauty. There is much still to be considered in this matter, much that seems inexplicable, but I steadily believe the first incident to be a black shadow cast by the light of the other and to be dissolved by it one day into radiance.

As to his difficulty about the injustice of the descendants of de Tracy suffering for their forefather's crime, to me with my Buddhist training that presented no difficulty at all. Those souls were naturally drawn by affinity into the sweep of the de Tracy karma who had something to learn, to suffer, or to perfect, by sharing that experience. It was not because he was their ancestor. He became their ancestor because their experience needed some training or experience from his. They were swept into his vortex because things in it made it their own necessity, and each turned it to account according to the stage of evolution which he or she had reached.

Wendover and I had many interchanges of thought before I left the ship, on Buddhism, the ancient Vedantic philosophy of life and death, and we each learned something from the other. He said on parting that he would let me know later what turn his life had taken.

This promise I thought he must have forgotten, for no letter broke the silence. 'Ships that pass in the night,' I thought, but did not forget him.

Two years later I received an invitation to attend the ordination of a *bhikku* or Buddhist monk – one who has renounced the world of transient appearances for the way of peace and renunciation.

It took place at a temple near a lake, where on a platform above the water a little hut decorated and screened had been erected, for the ord-ination must take place above pure water. I stood with the gathered people and watched the little procession of children carrying brightly decorated wands and leading the way. The yellow-robed brethren followed and with them the priest to be ordained.

Passing, he never lifted his eyes from the ground, but I saw the face of Stephen Wendover. I cannot say it was either a surprise or a shock. At the moment it seemed the right, the logical conclusion to all pain and trouble of mind. More I cannot say, though I know much more. The monks crossed the bridge to the hut, none others following them, and there the ceremony was performed. It was a long time before they emerged, the new brother walking gravely, the white European shoulder emerging strangely from the flaming yellow of his robe. They proceeded to the white tent where he would receive congratulations.

The faithful bowed before him and kissed the ground at his feet. I myself made salutation with joined hands, remembering very strangely how often we had sat side by side talking as friends of matters which I alone of those present knew had influenced him to this high decision. Our eyes did not meet. A whole world of experience divided us now, and yet never perhaps had we been so near in thought and purpose.

He repeated the necessary prayer. The tom-toms beat their guttural music and it was ended.

A week later he wrote me a few words which included these:

Your kind interest in my singular fate bids me inform you that I have made a fuller study of the Buddhist faith in the past two years and have found in it an answer to all my questions. You will recognise the words of the Perfect One with which I end and you will ask no better.

'Tranquil is the thought, tranquil the word and deed of him who is delivered and brought to quiet through the perfection of wisdom.'

I have found the Peace. May you also find it! I thank you for your presence on the happiest day of my life.

For the last time this was signed with the initials of the name he had discarded on passing into the quiet life. It is because he has done so, and the noise of this world is less to him now than the little sounds in the inside silence of a grave, that this story can be written. If he read it, it would be with the indifference with which a man reads the history of an alien whom he will never know.

Of Cicely Thorold I know nothing, but I believe I shall know one day.

The House of Fenris

JOHN COOLING

'Each night is the same, Morrow. I begin to find sleep, hoping that at last I shall be spared the awful vision. My mind drifts away from the waking world, images play at random and then with a sudden burst my thoughts are focused as if through a funnel, and I see suspended above me a severed hand, dripping with blood. And I hear, like a great gust of wind, a terrible howling. It seems to last for many moments, though in fact it is a few seconds only, and then there is a cold, brittle silence.'

Dr Morrow, of the School of Comparative Mythology at the University of St Edmundsbury, frowned. 'How long have you been at Thorsby, Overbury?' he demanded abruptly. He placed his thick spectacles upon his nose with meticulous precision, tugged at his waistcoat ends and peered at his old school friend.

'Only a few weeks. I'd been scouting around for quite a while since I came back from the Yukon, and I made up my mind I wanted a place full of history. After so long out of the dear old country, I felt I needed to be part of its deep-rooted past once again. The agents offered me all sorts of very commodious new red-brick constructions but I fairly spat at them. In the end they got the message, and said that Thorsby would be just the place for me. There has been a settlement there since before the Norman Conquest, or so they claimed. The name, anyway, is Old Danish in origin. That would meet my requirements. Why they have to build new stuff when there's plenty of old places like this lying empty, I do not know. I said as much to the chap who leased me Thorsby, and he quite agreed, though he did say sometimes tenants have strange prejudices about old empty houses. And then he smirked. I think I see his point now, but I tell you Morrow, I'm not giving up. Will you come down and help me sort this thing out?'

Morrow eyed his friend cautiously. 'I need to know more. Have you had any changes made to the house since you took it?'

Overbury considered. 'Very few. But I did have the wine cellars opened up. I could not understand what was the point of having such excellent storage and barring it all off. The steps led down to a stout door which had been sealed and all its handles removed. I mean to live in some comfort after all the hardships I had out in the Yukon, and a good cellar is high on my list. I had them break open the door and start building the pipes and racks for the bottles I shall acquire.'

'Did you indeed?' said Morrow. 'Anything untoward happen?'

'Beastly smell when we first got the door open, if that's what you mean. Not surprising considering it's been closed up for years.'

'Just damp and rot, then?'

Overbury paused. 'Yes, just so. But some foul vermin smell too. Put me in mind of some of the rank-smelling dens we found out in the wastes of the Territories – wolves' leavings and suchlike. However, I don't see how that could have affected my dreams, old man .'

Morrow considered, and moving surprisingly quickly for a man of his girth, mixed two more drinks from the choice selection in his cabinet and handed one to Overbury. He then opened an old oak cupboard and picked out, from what was hung on the inside of the door, what looked like a series of curious letters in iron.

'The cellars are only to be used for storing wine?'

Overbury replied, 'I moved various old pieces of junk and other "heirlooms" left lying about in the house into the cellar. Some were almost wholly defaced, and I thought about getting rid of them. I only kept them to take to the museum as I have no use for them. The cellar seemed a good place for them temporarily. I cannot think that they can have anything other than historical value and even then I think it is doubtful.'

Morrow said, 'I will look at them when we go to the house. This, however,' he continued, 'is one set of old objects which I believe may come in useful,' pointing to the items he had taken from the cupboard.

On arrival at Thorsby, Morrow was surprised to find that it looked tranquil from the outside. It was pale, solid, with well-maintained grounds, and had been carefully preserved. He walked slowly around it to get a better impression. Also his habitual caution in matters of the occult made him desire to know what he was getting himself into.

He was somewhat peevish. 'You said this was an ancient place. Perhaps. But I could not understand why a place with a Danish name should be still standing and still in use now, as they built in wood rather than in stone – and this is a stone building.'

Overbury replied that he not yet delved into the history that much. Morrow walked around the house again. The aspect of the house itself was not at all daunting. Rather it seemed to be built with the idea of renewal in mind. The austere, almost classical lines reminded Morrow of Roman architecture.

It was in the interior that darker thoughts seemed to come into Morrow's mind. Certainly, the builder had a clear idea of perspective and beauty. The original conception of the house appeared clever. It was the use it had been put to which seemed the problem. Morrow felt the filaments of unease steal upon him as they always did when his researches led him into the presence of something genuinely uncanny. He fought off the urge to fling these sensations from his mind, and let them creep insidiously further into his consciousness, awaiting the first hints of revelation that might come. As he stood in the lofty entrance hall, the feeling of an all-seeing mischief-making mind and an inhuman one at that, made Morrow shiver against his will. He cast about for some more fortifying force to sustain him, and found it in the fine harmony of the house. The amount of care that had been put into the original construction gave it a contrasting aura of serenity and reminded Morrow of a temple.

He knew where he must go. Overbury conducted him down the bare, neglected staircase to the cellar. A rank odour rose up and pervaded his senses, just as the first encroachments of fear had done. The feeling of some vast inhuman mind also persisted. It was the feeling of being watched by a malevolent will that was the most disturbing feature.

He stood in the empty, hollow, low chambers of the cellar, and saw that on one slab, his friend had put away a disordered collection of items from the house above. He sifted through these carefully, discarding a broken umbrella, a cracked port flask, rusting keys, a ball of twine, several dull vases, and other left-overs. Then something made him pause. It was a tablet in terracotta, with blurred figures upon it, perhaps a pair of *putti* or cupid-type figures and some heraldic animal. Probably used as a garden ornament, Morrow mused to himself, yet the figures were either very primitive or very debased. He put this item back with a puzzled expression on his face.

'Michael, this is one of the things which you brought from upstairs?'

The tone of voice turned this into a question, and Overbury nodded his assent.

Morrow became thoughtful.

He paced about the cellar a little, then looked up at his friend, who was expectantly awaiting his advice. 'Well,' cautiously offered the Professor, 'the first question in my mind is whether these are simply dreams you experience, or whether they are visions. Although they appear in the room above I think it is more likely that the origin is here below. And – I think that the only way we can find out for sure what is going on is to observe from the cellar itself at night.'

There was a brittle silence, as if the cellar itself were waiting. Overbury replied, 'I understand. Yet I am beginning to think I was wrong to stay in this place and that actually spending a night in the cellar may be highly dangerous.'

Morrow said, 'There are parts of the entire manifestation which I do not understand, but I begin to see glimpses. There are measures which we can take to ensure our safety. The iron characters I have brought with me may offer us some form of safeguard. We will be in the cellar, but I am determined that we will have torches with us as well as those. I fear it may in any case be too late to stop what is emerging here. We must face it.'

They waited that night in the dank echoing cellar. At first it appeared that nothing was going to happen, and after some desultory talk to keep themselves awake, their eyes began to weaken and their heads to nod, as they crouched upon the floor. But they concentrated hard on the four faltering torches of flickering fire, which cast curious shadows upon the walls, like a weird dark drama of misshapen things. And from those shadows, as the two men watched transfixed, figures began to form. At first there was no more than the stealthy movement of a slight gathering of darkness in the door from the passageway, but this writhing shadow grew until the shape of a black spectral chain could be distinguished. Then other forms followed quickly, and some had the semblance of the human, and some that of the creatures who go upon four feet. Then all this wavering, pulsing gloom was pierced by two great red orbs of light, and around these the vast lineaments of a ravening creature coalesced – a great jaw, a pointed snout, pointed ears, and a lolling tongue. The shadow-wolf's eyes gleamed with the nearest thing to pure evil that Morrow had ever seen, in all his encounters with the abnormal. He shrank back against the bare walls, forgetful of all his learning and all his caution, until his hand touched the cold iron of the black characters he had brought with him. He drew these out and raised them above the spot where he and Overbury crouched in terror, chanting and using them to ward off what was before them.

But the vision had not finished. The great wolf was held by the chain they had first seen, and the chain was held by another being, deeper in the shadow. This being, which had the form of a man, was tugged to and fro by the beast whose leash he held. Morrow forced himself to allow his preternatural alertness to the psychic world to reassert itself, and with a rush he felt an ingress of reassurance. He felt fixity of purpose, the grim struggle of a brave man who knows fear but has succeeded in conquering it.

Then there was a hideous lurch in the course of the vision. The great wolf-shadow rose up and lunged towards the master that held it on its chain of dark air. The shadow-man did not hesitate, but threw off the assault, putting his hand deep into the wolf's maw to prevent it from closing upon him, and working furiously to weave the chain in great circlets, so that it was fully wrapped around the wolf. The wolf attempted to shake the chain off, but found that each attempt merely wrapped the chain more tightly around it. It was as if the very efforts of the wolf made the chain more able to resist him. The wolf's convulsions became more and more furious, and in its extremity of hatred and anger, it closed its great jaws upon the shadow-man's hand. Morrow gestured again and again with the iron runes he held and in his anguish bellowed them aloud.

The image of the bound wolf and the man holding his maimed hand started to recede. The pair staggered up the steps and were able to get through the rest of the night without further incident.

In the morning, Morrow eyed his friend over the hasty breakfast they had contrived, each preoccupied with his own thoughts. Michael Overbury caught his stare. 'Well, you see? What I have seen each night has been the aftermath of all that cursed shadow-show – the dangling, severed hand. Nothing for it but to get out and let it carry on its crazy ritual all to itself again. Perhaps one of those nice new red-brick sheds might not be such a bad idea after all.'

Morrow cleared his throat, and bit with care into a slice of toast and marmalade. After he had absorbed that, he remarked, with studied carelessness, 'Oh, it is all quite clear so far. You do evidently have here a most ancient temple of the Danes: those agents were not for once bluffing. It is evidently a place of ancient power. And all that vision came from Norse mythology, of course. The Norse gods faced peril from a son of the god Loki, who had taken the form of a wolf and was called Fenris Wolf. He was taken by Loki to Asgard, and shown the iron bands the gods would use to hold him. Fenris laughed at them and when bound easily shook them off. The gods came with a special bind which was made by magic and at this point Fenris refused to let the gods bind him. He said that one of the gods would have to put his hand in his mouth before he would allow himself to be bound. Brave Tyr did and had his hand bitten off. But Fenris Wolf was bound.'

He paused. 'Something here is in danger of unbinding him. We were only saved last night by those iron rune-letters I had brought, which came from the excavation at Gothborg – Hardrasson gave them to me as thanks for the help I gave him in identifying some of the finds there. They are the runes of Vidar, son of Odin, the only being able to withstand the might of the wolf.'

He helped himself to more marmalade.

'However, the problem in this case is why the Fenris has become active again. I believe the answer lies in this tablet, which you had deposited in the cellar. I do not know if any actual records can be found, but there is something in the fine dimensions of this house which suggests inspiration from a Roman temple. Perhaps the site is older still than the Vikings, and – just as the heathen worship has returned here in such full force, so has that older paganism. I have studied this tablet carefully and believe it shows Romulus and Remus, founders of Rome, who were suckled by a great she-wolf. By taking this icon into the lair of Fenris you invoked more than you knew, and reawakened the wolf-form, with the consequences we have seen. By removing it, and by leaving in its stead my runes of Vidar, to grow in strength, we shall stop the visions below.'

'Even so,' he added, with characteristic caution, 'I should abandon those plans for a grand wine-cellar if I were you . . .'

The Prince of Barlocco

MARK VALENTINE

A great luminous yellow moon hung low in the sky as I made my way to the secluded rooms of my friend the Connoisseur on one late October day. I found him contemplating this apparition through his quaintly arched windows as I entered. 'Very remarkable, isn't it?' he commented, 'Almost an alien moon, almost not the moon we normally know. One could imagine anything might happen under its sway . . . '. He beckoned me to my accustomed chair and poured into two delicate glasses a rowanberry liqueur which he had acquired some time ago and which he eked out sparingly since the supply was uncertain. As we sipped, he assumed that meditative air which I knew often presaged a story of one of his encounters with the curious: so I remained silent and waited.

'Early in the summer of last year,' he began, gazing at the little yellow fire which murmured to itself in the old stone grate, 'I received a handmade envelope of Archenfeld paper, strong and well-textured, which bore the distinguishable postmark of Kirkcudbright, in South West Scotland, impressed upon two stamps. One was the standard British issue, the other an unserrated black and white label which had a picture of a domed island, with the waves of the sea pleasingly delineated in fine plumes of pen-strokes: and which bore above this the legend 'Barlocco' in strong clear lettering, together with one or two lesser inscriptions. Greatly intrigued, I nevertheless opened the envelope very carefully with my brass, serpent-hasped paper knife – ' the Connoisseur reached behind him and wielded this instrument in emulation – 'and took out the letter inside.'

'It proved to be from the illustrator Edward Kesteven, an old friend from when we had both worked on a short-lived arts journal. He was writing to say that he had discovered a rum old place he thought I should rather like: Barlocco, one of the Isles of Fleet, just offshore from a bay in the Solway Firth. Needing some solitude and time to think, to revive his art, and also being rather down on his luck, he had been introduced, through a set of mutual acquaintances, to a most unusual opportunity. He had been appointed, for the months of Summer only, the steward of this otherwise uninhabited island, which boasted only a little white bothy, a couple of freshwater wells, a withy pool, and the rounded hill, with its earthen banks. In return for the rudimentary shelter of the bothy and a weekly delivery of decent provender, he was to undertake quite light duties: a certain amount of maintenance of the tiny estate, showing round the few day visitors and taking their landing fees, and keeping an oil light glowing in the window that faced the shore – not, as he added, for the benefit of any shipping, since it was too weak for that, but simply because it was the owner's fancy.

' "As you will see, however," Kesteven went on, "I have also appointed myself the Postmaster of Barlocco, and designed a few stamps for the island. The fisherman takes them off when he delivers my weekly supply." He added that the owner was a very game old doyenne who occupied a run-down castle on the mainland and who was styled – he thought I would like to know – not as the Lady, nor even the Laird, of the place, but as the Regent: The Regent of Barlocco. Kesteven went on: "She makes rather a game of it, but when I asked her, Regent for whom? she became somewhat coy and merely said 'For the Prince, of course', and would not be pressed to say any more. I think," – he went on – "you should intrude yourself up here – I shall bespeak you – and see if you can't draw her out a little. Quite apart from all else, you will be greatly taken by her minor castle, an early nineteenth century *jeu d'esprit* of some bizarrely ugly beauty. And furthermore I need company, for there is something about the gloaming of this place that makes one overly thoughtful. So if you can rough it for a few days in my cottage post office, so much the better." This was just like Kesteven. I was glad to see that he was evidently in good spirits, because the last I had heard from him he was moping about his inability to make a living from his illustrating. I wondered a little how long his delight in this singular hermitage would last, but at least in the meantime he seemed contented.'

The Connoisseur paused and took another taste of the glistening scarlet decoction at his elbow. 'I was glad of the chance to see Kesteven again, of course, but you can probably guess what else drew me up there: the scent of the Old Cause. The mention of an absent Prince suggested to me some relic of Jacobite folklore, which would be unusual, but by no means improbable, so far south in the Scottish realm. I therefore arranged matters here so that I could be absent for a while, wrote to Kesteven to expect me, and made my way up. The journey from the serene old harbour town of Kirkcudbright to Castle Barlocco – for it bore the same name as the islet – took me through very bare country indeed. At last, however, on the blind corner of a very narrow road I caught sight of the little Castle and was immediately taken aback, despite Kesteven's forewarning. You have heard some Rhineland castles described, no doubt, as having 'pepper-pot turrets'? Well, Barlocco had those all right, but it also had all the rest of the condiment set. There were towers like tapering salt cellars, lantern-like vinegar bottle affairs, and rounded plump mustard-pot extrusions. A wild profusion of corbie-steps jutted from many gables. Vanes and finials and several naked flagpoles stood starkly against the sky. Windows were rounded, lozenge-shaped, ogee-arched, fish-eye, lancet, anything but square. And it was all done in that dusty musk-rose of the region, a stone that for all its bright hue always seems to be brooding, somehow.'

' "Welcome to the Pink Elephant!" a clear, soft-tongued, feyishly genteel voice greeted me as I walked up the rhododendron-encumbered path towards the slightly zigzag steps leading drunkenly to the broad, hooded doorway. I turned, rather startled. Kesteven had made no mention of anyone other than the ancient Regent, and in my mind's eye I had imagined her tended by some equally elderly companion. Yet it was a young woman who came into view from behind a clump of bushes and regarded my approach. She was tall, tawny-haired, and a little awkward in her comportment, but what struck me most as I drew nearer was a very wry, quizzical smile and her pale, pale harebell-blue eyes. Taking my case, she leapt lightly up the steps, at ease with their quirky gradients, and flung open the thick and gnarled door, beckoning me in with a half-bow of pleasing courtesy.

'But she flung open the door upon emptiness, an emptiness that seemed to reach out and enter one. I don't just mean that the entrance hall was nearly all bereft of furnishings, though it was, nor that it seemed hollow and cavernous, which it did. There was, in addition to these physical absences, another absence which I felt strike me as soon as I entered in. She felt it too, I know, for something of the liveliness with which she had greeted me subsided once she was inside. "You will find us rather spartan, I'm afraid," she observed, in a low murmur. "The place is outlandish enough without festooning it inside as well." I relished the musicality with which this phrase left her lips, garnished as it was with the long vowels and soft sibilance of the region and, so that I could hear her speak again, I said how grateful I was for the invitation to stay: but this remark was evidently too lame to warrant a response other than a little acknowledging tilt of the head.

'She ushered me into a room leading off the hall, which was altogether more comfortable, but still somewhat bare. As I entered, there rose from a straight-backed chair, a lofty elderly lady topped with a great bun of hair in which fine silver and the faded gold of the brocade of old tapestries were admingled. A very decided nose, long ears, and eyes as of slightly dimmed blue topaz added to the distinction of her bearing. She was simply dressed in rustling umber bombazine, but wore at her collar a brooch of many-hued and softly subdued Scottish agate, like a rose-window of stained glass seen at twilight. I said how pleased I was to meet her, to which the young lady replied, "My Aunt", so I added, somewhat confused, that I was, no, truly. Then it emerged that this beldame, whom I liked immediately, was "Rosemary" – "for remembrance, so you will remember won't you? Just Rosemary, not Miss this or that, and certainly not Her Excellency the Regent, as that foolish boy Edward insists – Rosemary Wriothesley. Trips off the tongue rather does it not? And this is my great-niece, Grace, I don't suppose she told you that, she is rather bashful, who is all I have left in the world, or at any rate as far as we know, certainly in this world, anyway . . . ", the which peroration was delivered in a great rush of tumbling melody rather like a waterfall in spate.

'I soon discovered that this was The Regent's – for I could not in fact think of her as anything else, so aptly did she seem to suit the title – habitual mode of address, and I was glad of it, for I was a little afflicted by the sense of forlorn-ness which pervaded the place, and Grace too seemed sparing of tongue, much to my regret, except (I observed) when on occasion the talk turned again to my friend Kesteven. After we had taken a simple supper, augmented by some gifts of heather honey, Abernethy biscuits, and creamy, unduly ripened Galloway Blue cheese that I had brought from Kirkcudbright, Miss Wriothesley and I returned to the parlour to discuss my visit, while Grace went about her own way.

'I learned that Barlocco, the headland, the shoreline and the island, had been in her family for many generations, sometimes through the male and sometimes the distaff line, but at any rate with a kind of continuity as far back as anyone could reasonably tell. The estate had once spread itself over much of the neighbouring moorland and pasture-land, but that had now all gone, sold off, as – this was no

more than genteely hinted at, but I divined enough for myself – the
fortunes of the house had been in decline for many a year, since the
last War. There was a little income from a few outlying cottages, but
she did not think it fair to charge very much for these as they were all
in a state of some disrepair, and some field-rents, and some fishing
rights, but they did not amount to very much and probably had not
changed since her father had the place so long ago now, as it seemed,
and of course there was no Factor now, nor the reason to need one,
but she had decided, she had most certainly made her mind up, that a
steward on the island was only right and proper, if only she could
find someone willing to take it on, and then a friend of Grace's from
college had told this Mr Edward Kesteven about it and he had been
most amusingly keen and so it had worked out very well, but whether
he would really want to stay there all that time she hardly liked
to think, but she was glad that he had a visitor as that might help
him see it through. And as for these postage stamps for the island,
all done by hand in very neat black and white, why, well, it was a
charming idea. Very whimsical. Just like Barlocco the castle itself,
which had been put up mostly by an antecedent who for some reason
had become completely obsessed with fairy tales, was convinced by
some wild theory that Barlocco was the scene of some of them, and
so not unnaturally decided he must build a fairy tale castle there,
during the days of the landscaping craze: but perhaps had been
somewhat over-zealous in this regard.

'As she said this, I had an idea about how Kesteven's designs might
help bring in some more money for the place, but I kept it to myself
for the moment. I turned instead to the other subject of my visit – as
well as meeting up with my friend again – and said that despite her
disclaimers I should really like to know how it was that she came to
be called the Regent of Barlocco. At this, she slanted her great head
to one side, looked down her long nose at me, and fingered the agate
brooch at her throat. Then she began a cautiously expressed tale in a
careful diction unlike her previous tumult of words: "Edward said
you would be interested in this, so I see I shall have to tell you what
little I know. Bear in mind that I did not live here for most of my
life – I taught History, you know, at Durham, and before that I was
away at school. I only came back after my retirement and when all
the rest had passed on. Well, I dare say there are a good many
explanations. But I was always led to believe it was just a piece of
rustic fun. A castle such as this seems rather to call for it, does it not?
My father, who was not a man of much imagination, always said it

was simple. Every year one of the farm men would be deputed to go and tend to the island, where in those days there were sheep, a goat or so, and some fowl. They chose him by a kind of lot-taking from among the men without family. Whoever it was would be alone on the island for the Summer months – always from the first young moon of May to the day before the last old moon of October, as I distinctly remember being told. And so, because he was the sole inhabitant, the monarch of all he surveyed, so to speak, he was given the jocular name of the Prince of Barlocco and sent off with all due mock-ceremony, accompanied, I have no doubt, with plenty of drinking of the ale. It followed that upon his return, during the months when the island was uninhabited, there was no Prince: and so in his stead the domain must needs have a Regent. What do you think?" she concluded, somewhat artlessly, as if asking my opinion of something she had just made up.'

The Connoisseur rose from his chair and gazed out of the arched windows again.

'I said of course that it might very well be so. Or it might be that this explanation was what place-name authorities call a "back-formation", a retrospective way of accounting for a curious old name, which sounds convincing but is in fact wrong. The evening had worn on by now and the shadows clustered around the room. She had told me that the first chance I should get to go across to Edward would be the day after next, since the fisherman who did the crossings was away until then, for his mother, who lived over by Muraghty, was not so well: but in the meantime I should feel free to wander the grounds – "such as they are, now" – or to look in any of the lumber rooms – "for I am afraid that is all we can call them now, as all they hold is what we could not, or would not, sell: our dearest and our daftest things, that is what is left. And that is not such a very bad thing to have, after all" – this with a bittersweet smile whose echo I had seen, as I remembered quite well, on the fair face of Grace, her great-niece, when she had welcomed me.' The Connoisseur sighed, and resumed his seat, inhaling absently at the almost empty glass of rowanberry essence.

'I slept that night in a room which had once been painted in a rich cinnamon tint but had now faded to the colour of old blood. It was embellished by cornices of extravagant swaggery in which wings, bows and vines seemed to play a riotous part. The whole effect was very curious, and I was frankly restless to do some delving into my pet theory about the missing Prince – for I had not been convinced by the possibility vouchsafed by the Regent – so all in all I did not sleep well. But even that, I think, could not account for a feeling of desolation that afflicted me as I lay awake, a sense that some inner spirit in the house had been withdrawn, leaving it a mere empty theatrical prop.

'After breakfast, Grace gave me a quick tour of the house, opening and shutting doors swiftly to give me just a glimpse inside, as if she were a little abashed by the hugger-mugger of things that were more stored than placed in each room. She also gave me a sealed lavender envelope to take over to Kesteven, with a rather elliptical look in her eyes as she did so: and she asked me some seemingly casual questions about my friend, which I was glad to answer for the sake of hearing her finely inflected voice again. Then she said she had to be away doing some book-keeping for the estate, and I asked her if the old account-books of past Factors were still kept and where I might see them, taking the Regent at her word about my license to rummage anywhere. She told me where she thought they might be, in a sort of muniments room in the stout mustard-pot tower, and I made my way there.

'It was a dry old business in that dank, bare room, with its unsteady table, hard wooden chair and shelves of green leather volumes, but after squinting at the manuscript entries of successions of Factors, I at last found what I was looking for. Or, to be more precise, I did not find what I did not expect to find. There were no entries whatever denoting wages paid to a farm hand to tend the island of Barlocco, only occasional inscriptions about repairs to the bothy or the purchase of items for the bothy, including oil lamps, a camping stove and a rainwater barrel. And there were just a few entries which led to a tentative conclusion of my own. For example, one said 'Master Alexander asked if he might have a brass spyglass to take with him to the island, and the Regent approving this, it was sent for, 4 guineas paid to Thos. Tompkins & Co.' and another, 'After a delay, the steward of the island was found, who is a cousin-german of the Regent, young Mr Anson Gair, and the Regent made his own private arrangements with him, as is usual, but required me also to find a new pallet for the bed', and then an indecipherable sum. A few other such remarks, scattered here and there, took me the best part of the morning and early afternoon to track down, and I rose up, reasonably well-satisfied, but feeling cramped and musty-headed, and decided I needed a walk.

'The garden of the castle was narrow and not at all extensive, and moreover was highly overgrown, so I strolled down the rutted road which petered out into a thin shore of tawny sand. There was a small wooden jetty. The bay opened out before me and I gazed with keen pleasure at the three Fleet islands lying out within easy distance, as it seemed: the grey crag of St Elen; green-domed Barlocco with its ridged turf banks, scattering of trees, and the white cottage just visible; and the Fleet Isle itself, with its lighthouse, farmhouse and ruined priory. Islands always seem to put a spell upon the eye of the mainlander and I watched them in a reverie for a while, refreshed by the slight sea breeze. At last, I pulled myself away and returned to the Castle. Then I began my search in earnest amongst all the bric-a-brac and heirlooms of the many rooms, all at odd angles and up unexpected flights of stairs. The Regent kept mostly to her parlour, one of the few places that had any semblance of accustomed habitation to it, but she did at times emerge to observe my careful scrutiny of various objects, with that wry smile upon her lips which seemed a family trait.

'Later that evening I returned to her with, I confess, a tinge of triumph about me. I told her of my conclusion, from the Factor's books, that the tale of the farmworker "Prince" was unlikely to be the true explanation, and of my inference, a hesitant one, but sustained by a few comments here and there, that in fact it was usually members of the family who went over to Barlocco isle and stayed there over the summer months: and at this she tried not quite successfully to conceal a flicker of anxiety across her long, watchful face. Then I told her of four things I had found which led me to believe I could identify the Prince for whom she was Regent, and her expression became even more guarded. "Go on," she urged, "I did say you might explore where you would, and I am glad you have found what you were looking for."

'The four things were: an engraved glass bowl with a white rose carved in its base; a walking-stick in white ash with a handle in the shape of a hound, though oddly someone had tinted its ears red; an oil-painting, gashed in one corner, of a grave bearded elder solemnly shaking the hand of a younger man, probably his son, but with his left hand; and a piece of withered dry purple heather in a locket with an indistinct inscription that had evidently been worn away by frequent touching. "A pretty collection," the old lady observed, "I wondered where that locket had got to. Where did you find it?" I told her it was in a box beneath an array of keys and other oddments, where I had been searching for the key to a clock-case. "Well, then, what do you conclude?" she asked me, a little banteringly, adding, "Though I think I can guess."

'I told her that I thought all of these were Jacobite relics. The white rose and the white hound were emblems of the Cause; the portrait depicted MacMurdo, the last man to shake the hand of the Young Chevalier on Scottish soil, who never again used that hand to greet anyone, not even his son; and the locket contained heather from Skye and would probably have been inscribed with the royal sigil. In short, I said, it seemed to me probable that the Prince of Barlocco was Prince Charles Edward Stuart, and she and all her forebears were Regents for his return or for the return, more symbolically, of his heirs and his Cause.'

'That grand dame was not ruffled by my revelation, indeed it seemed to me that she was somehow relieved by it. She nodded her head slowly. "It all makes a very good deal of sense to me. Indeed, I believe the Wriothesleys were loyal. There were not many of the lowlands who were, I know it is said, but we have always been independently-minded here in our little enclave on the bay, and left very much to ourselves, and so I should not be at all surprised, not in the least surprised, if we helped fugitives away over the Firth after the Forty-Five. I do not frankly ever recall my father speaking of any such thing, but as I have said, he was not a romantic man, and these things you have unearthed do rather give the game away, don't they?" Then she paused, before resuming: "May I confide in you? I expect you have noticed that this house is not what it could be." I uttered polite protestations. She waved a hand vaguely. "Oh, I do not mean that it is all out of order and needs a good freshening, though we do our best. That is merely material. I mean – well, it has been dismal, frankly dismal in its atmosphere, for as long as I can remember. There is some ban upon this house, some chill pall that try as I might I cannot dispel. It is scarcely fair upon poor Grace. She must sense it too, though she says nothing." Then she leant back, and touched again her agate brooch. "It will sound absurd to you, I am sure, but that is why I so wanted a steward upon the island again. It has been years since we sent one there, and yet it is surely our duty to look after it, and I simply had this sense that if one neglected one part of the domain, then it would surely tell upon the other. Does that sound too foolish, too curious to you? Well now, Edward is there, and I do feel it has made a difference, a little difference. Who knows whether in time all might become well? But as to your theory about the Prince, all I can say is that you might very well be right. Do share it with Edward tomorrow: he will be delighted." I had the impression I was being courteously dismissed and I left the distinguished old Regent pondering to herself.

The Connoisseur yawned and stirred up the fire with a gargoyle-headed poker, then stared into the newly-quickening flames a while. 'Well, I took the fisherman's ferry over to the island the next morning, leaping out into the shallows as we approached, and was much cheered to feel the fresh sea-fit through my flesh and taste the hint of salt tang upon my tongue. Kesteven, looking more fit and limber than ever I saw him before, came down to the shelving shore and helped to haul me up, threw a wrapped-up bundle to the fisherman, with a fair word to him and a question about his mother's health, and took from me the basket of victuals I had brought across: also, a little too self-consciously nonchalantly, the lavender envelope from Grace. After a swift look at the rather tumbledown white bothy (or "Post Office" as he called it), where on a rough table I saw evidence of the artist's continued work on striking monochrome sea and island scenes, Edward took me on a roam around the whole island, which was, I should say, not more than a mile and a half in circumference. First we skirted the shoreline, shoving through gorse, heather and fern, and chatting all the while of our news. Then, as we came to a rocky gully, Edward halted and pointed upwards with his walking stick, saying that this was the best route to the crest of the hill, the top of the island. It was only then that I noticed, for his hand had been covering it before, that he too had a stick carved with a hound's head: and that again the ears had been tipped in red. I asked about it, and he said he had found it propped inside the cottage, and dashed handy it was too. This started me off on my account of its pair in the Castle, and all the Jacobite relics, and my surmised explanation of the Regent's title, the which Kesteven listened to with mild interest as we climbed upwards.

'We reached after a while a deep furrow in the great mound of the hill, which seemed to weave all the way around it: and above it a bank rose to a similar circular ridge; and again above that there was another. "Now we go this way," said Kesteven, leading us along the path of the furrow. I said surely it was quicker just to go straight up – feeling somewhat winded by then, what with the ascent and my rapid explanations – but Kesteven said we should enjoy the all round view. Then, after we had completed the first circuit, it transpired that we had managed to slope up to the second highest bank, and my friend started again to go round this. To my further remonstrations, he stopped, regarded me gravely and said: "I don't know how it is, but whenever I come up here, I always go this way. It just seems to be the way. I tried the straight path up a couple of times when I first got here, but there always seemed a hell of a gale in my face as I did it. Haven't a clue why, but just go along with it if you will." So I did.

'When at length we reached the last turn of the last path and came out upon the rounded summit, I was grateful to see that there was a little hollow in the earth which provided a certain amount of shelter, so I sank down in this, and after a slight hesitation, Kesteven joined me. For a Summer's day, the wind was somewhat keen, even allowing for the influence of the sea, and it seemed to rake its fingers through the wild grass and whisper in the ears of the haggard clinging hawthorn trees. We took a pull each from a silver hip-flask that I had brought with me and Kesteven began to say how much he relished the life of the island, though he would not want to be a hermit forever, he added hastily, his fingers (I noticed) stealing to the lavender envelope that he had secreted in the inner pocket of his tweed jacket. He told me that he had now completed to his satisfaction five different postage stamp designs as well as a deal of other work – sketches and illustrations that he thought he should be able to sell when he returned home. I outlined to him my plan to get the postage stamps printed up as limited editions and he liked the scheme, so we agreed I would take away such as he had done to put this into effect. So the talk went desultorily on, pleasantly enough, but it seemed to me that I sensed some reservation in him, something that he was not sure how he should broach. After a while, he suggested that we return to the "Post Office", and I was not surprised to find that he took us by the same circuitous route back, as if we were unravelling what we had walked before. This time I held my tongue on the matter. I asked instead if he knew the age and nature of the earthworks – defensive? quarrying? lynchet strips? Kesteven said that this was not his province, but that the Regent, who was, after all, an historian, thought they were very probably the signs of an Iron Age hill settlement, perhaps an outlier of the old realm of – was it Rheged? – but that they might be earlier. I emitted noises of interest, but actually this started me thinking. Yes, the old dame had said she was an historian. Why then had she not made the fairly likely Jacobite connection to her house, herself? Not her era, possibly, they all tended to specialise: but even so . . .

'The boat was coming back for me at seven, so we spent the rest of the time over a pleasing meal of the simple but good fare that had been sent across, and in making all sorts of unlikely plans for the promotion of his illustrations and even for the revival of that long-lost arts journal which, I am glad to say, never came to anything. There was just the first faint hint of dusk as we stepped out of the door and I remembered Kesteven's passing remark in his letter, so I asked him what it was like after dark on the island. "Well, of course," he replied, a little hesitantly, "there is always the lamp that the Regent made me promise to keep lit . . . " – he indicated its dull glow through the shore-facing window. "But aside from that it is devilish dark here I can tell you. Never known it so deep. In towns, there's always some light somewhere and even in the country there might be a farmhouse lit up or a stray street light or two. But here – nothing. Just very dense black. If I step out for a stretch after working late on a piece, I look up to the top of the island and I can make out its shape all right, if there is starlight, but it just seems a great dome of darkness. It does make you think, as I said. Standing here, just as we are now, it's as if that there – " he pointed to the hill, "is another kind of place entirely than during the day." He made as though he might say more, but held back: and after giving me messages to take back to the Regent and to Grace, he accompanied me down to the landing-place and we parted.

The Connoisseur allowed me to catch up with my note-taking, and proffered me a shallow dish containing walnuts-in-ginger, a favourite delicacy of his, which I declined so as to concentrate upon his story.

'After my return from my first visit to Barlocco, I made myself busy in arranging the printing of a limited edition set of the postage stamps from the island, which Kesteven had designed, showing scenes of the island from the sea, the "Post Office", the White Well and the Black Well, as they were known, a (somewhat imaginary) view of the Castle, and so forth. I knew that "private issue" stamps from Britain's offshore islands appealed greatly to certain collectors, both here and overseas; and that Lundy, Sanday, Colonsay, Bardsey, Bernera and others had all issued these. Some collectors preferred them "mint", direct from the press: others liked to have them on envelopes actually dispatched from the island: between us, Kesteven and I could cater for both. The quality of the design was an important element for these collectors, and since my friend was refining his draughtsman-ship very well indeed, the stamps soon found a following. Further-more, I contacted those I knew were appreciators of his artwork and they too were eager to acquire such unusual and ephemeral examples of it, so that, all told, we soon found we had a decent subscription list. Over a few months, as the orders came steadily in, I handed over the administration of it to Grace, and so from this and from the "duty" that Kesteven insisted he pay, there was an extra stream of income for the Castle.

'I also began preparation of an article on the Jacobite folklore I thought I had found in connection with Barlocco, and sent it to the Regent for her approval. She replied most tactfully, but intimated that she did not want to draw attention to the Castle because of its condition – this was italicised, so that I apprehended she did not merely mean its physical condition – which, though better than it had been, still caused her concern. Also, I have to admit, there was something nagging at the back of my mind which told me I had overlooked an obvious discrepancy. I therefore laid the work by and turned to other things. Just as well.

'As the year wore on, the letters that I got from Kesteven, though they were firstly concerned with the postage stamp side of things, nevertheless became increasingly edgy about his solitude on the island, even though Grace and a friend had been over to visit a few times. The nights crept in, of course, and he found it harder to just shut himself up in the bothy for longer, but neither did he relish walking on the rest of the island in the deep, deep gloom, even armed with a flashlight. There were more and more allusions to the great engraved mound of the hill and how it seemed to him a place apart that he now found himself reluctant to visit even in daylight. At last, he said plainly that he would like company again for the last days of his stay, and urged me to join him. In late October, therefore, I made my way again to the domain of Barlocco, and renewed my acquaintance with the Regent, and with Grace, who was brimfully keen on the stamp business and more especially about Edward's part in it. The old great-aunt, I found, was pleased too with how well it went, and there were little signs of revived fortunes here and there – the gardens for one had been cleared and trimmed well – but I could not help notice a reserve in her. She seemed, too, more tired than when we had first met, and we spoke only briefly in the parlour on the evening before I went across. I thought at the time that her speech was more wandering, though just as beautifuly intoned, and it was as if her watery blue eyes were gazing inwardly not out at me at all.

"Things are better," she began, "thanks to you and Edward. There is a change that I am sure you can feel too. But yet the ban has not fully gone. Whatever a little extra prosperity can do, whatever the excitement a new venture can bring, whatever the joy that young love imparts, has worked its influence upon this house: and now as I walk around it, even in those rooms I could not bear to enter before, for all their coldness and decay, now I find a new atmosphere which hints of hope and fortune. And yet I sense an omission, an abeyance in all this: and I fear for what will happen in future. Am I really, do you think, the Regent for a long-dead lost cause? It seems so fearfully apt. You found the evidence, did you not? All there. The bowl, the painting, the locket, the stick. Yes, the stick. You shall take the stick I think, over to the island, so that you can – compare it with the one that Edward has. Take it when you go walking. You'll need it going up that hill. Edward will need his too." With that she relapsed into a silence, as if overtaken by her thoughts or, perhaps, visions. I took the stick as she had insisted and stole out.

'I went across to the island the next morning, when it lacked just two full days and a half day before it had been arranged that Kesteven should leave, according to the old lady's calculations. I found him still as bodily fit as before, and still working at his drawings, but the odd shadows in his ways of thought that I had discerned when I first met him there, had crept closer into the forefront of his mind, and he was eager to be away. He asked me, for example, if I had ever thought where darkness came from and was unsatisfied by my rather too ready answer. "Absence of light?" he repeated. "Yes; or presence of darkness. Which? Is it what goes? Or is it what comes?" I tried not to encourage him in these abstract speculations, but it was clear that the last dark nights of his time on the islet had burdened his soul. It was with some anguish, therefore, that he waited in vain on that last afternoon for the ferryman to come and collect us.

'The first grey veils of dusk descended and still there was no sign of the fisherman's boat. It was long past the time when he had been due to pick us up. Kesteven was very restless, having made all his plans to depart. We waited until it began to become too dark to descry very much anyway, and then I said that it seemed to me we must take the flashlight up to the top of the island, where it would stand more chance of being seen, and signal. The crossing could still be done at night, for there were no hazards, and perhaps someone might alert the fisherman or one of the other boat-owners, and come and get us. But Kesteven was curiously obstinate, saying we must wait where we were in case anyone came. I said we could see that no-one was coming, since there were no lights, and if we climbed the hill on the landward side we could keep an eye out for any that did set out, and scramble straight down again. He replied that we could not go up the hill that way nor could we go down that way, remember? and I chided him for clinging to this custom of his in such pressing circum-stances. At length, and I think only because I said I would go up the hill alone, and he did not like the idea of this, he consented to my plan and we returned to the bothy to get the flashlight. As we stepped out of the door, I remembered the words of the ancient Regent, stepped back inside, retrieved the two pale hound's-head sticks, and, giving Kesteven his, strode on. It was a rough climb. We stumbled frequently even with the torch and there was a sullen told-you-so air about Edward. There were great massifs of dark cloud on the horizon and fleeter-shifting emanations from these, which were fitfully lit at intervals from unseen beams. Yet if they were so wind-driven, how was it that the air where we were was so very still, and the sea, by the sound of it, so calm?

'As we reached the first ridge, Kesteven made as if to circle round and it was all I could do to stop him and make him trudge straight up the incline with me. Leaning heavily on our sticks, we clawed and lumbered our way up to a gap in the next ridge, and halted for breath. Then the black cloud on the eastern edge gave way and there emerged, vast, veiled and oddly luminous, the great old moon of October, the last moon of October. The way to the earthen bank above us seemed strangely lit, with each blade of the sward, each pockmark of rock, each burrow-hole, each pebble even, picked out in a rich, bright illumination. This sudden irruption of light after the deeps of the darkness caused our vision to waver for an instant, so that we had to blink and to refocus not so much the optical apparatus of the eyes but the inner comprehension of what we saw. It was in that instant, an instant that seemed then, and seems now, the sort of instant that sometimes in our lives we experience as stretching on for far longer than our watches would tell us, that the great glow of the moon, the lesser light of the few revealed stars, and the chasing of the high clouds was changed in our sight into something else . . .

' . . . into a great streaming procession, all gold and silver and white and shapes of black, that seemed, in that long, long moment, to storm from the sky in a vast cascade, led by a magnificently-clad horseman whose form twisted and glimmered and turned from a dazzling radiance to a dense darkness in quickening succession, like the moon when it dons and doffs the mask of the clouds. And flailing behind him was a cloak of black seeded with silver stars, and its wrought shoulder-clasp bore upon it all the colours of all the agate that there is in all the islands that there are. The rout that he led was vast, and there were faces and figures in it that were human, and some that were animal, and some that were neither of these, and floating above all there were shards of darkness, like black pennons on unseen lances, and leaping around all there were long graceful hounds, white in the coat and with red-tipped ears: and I clung to my stick and crouched quickly to the ground, and put my hand on my friend's shoulder and made him do likewise, and in this wise we saw through our veiled eyes that wild high retinue pass from the skies into the earth, into the hollow of the crest of the island that belonged to a Prince that I knew now was no mortal Prince. And we knelt there, shivering, for longer moments than the moment which had just passed as we saw the descent of the vision, but these moments seemed to flicker by, like a missed heartbeat.

'We made our way haltingly down, straight down, murmuring to each other glimpses of what we thought we had seen, neither quite able to really believe it was so: and yet it was so. And we waited, awake, in the white bothy until the dawn when the boat came, rowed by Grace and the old gardener they had taken on, with news that the fisherman had been called away at once to his ailing mother, and they had tried to signal that they would come in the morning, yet knew in their hearts that the lantern-flashes would be lost amid all that sudden storm of summer lightning which they could see crackling over the isles. And her great-aunt had been beside herself and had said over and over that they must get them off the island, that it was the day before the night of the last old moon of October, and the steward never stayed on the island on that night, never as long as she ever knew. Grace had placated her only by suggesting that they keep vigil over the island and watch from the highest tower: and the old lady had at last agreed and sat there gazing out, all the while fingering her brooch of agate, while Grace simply thought hard of both of us. And I for one was not wholly fooled by that "both", and the old gardener and I suddenly found much to admire in the view of the priory isle, while Grace and Edward embraced.'

The Connoisseur got up from his chair and walked over to a bookcase, plucking out a narrow volume in black, with no lettering upon its spine or covers, which he placed beside me. Then he stirred the last embers into a fitful crackling, and warmed his palms before the sullen golden tongues. 'I was never sure how much the old lady consciously knew and how much she arrived at by family instinct, as it were. I don't think she had ever been told anything directly by her father, who seems to have shunned it all and hoped it would go away. But we can piece together these things: that her ancestor who became obsessed with the idea of a fairy castle for Barlocco must have heard some dim memory of the true fairy castle, the domed earthwork on the island, one of several such embanked hills around our coast, which some trace to the spiral "Caer Sidi" of the old poems of the bards; that her family had a tradition – one might call it a feudal duty – that they must keep the island in the Summer months, the months of light; and that they were there merely as Regents for a Prince who must never be named, but who would claim his realm on the appointed day each year. And they knew too, or had been told, that the Prince's guards were white hounds with red-tipped ears, and their staffs were fashioned so to show that they were already enranked in his service and should not be rounded up with the rest.

'We can surely deduce too that the ban upon the house that the old Regent sensed and knew, and which even I felt, seeping out from the stones, was because for so long her family had failed in their duty to tend to the island, that strange realm. And her instinct was right that the return of a steward would in some measure remedy this: but to truly remedy it, the steward must be of the family. He was not: but now he is. For Edward Kesteven and Grace Wriothesley were married last May and made their troth both in the usual way and upon the top of the island, each holding a pale wood stick with a hound's-head handle, the hounds having scarlet ears. Some days they stay upon the island, not least to deal with all the postal transactions: other times they pay a passing visit; but what is sure is that they tend it with great care.

'What you have there,' concluded The Connoisseur, 'is the rarest stamp of all the offshore islands, since there is only one copy, and it is not for profane eyes: we call it the Dark Barlocco. Open its album and see.'

I untied a black silk fastening on the boards and gently lifted up the cover. Beneath frail paper, and protected again by a sturdier transparent film, was framed a single postage stamp, of the usual commemorative scale, with the neatly incised lettering, BARLOCCO, across the top, and below a drawing in black and white, done in the woodcut style, in which the clear, swift, swirling lines depicted with intricate detail the moon-illumined descent upon the domed hill that the Connoisseur had described to me with such fervour, though only a single dark flicker of the pen, as of a great cloak of darkness, intimated the nature of the Prince: and for this I felt strangely glad.

The Legacy of the Viper

C. P. LANGEVELD

'The Prefessor to see you, sir' announced Ned Amiss, once boat-swain of His Majesty's warship, the *Vindicator*.

'Why, send him in at once, Ned. Ah, there you are Sam, how very happy I am to see you. How is Scotland, How are you, my dear sir? Sit down. A bottle of claret? A pint of sherry? Some tea?

'Scotland, as ever, is chilly and somewhat treeless – a dish of tea will be capital, Thomas.'

'Do you hear him, Ned? A dish of tea, and haul up the steak and kidney pudding from last night.'

'Thankee kindly, but no – I have just this minute dealt with a prodigious mutton pie. Just the tea, Ned, just the tea.'

Professor Samuel Benskin sat back in the elbow-chair he usually occupied on these occasions. He covertly took note of the change that had taken place in his friend during the three months of their separation.

Yes, the hair (for Captain Thomas Gaunt wore his own), though shot with grey, was still blue-black and thick. The destructive pain in the dark blue eyes was gradually being replaced by the mirth-ful twinkle of old. His weather-worn, aquiline face was losing the terrible scars of anguish.

'Well Thomas, these last few months on shore have worked their wonders. How long before you return to sea? Have they given you a ship?

'Aye: but I am finished with the sea, I have lost the taste for it, my heart can never again be in it. Too many bad memories, Sam, too many.'

Benskin, a slight, dainty man of forty-five with a perpetual look of curiosity upon his genial features, lifted the dish of tea and gently blew into it. 'To tell the truth, I am heartily glad to hear it. How do you intend to live?'

'As far as my living is concerned, the prize money, if handled with caution, will see me through. But that is of little weight.' Gaunt's face brightened and he became visibly animated. 'I have discovered a new edge to my life, Sam. If you have the time to spare, I have a wondrous tale to tell.'

His old friend bowed his bewigged head in tolerant acquiescence.

'After Bess was killed,' began Gaunt, 'I lay in this house, neither caring if I lived or died, I would often drift into what can only be described as a deep swoon, whether induced by my wounds, or by the ministrations of old Phillips, I will never know.

'Upon one of these occasions, Bess appeared to me – no, old friend, I am not yet ready for Bedlam. I shall not enter into the details of what she told me; sufficient to say, her assurance that she apportioned no blame to me for her death and that she was very content where she now abides, was of great comfort to me and ultimately served in the deliverance from my many wounds, of the body as well as the mind.'

Benskin well recalled the day Gaunt had been brought into this house following his last battle; the body, a bloody battered wreck, hardly recognisable as his closest friend. Captain Gaunt and the *Vindicator*, a warship of 74 guns, had been on a return voyage from the West Indies. On board was a single passenger, his new bride Elizabeth, eldest daughter of John Randall, a wealthy plantation owner. The cruise proved to be an easy one, a voyage in which each day brought Gaunt and his Bess closer. Then, ten days out, a frigate, sailing under Swedish colours, was sighted, smoke billowing from her stern. Gaunt approached cautiously, aware of the presence of French privateers in these waters.

They were well within hailing distance when the frigate, now blanketed by a pall of white smoke, opened fire. Seven hundred pounds of iron roundshot crashed into the side of *Vindicator*, pulping flesh and scattering a hail of deadly splinters. As a precaution, Gaunt had ordered the decks to be cleared and the guns run out. The fight was brief and vicious, ending with the badly mauled privateer beating a hasty retreat. But the *Vindicator* too had suffered badly with her captain terribly wounded. There were eight dead, Elizabeth being one who died.

'And what has been so amazing, Sam,' Gaunt continued, 'is that I have discovered an ability within my person to help others who are similarly plagued by doubt, guilt, and worse. Why, not two days ago, I eased the mind of a banker no end who was tormented by a shade that stalked his vaults.'

'I am so very deeply relieved that your uneasiness is removed, but what a fellow you are, Tom, to take the burden of others upon your shoulders.'

'No burden, I assure you, old friend. I find the whole business most satisfying . . .

Gaunt's reply was cut short as Amiss entered the cluttered room. 'Begging your honour's pardon, but John Mallet as served with me on the old *Morgan*, seventy-four, and is supposed to call at three prompt, is a-waiting in the hall.'

'Lord, here I am with moss growing under me. Forgive me, Sam, while I see to this fellow. You will stay, will you not? Show him in, Ned.'

John Mallet was indeed a seaman; the tarred pigtail may have been shorn, the diet of salted horse and ship's biscuits replaced by what some considered to be more palatable fare, but seaman he was. The large, rough hands, the weathered features and the gentle roll of his gait as he entered the room proclaimed it so.

'Sit ye down, John, sit ye down, no quarter-deck proprieties here. Ned, heave up a bottle of Jamaican,' said Gaunt affably. 'Now, what can I do for you? What ails thee, John Mallet?'

'Why, sir, it keeps knocking at the doors, you see, knocking, a-banging, a-thumping . . . '

'Easy does it, John. I think starting somewhere near the beginning would be better. The gentleman sitting yonder is Professor Benskin, a scientific cove who, if you have a mind, would also like to hear what you have to say.'

'Easy it is, sir,' began Mallet with a hasty side-glance at Benskin, 'Well, me and Jed Towers have recently taken over The George that lies on the Kent Road. You might have passed it, sir, a pretty place with good ale.'

'I have indeed, a handsome place as you say, must have cost a pretty penny.'

'Aye, sir,' replied Mallet proudly, 'took a big slice out o' our prize money it did, and making a fine profit mind, until this strange business began.'

'And, exactly, what strange business is that?' Gaunt's smile was restrained, patient.

'It all started six weeks ago, sir, we'd just moved in . . . why thankee, Ned. Your health sirs,' Mallet paused as his old messmate administered a liberal tot of rum. 'Jed Towers had not long locked up and turned in for the night. We had five guests staying over. All was quiet until I woke to the most dreadful banging coming from down below.

(I sleep in the attic, Jed's room is at the end of the corridor downstairs). Well, sir, I took those stairs three at a time only to find the place all ahoo. Guests in their nightcaps galloping about the corridor. By and by, the racket goes and I'm about to turn in when out comes Jed, tumbling from his room. "Why Jed," says I, "what's amiss?" but Jed, why old Jed he just stands there, looking silly, eyes a-rolling and shaking like he's got the yellow jack or something.

'It took three stiff brandies before Jed stopped shaking; but between me, you, sir, and the prefessor over there, he's never been the same man since. And then, two days later, it happens all over again, the same awful thumping and banging. The following week, the same. As you can imagine, sir, this does the trade little good and we've begun to lose custom. I have sat up, hoping to catch the rogue, but with little luck. And as for Jed, well sir, he don't spend much time at The George these days, and when he's here, he takes to walking around the place like a man run melancholy mad. It was then I started to thinking something queer was going on. Then as luck would have it, I runs into Ned here and he tells me that your honour might be able to help.'

'A sad business. And do these disturbances continue?' enquired Benskin addressing flame to clay pipe.

'Indeed, sir, it happens more often now, why only last night . . . '

'So, John, I think I should sample the hospitality of The George for a few nights, and if I may, bring Professor Benskin with me. How say you, Sam?'

'What about a post-chaise?' beamed Benskin.

*   *   *

The George was indeed a 'pretty place', a smallish, ancient and solitary inn with many lattices and pointed gables. Benskin and Gaunt were established in a room of tolerable comfort. They saw little of Jed Towers, a sullen, thickset man in his late middle years, who made little pretence at avoiding them. He left for 'his sister's' later that day. 'There's something bothering that cove, Sam,' observed Gaunt, 'something in his eye that puts an edge on me.'

Following a detailed inspection of rooms vacant, corridors and cellars, it was agreed that the logical course to pursue would be an all-night vigil.

The surveillant would sit upon an elbow-chair, conveniently placed so as to provide him with an unrestricted view of the corridor in question. He would be relieved after three hours.

The first night proved to be peaceful and brought nothing but frustration, as did the second. It was on the third night, however, while Benskin sat with a small sword across his knees and two huge pistols cluttering up his coat pockets, pondering the likelihood of an eighth planet and the possible effect it might have on the rest of the solar system, that the assault came, abrupt and frightening in its intensity. Benskin leapt to his feet as a frenzied thumping reverberated down the low-ceilinged corridor.

Consternation followed as doors were thrown open. Angry night-shirted guests voiced shouts of reprobation while poor Mallet attempted the unenviable task of simultaneous recantation and appeasement. Gradually the clamour died down and the corridor emptied, leaving Mallet mopping his brow with an enormous neckerchief while Gaunt and Benskin clumped up and down, inspecting the gloomy gallery.

'It started over here,' said Benskin, 'and was working its way up to . . . ' Both men turned as a door at the end of the corridor burst open and a man, naked to the waist, staggered into view.

'It's Jed Towers,' cried Gaunt. 'When did he . . . ' he stopped as Towers lunged towards him. The man was raving, murder dominated his eyes, the reek of spirits, strong on his breath.

'You is it, Davie? Curse ye.' Two huge hands reached for Gaunt's throat and – stopped. Towers shook his head and sanity gradually smoothed his contorted features. He dropped to his knees at Gaunt's feet.

'Ah, now God help me, has it come to this? Your pardon, sir, I have not been well these few weeks, and was having a nightmare. I beg you, please do not send for the night-watch.'

Mallet gently raised Towers to his feet and with diverse 'tuttings' and 'hushings' led him back to his quarters. He returned, gloomy of aspect. 'A terrible business, sirs, terrible. I would not blame you if you wish to take action for this night's doings.'

'Calm yourself, John Mallet', said Gaunt. 'We are not here to prosecute, but to peruse and ponder; to put an end to your troubles. Now, what can you tell me of Jed Towers?'

Relief brought the huge neckerchief back into play, 'Why, sir, me and old Jed have been together – on and off – these twenty years or more. Jed, me and Matthew Pratt and poor Davie Quarles, lost at sea these twelve months: good shipmates all. Made our packet on our last trip when we took the *Lydie*, a Frog merchantman.

'This Matthew Pratt, what of him? Did he not have a share of the prize money?'

'Oh, aye sir, that he did. But Matthew,' the old seafarer paused, shaking his head dolefully, 'well, old Matthew's gone and taken queer in the head. Not bad enough for Bedlam, mind. He settled in Pluckley, his old village, and lives on church grounds in a hut which is owned by the parson. Does the odd job, you understand.'

'I understand, said Gaunt. 'Bye the bye, at what o'clock did Jed Towers get back? I was not aware he had returned.'

'Jed came back about an hour ago, came in through the back door so as not to disturb the customers.'

'Thank'ee, John, you have been most helpful. Good night.' Mallet turned to go but was stopped by Gaunt's hand on his shoulder, 'One more thing, is Jed a Catholic?'

'Who, Jed, a Papist?' Mallet's eyes widened with shock. 'Why, bless you sir, he's no more a Papist than King George is. Now, if that be all, I'll be bidding you gentlemen a good, and I hopes peaceful, night.'

*   *   *

'Well, I'm hanged if I know what to make of it, Thomas,' conceded Benskin as they sat at breakfast in the genial taproom. 'There's no trace of your trapdoors, your secret tunnels nor hidey-holes. Yet, before that racket started, I swear not a living soul was to be seen in the corridor last night – 'pon my word, this is good ale!'

Gaunt glanced up from his broadsheet, a grim smile ghosted his lips. 'And there you have it, Sam – not a living soul. I nabbed Mallet earlier and from what I can deduce, these disturbances only occur when Jed Towers is staying here. There is, without a doubt, a connection. Now, what say you to a canter over to Pluckley?'

The late summer roads were dry and dusty and the journey was completed in reasonable time. Following a draught of beer at the inn that, with some brick cottages, formed a square in front of the thirteenth-century church, Gaunt and Benskin sauntered over to the parsonage. The incumbent, a kindly man sporting a white horsehair wig of impressive proportions, conducted them to a small but neat hut that backed on to an abundant garden.

'I would take it kindly, gentlemen,' whispered the cleric as they approached the rough-hewn door, 'if you would tread softly with Matthew. He is not a violent man but is open to fits of the mopes.'

The interior was neat, the floors scrubbed to a near white, a distinctive trait of men with many maritime years under their belts.

Introductions were brief, and the parson departed to attend to whatever parsons are supposed to attend to. Gaunt's unintrusive manner soon calmed the highly agitated Matthew Pratt. 'Now, Matthew, I am here because your old messmate, John Mallet, is sailing in dark waters.'

Pratt's eyes widened in fear as Gaunt told of the strange disturbances taking place at The George.

'Aye, sir, dark waters it is,' agreed Pratt with vigour, 'dark waters for me and Jed Towers, for 'tis God's judgement on the likes o' us, but why so for John?'

'That is why we have come to you,' said Gaunt, clutching at the straw fortuitously cast his way. 'Can you tell us why John should not share in His judgement?'

'Why, now look'ee sir, if old John is a-suffering, then it is time the tale was out. Indeed I do think I shall run mad if it is not. Come closer, sirs,' whispered Pratt looking furtively about his meagre quarters, 'and I'll tell you o' doings that has near drove me to the steps o' Bedlam.

'It was while me, Jed Towers, Davie Quarles and John Mallet, top-men all, were serving on the frigate *Viper*, Cap'n Edward Gwilliam, that our luck came in. We had overhauled a French merchantman, a two-decker, much bigger than us, the *Lydie*, topgallants and mizzen all shot to pieces. Then Cap'n Gwilliam shouts, "Boarders away, mates!" and me, Jed, John and Davie are first on the merchant's deck. Ah, but them Frenchies were ready for us, muskets, blunderbuss and carronade. And now follows a sharp set-to at close quarters, cutlass, pike, axe and pistol. Well, to cut things fine, sir, I sees Davie down an officer, a wealthy-looking bully. Just then, the Frogs strikes their colours, and Davie, always quick with his mitts, goes through the officer's clothes like a dose of salts, if you'll pardon the expression, sir.

'We lost some good men that day; but such takings, sirs, such takings! Gold, silver and mercury, not to mention spices a-plenty. That evening we sat in the bilges (we had just come off the middle watch and was not due on deck till eight bells), drinking wine we'd lifted and making plans for the days to come. By our reckoning, we'd made enough to set us up for life. You see, sirs, Davie had lifted a thick money-belt off o' the Frog officer. Then he brings out this sparkler, as big as a duck's egg, and says as how he'd cut off the officer's finger to get at it, and brags as how he'll be able to buy the *Viper* if he so wishes.

'I must have dozed off because the next thing I sees is Jed and Davie a-rolling on the deck, knocking empty barrels all over the place and Jed with his hands around Davie's throat. I tried to stop 'em, sir, God's truth: but the wine lay heavy with me. Then, suddenly Davie gurgles, ah terrible to hear, and after a while he stops kicking and I sees Jed lift the ring and pocket it and has a good rummage about Davie's clothes. I must have made a noise, for he turns and says "Now, curse ye, Matthew Pratt, not a word, for by God, ye'll surely hang with me. We'll share the money-belt with John Mallet, but I keeps the rest, mind. Now help me put Davie into this barrel."

'And Heaven help me, so I did. We shoves poor Davie down into that stinking barrel and hammers down the lid.'

'And what of John Mallet? What of him while this was going on?' queried Benskin.'

'Why, sleeping like a babe, your honour, being as he never could take much o' that Frenchie wine.'

Gaunt asked, 'How did you do away with the evidence of that murderous night's work?' But seeing the distressing affect his question had upon Pratt, added, 'Come now, Matthew, if you play it right with me, I swear that all you say shall go no further.'

'Well, sir,' said Pratt, somewhat mollified, 'we hauls the barrel up to the main deck; a gale had sprung up so little heed was taken of any bumping and groaning. There was no moon that night and we reaches the gunwales without being hailed. Then, as we lifts the barrel to throw it overboard, I hears him, Oh dear Lord, I hears him.' The seaman buried his face in his hands and rocked in his seat. Gaunt allowed him to recover in his own time.

'"Let me out, messmates," he calls, all muffled like from inside that barrel, "I can't see, I be sufticating, mates, in the name o' God, let me out!" Then he goes to a-banging and a-thumping – horrible, sirs, horrible. But Jed pays no mind and shoves me out o' the way and throws the barrel over the side. I swear I could still hear old Davie a-thumping away as the barrel drifted past. Then Jed, all crafty-like, waits a while before he shouts "man overboard!"

'They put a boat out but it was no use, a storm was coming up fast, so Cap'n Gwilliam says a short prayer and tells as how good a seaman and messmate Davie was, then we all goes back to our duties. But I never touched a penny o' that belt, sirs, God curse me if I lie. And here I sits and waits for the dark night when Davie shall come for me, though I have said a prayer for him every day since that terrible night.'

Pratt did not acknowledge their farewells, instead continuing to rock back and forth while mumbling dark obscurities.

* * *

The sun had set by the time they dismounted in the spacious court-yard of The George. Following a cold supper, Benskin took the first watch and painfully surrendered his seat to Gaunt three uneventful hours later. Gaunt had refused the offer of Benskin's two pistols, but as a compromise had taken the small sword that now leaned against a tall clock that ticked away in lugubrious monotony. The day's hard ride now began to tell on his body. The candles flickered; he began to doze.

Suddenly, Gaunt became aware of a change. No subtlety here, but instant, almost violent in its spontaneity. Then he saw it.

A grey mist, roughly human-shaped, that flitted from door to door like a bee seeking nectar. And the assault began, louder now than ever, brutal, vicious, obscene, a deep thudding that reverberated the length of the corridor. Gaunt turned sharply as something approached him from the rear – and relaxed as Benskin and Mallet, breathless from their dash, took their places by his side.

'See him, Sam, there by the middle door!'

Benskin spun round twice, a bewildered expression on his kindly features, 'See what, Tom? I see nothing. What of you, John?'

'Nor do I, sir,' affirmed a terrified Mallet.

Exasperation outweighed caution. Slowly, Gaunt approached the restless, darting shade. If it would be still for one moment . . . The door on his left opened and he found himself, once again, facing Jed Towers.

This time, the frenzied man gripped Gaunt's throat with hands strengthened and toughened by a lifetime of iron hard-ropes, violent recoiling cannon and vicious ice-drenched flapping canvas. Instinct-ively, he gasped – nothing entered his lungs. Through a darkening mist he saw Benskin and Mallet struggling with the madman. Then the grip on his throat eased. Through pain-filled eyes he saw the change taking place on the features of Jed Towers, features that must have mirrored his own.

During his naval career, he had witnessed the hanging of mutin-eers and pirates, but always from the quarterdeck. Now he was seeing those last moments at close quarters. The face turning from crimson to black, the veins ready to burst from the head and neck while blood forced eyes to pop like some ghastly made-up clown.

Towers collapsed. His back arched and his heels tapped a macabre staccato on the floorboards. By the time Benskin had loosened the man's vivid neckcloth, Towers was dead.

'Bless my soul,' gasped Benskin, 'Tom, look at this!'

Circling Towers's neck was a vivid, narrow red line.

* * *

Gaunt, sore of gullet, weary of spirit, rested for most of the following day. They met for supper in the somewhat noisy taproom. A fire glowed and candles twinkled upon glass. 'So, ghosts is it? Phantoms and shades. Not something a cove scientifically bent likes to hear, though it is said that the ghost of Sir George Villiers has been seen to walk.'

'I'm afraid, a ghost it was, Sam,' said Gaunt somewhat apologetically.

'Say no more, Tom, for I have smoked it. It was poor Davie Quarles who came back to take revenge for his terrible murder.'

Gaunt shook his head mournfully, 'Indeed, I must correct you – Lord! Towers has played old Harry with m' windpipes – you will mind how I asked if he was a Roman Catholic?'

'I do, and thought it mighty odd at the time.'

'Well, the first time Towers went for me, I noticed a crucifix about his throat. Oh, and by the bye, he mistook me for Davie Quarles. That is what led me to Matthew Pratt.'

'So – you are saying?' Benskin sounded miffed.

'I am saying that just before Towers attacked me, I *saw* the shade that walked these corridors. It was that of a French naval officer!'

'But what would he want with Towers? Towers had not laid a finger upon him.'

'I have heard of how the dead, if refused a burial service performed in the manner of their own faith, are unable to rest easy. The Frenchie would have been tossed over the side, like so many others that day. The crucifix must have been an ancient, and powerful, icon. The fact that it has vanished must surely mean that the poor creature has found peace.'

'What about a post-chaise?' beamed Benskin.

The Sheelagh-na-gig

MARY ANNE ALLEN

When William Haydn became rector of the parish of Applestone, a little village a few miles from Thaxted in the rural part of Essex close to the borders with Cambridgeshire and Hertfordshire, he quickly realised that the inside of the small fourteenth-century church, complete with timber belfry, was badly in need of repair. In particular, the rood screen, with its pretty tracery, and two late seventeenth-century monuments, were covered with the grime of many years, obscuring what appeared (to his admittedly untrained eye) to be their original colouring.

William's plan to have the furnishings restored easily gained the support of the parishioners, the female half of whom were won over by his youthful enthusiasm and good looks. Even the men admitted that, in twenty years or so, when he wasn't such a newcomer, the young priest would make a good replacement for the former rector, recently deceased. The ladies were full of money-making schemes, from bring-and-buy sales to sponsored bike races for the children. There was also the likelihood of a 'top-up' grant from an august body, so paying for the work would be little problem, though William was soon sick and tired of the formalities and paperwork involved. I think he was relieved, therefore, when I, the restorer recommended by the Diocesan Advisory Board, arrived at Applestone to spend a couple of days at the rectory and do some preliminary tests in the church.

It was just after Christmas, and pretty chilly, but at least it wasn't snowing as I drew up my red mini in front of the rectory as dusk started to fall. Of course, no work could be done that night, but the rector met me at the car and insisted on helping me to unload the cleaning materials and carry them over to the church right away. I knew the signs: here was a cleric so excited about his new living that he would insist on giving me the guided tour immediately, and no plea of a tiring journey would deter him. Best to get it over and done with; and, anyway, churches at dusk have their own particular atmosphere which has always appealed to me.

Some forty-five minutes later, having made approving and admiring noises about everything in the building that William Haydn pointed out to me (which did, indeed, seem like everything), I stood outside the church, waiting while he carefully locked the door. In the silence, my stomach rumbled embarrassingly, reminding me that I had not eaten since breakfast. I hoped that whoever cooked the meals at the rectory had been told that I was vegetarian.

Although by then it was quite dark, I could still make out most of the details of the church's exterior, and one thing in particular caught my eye. Under the eaves, to the east of the porch, was as fine an example of a sheelagh-na-gig stone carving as I had ever seen. These rather gross symbols of female sexuality, usually depicted as a naked, pregnant, and very busty woman, holding open her genitalia, are quite rare, and no one really knows what they represent. In most cases, I tend to favour the prosaic explanation that they are charms to protect the church against being struck by lightning.

I made some remark about the sheelagh-na-gig to William as he joined me, and noted with amusement that he was blushing fetchingly, if somewhat anachronistically.

Mrs Chapman, the housekeeper, served me with a pleasant mushroom omelette for supper, though she made it evident that such a meagre repast wouldn't do for the rector, who instead had a large plate of chops. There was a further hiccup in our relationship when Mrs Chapman said, 'I've got a nice bit of fish for you tomorrow, Miss Bradshawe,' and I had to explain that vegetarians don't eat fish. Nevertheless, the good inroads I made into the apple pie she provided for pudding seemed to improve her mood considerably.

Feeling replete, I settled down with coffee, while William searched through his bookshelves for something. Eventually he found it and handed it to me, saying, 'I'm afraid this is the only published history of the parish, but it's not without interest.'

L. G. Beddoes's *History and Antiquities of Applestone* (privately printed in 1907) proved to be rather charmingly filled with line drawings of the village; drawings which might be better described as enthusiastic rather than skilful. Here, for instance, was a picture of the sheelagh-na-gig.

'Look at this,' I said. 'It doesn't look a lot like the real thing, does it?'

'Now you mention it,' the priest replied, 'you're right. I suppose Beddoes's artistic abilities weren't quite up to it.'

'I think there's probably more to it than that,' I said. 'The differences between this and the actual carving are mainly of only one kind. The artist has toned down the sexuality of the original: see, the stomach is slimmer and the legs are not spread so far apart. This is nothing more than a fine example of Victorian prudishness. Beddoes may have been writing six years after Queen Victoria's death, but nineteenth-century morality didn't die with the turn of the century.'

'That's really fascinating,' said the rector, squirming a little. I quickly realised that nineteenth-century morality was still alive in the 1990s, especially among young men who had gone from public school straight into theological college, and had probably never had a girl friend.

I should have slept well. The location was certainly perfect. Applestone Rectory is two hundred years old, and adorned with delightful pargetting – that plasterwork decoration which is so common in northwest Essex. It is a particularly fine example, with patterns, flowers, and the occasional pink sheep and fox frolicking joyfully across the front of the house. What's more, the inside of the building has been carefully modernised, and my bedroom even had a bathroom en suite. I have stayed in everything from hideously drafty Victorian monstrosities to the tiny 'executive homes' which often replace them. If only all rectories could be like this one, I thought.

But sleep was slow in coming and, on the edge of it, I had to endure more than the usual number of hypnogogic dreams, which took the standard form of a familiar shape slowly transforming itself into something hideous. I have often thought that the scene in M. R. James's 'A View from a Hill', where a perfectly ordinary arm rises out of the ground and then begins to grow 'hairy and dirty and thin', must have been based on a hypnogogic dream of Monty's. Mine at Applestone, though, mostly concerned the sheela-na-gig, sometimes as portrayed by Beddoes, sometimes as it was in reality, and sometimes even grosser than that.

Nevertheless, I woke in a good mood, and started work in the church straight after breakfast. The morning passed uneventfully, but when I returned to the rectory for lunch I found that William had a visitor. Every village has its local historian, who likes to think of himself (or, indeed, herself) as the sole reservoir of accurate knowledge on the area. Mr Harvey was Applestone's. Apparently he had decided that I would need to see his huge collection of old photographs of the church in order to do my work properly. Not that I had any real objections to this – I like old photos as much as anyone, and they can be a valuable source of information – but I knew that I would need to get back to the church as soon as possible to take advantage of the light before it started to fail.

It was only polite to have a quick glance through the pictures, though I almost skipped straight past it when I came upon the sheelagh-na-gig photograph, but something odd struck me. Yes, there was no doubt about it: the carving in the picture differed from its present form. The female figure was distinctly less gross. By no means as decorous as in Beddoes's drawing, but not so fat as she was now. The photograph was, I noticed, dated on the back: 1945. Perhaps my dreams of the previous night had predisposed me to this revelation, but somehow I did not feel terribly surprised. Racking my brains for an explanation, however, produced only a – not terribly useful – memory of Walter de la Mare's 'All Hallows', in which evil forces progressively alter and restore a cathedral according to their own design.

Presumably whatever transformation had taken place had happened so slowly that no one in the village had noticed. Mr Harvey might have spotted it, since he apparently knew every single detail of every one of his photographs, but questioning revealed that he was severely short-sighted, and had not been able to see the original carving for years. In the face of the inexplicable, it's probably always the best idea to get on with the mundane, so I returned to work that afternoon and quite forgot the sheelagh-na-gig in my preoccupation with the cleaning tests on the monuments, which confirmed my suspicions that the colouring was almost certainly contemporary, though retouched at a later date.

The next day I expected to complete my assignment, but meanwhile that evening, with nothing to do, I returned to pondering on the mystery. Given William's response on the previous two occasions when the sheelagh-na-gig had been mentioned, I decided not to raise the subject with him and, as a result, conversation tended to flag after supper. In the end, he suggested a visit to the local public house, and I happily agreed.

The Green Man seemed a pleasant enough country pub, although I noticed with some irritation that the inn sign depicted a very ordinary Robin Hood instead of a portrayal of the ancient fertility symbol (the male version of the sheelagh-na-gig, I recalled, but quickly put that thought from my mind).

I was introduced to Johnny Fryer, the village gossip and storehouse of local stories for the past sixty years. I'm not quite sure how, but, despite my best efforts, the conversation came around to the subject of the stone hag; or 'Nagging Sheila', as Johnny called her.

'They did used to say,' he chuckled, 'that she were an old goddess who the vicar had trapped in the stone and wouldn't let out. My old grandparents would take a pear or apple or some such every year at Harvest Festival time and put it down by the wall under her, instead of in the church. A lot of other folks did the same. Us young 'uns thought it were all very silly, but we did get a beating if we tried to take some of the fruit, so it were left to rot. Do you notice when you go to the church tomorrow how good the ground is there for growing things.'

The codger paused for a drink (he could see that I was really interested, in spite of myself, and reckoned I'd be good for another pint at least). 'No one puts fruit out for her nowadays, but if you can believe the story I heard from my old gaffer then perhaps we oughta. Grandpa Fryer used to say that, while Sheila herself could never get free, she were pregnant, and if people stopped giving her her due, she'd get angry and eventually have a baby who'd take over the world. He said there were a bit in the Bible about it – Revelations, it were.'

William, who had just come up and was listening pink-facedly to the conversation, opened his mouth to correct him, but Johnny wasn't going to let anyone interrupt his tale, especially now that he'd reached the punchline.

'Some do say that the Sheila is growing and getting bigger and bigger with child, though I don't see it myself.'

'That really is quite enough,' burst out the rector. 'Don't you believe a word of it, Jane – he's the best story-teller in East Anglia.' As we walked back to the rectory, William broke the silence.

'I hope you didn't let what Johnny said worry you. He really is a great liar; or maybe it would be more charitable to call him an embroiderer of facts.'

I was less sure about that, but the rector was hardly the right person to discuss it with. I made some comment about there possibly being a basis of truth in Johnny's story, and if so it was a remarkably late survival of goddess worship, and left it at that.

I left it at that over breakfast the next morning too. In fact, I was so taciturn that Mrs Chapman took offence and clearly decided that her initial impression of me had been the correct one after all. I desperately wanted to complete my work in Applestone and get away as soon as possible. The whole village had taken on a nightmare quality. Whatever was happening, there was nothing I could do about it, and I felt that if only I could leave, I would return to the real world. I had already decided that, were I to be offered the full restoration job, I would find some reason to refuse it.

But my best-laid plans to avoid looking at the sheelagh-na-gig when I returned to the church to finish up came to nothing. As I passed it, I was unable to resist a swift glance in its direction.

In a way it was a relief, as I had almost expected it, although if Johnny Fryer's stories were even half true, the consequences don't bear thinking about. The sheelagh-na-gig had been transformed. It was no longer a grotesque female caricature. The new carving was crude and unformed, but there was no question about it . . . now it portrayed the Madonna and Child.

The Black Veil

A. F. KIDD

'I asked him whether he would object to my drawing a pentacle round him for the night and got him to agree, but I saw that he did not know whether to be superstitious about it or to regard it more as a piece of foolish mumming; but he took it seriously enough when I gave him some particulars about the Black Veil case, when young Aster died. You remember, he said it was a piece of silly superstition and stayed outside. Poor devil!'

William Hope Hodgson
The Horse of the Invisible

We had all seen the newspapers, although each of us knew that what we read there could only be a part, at best, of the full story. So none of us was surprised to receive a card in the usual vein from Carnacki, and none of us would willingly have refused the invitation.

No sooner had the four of us – Jessop, Arkwright, Taylor and myself – all presented ourselves at No. 472 than we were ushered in to dinner, during which our host was even more taciturn than was his wont. Afterwards, however, he settled himself comfortably in his great chair much as usual and waited for us to take our accustomed places.

'I dare say you fellows have seen the newspapers,' he remarked, puffing at his pipe. 'Though you won't have got much sense out of them. But you know that, of course. It's entirely due to that sort of materialistic scepticism that Aster died. An altogether curious and unpleasant affair and I can't say I am entirely blameless.

'Charles Aster was a newspaper reporter. Now as you know I won't, as a rule, have any truck with them, but there was something about his persistence which was rather – endearing, for want of a better word. The man was more like an importunate puppy than anything else, and he pestered me until I began to think I'd have to take him along on a "safe" case – as much as anything in this line could be termed "safe". As you know, it's a rather relative description!

'However, before a suitable case presented itself, Aster himself sent me a rather intriguing letter. It appeared that an uncle of his, a Mr Jago, had recently purchased a property in the West Country and was experiencing what Aster described as "some odd trouble" and begged me to come and investigate. In view of what I had been thinking, I decided to agree to this request.

'It appeared that the house had a long-standing reputation for being "queer" but Jago, far from being discouraged by this, had apparently viewed it as a positive asset! This is just the sort of thing I meant about the newspapers. However, one night spent in the house had been sufficient to disabuse him of these notions and convert him into a fervent believer in the power of the Ab-natural, with the result that Aster had suggested contacting me.

' "What exactly was it that happened?" I asked Aster when he met me on the train.

' "I can't tell you, exactly," he replied. "But there's something about the silence in that house that makes a chap beastly frightened."

'It was clear that Aster's uncle was in quite a funk. He was one of those big, fleshy men – you know the type – who bluster a lot, but when they snap, they've nothing to fall back upon. He was almost pathetically glad to see us when we arrived at the station, and prattled nervously all the way to the house.

'When we turned in at the gates – the house stands in its own grounds – Jago began to cast quick, tense little glances at it as if he were trying to catch it unawares – as if it were doing something furtive that he only suspected. Then suddenly he caught Aster's arm and whispered, "Look, look, the upper window!" His voice was that of a man who expected some horror, but who is still surprised by its appearance. Do you know what I mean?

'By that time, it was twilight, and logically it was quite absurd to suppose that either of us saw anything, for the windows were all in deep shadow. Still Aster and I were both convinced that we saw the figure of a woman silhouetted in the window Jago was indicating. Not only that, but I had the distinct impression that she was a young woman, although her features were obscured by a long, black veil. Now as neither Aster nor I had any indication of what form the "haunting" took, there was no suspicion of auto-suggestion – indeed, had it not been for the very odd fact that we could see her at all in that light, I for one would have taken her for the housekeeper.

'However, the effect which the sight of this woman had on Jago was extraordinary. With a cry of "The Woman, the Woman!" he shrank into the corner of the carriage, his face as white as cheese. But curiously enough, neither Aster nor I felt, at that stage, any sense of fear or even revulsion.

'As soon as we entered the house, though, the silence overwhelmed me. It was like an ocean swell – wave upon wave of it. I can't begin to describe the suddenness with which that sickening feeling overwhelmed me, and I recalled Aster's words. I knew there was something merciless in it – something brutal. My hands started to perspire, and glancing at Aster I could see that he, too, was sweating. He turned to Jago, who stood behind us outside the doorway, unable to cross the threshold.

' "What is it, uncle?" he asked, and his voice was not quite steady. "Is it that Woman?"

' "Not just her," Jago whispered. "I thought it was just her at first, and she couldn't harm me. I thought I'd give her a bit of company. But it isn't just her." He had actually decided to sleep in the haunted room out of sheer perverseness!

'After a while we got him indoors and I managed to extract the story from him. Having seen, as we had, the figure of the Woman from the outside, he had gone up the stairs and located the room whose window it was, with the intention, as I said, of spending a night there. I must say I marvelled at his nerve, because I had not been in the house an hour and the "creep" was crawling all over me. But according to Jago, it was not until he actually entered the room that anything happened to him.

' "As soon as I stepped inside the door of that Room, I began to have my doubts," he said. "It was so beastly quiet in there that it made me think – though I'm not a fanciful sort of chap – that Something was holding its breath, and waiting. And then, you know, everything went black. I don't mean I passed out – I don't think I was scared enough for that, then. No, it was as if I'd been struck blind, and if I hadn't had my hand on the doorknob, I think I wouldn't have got out. As it was, I gave a kind of backwards leap out into the corridor and slammed the door as I did it. And then I was outside and I could see again. I haven't been near the room since."

'You remember what I told you about "making a darkness"? At first I thought that was what Jago meant, but he was quite insistent. His candle had not gone out. He repeated the words, "struck blind".

'By then it was too dark to do anything about investigating the room, although it was not late by any standards. I have to admit I was grateful for this excuse. Now I've gone into too many cases connected with "ghostly" things to be accused of being a cowardly chap; but sometimes, you know, there are things you just can't face. That was one of those occasions. There was something pretty unholy in that house, and maybe I was being warned against tackling it without proper preparation. You never know, do you?

'So I didn't feel too bad about funking matters, but decided to go to bed and start fresh in the morning.

'I waited until full daylight before beginning my investigations – which at this early stage consisted simply of sealing up the room in such a way that I would be able to tell instantly if something material had entered it during the coming night. First I checked every inch of the walls, ceiling and floor, tapping then with a little hammer – the room was completely empty of furniture save for a wooden window-seat.

'Aster was tremendously interested in all this and I told him I didn't mind him watching, as long as he kept out of the way. Even in daylight, the atmosphere in the room was pretty beastly, and I didn't want any distractions of any kind.

'The room was not too large – only about twelve feet by ten – but it still took me a long time to cover every surface with the colourless sticky wafers I use to detect any material activity. I find then pretty foolproof for this purpose; I used to use chalk, as you know, until that "Locked Room" case in which the hoaxer was using the ceiling rose for access to the sealed room. After that I stretched hairs across the window and the window-seat, which had registered as hollow, of course, but resisted all my attempts to open it. The house was only about a hundred years old and therefore unlikely to contain such things as priest-holes, but the builder could well have put in secret passages for his own purposes. You can never take anything for granted in this sort of case.

'As I was in the process of sealing the door, Aster asked me why I used hairs for this purpose, rather than, say, cotton thread. I explained briefly, but he seemed unconvinced, and I was too busy with my work to pursue the matter further – I wish I had realised what it would mean. After that there was nothing to be done until the following day, so I convinced Jago that he should put up at an hotel for at least the next couple of nights. It was not difficult to persuade him, and shortly I prevailed upon Aster to accompany his uncle into town.

'You can imagine that I felt pretty small and lonely after they had gone. The winter evening was already darkening the sky, and I sat downstairs in the library with my revolver to hand, although I was more than half convinced by this time that this was a genuine "haunting". I spent the time reviewing the notes I had recently made from the Sigsand MS. You know what I told you about the "Defences" he mentions? Naturally I had assumed them to be simply the superstitions of the time, which had been superseded by other methods of protection – the Circle of Soloman, for one. But it occurred to me subsequently to wonder whether these old, old formulae would still be valid today, in the twentieth century; and I have, as you know, tried some of his suggestions before, with modest success.

'Still it is one thing to seal a door or window with hair and certain signs – quite another to trust one's own self to a type of barrier unused since the fourteenth century. And that is what I was contemplating, if the seals were unbroken in the morning. I had provided myself with the requisites for constructing such a barrier – certain herbs, for instance, candles, water vessels, and some things which I might call "creative interpretations" of Sigsand. But I am anticipating, here. There was nothing further that I could do that night, and so I went to bed.

'About midnight I went up to the room and loitered in the corridor for a little while, but that malevolent silence got on my nerves. I had intended to open the door and have a quick look inside, and had popped a couple of cloves of garlic into my pockets for protection – but I tell you, it would have taken more pluck than I had that night to open that door, in the end. I had the feeling that Something rotten and monstrous was waiting on the other side, and that it was *smiling* at me – smiling with a kind of mean, gloating anticipation. What an odd thought – eh?

'Of course, there was no sign of any disturbance the following morning. I had hardly expected it, but I went over the room very carefully, nonetheless, as I cleared away my paraphernalia.

'I had just unsealed the window when a cab drove round the corner of the drive and came to a halt in a flurry of gravel below me, to disgorge young Aster. He stood looking up at the window where I was, and suddenly I wondered what it was that he could see – me, or the Woman? I thought I had better hail him, and knelt on the window-seat to attempt to open the casement.

'The catch was infernally stiff, but at last I got it dislodged with a shriek of disused metal and leaned out to call to Aster. As I did so I heard a sharp "snick" – like the tumblers of a lock being turned – but ignored it for the moment.

' "Aster! I called

' "I say, Carnacki, is that you?" he cried. "I've found out some- thing about the ghost. Any luck your end?" But he was gone out of sight into the house before I could reply. I stood up from the window-seat to try and see what had made the noise; and, do you know, it was loose! The sound I had heard was the releasing of some internal catch, which had snapped open when I opened the window.

'Carefully, I eased open the lid. Remember, I had no idea of what, if anything, I should find in there; but I admit I was disappointed to see that it contained nothing but a mass of sooty cobwebs – or so I thought at first.

'By that time Aster had arrived. I heard his footsteps clattering down the corridor – at least, I hoped they were his! – and now he put his head round the door and asked if he could come in.

' "Come and tell me what you make of this," I said.

' "By Jove! you've got it open," he exclaimed, and before I could stop him he had reached into the window-box and brought out a handful of the black stuff, revealing it to be not cobwebs at all, but a couple of yards of cloth so fine or so old that his fingers tore through it as he lifted it.

' "The Black Veil!" he cried excitedly. I begged him to calm down and tell me what he was talking about, and at length he explained, and explained, too, why he had returned so soon. He had got the story of the ghost from some folk in the town, where apparently it was common knowledge.

'It was a nasty little story of the sort that one hears all too often as being behind "hauntings". The original inhabitant of the house, one Arthur Green, had been the worst sort of brute, given to beating not only his servant and animals but his unfortunate wife as well. She, poor woman, had appealed for help to some young man, and Green, assuming that she had taken a lover, had thrashed her so savagely that he blinded her. Green then imprisoned her in her room, where she remained until her death, but was often seen standing at her window clad in a long black veil; and after she died, she was to be seen still.

' "This must be her veil, Carnacki! What will you do with it? Bury it? Will that stop the haunting? Or does it have to be exorcised, or blessed, or something?"

'I told him rather shortly that I knew my business better than he did, and that I intended to burn the thing, but that it was by no means certain that this would put an end to the manifestations in the house.

' "There may be other circumstances we are not aware of," I told him. "We shan't know one way or another until tonight."

' "Do we spend the night in here?"

' "I can't tell you at this stage. First of all this Veil must be burnt."

'I had, as I have told you, equipped myself with a number of items out of which to construct a "Defence", and I employed some of these to construct a Pentacle around the Veil before burning it. Aster watched these proceedings with a very queer look on his face, but said nothing.

'When we went back into the house, I could tell at once that *something* had changed, but it seemed like a change without direction – I could not tell whether it was for the better, or not. It was just, somehow, different. I wonder if you know what I mean?

'I spent some time checking the room once more, and by about midday had more or less decided to chance it and spend a night in there. I was fairly sure that I had achieved at least a partial advance against the haunting, and it seemed like an ideal opportunity to test the Sigsand barriers. I told Aster what I intended, and invited him to observe the preparations which I should be making. He nodded thoughtfully, and after a scratch luncheon I set to work.

'Now as you know the powers and properties of herbs are well-documented, and so I felt quite justified in using certain of then specified by Sigsand – hyssop, vervain, St John's wort, and so on. To this I added garlic, which I have found to be most efficacious, in a limited but most specific sort of way, and ended up with a form of protection which I thought – I hoped! – would be peculiarly powerful.

'First I inscribed a circle, the outline of which I rubbed with garlic and swept with a spray of hyssop, the Holy Herb. Inside this I made a "Ringe of water and fyre" joining lighted candles with crescents of water using the Second Sign of the Saamaa Ritual; and then drew a Pentacle, making sure that each of its points touched the circle. In each of its five points I placed a wafer of certain bread and in the "vales" a small dish of holy water.

'All this took rather longer than I had anticipated, and by the time I had completed these precautions the sky outside the window was growing dark and I was glad of the light cast by the candles in my Defence. Then Aster, who had grown bored with watching, put his head round the door and remarked, in a conversational sort of way, "Are you going to let me into the joke, old man?"

' "I assure you this is quite serious," I replied curtly.

' "Well, it ain't science," Aster retorted. "I thought you were a scientist, Carnacki."

' "I don't discount things simply because modern opinion laughs at them," I told him. "Nor should you, Aster; an open mind is the best asset a journalist can possess."

' "The best thing this journalist possesses is a flashlight," he replied, drawing one from his pocket and switching it on, "not a piece of silly superstition."

'The bright light dazzled me momentarily, and I screwed up my eyes against it, but before I could admonish Aster, an awful chill swept over me. I knew what it was at once.

' "Get inside the barrier – or get out!" I shouted at him. "*Hurry*, Aster!" He turned a puzzled face to me, and I actually reached over the Defence to try and seize his arm, fearful of breaking the barrier but somehow more fearful for Aster himself.

'Then, just as Jago had described, everything went dark – a stifling blackness that you *knew* would not admit any light, ever. And in that Stygian darkness I heard Aster scream, followed by a thud and soft rumble as his flashlight hit the floor and rolled away somewhere.

' "I've gone blind – blind!" he cried. I tried to call to him, but my throat had closed up and I could not make a sound, although I was in mortal dread that he would blunder into my Defence and make a path for Whatever was in that room. Then he screamed again, and the sound was one I hope I never hear a man make again. All semblance of humanity had gone from his voice – I can't begin to describe the sick feeling of horror I felt at it. It was the negation of all that is clean and sane and wholesome to us, as is the touch of the Outer Monstrosities. No, it's no good – I am quite unable to convey to you the sheer *depth* of vileness in it.

'I crouched in the centre of the Pentacle, all sense of direction lost. I had no idea where the door was, or the window, or even Aster – the thing which had been Aster – although I could hear him crawling round, making a sick, inhuman moaning noise which was somehow worse than the scream. In the utter silence it sounded like a voice from the Pit.

'Even now I do not know how I got through that night. I felt physically and spiritually ill, and almost paralysed with fear – although if I had been able to see the door, I think I might have made a run for it. Thank goodness I didn't.

'At some stage the noises coming from Aster ceased, and at long last light began to grow outside the window – the cold and whole-some light of a winter morning. I found I could see again, and sure enough, my candles were still alight. Aster's body was huddled in a corner, and his flashlight glowed where it had rolled, just outside my outer circle. I made a move to pick it up, and then, you know, the most horrible thing of all happened.

'What made me look in Aster's direction then I don't know, for I was sure he was dead. But as I moved, his eyes snapped open, and met mine. Their very *lack* of expression was so monstrous that I was paralysed, not with physical fear, but with the hideous conviction that I was actually on the brink of being dragged down into some foul depths beyond anything we humans are ever meant to know. And all that stood between me and the instrument of that descent which stared at me with its dead and gleaming eyes was a Pentacle and a ring of garlic!

'Aster began to shuffle towards me, with an odd, broken-limbed crawl. I fumbled for my revolver, and then paused. Aster's progress had halted. As I watched, he snuffled at the outer circle of my Defence, and drew back; crept around a little way and sniffed again – I felt a thrill of hope. The barriers ware holding him back! The pathological, spiritual change which he had suffered – put simply, soul destruction – had transformed Aster into something so totally un-human that he was as unable to cross as any purely aetheric manifestation.

'Then, as suddenly as it had become animated, Aster's body went limp and collapsed in front of me. It took me an instant to realise that it lay in a beam of weak sunlight which had just that moment struck through the window. Nevertheless I waited until full daylight before venturing out of the Defence, and even then I had to "take my courage in both hands" before I could bring myself to touch Aster's body. He was quite dead.

'The house was demolished last week. There was absolutely noth-ing in the way of physical remains to suggest how the haunting had reached such a tremendous pitch.'

'No pathetic little skeleton buried in the cellars, then?' queried Arkwright.

Carnacki shook his head. 'Possibly the simple fact of the woman's dying a lonely, painful death in that room was sufficient to imbue its fabric with the feelings of her last months.'

'And Aster?' I asked. 'Do you think the Defence would have protected him, since he didn't believe in it in the first place?'

'That particular brand of metaphysics is not my field,' replied
Carnacki sternly. 'Out you go! I want a sleep.' And he ushered us all
out on to the quiet Embankment, as always.

Like Clockwork

R. B. RUSSELL

I made the acquaintance of Mr Magarshack in his declining years, in a small hospice where I would visit my late grandfather. The two men were unlikely friends; my old relative had lost the power of speech through a stroke, and Mr Magarshack was able to talk endlessly on a wide variety of subjects. The latter had been a geologist, but the topics of his conversation ranged wider than one might have expected for a man who was so obviously proud of his profession. It was in the last couple of weeks before his death, and a whole six months before my grandfather died, that he told me a tale that left me wondering whether any of his anecdotes could be trusted. Of his most outrageous story he claimed to have offered me proof, but a few old pages of yellowed writing paper mean very little . . .

He had been prompted to talk about some very curious experiences by a remark that I had made about a dream I remembered from the night before. I told him that I had bought an impossibly rare book for a few pennies, and was annoyed on waking to find that the acquisition had not really occurred. Mr Magarshack shook his head and announced sententiously: 'The dreams that turn out to be reality are far worse, believe me.'

I could not help but ask him to explain, and for a change he suddenly became unwilling to talk. However, after a few seconds his garrulous nature got the better of him: 'Many years ago, when I was quite a young man, I had a friend in the police force who was troubled by an inexplicable murder. He became frustrated by it, and on the first night of my return to the city, after several weeks away surveying to the north, he insisted on taking me to the scene of the crime. It was a sordid little house in a disreputable quarter, and the walls were still stained with the blood of the innocent victims. I remember the way that the moonlight came in at the window and made the scene all the more ghastly. There had been a struggle, and the furniture was broken and strewn all about the floor. It was no surprise that I dreamt about the room that night, and quite natural that I would relate the details to my friend the next day. Only, I didn't just dream about the room, but of the tragedy that had so lately been played out in it. If I recall correctly, I was able to describe the killer with some degree of minuteness, and I said that in my dream the murderer had run out and across the back yard to a house directly opposite. There he had hidden the weapon under the floorboards of his own kitchen.

'I thought little more of the dream, but the next night my friend came to my rooms with a bottle of wine to celebrate the fact that the murderer was in custody, apparently as a result of my dream. It was a wonderful coincidence as far as we were both concerned. My description of the murderer bore a certain resemblance to a suspect who lived opposite the scene of the crime. My friend had visited the man to ask a few routine questions and became suspicious when he spotted an uneven floorboard in the kitchen. The discovery of the murder weapon just where I had dreamed it would be resulted in his arrest.

'My friend took me to the scene of the next violent crime he investigated, perhaps by way of a joke. It may have been that his odd sense of humour was hiding a certain amount of desperation because again the investigation was at something of an impasse. It was not a murder, but an attempted strangulation in which the victim had not seen her attacker. My subsequent dream led to the detection of the villain, and the poor woman's jewellery was discovered in the possession of his wife.

'At this point my friend dropped me. He did not find my dreams amusing any longer. He became more than just wary of me but actually suspicious, for how on earth did I know these things? We had been close friends from childhood, and until that point both of us would have trusted the other in all things. But now he would not visit, and was always unavailable when I tried to visit him. My surveying took me away from the city for several months and it was only *in extremis* that he asked me to come back and aid him. Some important state papers had been purloined and he had been given the case. Again, he was making no progress.

'I dutifully accompanied him to the house of the politician who had been burgled, but if I dreamed of anything that night I did not remember the details the next morning. At the time this caused considerable frustration for both my friend, who was desperate to uncover the crime, and for me, because I wanted to help someone whose good opinion I craved. It appeared, subsequently, that I could only dream of crimes where there had been a vast upsurge of emotion, such as a bloody murder, or a brutal assault in the heat of an argument. These violent crimes were especially vivid. Cold, calculated, callous wrong-doing did not seem to register with me. And I would always see events from the vantage of a disembodied observer.

'My friend used me for information on any number of cases over the years, and rose up through the ranks of the police force because of his apparently uncanny ability to know just who the villain was. On many more occasions I was called in by him from where I was working, sometimes many hundreds of miles away in another part of the country, because he was getting nowhere with a case.

'But, of course, it has never been a question of simply identifying the guilty party; you need proof if you are to convict. It always sur-prised me that the majority of criminals broke down and confessed when confronted with details of their story. As time passed, however, there were several who refused to admit their crimes, either to the police or, I suspect, to themselves. Often I could help, saying where the murder weapon was disposed of, or how they had made an ingen-ious escape from the scene of the crime. But I was also able to prevent several miscarriages of justice, and this frustrated us.

'My friend came to be so confident of my information that he was more than ordinarily angry when we knew who the perpetrator of the crime was, but could not prove it. He hated to let anyone escape justice where he felt it was due. He was finally asked to look into the case of a society gentleman whose wife had fallen from a height and had died. I saw that it was murder, he believed me, but there was no way of proving that she had been pushed by her husband. In his desperation my friend forged a letter and claimed it as evidence. He was discovered, and thrown out of the force, mainly at the instigation of the murderer, who had powerful contacts in the judiciary.'

Mr Magarshack shook his head in sadness, and for once, unchar-acteristically, excused himself from our company. On his two sticks he hobbled back to his own room, leaving me and my grandfather to look mutely at each other and shrug.

On my next visit, my grandfather was in Mr Magarshack's room, being talked to, and I joined them, noting that the old man in the bed did not look well. He broke off from some apparently interminable tale of surveying mines in the east to say that he wanted to make some explanation of the story he had told me on my previous visit.

'I do not believe in the paranormal, the supernatural, or the occult,' he insisted. 'That's all so much mumbo-jumbo . . . '

'So how do you account for your dreams?' I asked.

'I don't,' he said firmly, if unhelpfully. 'I don't understand them at all. If they bore any relation to what really happened, I was never in a proper position to check. For all I know, my friend may have taken my word for exactly who the criminals were, and convicted many innocent people. He claims that many of them confessed. I don't know . . .'

Although he now broke off his address to me, it was obvious that he had more to say. I waited patiently until he finally told me to look in the cupboard where he kept his private documents.

Here I found a profusion of ledgers and books, maps and charts, but also many, many sheaves of papers, some tied up in string, some in collapsing piles, others in old files and envelopes. The confusion of old, yellowed paper was almost overwhelming, and not easy to sort through because I had left my reading glasses at home. Eventually I found the large manila envelope that he told me I should unearth somewhere towards the bottom of the heap. I passed it to him.

'I am a sceptic,' he explained, as, with shaking hands, he took out and looked over a few thin pages of paper, 'but one case seemed to prove that I was able to precisely dream of violent events of the recent past. I don't have any explanation of this.

'I was never directly involved with any of the criminals, or their victims. I just reported what I had dreamed after a brief visit to the scene of the outrage. And then a curious case came before me. It was not classified as a murder because nobody knew quite how the poor woman had died. Or, rather, they knew how she had died, but not what had caused her death. All they knew was that it was highly unnatural, and all felt that a particular gentleman was somehow responsible, but could not prove it. He refused to confess to the police. My friend was not directly involved with the case, but hoped that I might throw light on it and thus help a colleague of his who happened to be the city coroner.

'I didn't view her corpse or anything dramatic like that; she had already been buried for some months when I was asked to help. Besides, I simply needed to see *where* she had died. I was therefore taken to a large and respectable house on the edge of the city by my friend. The old man of the house was at home but unable to receive visitors (his health had deteriorated since his wife's death.) No other family members were present, but an old servant let us in and showed us where the woman had died. It was an unremarkable room, a study, and seemed to make no impression upon me at all. However, the following night I dreamed of what had happened . . .'

'It must have been distressing to have such dreams?' I suggested. 'To see murders, attacks . . .'

'Yes, every time it was upsetting. I never became used to them, or "hardened", as you might say. And in this case the woman's death was really very horrible. But my first dream was of little use to the police. I saw her death, but nothing useful of the events leading up to it, or immediately following it. I could only really tell them what they already knew.'

'So you didn't see her murderer?'

'No. Or perhaps I did, but couldn't remember him because of the horror of the death itself.'

'You said "first dream"?'

'Yes. I became a little obsessed, and desperately wanted to help. What little I could tell the police sounded so unlikely . . . So I returned to the house on my own, and met the younger gentleman of the house, the old man still being indisposed.

'I expect that was enough – meeting him, I mean. I am not spoiling my story by telling you that this younger gentleman was the murderer. It was clear from his face. He demanded to know why I wanted to visit the study, and I told him about my dream. I'm sure I shouldn't have done, but because of what I could tell him his defences fell apart and he admitted the crime. He became distraught, and tried to make a confession to me. I could not hear or understand a word of it because he was so overcome with emotion. I left him prostrate on the floor of his drawing room.

'I went to inform my friend in the police force, but by some mischance he was unavailable until the next day, and I wasn't in a position to talk to any of his colleagues. That night I dreamed of the whole affair again, but in greater detail, and the following morning I received a letter, a full confession, from the gentleman I had seen the previous day. He had added a note to say that I should pass it on to the police, if I saw fit.'

Mr Magarshack tried to pass me the papers, but I pointed out my lack of glasses. He fumbled for his own on the cabinet beside his bed.

'I never did give this statement to the police, or tell my friend in the force of my second dream,' Mr Magarshack admitted. 'Rather than see events as a disembodied observer, my second dream was from this poor fellow's point of view, and was identical to his confession. This is what he wrote.

'My dear Sir,

'I realise that you are not a detective, but somehow you have discovered the details of the death of Lilly Cardigan. Those who have interviewed me have failed to understand anything thus far, although some firmly believe that I was responsible for the death of Lilly Cardigan. The more generous men I have met believe I may be suffering from some nervous disorder as a result of witnessing her death, but their generosity is misplaced. I do look pale and wan; cadaverous is a better description, and I have no doubt that guilt and grief play their part. But it is also due to lack of exercise, and the fact that I have the most insipid of diets: I simply do not wish to excite myself. I can only shake my head, slowly, at their attempts to understand what occurred on that fateful night. I would laugh at their suggestions, but I must not make any violent movements. How I survived the exhibition I made of myself yesterday I do not know.

'Let me explain my circumstances. My income is sound, and is based upon the watch-making business in which I have lately become a partner with William Cardigan. Since the death of his wife he has been unable to continue in the business which I now administer on his behalf. We have good men working for us who are now paid very well indeed (I have ensured their loyalty and trust by also giving them a financial stake in the firm.) All have good eyes and quick minds, and the watches made by Cardigan's are very well respected. This was not always so. Mr Cardigan, who founded the business forty years ago, was a devious business-man, but not a good watch-maker. He employed cheap labour, and cheaper materials, and his watches were but poor imitations of the art.

'I came to work for him at fourteen. He had worked from out of his premises for many years, and had never raised the wages of his employees once. I was employed for but a few shillings a week.

'My eyes were good, though, and my mind agile. I made some startling innovations and excelled at my work. A rival employer tried to tempt me away from Cardigan, but the shrewd man gave me a rise to match their offer and I remained. Cardigan was a cheapskate, but he was not a bad man to work for. In fact, as he came to recognise the value of my labour he showed me a great deal of respect, and I was given some of the most import-ant commissions. My wages became quite reasonable when he realised that I was tempted to take up more lucrative positions elsewhere. Had he continued to pay a pittance, however, I would still have stayed. But I will explain more in a moment.

'Watches were my life. I loved the intricacy, the precision, and the art. At home, in the evenings, I tinkered with watches, and after a while I became taken with the creation of small automata. I started to make miniature toys, and for the daughter of a colleague I created in metal a dragonfly with working, fast-moving wings. I evolved a mechanism whereby these wings could be folded into the dragonfly's body, and the toy could then be snapped shut on itself. It was a beautiful piece of workmanship, as all agreed, but even as I built it I realised the refinements that could be made.

'As I said, I would have remained in Cardigan's employment no matter what wage he paid. You may guess that a woman was involved. And most would assume that I was interested in Cardigan's daughter, who, in a very quiet ceremony, has lately become my wife. But no. His daughter, was, and is, God bless her, a plain little thing, and uninteresting to me. It was Cardigan's wife, Lilly, who fascinated me. She was a tall red-head, with slender hips and small breasts, and the deepest of deep green eyes. I often tried to find ways of describing her eyes, but my imagination was not up to the task. Her eyes were not like emeralds, for emeralds are too cold; they were not like holly leaves, for they are too prickly . . .

'My dragonfly toy was shown to Cardigan, and he shook his head. He admitted that I was bound for great things. He increased my wages, invited me to dinner at his home, and said that I would be the making of his firm. He asked me to make another as a gift for his wife, and I was happy to oblige. I immediately realised how the next model would unfold on a small spring, and how the act of unfolding would wind up the mechanism which would cause the wings to move. I was inspired by the woman who would receive the gift.

'This was the first time that I had been to Cardigan's home, and I discovered that his house was a great gothic affair of red bricks, perched on the edge of a suburb to the north. A maid opened the door, but Cardigan himself strode out into the hall to meet me. I should describe the man.

'Francis Cardigan was a little over six foot, with greasy greying hair which left a small dusting of white over his broad shoulders. He had a large moustache, and the style in which it was worn enabled his employees to tell his mood. Cardigan was only in his middle age, but that night he suggested that he would some day need a junior partner to pass the firm on to. He was also a great drinker of port wine, and it was after he had drunk rather too much that this suggestion was made.

'Cardigan's wife I have already described, but I ought to mention that I had seen her just a short while before I ever found work with her husband. Early one morning I was travelling into town in a second class railway carriage and I put my head out of the window in a break between the smoke. The air was like Imperial Tokay, too cold but sweet and clear. From the first class carriage just a few feet away a woman also put out her head. The wind streamed her red hair out behind her. I was dumbfounded to see the golden morning light shine through it and it was not red at all but copper and russet and hazel and aflame. She turned her head in my direction and it blew into her face. As she pulled it away I saw Lilly Cardigan for the first time. She hastily withdrew her head into the carriage.

'She now looked at me over the dinner table as her husband made these suggestions of partnership. Their daughter was a plain little thing, as I have said, and she stared at me pathetically from beneath drooping eyelids. In gratitude to the old man I outlined an idea for a watch that I wished to make for him. It would be a lady's watch, shaped as a semi-circle when closed, engraved as a half-moon, but which would be opened to reveal the full face of the dial. It took a year to perfect, and it was over a similar meal with Cardigan's family, that I revealed my creation. He marvelled at it. He went over it in detail, hoping to suggest refinements or make alterations, but after two weeks deliberation told me that I was to make a dozen of my half-moon watches with as many jewels as I needed, and that I was to instruct the silversmiths in all particulars so as to create the most sumptuous appearance for my watch. We were to employ a particularly fine firm in Paris to carry out the enamelling for us, which was to be a delicate sky blue.

'Of course, inevitably, as it went into production I realised that there were further refinements that should be made. This was always the case. I was still trying to perfect my mechanical dragonfly for his wife and had lately realised how to improve that once again. My automaton could unfold from a metal disk the size of a shilling, into a creature with wings that would span your hand. I also saw that this technique could be adapted to the watch that I was already in production; simply closing either the watch or the dragonfly would wind it up.

'The morning after this discovery I boldly strode into Mr Cardigan's office to tell him of my plans and suggest that the watch be redesigned. However, he was not at his desk. A little annoyed that I would have to wait to share my enthusiasm with a willing audience I impatiently looked at the trade journal open on his chair. I was not really in the mood to read it, but the headline caught my eye: WM. CARDIGAN'S INNOVATION. The article praised the intricate mechanism of my half-moon watch, and my employer claimed the invention as his own.

'I did not know what to make of this. As my employer did he have a right to claim the credit for my work? Surely not, for the invention had been the product of my leisure hours. If he had returned to his office at that moment an unpleasant scene would have arisen, but he was detained elsewhere for another half hour, by which time my passion had abated, and was replaced by a devious desire for revenge.'

At this point in his reading of the statement Mr Magarshack lowered the fragile pages and looked over his glasses at me. 'If I remember correctly, this was the first element in my second dream. I felt his anger towards the old man. Now I knew why this was so.'

Magarshack took a second to find his place in the confession once more, and continued.

'Cardigan made no mention of the article, and I did not offer my true reason for wanting to talk to him. We talked as friends rather than employer and employee, for he was in a fine mood, and, praising my work to the highest degree, he offered me yet another small rise in my wages and a promotion of my position within the firm. I convinced myself that this was neither generosity nor guilt, but sound business sense: he did not want me to move to his competitors.

'That season my half-moon watches were a success; they could not be made quick enough to meet the demand, and the formerly cheapskate Cardigan even allowed a very limited *de luxe* edition which involved his purchase of the very best metals, jewels, and even some extra-fine enamelling work in several colours. I bided my time and worked on my automaton, and my method of revenge.

'Looking back on that time I became obsessed. I can see that very clearly now. It was only a watch, and it was only my pride that had been attacked. I should have confronted him with the theft of my idea, or I should have left it and put the effort into the winding refinements for which I would receive the credit, and not just my employer. But I became fanatical, and while I was considering the clever ways of avenging myself I was also obsessed by the mechanism of my dragonfly. Intricate changes and subtle adjustments were made to my plans for both, and in so doing I rather lost my way. I believe that I may have actually forgotten the cause of my ill-will towards Cardigan, and I certainly forgot why I was meant to be making my toy.

'The latter needs to be described; when folded away the finished device was the size of a shilling, though somewhat fatter, and with a soft, rounded edge. A shake or a jolt would prime it, then another would cause both the top and bottom to unfold like flower petals, and then it would appear to turn itself inside out once, and it ended up roughly the size of a matchbox. Suddenly it looked like a finely wrought, bizarre insect. I spent so much time on the devious mechanics of the thing that I gave little thought to its appearance and my evolving mechanical contrivance looked less like a dragonfly than a wasp. Legs would appear, but I had not thought about their aesthetics at this point and they had sharp barbed hooks on the ends. Immediately, the precious, skeletal instrument fizzed and buzzed, and it would proceed to walk over any surface, and with the unfinished legs, even a sharp incline. Where I planned to construct the beautiful wings, as in the previous attempt made for the daughter of the colleague, at the moment two sharp blades flicked to and fro. After a full half minute of elegant but fast movement the blades were gone again into the back of the creature. The actual design of the wings was for later; I simply needed to leave enough space for them inside the folded-up case. It was designed to continue to walk for another half minute until the mechanism wound down.

'My automaton was far removed from the quiet and easy movement of my watches. It was impossible at the time for the indulgent eyes of its creator to see that it had become a rather frightening little creature with its delicate cutters. Rather than a dragonfly I had created a furious beetle, or a demonic lady-bird, but I was very proud of my mechanism. The minute machinery was so intricate and delicate, every part of it moving swiftly and smoothly, and yet it could be folded up so small and hidden away.'

Magarshack coughed and I had to fetch him a glass of water. 'I can still see that little device of his, with its delicate cutters . . . The poor fellow then wrote in his confession:

'For several months I considered how I was to avenge myself, and it was not a lack of courage that stopped me but a lack of ideas. Somehow, in the depths of my unconscious mind, I knew that my automaton would have to have a part in my revenge, but I did not know how. It was while I was still trying to evolve a plan that another indignity, something petty and minor compared to any previous indignities, made me loose my reason. But I had become so devious by now that I was able to hide it. My chance seemed to present itself immediately; that very afternoon I was told by Cardigan himself that he would be alone that night; his wife and daughter were leaving for the country and his servants all had the night off to go to a local fair. I did not have any plan in mind when I rang his bell, and it was indeed he who answered the door to the quiet, dark house. He was surprised to find me on his front step, but asked me in, civilly enough. I said that we had a matter of horological innovation to discuss and I could see that he immediately imagined the possibility of increased profits through some new design of mine. He ushered me into his study and poured us both port wine. I wasted no time.

'I immediately confronted Mr Cardigan with the article in which he had claimed my half-moon watch as his own. He made a number of pitiful excuses and was obviously prepared for a fight. I listened patiently and was reasonableness itself. I did not argue, but asked a number of pertinent and incisive questions which made him so uncomfortable that he offered me the junior partnership that he had suggested some time before. In my presence he even made out a letter to his solicitor instructing them to draw up the relevant papers. After all that I had imagined I would have to do to receive justice from this man, it had been delivered into my hands through simply asserting myself! I was to get what I deserved, after all, by simply confronting him, but somehow this was not enough. I could not simply forgive and forget.

'The papers were signed the following afternoon, and I was a partner in the firm. There had been a number of people on the premises, solicitors and witnesses, and I had not yet seen my chance to take the matter any further. I knew what I wanted to do, and suddenly we stood alone in his office, the building empty due to the lateness of the hour. I had been hoping all afternoon that he would open the bottle of port and propose a toast but he was being uncharacteristically temperate. In a flash of inspiration that was my downfall I humbly told Cardigan that I had fallen in love with his daughter, and asked his permission to court her. He was surprised but then delighted, and, of course, could not resist the toast. The deep red wine was poured into two large glasses and the toast was made.

'As though good fortune had marked me out for special attention there was suddenly a sound at the door and he put down his glass. The moment that he turned his back to investigate I slipped my little automaton into his glass. It disappeared into the rich darkness of the wine. I had no doubts that when he returned he would take his usual deep draught, head back and throat open, and the contents of the glass would be downed in an instant. He returned, however, with his wife and daughter.

'Lilly Cardigan looked stunning in a black velvet gown, her collar bone and throat a perfection in ivory. Their daughter was unremarkable in a grey dress of some coarse stuff. Both looked harassed, but their faces were bright when Mr Cardigan immediately announced that I wished to go a-courting. When two more glasses of wine were poured I was unable to move. I was so astounded that my declaration of counterfeit love had been revealed to others that I could say no word. In the moment of confusion I even put down my glass and now had no idea whose drink contained my automaton.

'Dropping it into the wine would have jolted the device and primed it. Cardigan threw back his wine with gusto, and in desperation, not caring, I did the same. In her excitement at the news Lilly did the same, and their daughter looked pathetically into hers and took a single sip.

'Of course it was Lilly who swallowed my device. The pain must have been unbearable. She did not writhe for long. Blood came from her mouth, her eyes, her nose and ears. She lay among her red hair and her red blood as her husband and daughter wailed and screamed ineffectually. He dashed out for a doctor, and she hugged her mother's chest sobbing uncontrollably. I saw a blue blemish appear under the white skin that was taut over her collar bone. It darkened, then became violently red and split. My automaton calmly walked out and over the floor and stopped by the wall, where it folded itself up. Almost unbelievably it had not been seen, and I picked it up and placed it in my pocket.'

Magarshack paused, and then said: 'In my first dream all that I could remember was that the woman had swallowed something with her wine. She knew she had swallowed something, and was surprised. I didn't know what it was, and I saw her die, perhaps assuming that the two things were unconnected. I was wrong, though. As soon as I saw something cut its way out I knew that it had caused her death, and knew how horribly she had died. I awoke without seeing quite what it was, though; without seeing it walk across the floor, or be picked up . . .

'In my second dream I saw everything, including the man picking up his clockwork device and putting it in his pocket, not casually, or with satisfaction, but in terror. And then my second dream ended. The little extra information came at the end of the confession. He added:

'That night I found myself alone in Cardigan's study, drinking his wine and playing in misery with the little device that had been the instrument of death for such a lovely woman. The insides of the metallic insect would contain her blood, fragments of her flesh and bone, but I could not open it. I despaired to think that she could have so easily swallowed it. I placed it on my tongue and thought what a large object it felt, how nobody could possibly have swallowed it without noticing. I took it with my tongue to the back of my throat, not believing that she had not realised she had swallowed this alien object. And suddenly it was gone.

'So now you understand why I take no exercise, and have the most uninspiring of diets. I do my utmost not to excite myself for fear of activating a mechanism which has never passed through my body. There are times when I wonder just where it has lodged, and whether I would survive its exit.'

Mr Magarshack smiled weakly as he put down the confession and took off his glasses. He rubbed his eyes and said: 'Old Mr Cardigan lived to be a very old man, a perpetual invalid, under a joyless roof shared by the pathetic young man and his plain wife.'

'Did you continue to work with the police after that?' I asked.

'Yes, I did, in my very unofficial capacity. But I took every precaution not to meet the perpetrators of the crimes I saw in my dreams. You see, I have a terrible feeling that if I had met any of them that every one would have had an equally appalling tale to tell. Perhaps, like that young man, they would have suffered just as many agonies, daily, if most of them had not been blessed with the effective balm of the hangman's noose.'

Spirit Solutions

ROSALIE PARKER

January 23

It has been snowing all day – the trees in the garden are hung with
icicles and Graham and Simon had to shovel off some of the thick
white blanket that coated the drive so that Clive Mason could inch
his car up to the house. I could see him peering over the steering
wheel from the hall window, his glasses perched on the end of his
nose. I always had the impression that father enjoyed Mason's somewhat obsequious professional manner – I suppose that is why, after
the rumours began circulating, he allowed him to continue handling
his affairs.

Mason looked us over one by one as if we were still small children
arranged for his approval (we had gathered in the hall when we heard
his car turn into the drive). Fay took his coat and Graham, snapping
out of a reverie, led the way into the music room. It was as cold as the
grave. You could see your breath in front of your face. I felt like
fetching my duvet.

There were no surprises. At least I think we all knew what father
would do. Mason droned through the preliminaries. The money
went into mother's years of care. All there is left is the house, and
that father has bequeathed jointly to the four of us. Fay snivelled
discreetly into her handkerchief. Simon tapped his foot against
the table-leg. Graham cleared his throat as if about to speak, then
thought better of it.

I wondered how long it would take him, but at least he waited until
Mason had left. The kitchen is still the only warm room in the house
and, as Mason pootled his way back up the drive, we regrouped
around the Rayburn. Graham gathered himself up and began.

'Well, I believe you all know what I think we should do, and I'm
sure it's what Father would have wanted. This place has got to be
worth a tidy sum, even in this condition. We'll do well enough out of
it. I'll ring Ratcher and Flimcock in the morning, shall I?'

There was an uncomfortable silence. Simon frowned. 'Hold on, Graham, don't you think you're being a bit hasty, even if we decide that's what we want to do in the end. Anyway, the will has to go through probate first.'

'And', put in Fay, 'how can you be sure that's what Daddy wanted? He carried on living here right up to the end, didn't he? Don't you think he wanted one of us to live in the house. Otherwise he could have sold it and bought somewhere more convenient.'

'He knew and you know that no one of us can afford to buy the others out. We have to sell.'

'Not necessarily.' I said. 'One of us could rent it off the others.'

No one except Graham felt like talking about it any more after that, although I suppose we'll have to sooner or later. Simon offered to buy us a take-away curry for supper, but in the end we decided to make do with tinned meatballs and rice from Father's larder.

We are sleeping in our old bedrooms. I am sorely missing my central heating. I'd forgotten how cold the house is, even in bed under the duvet with a hot water bottle. I hope it has stopped snowing by tomorrow.

January 24

It snowed through the night and was still snowing this morning. I got up early and found Graham in the kitchen shivering over a cup of coffee. The Rayburn had gone out.

'When are you going home, Graham?' I asked.

'Going anywhere may not be easy if it carries on snowing. And I think we need to sort out what we're doing with the house first. I'm going to call a family meeting.'

He was looking uncomfortable. 'What's up, bro'?'

'Oh, you'll find out soon enough anyway. It's started again'

'What?'

'You know. The noises. The music. I heard them last night.'

It seems that he heard the full range – the clumping footsteps along the landing, the whispering, the piano-playing in the music room – everything we used to hear when we were children. I've never been able to properly explain what happens in this house, although I've tried often enough, usually when I've drunk too much at dinner parties. When we were children it didn't seem threatening, we just accepted it as part of the way things were. And there has never been anything to *see*. Just the sounds – of faint, far-off music, indistinct voices and the occasional heavy treading upstairs. A poltergeist, although it was a long time before we learnt to call it that.

Fay and Simon didn't hear anything either.

'Perhaps it's never gone away,' said Fay.

'But father didn't mention it,' put in Simon.

'He wouldn't, would he?' said Graham.

Graham's family meeting began over breakfast, and continued, on and off, all day. Early on, I wondered aloud whether the presence of the poltergeist would enhance or detract from the desirability of the house to prospective buyers. Fay wants to live here, but even if the rest of us agree, she couldn't afford to rent it at the going rate. Simon will follow whatever Graham wants, although he likes to play Mr Reasonable while he pretends to make up his mind.

And me? Oh, well, I'm an undecided. A definite don't know.

We'll have to do some shopping tomorrow – we've eaten our way through most of father's meagre store cupboard. And at least it has stopped snowing, although the stuff has covered over the drive again and is weighing down the branches of the shrubs in the garden. If we have to stay here much longer, we'll run out of logs for the Rayburn. And it's so cold. I'm going to wear my cardigan and socks in bed.

January 25

It took a good hour to clear up the mess this morning. Fay thought we'd had burglars, but when she woke Graham he checked all the doors and windows (which he's locked and bolted each night since we've been here) and there was no sign of a forced entry. And nothing is missing, only broken. None of us heard anything – although you'd think that that amount of crockery smashing on the stone flag floor would have made enough noise to wake the dead. But I suppose the ceilings are high and the walls thick in this old house.

As far as I know, this is the first time we've experienced any activity in the kitchen. Fay was weepy again – 'But what does it mean? Is it angry with us?'

We were hungry after all the dusting, sweeping and vacuuming. Simon lit the Rayburn and I ventured out into the cold for some food. The snow is about six inches deep in the drive.

The supplies I found in the Spar shop cheered everyone up a bit, especially the bottle of Famous Grouse. After baked beans on toast and a couple of glasses of the whisky Graham recovered the power of speech.

'If there weren't enough reasons already, this has surely convinced even you, Fay, that we have to sell up.'

'Not necessarily. Maybe it's angry *because* we're thinking of selling.'

'Oh for pity's sake!'

'We could always get the estate agent to give us a valuation and take it from there,' said Simon. 'It would give us some accurate information on which to base a decision.'

'But I already have decided,' said Fay, 'and any amount of money isn't going to make me change my mind.'

Do we all have to agree, I wonder, or would a majority decision suffice?

Fay and I cleaned the kitchen this afternoon. This evening we stayed close to the Rayburn: the log supply is dwindling fast. Graham is sulking and drank most of the whisky without offering it to anyone else.

It has just started snowing again – our cars in the drive look abandoned, their roofs topped with snowy white crew-cuts. We're all going to bed early because we don't want to talk to each other any more.

January 26

Simon made the discovery when he went into father's study to open the curtains, which had stayed closed since the ambulance left. The ink is everywhere, in swirling flicks all over the wallpaper, on the carpet and the door. Nothing in the room has been moved except, presumably, the empty inkbottle on father's desk. We all had a long look and then closed the door – no one could face the idea of trying to clean up the mess. Graham says we may have to get in a professional cleaning firm.

Back in the kitchen, we couldn't look at each other. Finally, Graham broke the silence.

'This is getting beyond a joke. It has never been this . . . destructive before. What are we going to do?

Fay said 'Maybe we should just close up the house and leave it alone. Then it might stop being so angry.'

'Father would've called that giving up.' I said.

Simon left the room and came back a few minutes later with his laptop.

'What are you going to do with that?' asked Graham.

'I think we need some advice. This can't be the only house in the world that has this . . . problem. Let's see if we can find someone who can help.'

'How are you going to find anything useful on that thing?' said Graham. 'Exorcism online? Virtual Vicars? Ghouls R Us?'

The upshot is that, after some searching and several false leads, and as unlikely as is sounds, Simon has found a 'remote viewing' detective agency on the internet. They are called Spirit Solutions (mission statement 'exploring the inexplicable') and 'remote viewing' means, apparently, that they don't have to come to you, they just sit in Oregon or Winnipeg or wherever they are (their website didn't list an address, but we think from their writing style that they are North American) and come up with the answer to your problem. They claim to have assisted in successful outcomes for dozens of clients, and several case histories are outlined, somewhat opaquely, on the site. All sorts of dilemmas are represented, from hauntings to missing persons; love affairs gone wrong to burglaries.

Graham remains dubious, but came round a bit when Fay pointed out that they don't charge, but ask instead that satisfied clients make a contribution to 'esoteric studies'.

'And anyway,' she said, 'what have we got to lose.'

Fay and Simon are the most keen on the idea and set about drafting an email explaining what has been happening. In the end we opened a couple of bottles of father's small store of claret and all had some input into the document. It was almost fun. But after the email had been sent we realised that the time difference means that we will probably have to wait until the morning for a reply.

The rest of the day has dragged by. Fay went to the Spar and says that the shelves are half empty. She brought back bacon, eggs and sliced bread, so we had bacon sandwiches for lunch, fried egg sandwiches for supper. Graham has found a pile of coal in the outhouse so we should be able to eke out the fuel for another few days, if we have to.

Graham and Simon played dominoes all afternoon. Fay did her knitting and I read my book. Going to bed early is fast becoming a habit.

January 27
It wasn't as bad as it could have been. The groceries were strewn over the kitchen floor and the fridge door left open, a token effort compared to the last couple of nights. After breakfast Simon booted up the computer and collected his emails, amongst them one from Spirit Solutions:

> The answer is in your hands. There is an unquiet one among you, and the spirit feeds on it. The spirit will not rest until you have found the one and soothed away its energies or expunged it

from your hearth. Only you will know the solution. Seek and ye shall find. Be careful. We see danger.

Graham snorted. 'Is that it?'

'So they're saying that it's one of us?' said Fay, looking puzzled.

'Not exactly,' I explained, 'They're saying that the poltergeist takes its energy from one of us.'

'I don't get it,' said Simon. 'How are we supposed to find out who it is? "Seek and ye shall find" isn't very specific, is it?'

Graham stood up. 'You really are a bunch of gullible fools.'

'So how do *you* explain what's been happening then, Graham?'

It has stopped snowing, but there is no sign of a thaw. I have seen neither cars nor people crossing the bottom of the drive: the birds seem to have deserted the garden and even the Spar is closed. A leaden sky hangs over everything, threatening more snow later. I am so cold my bones ache.

Simon asked. 'Do you think we should email them again? Ask them for more specific advice?'

Fay frowned. 'But they seem to be saying that it is really down to us. "The answer is in your hands." We've got to work it out ourselves. Or we already know.'

'*Already know*? What on earth do you mean? Christ almighty!' Graham almost shouted. 'Don't tell me you're actually going to pay lip service to that rubbish. Anyone could have come up with one vague paragraph.'

'Well,' said Fay 'I see only one angry person in the room.'

'And what the hell's that supposed to mean?' Graham got up and stormed out of the kitchen. I could just hear the thud of his bedroom door slamming overhead.

Fay looked at me and Simon. 'Well, he *is* the angry one, isn't he?'

'He's only sulking,' I said.

We spent half an hour or so searching through all the kitchen cupboards and the larder for food, with very little to show for our efforts. Father catered only for his own tastes and all we could come up with was two tins of pilchards in tomato sauce, a bag of macaroni, a packet of rich tea biscuits and some withered, sprouting potatoes. These we added to our own supplies of sliced bread, cheese, eggs and orange juice. Fay and I were discussing possible meals when the door opened and Graham came back in.

'Look, I'm sorry. This is all a bit . . . ghastly, isn't it. Can we start again? I'll try not to be such an idiot.'

'Well,' said Simon, 'let's apply some logic to this. Work as a team. What we want is for it to stop, so what can we do to make that happen? If one of us *is* causing it, then how can we neutralise it?'

'Daddy would be proud of your reasoning skills, Simon,' said Fay. 'He taught you well. You always were his favourite.'

Simon looked at his feet. 'Oh, shut up, Fay.'

I said, 'Maybe we should stay up tonight and see if we can be in the room with it when it's happening.'

And that, after some discussion, is what we have agreed to do.

7.30 p.m.

We have washed up and cleared away after our supper of pilchards and macaroni and Graham has opened a bottle of wine. The electricity supply failed about an hour ago, so we lit the candles we found in the larder. The Rayburn is burning low – we are trying to save fuel – and I am wearing my coat. Late this afternoon, with the laptop switched on for only a few minutes to conserve the battery, we collected another email from Spirit Solutions:

> Sleep is the enemy of unreason, but you will not rest again until the act is done. The spirit will come in its own time and way – be ready, for you will need all your wits about you. Remember, the past is the key, the present the door. Who will know the future?

The night stretches out in front of us, and as we can't predict in which room our poltergeist will manifest itself, we will, at some point, have to take the candles and tour the rest of the house. Fay looks wan and tired over her knitting, which she seems to be able to do by touch in the semi-darkness of her corner, her needles clicking a staccato tune – it is too dark to read for long, almost too dark to write this. Graham and Simon are playing dominoes at the table, their shadows flickering on the wall in the guttering candlelight. I am shivering in my coat. Waiting, waiting – is this the boredom before the battle?

9.10 p.m.

It was hard to keep the candles alight in the cold draughts, so we processed at a slow walk, taking it in turns to enter each room. We listened at the door of father's study – no one would go in. The music room was icy, the varnished wood of the piano glistening like wet seal skin in the candlelight, the music stands arranged in a spindly quartet.

Fay shuddered. 'I haven't played a note since I left home.'

We could see through the French windows that it's snowing again, the flakes falling in thick clumps, further muffling the already frozen ground. Upstairs, the draughts are worse, the candle flames dipped and danced and we had to shield them with our hands.

The bedrooms are as we had left them – Graham's bed unmade, Fay's bedsocks and nightdress neatly folded. Simon collected his laptop from his room and back in the kitchen he checked again for emails. There was another one from Spirit Solutions:

> It is time. You are in control and cannot fail. All strength flows from the four to the one. Have courage and it will end well for you.

10.15 p.m.

I had forgotten how quickly candles burn. We found another box of them beneath the sink, but they may not last all night. After some discussion we have decided that we should patrol the house every hour or so. Time creeps by while we wait.

Simon said 'When this is over I am going to book a holiday.'

'Somewhere warm.' I shivered.

We began upstairs, and this time decided to leave all the doors open, except the one to father's study. All is quiet; there is nothing to report, except for the cat, a comfort, at least to me. It was scratching at the back door when we returned to the kitchen. Graham unlocked it and the cat stalked in, a plump grey tabby. It trotted, tail up, to the Rayburn and curled itself around a corner of its warmth.

'It looks quite at home,' said Fay. 'It must have been in here before.'

'Can you imagine Father letting it in?' snorted Graham.

It is licking its chest, the slight rasp of its tongue riffling the silence. A few minutes ago I crouched down beside it and gently stroked its head, which it tolerated, staring over my shoulder with its yellow eyes. We have nothing to feed it, but it doesn't seem hungry.

Instant coffee is keeping us awake and we are refuelling on cheese sandwiches.

11.25 p.m.

I think the coffee must be making us jittery. This time round, outside father's study, we could hear a faint, repetitive scratching, somehow familiar.

Fay gasped. 'It's father's fountain pen,' she whispered.

We looked at each other, eyes wide in horror.

'What is it writing?' She began her awful dry sobbing.

'No – No,' said Simon. It's the apple tree. A twig is tapping at the window, that's all. The wind is picking up.'

Listening again you could hear that he was probably right.

The cat is sitting on the table washing its paws. It has stopped snowing at last and the strengthening wind will be sculpting the laid snow into drifts. Graham has opened the second-last bottle of claret.

Perhaps it will not come tonight. Have we conjured it away?

12.10 p.m.

The cat is asleep by the Rayburn, and I can't bring myself to wake it, although I long for the solace that stroking it would bring. Graham is drinking the wine – the rest of us do not have the stomach for it. No one feels like talking.

The wind is buffeting against the back of the house, making the ill-fitting sash windows rattle in their frames. We should have conducted our twelve o'clock tour by now, but inertia has overcome us. I am beginning to feel sleepy, but cannot face any more coffee. Simon is dozing in the corner chair; Fay is in a dream, wiping the draining board; Graham slumped over his wine at the table. Shall I rouse them, or shall I let them rest for now?

I will give them five minutes more and then we will go.

12.30 p.m.

The door to the music room was closed. It may have slammed shut in the draught. The cat followed us and rubbed around our legs as we stopped outside each room, and when Simon opened the music room door it rushed inside. Through the French windows I could see some of the pale wintry garden, Father's shrubs a row of smooth white mounds, the trees tousled in the wind. The cat has hidden itself somewhere and won't respond to my attempts to call it out, so I have propped the door open with the piano stool. I am sure it will find its way back to the relative warmth of the kitchen when it is ready.

'We may as well go to bed if nothing is going to happen,' said Graham.

Back in the kitchen, Graham has returned from a trip to the lavatory and is opening the last bottle of wine. Simon is feeding the Rayburn with a shovelful of coal. Fay has just asked me if I would like another cheese sandwich. It's like a Sunday afternoon.

1.05 p.m.

I cannot think straight. Is she right? Is it over now?

We heard the cat miaowing. I assumed it was still in the music room and walked down the hall to bring it back. But when I reached the door it was obvious that it wasn't in there, and following the sound of its sad little cries I found myself outside the door of Father's study. There is no doubt about it, the cat is inside. I couldn't bring myself to open the door.

'So how did the bloody thing get in there?' asked Simon.

'*Poor* thing,' corrected Fay. 'Did you put it in there when you went to the loo, Graham?'

'Oh for crying out loud,' said Graham. ' I almost wish I *had* done, it would be far less peculiar.'

'No it wouldn't, I said. 'Look, someone has got to open the door and let it out.'

'If it were up to me I'd leave it in there,' said Simon. 'That would teach it to go creeping about.'

'I wouldn't leave anyone in that room, let alone a cat,' said Fay. 'Come on, I'll do it, if you'll come with me.'

So we filed down the hall, candles aloft, Fay taking the lead. The cat kept up its mournful cries as she turned the door-knob and went inside, shutting the door behind her. After a minute or so the miaowing stopped, and we could hear the scraping of heavy objects being moved. Then silence. The door-knob twisted and Fay emerged.

'It's all right. It's over now.'

Graham spluttered. 'What do you mean? Where's the cat.'

She smiled. 'Oh don't worry about the cat, it's sorted. We can sell the house. I don't mind.'

'But Fay . . .'

'He can't hurt us any more. I'm going to bed, and I suggest you do the same.'

She turned away and headed for the stairs.

It's cold in the kitchen now, the Rayburn has gone out. Overhead the heavy footsteps clump up and down the landing. Whispering and faint piano music fill the air. Simon has booted up his computer and the new message from Spirit Solutions is on the screen:

She is sleeping. Let her rest now, for she will need her strength. But you must stay awake, to face what is to come . . .